Usurper of Fire

The Kindling of Chaos

Adam Guthro

Prologue

"Am I the dumbest person in the world?" Drobo asked himself. He flicked through the pages he had written across his desk. Every word he read made his body cringe. He gazed around the room, noting the bits of food and dirty clothes scattered throughout his home in a hill. The stack of returned and unopened manuscripts of his first draft taunted him from the table by the door.

"Why bother? Why continue this?" frustration rising in his tone, "a first person account of heroism that exceeds *all* before it! A battle between demigods, powerful heroes and unrivaled villains! Love torn asunder and hate brewed to frothing despair! What more do these nincompoops want?" He punched his desk, and felt a burst of pain in his knuckles. "Mother of…" His teeth ground into themselves as he held back another blow.

He stood and paced the small room. Thoughts racing through his head, whispers past his lips, transcribing them in mumbled breaths. He stopped, motioning with his hands as he spoke. "Yes. I know I've talked more about writing this tale then actually writing it. I can admit that, pardon me." He turned to face the opposite wall. "However, I have now completed the tale at great labor. While my expectations waiver from insignificant prose to world renown at my own error. I at the very least expected those close to me to humor my labors!" He kicked at the chair, catching it with the tip of his toe and nudging it slightly.

He ripped a page off the desk and crumpled it. Walking over to the fireplace readying a throw. He stopped before it, his eyes transfixed on its dancing flames that reflected off them. The memories of his struggles quelled the pettiness of his current disputes. He lowered his arm, unfolding the page as he continued to stare into the embers. A solemn look on his face. "I've never fancied myself a skilled writer, nor could I say have sought tutorship. Admittedly. My hard work…is merely self aggrandizing drivel. A selfish endeavor, surely." The admittance was hurtful, but relieving. A weight lifted off of him. He shook off the embarrassment of the past year. Getting drunk at a tavern and loudly discussing his *art.*

He lowered his head to the page and read the final sentence aloud. "Then all again was therefore and henceforth, no questions to be ascertained, undoubtedly right with the entire world, greatly." A tear fell down his face. "But that's not true…is it." He sat at his desk and held a quill over a blank page. He licked his quivering lips. "I can find a solace in eyes never laying upon these pages. Inside these pages I will hide the truth I have yet to tell another soul." His hands moved with fevered haste as he wrote.

We said we saved the world. The witnesses endorse this claim. We have merely delayed the inevitable end. Now all of our hope lies in an impossible task. The usurper is more cunning than any person have right to be. The world will end. It will be because of me. I have brought you this doom. If fate or otherwise bids you read this, then you must be the one. You have to find—

A loud knocking at the door interrupted his confession.

“Coming!” He said.

The knocking continued in musical rhythm.

“I said I’m coming!” Drobo said, annoyance beset him.

The knocking increased in speed and effort alike.

“Stop!” he screamed as he opened the door. He gazed straight into the crotch of the tall man, his body eclipsing the afternoon sun. His slender body crouched in the door frame. His short auburn hair fashioned with great effort. He wore dark ill fitted clothes that seemed to hide a hundred secrets within the various pouches and loops upon them.

“Hello, Drobo! I’ve returned!” The man said as he waddled into the home. Pushing past a bewildered small man. “This house hasn’t changed one bit!”

“You’ve never been here before. How did you find this place?” Drobo closed the door as Teavis sprawled across a couch, causing it to fall to pieces.

“It was like that when I got here,” he said as he piled up all the pieces to sit on.

“Teavis…what are you doing here?” Drobo tightened his lips and lowered his brow.

"Well I'm not here to be roommates, so don't ask." Teavis said as he wiggled into the debris.

"I wasn't gonna—forget it. I ask again, what are you doing here? I haven’t seen you since…Oh, no.” His stern demeanor fell into shocked realization.

“Yes, my dear friend. This is indeed about *that*. The call of adventure nips at your ears once more my below-average height friend. We have yet another quest to complete.”

"Adventure? Like the time you kidnapped me and held me for ransom? I believe you traded me for a three-legged dog if I remember correctly." Drobo left the room to pour some tea.

"True. Probably could have held off for a four legged one but in my defense I felt bad for that enslaver. He told me his mother was sick and his horse was hungry, so I had to give him *something* so he could get home quickly."

He returned with two small teacups and handed one to Teavis. As Drobo took a sip of the steaming tea, Teavis threw the cup into his mouth and swallowed it whole.

"Oh my…" Drobo muttered.

"This cup taste like tea. Disgusting." He pressed two fingers down on his throat.

Drobo sighed. He turned toward his desk, glancing once more at the pages upon it. "So, I suppose you're here about the—"

"Yes indeed, I'm here for the orb. Hand it over to me." Teavis held out his hand. Anticipation upon his face.

"You know I have no idea where it is." Drobo's hands shook as he took another sip of his tea.

"Nonsense. I had you hide it!"

"Yes, that's true. Except you drugged me and pushed me into a raft heading down the Many Rivers. It was a week before I could have a sober thought. I haven't any idea where it lay."

Teavis sat up and stared into Drobo's eyes. He placed a finger on his shoulder.

"The answers are here, inside your heart."

Drobo rolled his eyes.

Teavis continued. "I'm well aware of the circumstances, which is why I thought this would be a fantastic call to adventure." He rose on bent knee and held up a fist. "I know you long for the thrill of the road, the rush of a fight, and the treatment for sores on your keister after a questionable night out. There is glory out there! Waiting for *you*. Waiting for you to grab the small of its back and give it unwanted advice. Children will scream your name as they throw rocks at the weird kid in town. Women will throw themselves at you if you lose a little weight because…what the hell is this?" He motioned toward Drobo's ill fitted attire. "Why by this time next month you'll be the most famous small to ever exist." Teavis clenched his fist and his grin widened as he nodded assurance.

Drobo's thoughts raced with ways to get out of this. He needed to convince this psycho from another life to leave peacefully.

Teavis's eyes shifted from friendly to malicious as a pendulum on a grandfather's clock.

"Teavis, I would love to accompany you but…but I'm afraid I have far too many duties here. And well, I can't leave behind all my friends and family so easily." Which *was* true. He had been running for mayor. He just hoped Teavis didn't mess it up since it'd be easy to convince the other smalls to send him away. It was known he was skilled at politics, but he had worn their patience thin in pursuit of beta readers. "On top of the matter, this really seems like the kind of thing you should bring Esby for. Not me." Teavis had written letters to Drobo mentioning her. The two were peas in a pod or a knife in the sheath in this circumstance.

Teavis lowered his head. "Well, nay to that. Esby died." He said with an uncomfortable lack of emotion.

Drobo immediately placed Teavis as her killer. A feat not unknown to him. He took a moment of silence before responding. “Still, my previous point stands.”

“I see…” Teavis frowned. Then he looked down with a smirk and lit eyes, and Drobo’s heart sank into his stomach.

“I know you'd hate to leave your friends and family behind, so I prepared a little surprise to perhaps…convince you.” He crawled over to Drobo, turned him toward the door, and put his hands over his eyes. “Are you ready?” He whispered into his ear, his lips brushing against his lobes.

Drobo realized the errors of his many years. Teavis was insane, but he was good at coercing others. It wouldn't be beyond him to gather them and have them send him away. Drobo sighed as he thought of his next move.

“All right…Let’s hear it.” Some form of encouragement wouldn't hurt, he thought.

With Drobo’s eyes still covered, they walked outside. Teavis then lowered his hands.

Drobo's breath fell out in a gasp. On his front lawn the smalls from the village were gathered. Their bloodied corpses stacked as tall as his own home, and their dead eyes penetrated his soul as his blood ran cold. The terror that coursed through him caused his body to stiffen. He fell to his knees, sobbing.

“I know! Isn't it great?” Teavis patted him on the back. Pride filled his voice. “Now you don’t have to worry about leaving behind friends and family! Because they're all dead! It’s great, right?”

“You’re a monster.” Drobo cried, pushing his face into the soft dirt and trying to catch his breath.

“Haha. Yeah…The important thing is that we can get moving soon. I’ll go pack some things for you while you say goodbye.” Teavis knelt and pointed at a small woman with blond hair on the top right of the pile. “She was a cute one eh? We’ll have to find another one like that for ya on the road! Probably one with longer legs too.”

Drobo looked at the woman he had been planning to propose to. Her neck was cut deep and the dress he had bought her was stained red.

As a whistling Teavis walked inside his hovel, Drobo looked at the flower garden that wrapped around his home to his right, spotting his sharpened trowel sticking out of the dirt. He slowed his breathing and gripped it in his hand. His breaths shortened.

“Oh wow! It’s like packing for a small child!” Teavis said as he placed various clothing and food into a bag. “What do you normally wear at a beach? I was thinking we might want to go on vacation after this. Drobo?” Floorboards creak behind Teavis, and he turned.

There stood Drobo with his hands behind his back.

“Ah, there you are my friend. I’m almost done here. We should probably bring some of your valuables to sell. Where’s your stash?”

Yet he stood still.

Teavis approached him and kneeled. “Are you still mourning? That was like minutes ago…It’s time to let go, my friend”

Drobo roared as he stabbed the trowel into Teavis’s neck. He wiggled it to pull it out. Teavis fell onto his back, grabbing at the wound. He got on top of him and stabbed him in the chest over and over. Rage overtook every fiber of his being. Teavis lay flat to the floor. He could only gurgle as his body fell still.

Drobo rolled off him, and lay on his back, his chest heaving. A wave of loneliness washed over him, and he sobbed once more. He berated himself for not spending more quality time with his friends and family. The silence of the village tormented him and he snapped. He sat up, placed the pointed edge of the trowel to his wrist and closed his eyes. “I’m sorry. I’m so sorry.” But before he could push down a hand grabbed his wrist.

“There, there, my boy.” Teavis said with a smile. “It seems you accidentally and repeatedly stabbed me, but as you can see…I’m fine!” He lifted his shirt, no remaining wounds could be seen.

“I never expected less, Teavis. You've stolen my hope with no prayer of reparations." Teavis had the gift of regeneration, Drobo knew that. He also knew Teavis when he was a valiant man, not this beast he had become. "You've broken me, Teavis. Just like my couch, you've broken me."

“Oh yeah. I apologize for the couch. It in fact wasn't like that when I got here.”

“That’s what you apologize for!” he screamed.

“Well, it was rather rude of me…So yes.”

“I dread ever learning about you hybrids.”

Teavis nodded.

The hybrids were relics from the Great War. People fused with the essence of something ethereal, that some considered gods. Others…thought them demons.

“Why…Why me?” Drobo dropped the trowel and put his head into his hands. “Why did you drag me into all of this? I never wanted this.”

“Drobo, you might not believe me, but I don’t have many true friends despite how well I dance or how cool I am. I trust you now, as I trusted you then. For one very simple reason.”

He looked up to meet Teavis’s eyes.

“And what reason is that?” he asked, genuinely curious.

“I flipped a coin.”

He stared at Teavis in disbelief. Then without thinking, he jumped on him, swinging and kicking.

Yet Teavis held him up with his arms and legs outstretched. “That’s it you little rascal! Nothing like a spot of exercise in the morning!” Teavis smiled as he swung Drobo through the air. “Weee!”

Drobo quickly ran out of energy and Teavis dropped him onto the floor.

“Alright, take a quick nap while I go bury the bodies. When you wake up, we’ll be ready to start our journey!”

He had no idea why, but at that moment he felt compelled to join him. If only for the chance to learn how to kill him. A new hope swelled as the thought permeated his mind.

“I can promise you one thing about this journey, Drobo.” Teavis said.

“What could you possibly promise me?”

“That murderous wish of yours. You'll get it.” His grin was wicked while his eyes were playfully inviting.

Their eyes shared an unspoken agreement. Amidst the madness he found a beacon of calming content.

"Teavis," Drobo said, "I wrote about our previous journey. If you wanna read it, go in my—"

"I'm good."

Chapter 1

The basement's odor singed at it's guest nostrils. Years of dripping wet rock walls and no ventilation. The dirt floor packed hard from years of storage as an old tavern. Which was now long abandoned and falling to disrepair above. An evil wizard with a darkened hood stood just beyond a doorway. A mask covered his scarred face, and a cloak hid the wretched body beneath it. The crowd of his henchmen chanted guttural hymns as he entered the room. Yet his shoulder pads got stuck in the door frame, a clang echoed throughout the room. He held up a finger to the crowd and twisted his body until he fit through. The chants grew more ominous with each step he took on stage.

Approaching the podium, he reached out a hand to silence the room. He waved to his guards and they turned to face the crowd. He then pulled out a piece of parchment to read from. His eyes strained as he realized he had only brought the piece of parchment with the boobs he had sketched earlier– a perfect replica of his mother's chest. It had taken several hours for him to get the shading on the nipples just right. His thoughts traveled to her tragic passing during the great war but five years prior. His vow to hurt the world that ripped his heart from his chest would begin with this performance. He'd have to perform his speech from memory.

"My brothers, the time is upon us," he said. He placed the piece of parchment back in his pocket. "The crescent moon has revealed the location of the final chaos gem." With all seven chaos gems, anyone could take over the entire world. Their essence offered power to those who were willing to pay the ultimate price. Or so it was told. "Sidival deciphered the code, Merciless planned the travel, and Jeff retrieved it."

The crowd all clapped as the three men stood up and blushed. What the men lacked in teeth, they made up for in patchy facial hair.

"Now we will put our final plan into action, and soon we will rule over the entire—".

The loud creaking and sudden bang of the front double doors opening and slamming against the walls interrupted his boasting. In the back of the room a man walked toward the wizard. He wore fashioned leather armor, light brown with silver inlays. His green hood fell over his face covering it entirely. His gait was determined and confident. He greeted the room with a wave and stumbled his way toward the podium as he tripped up the steps.

The speaker motioned for his guards to stand down.

When the man in the green hood reached the podium, he pulled out a dagger with a golden pommel and a dim ruby residing within it. He aimed it toward the speaker.

"You're Dark Lord Deathicus I presume?" He said, half yawning. He shook his head and slapped his cheeks to wake himself.

"Aye. You are indeed in the presence of a God." The man held up his hand, showing his gauntlet. Six magical gems embedded into it, and a magical frost surrounded them. "I control the legendary deathfrost, which is said to kill anyone who comes into contact with it. If you're here to fight, then I must warn you that no blade can pierce me. My skin is as hard as ice. My magic—gaw!" He let a groan out as he grabbed at the dagger that was thrown into his heart. "Dude!" He fell to the floor, blood pooling beneath him. “You can’t just stab someone mid-monologue…”.

The man in the green hood stared at his hand in disbelief, he shrugged. “Ah, dangit…I’m a bit new at this. In my defense that monologue did suck though, right?” He gestured toward the shocked crowd.

Though his words went unheard as Deathicus died.

“Yeah that’s fucked up,” a minion from the crowd claimed.

Others quickly agreed. The guards held their weapons out toward him.

“What’s this jerk’s problem?” another minion said.

The crowd erupted into a heated debate. Their voices traveled throughout the hall and into the dehydrated brain of the slayer of Gods. The ache from the night spent previous reached unbearable lengths.

The man in the green hood grabbed the podium’s gavel and rapped it against it.

“Hey!" he said, "you don’t know me and I don’t know you.” He reached down and removed the various colored gems from Deathicus’s gauntlet, along with the dagger from his chest. The squelching noise made the room wince. “Well, I’m a concerned citizen with despise for the wicked. A heroic man of mythic proportions. A bastard by all accounts measured. I also perform cool tricks…watch this." He placed the gems onto the podium and stabbed his dagger through them, shattering each one to pieces. A flickering light flashed the room with each gem destroyed.

Astonished, the crowd stared with wide eyes.

When he finished destroying the gems, he performed a dance with an awkward amount of knee movement. “Okay. So here’s the deal.”

He threw the dagger into the ground in front of him. “Your leader’s dead, I destroyed your gems, and I shat in the middle of your dorm rooms.”

"We *just* deep cleaned that! You monster!" a man from the crowd shouted.

"Do you have any idea how hard it is to get human feces out of tile?" another man shouted.

The man in the green hood grinned. "Your chores are the least of your concerns. Your very lives are at stake. We need to have a conversation, you and I," he said.

"Speaking of cleaning shit," a new man from the crowd said, "I don't need to be the only one replacing wiping towels. It's not hard to replace the towels guys. Seriously, it's like taking care of children around here!"

"Says the guy who never follows the chore chart," another man said, "also, stop reheating fish in the fireplace each day. You're stinking up the entire hideout!"

A heated debate erupted over chores and various odors.

The body of Deathicus landed with a loud thud on the floor beneath the podium. Interrupting the dispute of the roommates. “Anyways!" the man in the green hood said, "Boys, men…and other whatever.” A serious look overcame his face. “I don’t have a lot of time so I’m gonna give you two options here. Option one, I straight up murder everyone in here.”

A look of fear crossed the crowd. A few yelled their disapproval.

“Option two, if one of—”

“Hey! Wait a second!” One of the men called out from the crowd. “Isn’t that the guy from the tavern last night?”

"Pardon?" the man in the green hood said.

"Yeah...It's that Cadivus guy! The one who drinks beer with his asshole!"

The crowd erupted into chatter and laughter.

"Ass Juice! Ass Juice! Ass Juice!" they cheered.

Cadivus, in his green hood, examined the room more carefully and recognized various faces within the crowd.

"Oh wow. It's you guys? Charlicum, Sidival, and where is he?" He scanned the crowd and pointed at a man with a blond beard. "And who could forget Timotharian, my seventh greatest friend."

Timotharian stood and waved at the crowd.

"I still have no idea how you performed that disappearing pint glass trick. Absolutely brilliant."

"What are you doing Cadivus?" Charlicum asked, "I thought you were cool. Why did you kill Deathicus?"

"I told you I was a vigilante, did I not?" Cadivus said.

"*What*? No! You said you were gonna sign up and join, so we told you where our secret meeting was held," Sidival said. His bald head turned red. "If we knew your real plan, we would certainly have refused. You're a liar and a big jerk!"

"Jerk! Jerk! Jerk!" The crowd chanted.

Cadivus slumped his shoulders and broke eye contact.

"What was your plan anyways?" Sidival asked.

"Well, the plan was..." he pursed his lips and lost words.

"Oh, just be out with it then!"

"Kill the leader of the death cult and then kill all his henchmen..." The crowd's eyes widened and their groans exasperated his intent. The moment Cadivus had anticipated all morning fell flat.

"What the fuck did we do?" Someone called out.

"Um, have you forgotten the whole 'death' cult thing?" he asked.

"We haven't done anything yet besides snatch a few gems! Not even the king himself kills people for theft!"

He pondered this revelation.

"Hmm, I guess I just assumed you've been raping and murdering this whole time. You know what they say…"

"What do they say?"

"You know. All right, I may have gotten ahead of myself. What we need here is a compromise."

"What's compromise?" A man towards the front of the crowd asked another next to him.

Cadivus got on one knee in front of him.

"Compromise is when the woman gets everything she wants, and the man has to appease himself in the outhouse," Cadivus said.

The man in the front of the crowd smiled revealing his few remaining teeth.

Cadivus smiled and nodded back to him. "But of course in this setting, it will mean not killing everyone."

"I'll fight you scum!" A man with a tattered beard yelled out.

"Oh, fantastic! Anyone else with this man?" Cadivus pointed around the room and counted hands as they shot up. But he soon lost count and came up with a new strategy. "Okay! Let's do this. Everyone who wants to avenge their dead leader go to this side of the room." He pointed towards the left. "Everyone who wants to go home and swear to do no evil ever again on that side of the room." He pointed towards the right.

Squeaking chairs, footsteps, and conversation filled the room.

Cadivus glanced down, saw the parchment Deathicus had been holding, and put it in his pocket. As the noise died down, he looked over and saw the room was split almost evenly. "Okay! Let's bid a farewell to the reformed citizens shall we? How about a hand for these newly upstanding citizens!"

The reformed men walked out to applause, waving goodbye to the room.

"Please bar the door on your way out if you would!"

After the last man exited, a loud thud echoed as the door was locked from the outside.

"Now what?" one of the men asked.

Cadivus grabbed his dagger, sheathed it, and hopped down from the stage. He pushed all the chairs to the outer edges of the room, and the men ready to fight him followed suit, assisting him. He then placed himself in the center of the room.

"Alright, let's make a circle around me then."

The men took their places around him as he stretched his legs.

"Okay," he said, "so I figure this: you attack me one at a time for a few men. Then two at a time. And when there are three left…the last three attack in unison. Now, if someone could—"

"Charge!" one of the henchmen yelled.

The yell spurred all the men to attack at once. They threw Cadivus to the ground, punching and kicking him. He put his hands in front of his face, not wanting his teeth to get kicked out. Still on the ground, the blows and kicks rained down on him like a storm of anguish. They laughed and insulted him as they punished his actions. They kicked him until their breathing got heavy. With Cadivus on the ground unmoving, they backed off and caught their breath. They had a laugh and high fived one another.

"What a sissy," one man said.

"Imagine stretching to get your ass kicked. Dude's like a professional pinata." Another said. They all laughed and cast their insults.

Sniffles could be heard from the downed Cadivus. Their confused faces darted toward his body on the ground as his chest spasmed with the noise.

"Is he fucking crying?" one of the men asked. "Is this pussy really fucking crying right now? After everything he just did? What a loser." The crowd laughed loudly at the display.

Cadivus looked towards them with a scowl, his eyes and cheeks full of tears. "Screw you guys!" he spoke in his crying voice, "I just came here to be a vigilante and stop evil and you guys aren't playing by the rules and you're—" his voice became incomprehensible as he continued on. The occasional slur or curse word slipped through the mumbling as he wiped his nose into his sleeve.

"By the Goddess…just kill this guy already," one of the men said. He handed a spear to the youngest of the group. "Time to prove you're worth a damn, boy."

The young man grabbed the spear, his eyes moving between its tip and its target. "Totally…I…I got this." He moved toward Cadivus and readied an attack. "Any…uh…last words, man?"

Cadivus sniffled and wiped his face onto his other sleeve. He took a slow breath and calmed himself. He moved to a seated position as he stared into the young man's eyes. "Yes, of course." He cleared his throat. His red and wet eyes out of place on his stoic stare. "I no longer have a vested interest in killing you lot quickly. Justice will allow slowly to suffice."

The young man grimaced and shook his head. He thrust the spear forward and Cadivus dodged to the side, grabbing the spear end with both hands and breaking it off. He threw the spear head into the young man's neck. Who grabbed at the wound as he fell to the ground.

Cadivus stood and removed his dagger. "Now, let's begin…start…rain? Ah, fuck it!"

He charged the closest man to him and stabbed the dagger into his ear, twisting it before pulling it free in a fluid motion. He turned toward the others. He sliced at necks, stabbed vital organs, and punched in between his daggers swings. His dagger work had been practiced, but he had only trained with trees and dummies. Nevertheless, the motions felt natural to him.

The men also armed themselves with their weapons and charged, making wild swings at him. They fought with certain victory on their minds.

A grace flowed within Cadivus as he danced through them, every swing a kill. Every dodge and parry placed them off balance, begging for a counter attack. A part of him wanted the fight to last forever. He often surprised himself with his instinctual movements. His body forging past his thoughts painting his intent on the men around him. An excitement filled him as his long awaited moment became reality. Fear shadowed the anger of the crowd, their bodies becoming more timid from each man fallen.

He dodged an overhead mace attack, grabbed the man by the neck, and threw him into a pillar. The neck cracked as he bounced off it. He searched around for his next opponent…Yet no eyes met his own.

Only one other man was trying to stand, still upon one knee. He ran in for a strike and stopped himself right before his blade entered his neck.

"Oh! Last one?" he asked the man who now had his eyes closed. He poked the man's forehead to get him to open his eyes.

The man lowered his hands slowly. His breath quivered as he realized he was still alive. His eyes darted around the room and made the man vomit.

Cadvius turned his head away from him and patted the man's back. "There, there, evil henchmen. Get it all out now." The wet discharge turned into dry heaving. "Look, let me be quick. You always gotta leave one fella alive, so they can spread the word of a new hero. Just make sure you get my name right and describe me properly."

The man wiped his mouth and looked up, nodding.

"Yeah…I'm going to need to hear your description so I can make sure you get it right."

Baffled, the shaking man opened his mouth to respond but couldn't find the words.

"Just tell me what you want to be described as, and I'll just say that," the shaking man said.

"Look, Trevor?"

The man shook his head

"Well, I'm gonna call you Trevor. Now, Trevor, if I tell you what to say, you're gonna fuck it up. I need you to tell it in your own words, so I can hear how you're gonna do it. Just….pretend I'm a low-level hoodlum and you're telling this story and he asks what I look like, what would you say?"

"Well he was average height, short brown hair, skinny fellow. Not much of a jaw or anything. His arms are too long for his torso, his face is kind of asymmetrical. Not much of a looker this one. Dresses like a horrible actor from a shit play pretending to be a thief. Smells like the poor streets on 'toss your actual shit' out the window day. His eyes are yellow and pink. Although that could be because he funnels beer into his ass. Oh! Even though he's skinny, he has these chubby fingers and weird gut bulge. Average cock. Shaft is abnormally hairy. He–"

"Alright stop!" Cadivus grabbed the man's mouth and held it closed. "It's not my fault I tend to get naked after drinking. I'm an empath, after all." He collected himself and held his fist to his chest. "Anyways, first off, my name is Cadivus. Learn it proper. Secondly, Can't you say something about me being handsome in that speech of yours?"

"But sir, how would they recognize you if I did that…" Trevor said.

Cadivus closed his eyes and rubbed his temples.

Trevor continued, "It's not that you're ugly. You're just weird looking. Like a baby bird or something."

"*Okay*. I'm gonna need you to stop talking to me. Just when you're telling the story later, make sure you mention how nice my hairline is, or how fearsome a foe I am."

"Right, as long as you don't mean your gobbles and whatnot, that thing is freakishly hairy. It looks like a hairy hot dog. Why don't you just shave—"

Cadivus stabbed the man through the stomach. A look of instant regret took over his face.

"Ah, shit! Hey buddy." He spoke in a calm soothing voice. Patting the man's head. "You're okay. You're okay. Just a little friend in your kidney. You'll be fine. You got two…I think."

The man barely registered his words.

"Don't be a pussy and die! Come on Travis. Think of little Travis having to have a stepdad who doesn't really want him around and never opens up to him emotionally. That kid will never know how to display vulnerability and will never have a healthy relationship in his adult years." Cadivus slowly removed the blade, blood poured from the wound. The man fell to his back with panicked gasps. "Don't worry. I can cauterize this. I'm a fire hybrid after all."

The man groaned as Cadivus placed his hands to the wound. He stared at Cadivus's hands, waiting for something to happen.

"Just a moment please." Cadivus's hands trembled. He rubbed them together and focused once more. As he thought of a small fire, his chest tightened. His breaths shortened. Each sharp inhale brought a new bead of sweat to his brow.

"Come on then!" the bleeding man groaned out weakly.

"Oh! You think it's so easy? Then you do it!"

The man croaked and tilted his head to the side. He lay still in a puddle of his own blood.

Cadivus paused, yet he knew he had done his best and that was all that mattered. On the other side of the room, a piece of the ceiling fell onto a man's groin, and he let out a cry of pain.

Cadivus glanced over and smirked. He approached the man with a wide smile. "Ah, Timothy. Have I got the job for you!"

Chapter 2

Darion lay in his bed, staring at the axe hung above his head. Impatient.

The sun was just starting to creep in through the windows. The morning was as good a time as any. He glanced over at the candle he had placed under the rope that held the axe suspended. Yet he would have preferred to remain unaware when it would fall. The candle wax had burned too quickly. It only singed the outside of the rope, leaving it mostly intact.

He sighed and rolled out of bed to place it on top of a few books he had kept around until the flames engulfed the rope. He noted the top book was titled *Tranquility of the Mind*, he smirked, and headed toward his bed. As he lifted his sheets, the axe came crashing down. When the cloud of feathers dissipated, he could see it had landed squarely in his pillow.

He used his fingers to comb his straight black hair in front of his blue eyes then lay next to the fallen axe. "Me and you are one in the same my friend, tools that don't do what they're supposed to."

Yet the rope had caught on fire. Flames ran the length of it.

"Well, plan B it is." He closed his eyes and hummed a sad song to himself. His front door slammed open.

A woman entered the home. Half a head shorter than Darion. She styled her dark hair short to contrast her light olive skin. She wore light colored dresses rather than the previously preferred pants and tunic to allow the bump in her stomach to find more comfort. "Why the shit is it so smoky in here?" a woman's voice said. Seeing the fire, she ran inside and proceeded to snuff it out with a thick sheet she had previously placed near his bed. She looked at him laying next to the axe and shook her head. "You're getting more creative at least." She walked over to the window and moved the wooden planks leaning against it. "You'll have a whole eternity to be dead. Today you have work to do." She opened his dresser drawer. "Should we go with black or…black. Real smart, wearing black in a sun-laden desert. Such a genius you are." She threw clothes at him. "Get dressed genius. I'd talk you into a bath but we're already late."

"I'm not going." Darion said, rolling over onto his side.

"That's cute. I don't remember asking." She yanked him off the bed by his feet.

His head slammed off the floor, which, luckily for him, consisted of sand.

She grabbed the axe from his bed, brushed off the feathers, and put it back on the wall above his fireplace. "If you're gonna lose this debate, it's not gonna be because you didn't show."

Darion, not wanting to argue any longer, put the clothes on. He used a wooden comb to straighten his hair, and placed some charcoal around his eyes which he claimed kept the sun out. That last one in particular had struck a fashion trend with some of his supporters.

She placed a large bowl of water in front of him to wash up with. She left his bedroom and began tidying up.

"You can't just eat bread all day either. You're gonna get fat. I don't see a single piece of dried meat in this place." She lifted a sheet from the floor in a corner and found a stack of bottles reeking of liquor. "That part makes sense though. Hey, are you done yet?" She walked around the corner to find his head submerged in a bowl of water. She lifted his head out of the bowl, then dumped the water onto the floor. “Okay. That's three today. Used them all up already. On with it then, shall we?”

“Fine…” he gargled out.

She grabbed his hand and dragged him out the door as he flipped his hair in front of his face. Recently he had found that random eye contact made his eyes water, and he didn’t want to appear weak. The desert sand remained soft and difficult to traverse on foot. Yet their practiced steps traversed it with ease.

The town was still new to them, homes and shops were barren and poor. The wood was hard to come by, in some parts of town they had learned to build with sand, but it required water and mortar, which was even more difficult to come by. His idea to settle here now felt foolish after seeing how little could be accomplished in a year. Now, his leadership was under attack from his rival–Decan.

“Toonda, you can’t be dragging me by my hand when we approach,” he said.

She threw his hand back to him. Rolling her eyes.

“Look up when you walk dammit. It’s embarrassing to be seen with you when you stare at the ground like that.”

He gazed up through his hair. Half the people here hated him; he could feel their disdain. It was the same look he used in the mirror.

“Doban is gonna be there, so he’ll stand with us too.”

“*Great*. Nothing to garner support like a wench’s husband.”

“Call me a wench again, and I’ll bleach all your clothes.”

Darion shuddered at the thought of that.

As they approached the public debate, chatter grew louder. People arguing back and forth. He hated arguing, but he had a fondness for being snarky.

Decan, a tall burly man, was holding court. His hair and beard were long and blond from days out in the sun. His attire was bright oranges and reds, and consisted of tight pants and an open vest. He also noticed his large bulge. The mantra, *don't stare at it,* repeating over and over in his head.

"Eyes up here, lad" Decan teased. "Oh would you look at that? His make-up is running."

His crew laughed with him.

Darion rubbed the lower part of his cheeks and found the charcoal on his fingers. He sighed and rubbed it into his shirt.

"Good morning, chest hair." He extended his hand to shake. Decan hesitated but then squeezed his hand, hard.

"Good morning, city boy."

His crew chuckled to the retort.

Darion hated his crew more than Decan. Often thinking of them as diseased parrots. At least Decan had original thoughts, albeit far different from his own.

"We got started without you," Decan said, "since you're so late and all."

"Hi boys. Sorry to hear they slaughtered your favorite goat. I'm sure you'll find a new girlfriend in short time. If you're lucky she won't be delicious in stew." Darion waited patiently for their comprehension to catch up. Observing the critical moment where the insult settled into their ego. They scowled and pointed at him, uttering nonsensical noises. One of the men had to hold the other back from throwing punches.

"Watch it…city boy," the man holding the other back said.

"Irrefutably clever this one. Quick question: how does Decan like his asshole cleaned? Do you tongue it up and down or side to side?" Darion motioned with his hands.

The man seemed confused.

"I'm sorry. I'm sure it's more of a clockwise thing."

"Look Darion," Decan said, "We've already come to a decision. There is going to be an election." He got up close and whispered into Darion's ear. "Then we can finally end all the foolishness you've had us endure."

"An election…" Darion walked around with hands behind his back as he turned his words toward the growing crowd. "Well, that's interesting indeed. Our people, the Boudein, have their first election ever. Shattering *four hundred* years of tradition, because–and let me make sure I have this right–Because you believe I have abandoned tradition?"

"We thought it would be better than killing you. Unless you rather settle this in combat?"

Decan's crew laughed once more.

Darion considered the proposal but thought it unlikely to have a good outcome.

"So, we'll have an election then?"

"Remind me again what you plan to run on?"

"Gladly."

Decan's men placed a wooden crate in front of him, which he stepped on to address the crowd.

"We are nomads! We were not meant to build wooden homes, farm cactus fruits or lose ourselves and our connection to these lands. When he said we're going to build a grand city, I'll admit, I saw some sense in it. Look around, what do you see? After a year we have nothing. We don't have the resources to live like this, that is why it has never been our way. Ducian, Darion's own father, tried this once already. When he failed, he had us move to the green lands. I think we all remember what happened then, don't we?"

The crowd all bowed their heads, including Darion. Remembering the war that decimated their once great people.

"We must lose this place before we lose ourselves." He stood down from his box and everyone applauded. Approving chatter erupted from the crowd. He motioned for Darion to take the stand. Yet when Darion stepped up onto it, it broke, and he fell onto the ground. The crowd erupted into laughter.

"Even the furniture doesn't support you!" said Decan.

Doban, the hulk of a man that was Toonda's husband, walked over and pulled Darion up to his feet and dusted him off. Darion motioned for Doban to let him onto his shoulders. Doban nodded and got down on one knee for him to climb onto them. Darion addressed the crowd from the walking fortress.

"Look, let me be clear. My daddy ran this tribe, and when daddies die, their sons take their place! Especially when they're murdered!"

"Is falling asleep in your bed considered murder, boy?" Decan teased.

"That's not what happened..."

"We're being led by a child! Ghosts attacked his father in his sleep everybody!"

The crowd laughed.

Darion tightened his fist and stared at the ground.

"It wasn't a ghost…"

"Oh what's wrong, boy? Mayhaps you wanna run and cry some more?"

"That was one time…"

"Ah! He admits it!"

Toonda scowled. Tightening her fists as her body shook.

Darion wondered why he couldn't have just placed the candle properly earlier.

"All right folks," Decan said, "we'll be casting ballots in a month's time during the festival. I'll be out here everyday answering any questions you might have and, more importantly, taking your suggestions as well." He walked over and placed his arm around Darion. "If you need this one, go knock on his fancy door. Though ladies, I wouldn't ask him for any make-up advice."

The crowd slowly dispersed with a final laugh. Decan shook their hands as they left.

Darion sat in the sand and stared at his feet. He didn't know how much time had passed when Toonda tapped on his shoulder. When he looked up, they were alone–with her husband, of course.

"Why didn't you tell them everything?" she asked.

"Why bother? Nobody wants to listen to me anymore, maybe Decan should win the first ever election in Boudein history." He found footing and rose.

As he stood, she slapped him and continued to slap him until he grabbed her wrist. Even still he could barely prevent the assault.

“Pull the fucking hair out of your eyes,” she snapped, “then maybe you’ll see this isn’t just about you.”

“What do you want me to do exactly?”

“I want you to stop our scouts from never returning, killed by other tribes and beasts. I want you to form proper trade routes for resources. I want you to find wealth we can use for trading. I want you to live up to the dreams your father promised mine. I want you to stand up for your people! I want you to stand up for yourself dammit!” She ripped her wrist from his grasp and walked away past her husband.

Doban stood still as she past. "She really believes in you, Darion."

"Her faith is misplaced." Darion said.

"She's not the only one either." Doban nodded before turning to leave.

Darion simply stood there and thought about what she had said for a moment before walking home.

When he arrived home, the fragrance of smoke filled his nose. The stench made him turn toward his father’s shrine. It held the only possessions he had left: a necklace made of a black metal chain with a white orb hanging off it, a painting of him, and the sword he used in battle.

Darion removed the sword from its stand and ran his fingers along the blade. He gently slid the blade across his wrist, it bit into his skin, soft enough to not bleed. The last time his father had held it, his father had been panting heavily after a battle, two hands on the silver and black pommel. His father relaxed his stance. In the dust of battle there appeared those glowing wings outstretched from white armor. It gripped him, waiting just a moment before turning him into ash. He quivered now as he quivered as a child. That thing is dead now…it had to be. Not a single rumor of its existence ever came to him.

A sweat overtook him as his breaths halted. Darion dropped the sword. He squatted down and ran his hands along his face and past his hair. He collected himself before standing. He carefully placed the sword back above the shrine. He hung his head but had no words to offer. He laid down in front of it and fell to sleep.

Chapter 3

After returning south from Drisban to his home of Dreyhal. Cadivus sat with his three comrades in a tavern. The sun had been up for hours, which according to him, was the perfect time to imbibe his chosen ambrosia. Dark ale. The small town was alive with noise at all hours, loud voices and banging permeated the clay walls of the tavern. The horrible smell a distant memory to their now blind nostrils. Dreyhal could comfortably fit a thousand people, but it actually held about five thousand. Which meant the tavern was overcrowded as usual.

“Another caravan! This place is going to shit!” Toasty shouted. His eyes trying their best to focus on the glass of booze in front of him.

“Toasty, where the hell did that come from?” Cadivus asked, "didn't you arrive in an a caravan not two months prior?"

“The last good one if you ask me." Toasty drank the last half of his glass, slamming it to the table. "Pull the ladder up I'd say. These bastards are really—what the hell are you looking at?" His head fell to the table with a thud.

“The conversation.” Cadivus said, raising his glass to his lads, “was about how thanks to my latest exploits—I am sure I will be the most famous vigilante in the world once and for all.”

They all cheered to that. Their praise forced a grin on his face.

“Very soon the mention of my name will strike fear into the hearts of evil men and willing women. They will give my dagger a name and write stories and songs about my journeys. And they'll forget all about the hay incident."

The crew all grimaced and nodded.

Hedal stood. "I, for one, congratulate you."

Light clapping ensued.

"You know when I first, um. I…I'm too fucked up to remember what I was gonna say…" He sat back down and remembered why his second wife left him.

"Gentleman and the not so gentle and the not so men." Cadivus nodded toward the lady of their group. "It brings me great joy to know I am saving thousands–if not millions–of people from unknowable evil in our world. How I remain humble is but a mystery, however when I think of all the people, who can now live happy and comfortable lives because of me. How they can have families, and more specifically how they make those families. Well, there is no greater reward."

Everyone bowed their heads and raised their glasses.

"Also I stole their gold to be able to afford drinks today!"

They cheered.

An elderly woman approached their table. "Excuse me, sir, but did I just hear you say you're a savior of sorts?" With her head bowed, she removed her peasant's cap and played with it in her hands. "I come from a village not too far from here. The village is under the rule of an evil mayor who is going to execute my dear sweet child today along with dozens of others. Could you save them too?"

Cadivus rose to his feet, walked toward the woman, and gently grabbed her hand. "My dear nothing would bring me greater joy." He smiled at her.

She looked up and smiled, tears forming in her eyes.

"But right now I'm getting fucked-up with my boys!"

The group cheered and hollered as another round was delivered to the table.

"I'll tell you this though: a couple taverns down, you'll find a group of lads who would sack the capital city Afferium for a handy, so have at it ma'am!"

"What…what am I supposed to do now?" the woman cried.

"Oh it's easy, you just melt some butter in your palms and make this up and down motion here." He pantomimed the jacking off motion for her, feeling sorry for her husband.

Defeated, the old woman turned around and left the tavern.

"Cadivus, I gotta say it," Hedal said, "it was really messed up what you did back there. Someone of your renown and experience…" He gave a soft shrug.

"You're right," Cadivus said, "I should have shown her how to work the balls as well. I'll be right back." He turned to follow the elderly woman, but Hedal motioned for him to stop.

"That's not what I meant. We should go to this town, and save them from this evil that plagues them! I'm the perfect amount of fucked-up right now to get into a brawl!"

Everyone cheered for this. Alcohol was a great lubricant for praise in this group.

Cadivus gazed upon his friends, realizing one of his many faults was his enthusiasm for peer pressure. He paid the bill with the bloodstained coins, and the group set out to find the elderly woman. Outside, they took in the stench of body odor and urine that ravaged the city. They quickly headed to where they had pointed her toward.

But as they made their way, a figure on the ground caught Cadivus's eye. Down one of the alleyways, the elderly woman was lying face down on the ground.

"Lads, it appears the plot thickens," he said as he went to check on the body. He rolled her onto her back and gazed into her dead eyes. "It appears this woman is a drunk who cannot handle her liquor and may not offer reliable information."

"Nah, she's dead." Hedal said, pointing at the dagger, the blood, and all the other very obvious signs. "You can tell because of how unalive she is."

"Immigrants." Toasty muttered, making a fist. Lumpy–the lady of the group–bent down and tasted the blood.

"It's blood…" she said. "With trace amounts of dirt."

Cadivus smiled at her. He had always thought she was friendly, brave, and cool. He often wondered about settling down with a woman like her one day–but one without the hunchback. Which basically rendered her unlovable by anyone but a mule. Even Toasty said dating her would be dating down. So take that for what it's worth. Good ole Lumpy.

"It appears we have a new quest…" Cadivus said, "but it's a mystery quest, and those are lame." He lifted the woman and motioned for Lumpy to remove a lid from a nearby barrel. "In ya go, granny." He slowly slid her body inside. "I'm not trying to explain this to the fifty."

"Cadivus! What are you doing?" a voice shrieked from behind, sounding annoying, yet disarming. He recognized it before he even turned around.

"Oh, hey, Thermia…I just found a dead woman in a barrel and was about to alert the authorities." He dropped the corpse onto the ground, and an audible snap could be heard upon impact.

"Oh my god…that is so fucking rad." Thermia walked closer. In the noon light her red hair looked like a sunset, her round and pale face didn't fit the slim body she hid beneath her oversized plain blue dress. "Did she die from cold exposure or something?"

"Don't be silly Thermia. It's the middle of summer. The only thing that is going to be exposed here is evil doing." He thought for a moment about his predicament, then quickly changed the subject. While leading her away from the dead body. "So how are your cats doing?"

"Oh my god…Milky this morning…Well I don't know if you'd consider it morning. It was *way* after breakfast but before midday meal. Ohhh. You would have *loved* midday meal. We had this goat soup thing. It was like, so good, and then…"

"Right, right." Cadivus closed his eyes, feeling the aneurysm forming. "That is fascinating. Say, when's the last time you've seen my brother anyways? He's not skulking around here anywhere is he?" He looked around carefully.

"Oh, Hybie? Yeah last time I saw him he was passed out. I gave it to him good." She winked and made some awkward thrusting motions, hinting towards fornication. "Oh my god, I'm such an idiot, I didn't even tell you why I came here." She stopped thrusting, the group stood motionless not sure how to respond. "There's like a village or something that's—"

"Under the rule of an evil mayor." He stood up straight with a smug look on his face.

“Yeah, totally. How did you know that already?” With confusion on her face, which was pretty much her resting face.

“Oh, I, um, heard it from a child I saved earlier. From a tree. A mildly tall tree.” He put his hand on her back and walked her away from the alley, motioning for Lumpy to dump the body into the barrel.

Lumpy attempted to lift the corpse but fumbled and fell, getting stuck underneath it. It was at this point, she learned that dead bodies all shit themselves.

“Yeah, kids are pretty dumb,” Thermia said, tripping over own feet and face-planting the ground. She quickly got up and dusted herself off. “Well, I figured we could all go or something. I wouldn’t mind getting away from the smell of shit for a while.”

“Immigrants,” Toasty muttered once more.

“Absolutely. We are sober and concerned citizens after all,” Cadivus said, sneaking a shot from a flask he stole. “Let us set out on a voyage across the lands, and undo the evil that seeds into the soil of justice.”

Everyone agreed, and they set out on their voyage. Thermia told a guard where they were leaving and to tell her husband the details. At the main gate, Cadivus flicked a coin to the door operator. After the door closed behind them, they could breathe in fresh air for the first time all day. He flicked his last coin to a carriage operator, and they piled in.

“So, how far away is this village anyways?” Cadivus asked, taking the reins.

“We’re here,” Thermia said. Hopping out of the carriage, he looked to his left and saw a small village outside of his own town.

"My my. That is convenient evil. Why did you let me spend my last coin on a carriage if it is so close by?"

She laughed "Oh, because every time you rent one you get one of these collectible plates!" She held up a plate with a picture of an orange cat on it. "They are so cute!" Holding it with two hands, she skipped toward the village.

As they approached, they saw a crowd forming on the far side of town. They made their way toward the center of the crowd to see what was presumably the public execution.

"Wait a minute," Hedal said. "If this town is so evil, and so close to our own…why do people choose to live here?"

"Because, sticky leaf is legal here," Lumpy said. The group looked at her, and she shrugged. "It's good for my hump pain…"

"So, this icky is caused by the sticky icky, eh?" Cadivus said.

Looking at the stage he saw five people with black hoods on their heads and nooses around their necks. He scanned the crowd to get a sense of their temperament, but everyone just looked like they were staring at something far away.

"Interesting. We must learn the crimes of these people. We may have to intervene after all."

Shortly after, a well dressed man with long hair and a beautiful mustache took the stage. He put his hand up to silence the crowd.

"What's up mother fuckers?! Whoo! Who's ready for a little justice in Herbvia today let me hear it!"

The crowd cheered.

"I've gotta few mother fuckers here, let me tell ya. What have they done? I'm gonna tell ya. These, bitches, have been mellowing the vibe all gods damn week!"

The crowd yelled and booed. “No chill! No chill! No chill!” the crowd chanted.

“I know, dudes. And let me just say for a moment. In light of these crimes. Kevin makes like the sickest lemon pies I’ve ever had dude, everyone, let’s hear it for Kevin please. Love that man.”

The crowd cheered once more.

“These people are out of their minds,” Lumpy said.

“I know!” Hedal sighed. “Lemon pie sucks…”

“Indeed, lemon pie sucks,” said Cadivus “However, we cannot let these people die for such ridiculous crimes. We have to do something. Thermia, can you—” Cadivus turned his head and realized that she was gone. “Wait. Where did Thermia go?"

“She is chasing a kitten boss,” Toasty said. “Looks like we’ll have to handle this ourselves.”

Everyone nodded in agreement.

Cadivus motioned for the group to head toward the front of the crowd.

“Hey guys!” The speaker called out, stopping them in their tracks. “Yeah you guys. From Dreyhal.”

The group all glanced at each other and then at the man on the stage who was now making direct eye contact with them. “Yeah…What’s up bitches? I know who you are.” He took a hit from his rolled up sticky leaf. “Yeah. I’m gonna need these fuckers to hang tight for a minute. I’m gonna do a little monologuing here, and I heard you hate that.”

Cadivus did indeed have a disdain for monologues of others. But the crowd had squeezed him in, forming tighter and tighter around him and his comrades.

“Here’s the deal, bitch. I’m out of here, off to greener pastures. I’m taking my fabulous wealth and heading east.”

“Just tell me what this is all about!” Cadivus cried. “I’m so fucking bored right now!” He attempted to free himself from the crowd but he could not move freely. The pressure in his bladder rising and adding fuel to the chaos.

“Chill out a second, bro! I swear to gods!” He took another hit. “My brother was in that Deathicus cult. Remember Cavian, now I don’t think he deserved to have his neck stabbed, but maybe that’s just me.”

Cadivus grimaced. Where else was he supposed to stab him?, he thought.

“They were evil! And I delivered swift justice upon them!” His crew all audibly agreed.

“*Evil*?” The speaker spat. His tone softened.“You haven't witnessed evil yet. For you have yet to feel my retribution. I loved my brother. It was his dream to own a farm in the country. Now, his dreams fall to me along with a burning hunger for revenge that I fear can't be satiated."

He motioned for the five hoods to be removed. Underneath each were the five most beautiful single women in Dreyhal.

“Nooo!” Cadivus shouted. He struggled with all his might. “How dare you! All of my ex girlfriends!”

“We don't know you but please help us,” one of the women shouted back.

“And you've erased her memory of me!”

“Yeah. I heard you're a little fire bitch. Lame as fuck but works for me. I’m a top tier bitch mother fucker!” The speaker said. “So, do me a favor. Next time mind your own fucking business, kid. Enjoy the show."

With that said, he pulled a harmonica from his pocket and played an awful tune. The trap doors opened, and the women struggled in their nooses.

Heat formed deep inside Cadivus. His uncontrolled power burned. He couldn't stop it from gathering within him, no matter how hard he tried. He struggled to get away, to lift himself up on top of the crowd, but many hands from the crowd pulled him back down to the ground.

"Get away!" He shrieked. "Toasty! Lumpy! Hedal! Run! Get away from me!"

"Cadivus!" Toasty yelled out. He got onto the ground with Cadivus and wrapped his arms around him. "We got your back! It's gonna be o—"

Cadivus cried out as flames spread out from him in an explosion of heat. A fatigue he'd never felt before quickly overcame him. The vague familiar stench of burning flesh met his nose. He barely had the strength to lift his head. Nobody remained standing. His ears rang distortion into his blurred vision. His chest collapsed, making it impossible to breath. He wanted to scream. Not for rage but for the sake of terror.

Everything then faded to black.

Chapter 4

Cadivus awoke in a familiar dungeon cell. Large stones and bars were well lit by sun and flame alike in the cavernous design. Fatigue had left his body. He groaned as he stretched his aching limbs. He got up and peed into the corner of the cell.

"By the gods, Cadivus," the guard said, "couldn't you use the bucket we put in there for you?"

"Marking my territory Gerald. It would be a shame to waste such pungent piss," he said as he shook it off. He could hear pacing footsteps in the cell next to him. "Who's my roomie today?"

"Cadivus is that you?" a voice from the cell over called, "it's me, Thermia. Something horrible has happened."

"Yes, indeed. It seems we have been outwitted by a leafer. Our comrades have perished, our most beautiful women executed and–what's worse–my reputation is now going to be in shambles." He pushed a brick through the wall so he could see her.

Tears streamed down her face. "Yeah, and I have no idea what happened to my plate. It was the last piece of the set." She sobbed uncontrollably before looking back at him. "I didn't know your friends very well, but I'm sorry for your loss. You must be devastated. I can't imagine the pain you're going through right now."

"No, I'm fine. The blast didn't affect me whatsoever, and it appears I am none the worse." He checked his body for any remaining injuries. "Except it appears that a button is now missing from my jacket. I may become chilly soon." He took on a solemn expression.

"Gerald, why are we in here? We are the *victims*." Thermia took a deep breath. "And I freak out in tight spaces! The walls are closing in on me! Let me out!" She ran around the cell with her hands in the air making nonsensical noises.

She had officially lost her shit.

"Yeah Gerald, what gives?" Cadivus asked, "we tried our best out there, but we were bamboozled by an wicked man with an even more wicked stache." He grabbed the cell door. "Open this up, and we can go talk to my brother." He would've broken down the cells already, but last time he did that, his brother made him pay dearly. These cell bars also appeared twice as thick as the last time he had visited.

"No need for that," Gerald said, "he is on his way down now."

As the words left his lips, heavy footsteps that could only belong to one man echoed toward them. A symbol of fear and terror. The greatest hero the world had ever known. The unformidable, the legendary hero, known simply as: The Hybrid.

The Hybrid entered the room, dressed in dark cloth with dark gray metal greaves. A hood obscured his face. He lowered it, revealing his sharp features, short dark unkempt hair, pale skin, and bright pink eyes. Everything about his demeanor inspired capitulation. He walked toward the center of the room with those heavy footsteps echoing off the bounds of his dungeon.

"What is going on here you little shits?!" He strolled in front of the cells. "I decide to take a little nap and you have the audacity to sew chaos just outside my city walls!" He folded his arms and tapped his foot, waiting impatiently for any information.

"You tell us, baby!" Thermia shouted from her cell.

“Hey! Brother!” Cadivus called. “Flesh of my flesh, blood of my blood. Funny story…Me and my loyal henchmen were tricked into saving the world once again, and well, things got out of hand.” He got down on one knee “I ask your leave, so I may resume my duties of keeping this land safe once more.”

“This whole thing stinks of shit crap! By *got out of hand*, do you mean you murdered over a hundred people, including Gerald’s only son?!”

Gerald dropped his spear and shield.

“My son…my son has died? Oh my god…”

“Calm down, Gerald!” the Hybrid shrieked, slapping him across the face. “Control your emotions or, I’ll slap the shit out of you some more!”

He picked up his adornments and stood tall once more as he held back his tears.

The Hybrid turned back his brother. “You went to a foreign land–”

“I can literally throw a rock at it from the window,” Cadivus said, “you can see the smoke from here.” He stuck his arm out of the window. “Look. Everybody, wave.” He waved towards the men cleaning up the mess out the window.

One man slowly waved back.

The Hybrid walked through the cell bars, phasing into smoke, and losing the greaves on the other side. He slapped Cadivus, knocking his head to the side. “I’ve had enough, runt! A whole bunch of people are now smoldering ash because of you and your inability to control yourself! Not to mention we can smell booze all over your breath. Have you lost what little sense you had? Or should I slap you again?!” He raised his hand once more.

Cadivus turned away and put up his hands.

"No, no, no. Just wait a second here. This isn't my fault! I didn't activate my powers. The mustached man *forced* me to use them. I don't know how he did it exactly, but I think it has something to do with sticky leaf and a harmonica."

The Hybrid slapped him once more.

"I've never heard anything so ridiculous!" he cried in a high-pitched tone. "Do you understand what kind of position you've put me in as leader here? If I don't punish you two, this whole city is going to tear itself apart!"

"Wait. What?" Thermia said, "I didn't do anything! I was busy chasing a kitten! And then I found some incense…And before I knew what happened…my...plate…was...broke!" She sobbed.

"The guard told me you brought him there, which makes you just as responsible, missy." He phased back out of the bars, and into his greaves. "Almost everyone is asking me for a public execution, and others are asking me to find a way to sweep it under the rug."

"Put me down for the rug thing," Cadivus said.

"I'm gonna roll you up in one and smoke the shit out of you!" He walked toward the exit, but turned around one last time. "I'm gonna go talk to my advisors and figure out how to not spill any more blood today. Then things are gonna change. Big time! Mister!" He stormed up the stairs muttering to himself along the way.

"Well, all things considered that went pretty well," Cadivus said.

Gerald's gaze concentrated on him, a look he recognized very much: disdain and attraction.

"Now, now, Gerald. Like I explained to Smokey up there, this wasn't my fault. I didn't kill your boy. Well, I did physically kill him yes, but it wasn't actually my choice in the matter. Then again, I have told him on more than one occasion I was going to indeed kill him but that was more of a metaphor than anything. I surely didn't mean I would leave his smoldering corpse on the ground amongst a bunch of smoke sniffers."

Gerald grabbed his keys and opened the cell door.

"I'm going to stick my spear straight up your ass, then take my shield and liquify your balls!" Screaming, he charged at Cadivus, smacking his head with his shield and squishing him against the wall.

"Are you sure I can't talk you out of this? What if I buttered up my palms and...you know."

Gerald yelled once more, bringing back his spear to thrust it into him. Cadivus pushed on the shield and sent the guard flying back into the opposite wall, knocking him to his back. The spear left his hand and flipped into the air. He screamed as it came falling back–pointing down. He closed his eyes, preparing for the pain of the impact. But when he didn't feel the sharp agony, he reopened his eyes, and saw Cadivus holding the spear a smidgen over his wedding tackle.

"There. I have saved your jewels." Cadivus held his hand out and lifted up Gerald. "Are we even?"

Gerald sighed and nodded, rage having surpassed him.

"Good. Now you and your lovely wife can make a new boy! One who doesn't partake in freaky leafer festivals."

He screamed once more and Cadivus left the cell, and closed the gate behind him. He went to reach for his keys, but Cadivus twirled them on his finger.

"Sorry old man, but we can't leave our fates up to the fogies here." Cadivus turned to the next cell over. "Thermia, we need to get out of here. Now."

"But, I don't want to leave…" she muttered. "I love it here. I have servants, food, outfits, and your brother who just really boils my cauldron if you know what I mean." She raised her eyebrows at him.

"Thankfully I don't. However, if there is one thing he loves more than us, it is definitely this piss-filled shithole. If they decide to execute us, well, we're fucked. So we need to go. Pronto!"

He opened her cell, grabbed her hand, and led her outside. Luckily, most guards were busy either at the meeting or attending to the corpses in Herbvia. They easily crept through the halls–until a cat meowed.

"Milky!" Thermia yelled. "Who's a good boy or girl?! It's Milky!"

Cadivus sighed.

"What the fudge!" The Hybrid called from the conference room not far down the hall.

"Double time, Milky," Cadivus said. He grabbed Thermia and Milky by their scruffs and ran toward the exit. Yet, before he could reach it, a black cloud formed in front of it, blocking him from leaving. He turned around and found himself surrounded by guards.

"What the hell are you doing, deviant!?" The Hybrid asked. "Where is Gerald?"

"His balls are entirely intact, I swear it upon my life," Cadivus said.

"Well yours are about to be made into pudding!"

He dropped Thermia and Milky. The cloud of smoke from the exit formed a circle around them, starting from the ground and lifting over their heads. They coughed and gagged. Thermia threw Milky through the deadly column of smoke, and the cat hissed when it collided with a wall. When the coughing pain became almost unbearable, they found themselves able to take a deep breath. When they rubbed the smoke from their eyes, they saw that they were outside. Not only that, but they were outside of the city walls with no guards in sight.

"I'm going to do you both one last act of kindness and exile both of you!" The Hybrid said. "If either of you show your faces here again, I will be forced to slap you to death!" He raised his hand high into the air.

"Brother, I want to say one thing before we enter a life of exile," Cadivus said.

He folded his arms and turned away. "It's too late to apologize now!"

"No, it's not that. It's just well, we don't have any money for this exile–"

The Hybrid slapped him once more, much harder this time.

"I don't give a hoot!" He pointed toward the woods behind them. "Get lost!"

"Wait a smoke-ticking second here! What if I can prove our innocence?"

"And how do you plan to do that exactly?"

"I'll find the mustached man and bring him back here. Then I'll force him to confess to what he has done in front of everyone!" Cadivus said, faking a smile and trying to gauge his brother's reaction.

The Hybrid considered the proposal and gave a half nod, half shrug which indicated he approved of the idea.

"If you can get a confession from this supposed vagrant, I'll let you back into the city. If you come back without him though, I'll carve your ass up and feed you to the wolves. Don't test me on this!" he said, folding his arms.

"Of course, brother. Mother would want us together after all, right?" He got down on one knee and grabbed Cadivus's cheeks with his hand, and stared into his eyes.

"You wouldn't know anything about what she wanted, would you?" he said softly, "Because if you did, you would stop all this foolishness and stop forcing my hand."

Cadivus bowed his head and stared at the ground, speechless.

"Hybie…you didn't need to…" Thermia said.

The Hybrid turned his back to them and faced his city.

"Oh, and Thermia…" He said. "Be careful of your dark place. Take care of the deviant."

"Good-bye, my mist dick…" Tears formed in her eyes.

With that, he turned into a cloud of smoke and disappeared back over the city walls.

****

The two exiles wandered through the late afternoon, not entirely sure where they were going. They traveled through the forest that separated their city from neighboring towns and villages. The forest had several paths through it that were created by local wildlife and smugglers. They walked for hours. Hardly speaking to one another as the cold of night settled in.

"Ugh! Walking this much sucks!" Thermia shouted and punched a tree and broke her nail. "Dammit! I hate the woods!"

"Fear not my dear," Cadivus said, "we have one thing going for us. We are delinquent shut-ins. Nobody knows what we look like! Why, by midday tomorrow, we can enter the town of Motob. I shall seduce an elderly woman, and we can live off her until she has an 'accidental' death and leaves me all her earthly possessions." He nodded along with his own plan. "Then we'll use those funds to buy as much jerky and lotion as we can carry, and head out to find that leafer."

"Right…except for the fact that you are a famous vigilante! Everyone is going to recognize you!"

"Well, I don't think that will be a problem."

"Why exactly wouldn't that be a problem?"

Cadivus pursed his lips. "Well, in the past five or so years of me being a vigilante, I've only managed to defeat one death cult…"

"What? How is that possible?" she asked, "you'd disappear for days or weeks at a time! What were you doing?" Thermia asked.

"Well, I didn't have any leads and I didn't want to look like I was lazy, so I just got drunk in the woods and meditated. And by meditate I mean jacking off to lewd pictures and unusually sexy trees." He winked at one of those particularly curvy trees and sighed deeply. "So anyways, we should be fine."

As darkness swept over the woods, Cadivus lay under a tree, and Thermia lay against one near him.

"Well could you at least make us a fire so we don't freeze tonight?" she asked.

"I'd rather I didn't."

"Oh my gods. Why *not*?!"

"I don't remember if fire attracts or scares beasts. Best not to take the chance."

"Fine, whatever! I'll just make it myself!" She grabbed two nearby sticks and rubbed them together in an odd way. Nothing happened. "I don't know how to do this! Just poof one!"

“I can’t.”

“Give me one good reason why you can’t!”

With a look of defeat across his face, he took a deep breath. His head fell between his shoulders.

“I’m terrified of fire…”

Thermia stared at him blankly before giving up and lying back against the tree. Without uttering another word, they stared up at the stars until they fell asleep.

Chapter 5

The two exiles awoke from a rough night of sleep. Cadivus gathered some bugs and berries for breakfast and gave half to Thermia.

"This is going to be gross," he said. "Just pretend you're giving a slobby to get out of trouble." He tossed the mix into his mouth and chewed slowly.

Thermia reluctantly put the handful into her mouth and chewed. "Wow! This is great!" she mumbled through her full mouth.

"Reminds me of that time I came back to Dreyhal with that talking bird."

"Did you capture it in these woods?"

"Nope. Anyway, I have come up with a plan. That sticky hippy said he was heading east, so we'll just walk that way. We'll find him, kick his ass, break his harmonica, and then drag him back to confess."

"Yes!" she cheered. "Our love for our comrades will guide our hearts!"

"Well, yeah. Our *like* for our comrades will guide them certainly."

"What do you mean? They were your only friends for years!"

"Well, true," he said. "but they only hung out with me when I was paying for drinks. The other day was the first time we hung out outside of a tavern, and look where that got us."

"I never got that vibe from them but okay…"

"Fantastic! Now, let's be on our way. We will head to Motob and see if we can devise where in the east this leafer is heading."

The two headed toward the town that was now only a few hours away. Before they arrived, Thermia decided they should use alter egos so they wouldn't rouse suspicion. They decided to pretend they were fishers from the west coast, heading east for new opportunities. She made them grass hats from the fauna to sell the illusion.

As they made their way into town they noticed it was unlike Dreyhal. There were no walls, the streets weren't cluttered, and the smell of shit was thankfully absent. It was much smaller, sure. However each building appeared to double as a business and domicile for the workers within. The wide earthen streets allowed large carts to pass through the middle of town. Even though it was still the early hours of the morning, the town appeared to be very much alive.

The two approached a lone baker first.

"Dear baker," Cadivus said, "we are fisherpeople from the west. How do you do?" They both nodded to the baker, catching their grass hats before they fell off.

The baker momentarily stopped pouring flour over his breads. "You two don't smell like fish…"

"Just give me a few more days without bathing," Thermia remarked while nudging her elbow toward the man.

"Heyo!" Cadivus said, as they high-fived. He turned back to the baker. "My dear baker…My name is Kettlepot and this is my sister Brittlebuns."

They both bowed slightly.

"Brittlebuns…" Thermia muttered to him.

He nudged her side.

"We are seeking voyage to the east. Say…near good farming lands by chance…"

The baker eyed them up and down. “If you’re siblings, how come you look of no relations?"

“We’re also thespians," Cadivus replied.

“None my business what two ladies do at night…” The baker said while continuing to flour his loaves. "That being said, let me give tell–”

“Wait…” Cadivus put his hand up. “Wait a moment. Why are we getting exposition from a hideous, ugly man?” He grimaced and shrugged. “I’m not even going to describe you out loud or in my head but you sir are the stuff of nightmares.”

The baker nodded in agreement.

“No, no, no. What we need is someplace sexy, damp and dangerous. Some place like…” As he scanned the town, his eye became fixated on a dark building in the corner of town, the roof was falling apart and the guards seemed to steer clear of it. The sign read “Damp N Rousing.” “There! That is where we tick off this quest log.”

Thermia nodded excitedly.

“As long as I can use the bathroom there.” she walked toward it, swinging her arms wildly.

He grabbed her wrist and whispered into her ear.

“Not like that, dear. You walk like a gorilla through a thick brush."

She looked at him and blew out her cheeks.

He pushed them back in. “We need a good, confident, strong canter. Shoulders back, chest up and hips thrusting ever so slightly with each step. As you approach, they should be wondering whether you want to fight them or fuck them. Also, this head wear has to go." He took their hats off and threw them to the ground.

"Hey!" Thermia protested.

Cadivus pointed at her. "Proper. Posture."

Thermia nodded as she fixed her stance.

“So, what should I do with my hands then?”

“I don’t know. Never figured that part out. Let's go!”

He walked off with his arms and hands straightened toward the ground, unmoving. She followed suit, trying her best not to stumble and clenched her tongue in her teeth. They approached the tavern’s doorman, and Cadivus leaned in and whispered something to the large man. The doorman made a grossed-out face and waved them inside.

“What did you say to him?” she asked as they walked inside.

“I asked him if we could come inside because my racist cousin needed to take a shit.”

Her jaw dropped.

He pushed her lower jaw back up. “Careful, dear. They’ll think you’re advertising.”

They cantered to a table and sat across from each other. Afterward, she made weird faces and rocked back and forth.

“The bathroom is over there, love.” Cadivus said, pointing to the sign.

She shot up and ran off while he scanned the room familiarize his surroundings. He noted the tavern was old. The wood was rotting in most places, obvious traces of termites woven through each brace and table top alike. Newer columns were installed throughout to prevent what appeared to be an inevitable collapse. All the chairs were wobbly, clattering in a choir as bodies shifted in them. Everyone that was eating appeared to be enjoying their meals. Their eyes closing with elation with each bite taken. A waitress walked over and asked if he wanted anything.

He was about to order a round when he suddenly realized he was broke. “In a moment, my dear. Still looking at the menu.”

“We don’t have menus…” the waitress said, puzzled.

He waved her off and scanned the room once more. Seeing as how it was still mid-day, most patrons were just run-of-the-mill alcoholics. However, at one table came laughter, cheers, and clinking money. Gambling, perfect. He approached the table of seven with his patented walk.

A loud thud hit the table. “Ow!” a man yelled, “my elbow slipped.”

“You should stop licking it then!” another man shouted, and they all had a laugh.

The disgruntled loser tossed a coin across the table. The coin looked like a pebble in his monstrous hand.

“Don’t make excuses,” A softer voice said, “be a man.” The owner of the voice hidden behind a column.

As Cadivus walked over, his eyes shot open as she came into view. She was a beautiful woman with dark skin. An uncommon sight in this part of the world. Her curly hair sat at her shoulders, and her eyes…well, he was too far away to describe them properly. She wore light dark brown leather armor with decorative golden emblems embedded in it. She had a colorful beaded bracer with reds, yellows and greens. The bracer went half way up her forearm, oddly quiet with her movement. He adjusted his erection discreetly, putting it in his waistband as approached the table.

“What the hell do you want?” she asked in a familiar tone most women used with him. Her voice also carried a vague accent that he had not heard before.

“I couldn’t help but overhear. Slam hands is a game I have been wanting to try for some time now,” he said, gesturing to the table.

“It is called arm wrestling, you dumb twat.”

Everyone laughed.

“All the better,” he said, “wrestling is a pastime for me as well.”

“Where have you wrestled exactly?” she asked.

“Oh, just with my thoughts. Mostly at night.”

The men at the table winced, shaking their heads. One nodded.

“So, what is the wager for a round?” Cadivus asked.

“Normally it is a coin per round,” she said, “but you do not have any coins on you, do you?”

Cadivus tapped his pockets and shrugged.

She counted her own coins, not glancing up at him. “So I am guessing you want to bet that dagger you have in your waistband.”

“Well, I have two rules for gambling: one, never bet my manhood and–”

She held her hand up to silence him.

“I am not talking about your pathetic excuse for a dick in your waistband, muffin. I am talking about the seven-inch steel on your back.”

Surprised, he pulled the dagger from behind him and held it up, so she could see the extravagant metal work on the handle and blade. Their eyes lit up seeing the dim ruby in the golden pommel.

“I must be tired. It is a six-inch after all," the woman said.

“I do appreciate balance in my waistband.” He winked.

“Does that even make sense?” a man asked.

Another man grunted. “I think he’s trying to say his penis is—”

She slammed the table in frustration. “Okay! That is enough of…” The woman sighed as she collected herself. “Decent dagger…could probably fetch, let us say ten coins from a pawn.” She finally looked up to catch Cadivus’s eyes.

“I appreciate your low ball,” Cadivus said, “as I hope you would appreciate mine. However, this dagger is worth at least ten times that amount, I’m afraid.”

“Yeah? Well if you are scared to lose it, I understand why.” She rolled her wrist and stretched her fingers.

“Ten coins it is. Just wanted to make sure we’re all on the same page. By the way. I'm digging the beautiful but deadly vibe you have going on here.”

"I like your face smashed with a shovel but ignorant vibe that you have too. You adorn it with an unearned pride."

The crowd laughed and hooted as she smirked and gestured for him to sit. He placed his dagger next to her ten coins.

“Let me tell you something about me,” she said, “before you lose your only possession on this earth.”

He normally hated hearing people’s back stories, but they usually weren’t this pretty or threatening.

“I come from the lands to the far west, past the sea. From the plains of Naobi. Where men are warriors and women make babies.”

“Wow,” he muttered, “sounds like literally every other place ever but go on…”

“I grew up with many brothers and battled them each day and each night. I have been battle trained by the greatest warriors on earth since before I could walk. I am the second woman to ever make it into our warriors circle. I have never been bested in combat, I have never backed down from a fight, and I have never lost a test of strength. I am the warrior known by the name, Aries Ekio."

"Ekio!" the table cheered.

"Cool," Cadivus said, putting his hand out for the contest.

She looked at him puzzled but put her hand in his. The frayed calluses bit into him. She squeezed with sizable strength.

"Go on my count," One of the men said, holding both their hands. "Three, two, one, go!"

Cadivus slammed her hand down on the table before the first cheer. The table went silent.

"I have a brother too. That's probably why I won." He reached for his reward.

Ekio slammed her fist between his hand and the betting pool. He looked up from his prize to see her teeth clenched and her body shaking. "Double or nothing!" She said as slid over twenty coins.

"Look, I really don't want to take more of your money. Instead, why don't you buy your brothers a gift to thank them for all that training."

"Double or nothing!" Ekio said, grinding her teeth.

"If you insist…" He placed his hand in hers once more, her palms now sweaty.

The referee grabbed their hands.

"Three, two, one, go!"

Cadivus didn't slam her arm down immediately this time. He couldn't. Instead he stared into her gorgeous—yes now he can describe them—gorgeous brown eyes. The look of determination, the will of a warrior, and a light hue of…pink…*Wait.* His elbow slipped, and she slammed his hand on the table. The crowd cheered, patting her on the back. She had the smuggest look on her face as she stood there still as a statue.

Cadivus maintained eye contact with her. He knew his elbow didn't slip; it was pushed. Yet he still couldn't help but smile.

"Interesting technique you have there."

"As much as I would love to remain stoic right now…" She said as she got up, walked over to him, and brought her face down to his. "In your face! In your face! In your face!" she yelled, holding her hand in front of his face.

Everyone laughed.

He had no choice but to sit there and take it. The dagger had now become the least of his concerns. He stood up to shake her hand.

"Could we have a chat in private perhaps?"

She gave a single wave of her hand, and the group groaned as they were sent away.

After they left, he took a man's drink. "That is a good con you have going here. I have an admiration for creativity."

"*Please.* You tried to pull the same thing"–she lowered her voice softly, so others couldn't hear– "hybrid."

His heart raced and his waistband got tighter once more.

"The better warrior won. Just have a little humility and go back home," she said.

"I assure you that is not possible," Cadivus said.

"What? You do not know how to be humble, loser?" she asked, smirking.

"No, not that part. The home part is no longer an option for me. Not unless I finish the quest I am on."

The smirk fell from her face, and her eyes retreated into her memories.

"I have a feeling we share a similar past…Perhaps this meeting was not by chance, but instead of destined fate…"

"First off," she said. "Destined fate are synonyms and should not be used to describe each other."

Cadivus nodded.

"Second, I am not sleeping with you just because I am a hybrid and the only other woman you know the name of."

He opened his mouth to retort but nodded.

"Third, you have no idea of my past, or my future. It is bold of you to assume you could be of any use to me. The man I'm looking for is another like us. One who uses a harmonica as an instrument of death."

He laughed to himself, mostly through his nose.

"Did I say something funny?" Ekio asked.

"You're not gonna fucking believe this…" He explained what had happened with his run-in with the harmonica wielding man. Embellishing the story to make him look better in the process. "Like I said, this is fated destiny."

She rolled her eyes so hard they almost got stuck.

"We can work together! I already have one comrade with me. We can assemble a team and defeat this evil blowhard once and for all. But first, tell me what this man did to you?"

"I am not ready to reveal that yet." She turned away to gaze out the window.

"Good. It will keep this chapter of our lives shorter. Now, we need only to find a couple other good men or warrior women with brothers to assist us."

“Even if we wanted to, where would we find anyone like that here?” she snapped. “Those guys I was arm wrestling with are the strongest guys in here, and that is not saying much.”

“Hey ya’ll! Guess who’s a couple pounds lighter!” Thermia shouted as she ran toward them.

People glanced over toward her in bemusement.

“Not now, Thermia,” Cadivus said, “we are trying to devise a plan to find more comrades for our quest for absolution. Perhaps we can put up flyers or have a hand job sale…”

Ekio shook her head.

“We will just interview some people and go from there,” Ekio said, "does he always complicate things this much?" she asked Thermia.

Thermia nodded with wide eyes but halted when Cadivus turned toward her.

Cadivus shrugged. “Only if I get to make the poster,” he said. “I adore arts and crafts.” He tapped his pocket, where he kept a hand drawn picture of a curvy tree.

Chapter 6

The newest contraption was quite simple really. In the doorframe, the razor sharp sword was held in place at neck height. Secured with wooden planks and nails.

Darion braced his heel against a far wall. He stared at the blade allowing his focus to become his will. The darkened room glowed in his dedication. He ran toward it at full sprint. Yet he stepped onto a pile of dirty clothes and lost his footing. He tripped toward the blade and fell onto the ground.

The first thing he noticed was that he was still conscious. He ran his hands along his neck and face. No wounds. In his failure he tried to comb his bangs over his eyes, but they didn't hide his wounded pride. He tried using both hands in a frantic despair to no avail. Desperate, he ran over to a mirror and wiped it clean with his sleeve.

The sword had only cut his bangs. Severed follicles itched at his face.

His front door slammed open, and the outside light blinded him.

"It smells so…oh my god! What did you do to your hair?" Toonda dropped her supplies on a table and ran over to him grabbing his face. She smiled as she examined it. "It's an interesting look!"

"The strands are over there. Glue them back on." He pointed toward the doorway with the contraption.

She stared at it, looked back at him, screamed out a war cry, and punched his face. Catching his jaw, his cheek and finally his nose. He took a few steps back, wiping the blood escaping his nostrils. She breathed heavily then continued screaming wildly and clenching her fist. Her anger beyond words, devolved into tones and gutteral noises.

"What?" Darion asked, holding his bleeding nose.

"I can't fucking take it anymore! You entitled piece of shit! Why can't you just give a shit about anyone besides yourself for one second, you selfish cunt?!" She sent a searing high pitch scream through his home.

"Uh…my family's dead and I'm a failure. I'm allowed to brood."

She walked over to the shrine and punched a hole through the painting of Darion's father. She looked over to see his reaction. That same blank face looked back at her. So, she grabbed the necklace and began to pull it apart.

"Wait! Wait!" Darion said, falling to his knees and holding his hands up. "Please…don't!"

"There you go. You finally care about something. Now aim that feeling toward the men, women and children who trusted you."

"In three weeks, Decan will be the leader. Then we can all go back to the old ways, roaming the desert like we were meant to."

Toonda placed the necklace back down and spoke calmly.

"All but a handful of our warriors are dead. If we go on the move, the other desert tribes will slaughter us. You knew this then. Why don't you see it now?" She placed her hand on her stomach and tears filled her eyes. "I don't want my baby to die, Darion. Please, do something."

When he didn't respond, she walked over to the table and removed the few supplies she had been able to round up. He reached to his side, removed a dagger, and examined his face in the blade.

He held the blade's handle out toward Toonda.

“Start with fixing my hair please. Can’t go around looking like lake folk, can I?”

When Darion stepped outside he was forced to finally take a clear look around. A group of people walking by looked at him and smiled, complimenting his new look.

He walked over to a group of men sitting around and enjoying some water. “We need to build a perimeter wall.”

They all laughed.

“With what exactly?” one asked “we don’t even have enough materials for homes.”

He realized how ridiculous the request sounded, but could only think of one way to get it started.

“Tear my home down. Use what you can to start. Use the long piece for posts, and run ropes between them. We have plenty of rope.”

They looked at him and laughed once more.

“Tear your home down?” one asked before whispers and nods circled the group. “Okay. We’ll start tomorrow.”

“You’ll start now,” he said, “I just need to remove a few things first.”

Footsteps approached from behind him.

“Ah…The bat comes out of his cave…”

“Decan, it pains me to say this, but I don’t have time for this.”

“Three weeks, Darion.” Decan held up three fingers. “In three weeks, you’ll have all the time in the world.”

“If you told me that this morning, I might have agreed with you.”

“What changed then?”

“I realized something.” Darion turned toward him. “This was never about us.”

“Then what is this about?”

“You're the same as me Decan: a good son walking in his father’s footsteps. I found respect for that, but all the same, my dad could beat up your dad.” He smiled at that.

“Shame we never got to see that match, eh?”

“It is.”

“Scout!” someone screamed from far away in the camp.

They all looked over and saw a man pointing at another man running for the dunes. Darion pushed Decan out of the way and ran toward the scout, who was disappearing over the hill. Yet as he approached the top and looked around, he couldn’t see anyone.

Decan and his men approached the edge of the camp as Darion returned.

“This is bad,” Darion said, “we need to prepare for an attack.”

“We scared em off,” Decan said, “he won’t be coming back.”

“I Didn’t ask for your fucking opinion.”

Decan's men stepped toward Darion with malicious intent. He brought up a fist to stop them.

“He is the leader for now. We must respect our leaders. What is your play?”

“I already commanded some men to tear my home down and build a wall. We’ll fortify it in the direction the scout ran for. We’ll double the lookouts, and tell all fighting men to have steel on their sides. Put the most vulnerable in the center of camp. And for the love of the gods, comb that rat's nest of a beard you have before speaking to me again.”

Decan slightly bowed and smiled.

“You heard him! Get to work!” As his men left, he approached Darion. “It’s in my best interest to respect command, you know. When I am leading I can expect the same from you and any of your fanatics?”

“Decan, I command you to go fuck yourself.”

He nodded once more and walked away with his chin high and his hands behind his back.

Darion looked around the village, making sure his orders were being carried out. Hands wrapped around his shoulders from behind, hugging him.

“I should have beat your privileged ass a long time ago,” Toonda said. She released him, held out his father’s sword with the necklace tied around the hilt, knelt, and presented it. “Use the past to guide our future.”

He carefully grabbed the hilt and lifted the sword, examining the blade more carefully then he ever had before. In the sun, he saw all its imperfections from its many battles. He touched the blade, and dropped it on the ground.

“Oh shit! It’s hot.” He shook his fingers and picked it back up. Toonda untied the sheath from her waist and smacked his head with it before handing it to him.

“Never drop that sword again. You hear me?” She handed it over to Darion who quickly tied it to his own waist. He took one last look at the blade that protected their people for decades past before placing it into the sheath.

“Yes ma'am.”

Chapter 7

"Oh, I'm good at this." Thermia said after her, Cadivus, and Ekio set up a table in the tavern. The sign outside read "Seeking Adventurers: Become Famous and Guaranteed Maidens." "I helped hire all the servants back home."

"Isn't my brother always complaining about theft?" Cadivus asked.

"I let the people Hybie threatened steal… I'm surprised we owned anything, come to think of it."

Several people had lined up, waiting for their chance to apply to the team. The promise of adventure was an irresistible call to many.

First was a giant, shirtless man. His muscles were large, and his skin was unfathomably oily. He approached the group and placed a foot on the chair rather than sit. The decorated hilt of a large claymore protruded over his head.

"Greetings fellow adventurers," he said in a deep masculine voice.

At that moment, Cadivus knew he had to do everything in his power to prevent this man from joining them. He knew he would stand no chance of winning Ekio over with this living statue accompanying them. Lucky for him, the women were only making incoherent babbling noises, so he could lead the interview.

"I'm sorry. We didn't order a stripper. Perhaps you're meant to be in the next tavern over?" he said, pointing toward the door.

The man laughed. Even his laugh was attractive. *Damn him.*

"Forgive me," the man said, smiling. "It's hard to find a shirt that can fit over my chest and shoulders. I lost the last one I had while defeating a giant lizard that was terrorizing some monks near the Boromir Desert."

"Alrighty. So you have some experience. I should just ask– Are you flexing right now?"

The man shook his head.

"Where do you see yourself in five hundred years?" Cadivus asked.

"I suppose I will be long dead by then. Perhaps having died in my lover's arms."

"*Okay.* So, no goals…" Cadivus wrote down the answer. "And how often do you cheat on your girlfriends?"

Ekio and Thermia stared at him. Thermia also elbowed him under the table.

"Well, I've never been with a woman before, so never," the man said.

All their ears perked up, and confusion washed over their faces.

"Excuse me?" Thermia said, "how is that possible?"

"Well, probably because I'm a nice guy who doesn't treat women like shit," the man said, "so why would they want to be with me? Instead they go for the cool evil wizard or the mysterious assassin or the fat drunk guy at the bar!" The man's face became sweaty as his demeanor fell. His perfect posture now relaxed.

"Right. Well I think we are gonna go another way," Ekio said, "nice meeting you?"

"Pussy Slayer is what they call me." He winked at the women.

"I'm gonna call you… Irony Slayer," Cadivus said, "have a good one, Irony Slayer."

Pussy Slayer took his foot off the chair and turned to leave. But before he opened the door, he turned around one last time.

"Adventure tease…" He left.

An immense amount of relief filled Cadivus. Knowing he was still the hottest male group member. Albeit the only one, with luck that would remain to be the case. Still, he berated himself for not thinking of using the name Pussy Slayer for his own name. He had a new goal of acquiring a cool nickname before this quest was over. Which he marked down in the notes he was making.

A large dark-haired woman sat before them. Her face was bright red, and her skin was sweaty. "Hey," she said between deep breaths.

"Why do you want to be an adventurer?" Ekio asked.

The woman held up a finger, still catching her breath. She reached out for a cup of water and chugged it. Taking large, asthmatic breaths between gulps.

"I'm trying to prove a woman in my situation can be formidable," the woman said. Her face cringing in pain.

"Fat?" Cadivus asked meekly.

"Whoa!" the women cried out at once.

He sunk into his seat as the unexpected shame washed over him.

"That's not what I meant at all," the woman said, "I meant pregnant."

The trio glanced at each other before quietly shooing her away.

A skinny man in fancy loose clothing took a seat next. "Hello. I'm Sparklebutt." He tipped his fancy hat revealing his disheveled auburn hair.

"How long have you been an adventurer for?" Thermia asked.

He thought hard before answering.

"All my life really. I do this for a living. Been on hundreds of quests." He leaned in and whispered. "How much is the pay?"

“Pay?” Cadivus replied, “this is more of a paid in exposure sort of thing.”

Sparklebutt pursed his lips and got up to leave.

“Wait a moment.” The group whispered among themselves.

“All right. We have an offer,” Thermia said, “when we capture our guy you can take whatever gold he has, minus a bit for us for the journey back home.”

Sparklebutt looked over at them and mulled the offer over.

“Also, I’ll share all of my gossip with you.” She smirked.

He smiled.

“I’m in!” he said, “I just need to find a place to stash my baby before we go.”

“Excuse me?” Ekio said, clenching her fist. He laughed.

“Ah, I’m just yanking your clam. I shoot blanks.” He winked at Cadivus.

He got up and left the tavern.

"Wait a second," Thermia said, "shouldn't we have asked him more questions?"

Cadivus and Ekio tilted their heads. "Probably, but when he tried to leave I felt compelled to make him join us. Do you think he tricked us?" Cadivus asked.

"Probably not," Thermia said.

"I liked his hat," Ekio said. They all shrugged and continued with more interviews.

The next several men all asked for Thermia’s or Ekio’s hand in marriage. Apparently *adventurous* meant something else in Motob. They politely refused, but sensing a pattern Cadivus stood. He walked in front of the long line to address it. “Anyone here to ask the women for marriage, just leave now. We’re seeking justice, not suckstice.”

Several men and women left the line. Only a handful of people remained.

He shook his head at the leftovers. “Next!” he said with as much enthusiasm as he could muster.

A very skinny man entered the room with a wide, almost fanatical smile. He placed a resume on the table and sat down while staring straight through Cadivus as he read the resume over. He shook his head disbelief.

"Daniel. This resume is trash. There's nothing even remotely related to adventuring," Cadivus said as he handed it off to Thermia. "Just…get on out of here man."

"Wait!" Daniel said. His smile faded to a panicked frown. "I am your biggest fan. I came all the way down from Motob, and what do I happen to see? My hero is recruiting adventures." He held his palms out to the table as he stared into each of their eyes. "This has to be fate or destiny or…or…or fated destiny or something."

Cadivus turned to catch Ekio's eyes, who shook her head and sighed. "I take it back. This guy rules, your in!"

Daniel's eyes lit up and his mouth opened wide.

"No!" Thermia shouted, "you can't just bring along one of your fan boys. He'll die out there, and then you'll have no fans." She passed the resume to Ekio.

Cadivus placed a hand under his chin and thought on her appeal. "Have you ever been in a fight, Daniel?" he asked.

"Oh yeah, for sure. I fight my brother all the time. Almost won the last few too. Toddlers these days are something else let me tell ya." He folded his arms and sat back in his chair.

Ekio put the paper down. "This just says you helped your dad sell potatoes for a summer. I recommend you continue that trend for a few more," she said.

Daniel grimaced. "No offense, but I think I could take you in a fight," he said, "I am a guy after all."

Cadivus snorted. "Yeah, man. You can totally kick her ass, try it out." He elbowed Thermia under the table.

"No, no, no," Thermia said, "we're not doing that. Can we just move on?" She looked to Cadivus and Ekio who were both grinning ear to ear. Thermia threw her hands in the air in defeat.

"I could definitely take the noble bitch," Daniel said while pointing at Thermia.

"No…you couldn't," Thermia stated while crossing her arms.

Daniel grimaced and shrugged. "Pretty easily too I'd imagine." He mouthed 'sorry' to her sarcastically.

Thermia scowled and leaped accross the table. Daniel shrieked as she grabbed a hold of his shirt and threw him to the ground. She jumped onto his stomach with her knees and grabbed his hands and folded them across his chest. She growled? "Who can you take?" she shouted in his face.

"Mercy!" he cried out.

Thermia slammed his back repeatedly into the floor. "Who can you take?" she shouted louder.

"No one!" he yelled through his crying.

Thermia raised a fist to smash into him but Ekio pulled her off of him, and carried her back to the table.

"You're lucky, punk!" she said to the crying man on the floor.

Cadivus carried the poor soul out of the tavern. "Nice fight, champ. Almost had her."

The women took their seats once more. “Good one, noble bitch," Ekio said with a chuckle.

“Thanks for the save. I was in my dark place for a moment there.” Thermia hugged Ekio, catching her off guard.

Ekio couldn’t remember the last time she did more than shake hands with another person. The hug felt good and she closed her eyes and hugged her back. “It is a dangerous path you are on, but I think you will do well.”

Thermia smiled and nodded.

The group talked with several more people, unable to find someone they could bring along with them. As they were about to give up and leave, a short stocky man with a cowboy hat, trenchcoat and scaled boots walked into the room. His steps made the ground shake with an audible thump. His rugged face seemed to be adorned in a permanent five-o’-clock shadow.

Thermia yawned. “Name and reason for signing up?”

“Hunter,” he said. “And no, I’m not signing up.”

The group gave him a confused look.

“I’m joining you because I believe we are after the same man.” He removed a stack of papers from one of his several pouches and shuffled through them. When he got to the one he was after, he threw it onto the table.

Ekio grabbed it and read it aloud to the group.

"Wanted dead or alive, Captain Chronic. Illegal growing and distribution of nonlegal substances, murder, blackmail, invalid licenses, and other crimes." She passed the paper off to the others.

"My, my…" Cadivus said, "what a lame name. I cannot abide it."

"Lame or not, the man is powerful and influential. Heard you had a run-in with em already. Wouldn't mind a few extra hands here, willing to split the reward too." Hunter pulled out a cigar and lit it with a match that he sparked off his stubbly cheeks.

As Cadivus examined the paper, anger brewed inside him. He slammed it onto the table and caught his comrade's eyes. They looked back at him and gave a subtle nod.

"I think we found our…" His eyes widened. "Wait a second. Is that a gun?"

Hunter pulled his coat to the side and removed the dirty and uncared for weapon.

"All bounty hunters got one. Securing gunpowder was always a crown pastime, after all." He spun it on his finger and put it back in the holster.

"Can I hold it?" he asked, reaching his hand out with his tongue sticking out.

"Nope," Hunter answered, not even looking at him.

He frowned and went to reach for his own dagger before remembering he had lost it in a bet. He turned toward Ekio.

"Speaking of weapons, can I have my dagger back for the time being?"

"Nope," she said, staring smugly. "You lost it fair and square."

"Fair…pft." An uneasiness from being without a weapon coursed through him. "Well, I for one need a weapon. Is there a smith here?"

"None that make weapons," Hunter said, extinguishing the cigar in his hand and storing it in his pouch. "Not that it'd matter. Small towns tend to have shit smiths."

The group all stared at each other for an awkward amount of time.

Cadivus eventually made some popping noises with his mouth and rapped his hands on the table.

"Well, let's get going, I guess."

They agreed and stood.

"Thermia, grab our other member. We'll meet at the northern exit."

"You can count on me!" She ran off.

As they were putting the tables back, Hunter tapped Cadivus's shoulder.

"You oughta leave that girl behind. Roads ain't safe for a dame like that."

Cadivus shook his head and smiled.

"How chivalrous of you, but no. She stays with us. In fact, I'd choose her over you if need be."

Ekio walked over to the men staring each other down.

"I like her too. She comes."

Hunter glared at them both for a minute then softly chuckled, putting his hands into the air.

"Ain't that somethin'."

Chapter 8

Cadivus and his crew had wandered to the outskirts of town, far away from any prying ears or eyes. This new crew was far more attractive than his last one. And they had already made it out of a tavern without a dead body, which was a pretty good start.

"So as we are all aware, we are after a most mischievous hybrid bandit with a harmonica," Cadivus said.

"Yeah!" Thermia shouted. She folded her arms and nodded. "And with a little luck, you won't kill your crew this time!"

A look of bewilderment overcame the group. He moaned and rolled his eyes.

She, realizing her error, unfolded her arms. "No, no, no! That's not what I meant! I mean yes his powers *did* kill those people, but it completely wasn't his fault. The harmonica man made him do it. HE MADE HIM!" She grabbed her own mouth and shut it tight.

"Thanks?" Cadivus said. "Yes, this villain has a unique power, and he can apparently make you use your own powers. And believe me when I say, fuck that noise."

"Cadivus…" Hunter said, a sweet drawl to his voice. "Can I see your hand for just a second?" He removed his own glove and held out his hand too.

Cadivus saw no harm in the gesture. So he reached out and grabbed Hunter's hand. Both he and Hunter flinched, he couldn't move. His face looked as if it was concentrating hard. Or like he was threading a needle. A pained look overtook Hunter and he began to sweat. After a few moments, a disgusted look took over his face, and he turned to the rest of the group.

"Okay," he said, "this guy's a tad off his rocker, and definitely has blood on his hands, but I can't say it came from a place of immoral doings."

"Yeah, I'm a hero," Cadivus said. "Not a villainous criminal."

"Also, some of your memories are blocked from me. Not sure why."

"What did you just do to the loud one?" Ekio asked.

"Well, when I touch someone's skin I can see all the bad things they've done and feel their intent." Hunter said with a sullen look. "It's a curse more than anything."

"Does that mean…" Cadivus said, "does that mean you saw the hay incident?"

"Yep…"

Cadivus's face cringed. Hard.

"Okay…moving on." He shook the shame off his face. "So, what we need is a team of strong individuals, so we can head east, find the demonic harmonic–"

"Oh, nice one, Caddy!" Thermia said, giving him a thumbs up.

He waved back.

"And we must take him into custody, so myself and Thermia, can clear our names. Which is going to be difficult because well, as Thermia shouted earlier, he made me explode last time. And not in the cool way."

"Wait, wait, wait…." Sparklebutt said, "these two don't even have weapons?" he pointed at Cadivus and Thermia. "What are you? Wizards or something? Where's your wand?"

Cadivus pursed his lips.

“Oh, I lost my last weapon in a bet,” he pointed toward Ekio, “and she’s being a real blowhard about it.”

“Can’t say this is the best start I’ve ever seen. Then again, I don’t work with others much on account of the death rate being so high," Sparklebutt said.

“You know, for a guy named Sparklebutt, you really are a downer…”

“Mate, when you’ve seen the things I have you can talk to me about downers. Alls I can say is curiosity has got the better part of my sense here.” He shrugged.

“You know what?” Cadivus said, “keep that up and you're not gonna learn the secret handshake I have devised. And you're gonna feel real stupid when we’re all doing it and you’re not.”

“Yeah, boy!” Thermia said, waving one hand in the air toward Sparklebutt.

“Gods help me,” Sparklebutt muttered, “She's adorable.”

“Can I see that paper once again, Hunter?” Cadivus asked.

Hunter removed the stack and shuffled through it once more.

“Wait,” he said, standing over his shoulder. “Wait. Go back one…That guy with the long list of crimes. Who is that guy? I’ve never heard of him before.”

Hunter held up the page.

“This here? This is Teavis. Used to be a leader of a village of bandits. This guy has done it all: murder, theft, sodomy, arson, assault, public exposure. A real work-up alright. Worth a fortune if we come across him.”

“I heard he has a massive dick too,” Sparklebutt said.

The group gave him a funny look. “No it’s not that. It's just that I’m…gay.”

“At least the name makes sense now,” Cadivus said, “fret not friend, I will do my best to not set your loins ablaze.”

Sparklebutt gave him a thumbs up and a curt smile.

Hunter kept rifling through his documents and pulled out the one with the man they were looking for: the leafer with the wicked stache.

“I caught wind of this guy, after coming down here from the north. I must admit, this guy seems to be on a whole other level. Not only is his power extremely dangerous, he’s also known to be a gifted genius. After all, he did plan and execute that plan of ruining your life. A group effort would be better than trying to do this alone.”

“This man has brought ruin to me as well,” Ekio said.

Cadivus leaned toward Thermia and whispered “Back-story incoming…”

“My village was known for having the best medicines. This allowed us to have strong warriors who could train harder than any other and workers who get more done in a day than most can in a week. One day, this man showed up and said he can grow us an herb that would simplify our remedies, reducing many medicines to one plant. But it wasn’t medicine at all! And it just makes you lazy! Soon, we didn’t have enough workers to support the town. The warriors only played. And there was not enough food grown. We were weak!” She held out her arm and rubbed the beads on her wrist up and down with her finger. “Before long, our enemies learned of this, and slaughtered us in a single fateful day.”

Thermia’s eyes welled with tears.

“How did you escape this ruin?” Cadivus asked.

Ekio's eyes watered. She shook off the emotion and turned around exposing a large scar that went all the way across her back, top right to bottom left.

"I do not remember much from that day. All I know is at some point my injuries overtook me, I awoke to the aftermath. If it was not for a passing caravan, I would not be alive this day." She paused. "So, I come here. To kill this Captain Chronic. Then I will gamble to earn enough money to raise an army of mercenaries and take back my home."

"Holy fucking shit," Cadivus said, "I seethe with an angry rage of wrath for you."

She rolled her eyes.

"I swear on my honor now that once we are done here I will come back with you to help reclaim what you have lost. And hopefully, also help repopulate your village."

She slapped him so hard that he fell to the ground.

Thermia fist bumped her.

"In your face, creep!" Thermia shouted at the downed pervert.

"You know what?" Ekio said. "She *is* adorable, and I love her."

Sparklebutt nodded.

"Okay," Hunter said, "so, we need to come up with a plan. We need weapons, we need to learn the location of the man's farm, and we have to figure out how to defeat him without him using any of our powers against us. Not only that, but because he is a genius we also need counter-measures and plans A B and C. So first things first: weapons. Anyone know where we can get some decent weapons?"

"Yeah," Sparklebutt said, "I know a place that has lots of weapons a few days from here. *Special* weapons, if you catch my drift."

"And where's that exactly?"

"The armory in Pribbs."

"Hold on a minute," Ekio said, "you want us to break into a city and rob their armory? Might as well just kill ourselves now and save them the trouble."

"Don't worry. I have a plan. And I'll tell you when we get there." Sparklebutt grinned playfully.

"I don't like this one bit…" Hunter said.

"Are you saying this quest of revenge now has a *side quest* for a *heist*?!" Cadivus said, standing and dusting himself off. "I've never been more down in my entire life! How thrilling!"

He groaned. "Okay. So let's say that covers weapons. Next we need to be concerned about him using our powers against us. To do that, we need to know what everyone's powers are, so we can plan around it. You already saw mine, I can read people, but it does make me incapacitated for a few moments. Yours?" He pointed at Sparklebutt.

"Well, I don't know if you noticed back there. They don't call me Sparklebutt for nothing. My ass is the cleanest and most perfect ass you can imagine."

Hunter groaned once more, but then Sparklebutt pulled down his pants and showed them the most marvelous ass they had ever seen.

"Wow. Nice," Ekio said.

Cadivus crossed his arms. Feeling the sting of a pimple on his left ass cheek rubbing against his trousers.

"Yeah it's okay if you're into that sort of thing. Perfect male anatomy…"

"That's not a power…" Hunter remarked.

"Well, besides that, I'm really good with a flail," Sparklebutt said, "I used to practice all the time at home. It was a watermelon genocide! And, there is a really special one in Pribbs that I surely can't lose a fight with. Far better than this shit sword I have now."

Hunter eyed Sparkleblutt with suspicion. "Okay. I guess I thought you were more than human, but that could be good for us too. That just leaves Cadivus and Ekio."

Ekio stepped back from the group and threw a dagger into a tree. Yet her hair seemingly moved in a gust of wind, and the blade returned to her hand.

"Oh *wow,*" Cadivus said, "she's magnetic. That explains the attraction." He rubbed his chin.

She rolled her eyes, held out her hand and lifted the dead leaves from the ground around her. They formed into a sphere before she released them.

"I didn't know leaves were metal…"

"How are you this stupid? I can control air currents, so I can push and pull things like the wind does."

"That's pretty badass," everyone else said at once. No jinx was called.

"Hold on a moment," Cadivus said, "can you create a hurricane capable of leveling a city?"

"Why would I do this?"

"Can you fly like a bird?"

"Do you see people flying in the wind? Do people float around when the trees are swaying?" she replied, now irritated.

He thought hard for a moment.

"You know, I thought of something else, but I'm not going to say it out loud."

"Oh wow! He's learning to shut up. This is a great day indeed," Ekio said.

"Okay. I'm guessing Thermia doesn't have powers," Sparklebutt asked. "Is that correct?"

"Nope," she said, "just a boring and useless betch."

"That's not true at all," Cadivus said while placing a hand on her shoulder, "Thermia has the ability to lift morale and rally the cause. And most importantly, she is a people person. She can make friends with anyone, and that could come in handy."

She smiled at him.

"Well, that could be good for us," Sparklebutt said, "like me, she doesn't have powers, just skills. So this guy can't use them against us. However, in a fight that would mean she is more vulnerable. Every group needs someone with charisma, I suppose." He turned toward Cadivus. "So, what's your power? You can explode things with your mind or what?"

"Umm…Not exactly," Cadivus replied.

"Well, come on, out with it then," Ekio said, "we all told you ours."

He mumbled under his breath.

Ekio slapped his chest. "I am sorry. Can you open your mouth when you talk?"

"Fire…I'm a fire hybrid."

"Ugh. That's lame." Hunter, Sparklebutt and Ekio said in unison.

"Well, besides torching people around you, can your powers do anything else you can show us?" Hunter asked.

"Pass!" Cadivus shouted.

They all stared at him blankly.

“There are a lot of leaves, and wind, and I’m tired, from totally using my powers all the time which I certainly do…So let’s just move along, shall we?”

Thermia nodded at him and mouthed, “Nice.”

“So, anyways, let’s get on with it shall we? This has been an awful lot of exposition and I'm getting antsy.”

“Alright,” Hunter said, “we can head northeast through the forest tonight until the sun sets. The road would only take longer. If we don’t take too many breaks we can be at Pribbs in three days.”

Sparklebutt put on his gloves and wrapped a scarf around his neck.

“I like to wear travel gear,” Sparklebutt said, “helps get me in the mood.”

The companions set out on their quest. Embracing the danger that dwelled in the woods beyond.

Chapter 9

The forest became thicker and thicker as Cadivus and his crew traveled deeper into it. Even when the sun was up, it was hard to see through all the foliage above. They walked in pairs to manage their way through the numerous trees. Everyone wanted to walk with Thermia, and Cadivus just knew he was missing out on some killer inside jokes. Sensing a lack of attention, he decided to stir up some drama.

He increased his pace to catch up to Hunter, who was leading the band of adventurers.

"Hey," he said, strolling beside Hunter. "I've noticed something peculiar going on here. So I thought we should settle it now."

"And what almighty is that?" Hunter said, already annoyed.

"Well, it's just that it seems you're trying to become the leader of our group. And well, that's my job, rightfully."

Hunter groaned.

"It's just Thermia and I started this quest together, and I was the leader then. It doesn't make one lick of sense to switch now. It would be far too confusing for her."

"Yeah, confusing for *her*. And no, I'm not trying to lead anything. I just happen to know the way, and I just happened to be up front."

"And I just happened to be in my maids closet wearing her underwear and calling myself Dorothy. I know you saw that one when you mind-tapped me…"

“Actually, I didn’t. And with all my heart I wish you kept that to yourself.” Hunter shook his head and walked faster.

Cadivus was starting to get the sense that he and Hunter would never be best friends.

“Right! I order you to go ahead, and I’ll lead from the rear!”

In the rear, Thermia and Ekio walked together. She bit her tongue to help her concentrate on walking through the difficult terrain.

“So, are you really a queen or a lady or whatever they call it here?” Ekio asked.

“You should address me as, your Majesty,” she replied, holding her chin high and squinting.

Ekio sighed.

“I’m just fucking with you girl!” She cackled. “My husband is the one who demanded respect, but it always made me feel…so…pfft.” She blew a raspberry and wiped the extra spit from her chin.

“Is it not a great honor to be chosen by such a man?” Ekio asked.

“I’m sure it would be, but I wasn’t chosen by him…Not like that anyway.” She fiddled with her ring.

“Did you choose him then?”

“Well, no. My country offered me as a reward to him.”

Ekio glared at her.

She looked back and spoke in a deep voice. “I’m the prize!”

“Sorry,” Ekio said, visibly confused. “I guess I’m not as familiar with your history or customs as I had thought. Does marriage only come as a reward? What did he do to earn such a reward?”

“You don’t know The Hybrid? He defeated a great evil, ended the great war, and basically saved the world.”

“We have never heard such a story across the ocean, but I can see why you would be considered a great offering to a man such as him.” Ekio put her arm around Thermia and pulled her in for a side hug.

Thermia blushed.

“So anyway, after Smokey defeated the evil, I was given to him by my father as a reward. And as a way to *unite the kingdom,* as he would say.”

“That must have been scary, leaving your home and going to a strange new place,” Ekio said, “it can be hard to adjust to something different like this.”

“Well, lucky for me, fitting in is my superpow–” She tripped and quickly got back to her feet. She took a beat to collect herself. “I’ve always been good with people. It just comes natural to me.”

“It is a great gift, Thermia, to be a pleaser of people.”

Thermia tilted her head.

“You make it sound sexier than it is,” she said.

“Maybe that’s *my* gift.” She raised her eyebrows.

As the group made their way through the woods, the conversations winded down, especially as they found themselves walking over even more uneven terrain.

Cadivus noticed everyone seemed sort of down and decided that, being the great leader he is, he would lift the spirit of his companions.

“Normally, this is the part of the day when I would say let’s get shitfaced. However, we are without a drop of ambrosia. So, instead, I offer to get you drunk off these sick pipes.”

Everyone groaned except for Thermia, who clapped excitedly.

He sang in a not quite good but not quite bad voice.

The sun, must rest, so it can shine

The moon, must succeed the one true light

Today's troubles, are fading away

Without words, I hear you say

Goodnight, and know

For you, my soul

Hunter laughed. "You do know that's a nursery rhyme for kids, right?"

Everyone else smirked along.

But a scowl overcame Cadivus's face. "What? So what if it is? It's a good song."

"I just want you to know how ridiculous it is to sing a bedtime song for youngins' to a group of grown-ass adventurers on what could potentially be a suicide mission."

He ran up and pushed Hunter into a tree, getting into his face.

"I like the song! So, zip it."

The group's eyes widened. Hunter put his hands in the air. Cadivus let him go and continued walking onwards, not looking anyone in the eye.

"Is anyone else hard right now?" Sparklebutt asked.

"Easy there, partner," Hunter said, "was just a playful jest. My mistake. Maybe someone else would like to sing a more appropriate song though, given the situation?"

"Um, I think I know a song, " Sparklebutt said, "hey, Thermia? Can you give me a beat?"

She put a hand over mouth and began beatboxing.

He sang rapidly.

This is world is vicious

these words litigious

I probably embody my outer body like anybody
I'm on the verge of lost and found
of hope and doubt
Regulate the love and hate no more debate
I'm Just trying to get by in my inner state
I'm defiant to whims of a god with a plan
I'm reliant to pimps who are on the fence
I'm prophetic if you got the programming
I'm sardonic if you wanna take the offense
I see all these demons, where are the angels
I've seen the whole plan, aware of the angles
I've see all these sinners, where is the virtue
Trust is worthy, but only trust can hurt you
Half full of despair, half empty of hope
Tied down in the lair, I chewed through the ropes
My allegiance internal
This struggle eternal
My rage infernal
My words they burn you
Why bother being grown, probably never known
Why bother being free, in a world of destiny
I'm just trying to lean forward
Until I reach your mind, end it now

Having never heard a song like that in their entire lives, the group stopped in their tracks and cheered. Even Cadivus had to admit the song was good.

"Oh my gods!" Thermia shouted, "where did you learn that? I've never heard anything like it!"

“Oh, it’s called freestyle,” Sparklebutt said, “we used to do it all the time back in my homeland. Anyone can do it with a little practice. In fact if you really–”

Loud banging and crashing echoed through the woods. A large dark figure crashed through them, knocking everyone to the ground. It grabbed Sparklebutt in its mouth and carried him off.

“Get him!” Hunter yelled, jumping up and racing after him.

The others quickly followed. The beast had cleared a path through the woods, knocking any trees and plants in its path aside.

Sparklebutt yelled in the distance. “Stop it, you fuck!”

As they ran, the echoes of destruction halted, and Sparklebutt’s screams grew louder. They traversed over the last hill. A dark, hairy creature that moved on all fours with stripes of white on its side, paws in the rear, and more monkey-like in the front. Its hairy face had a large mouth, a snout, and glowing yellow sunken eyes. Its pointed ears twitched as it pushed Sparklebutt back into a dirt mound with one of its front paws. And to the group's surprise, was sniffing at his rear.

“Oh shit, a chimera! Sparkle!” Hunter yelled, “hang on! We’re coming!”

The beast's nose pushed Sparklebutt deeper into the dirt mound, its ears twitching wildly.

“Either kill this thing or tell it to give me a reach around!” Sparklebutt yelled.

As the group got closer, Hunter stopped Cadivus and Ekio. “You two go left. I’ll go right and–”

“I got it!” Cadivus yelled as he took off toward the monster’s head at full speed. “Nobody tosses our friend’s salad forcefully and gets away with it!” Cadivus leaped into the air, preparing a powerful punch. As he was about to make contact, a giant tail came out of nowhere and slapped him away, sending him flying through a nearby tree.

"That fucking–" Hunter gritted his teeth. "Ekio, I have one more plan. Come here." He spoke softly into her ear.

She nodded and ran into the woods.

He circled the monster, taking careful shots with his gun. He knew his bullets would not penetrate, but they would still hurt enough to draw some attention. "Come on, beast!"

The monster continued sniffing, unaffected. He brought his possum-like tale to his front and gripped Sparklebutt around his waist with it. He flipped him over and growled in his face.

"What the hell is it doing?!" Hunter asked.

"Oh no!" Thermia yelled from the back, running toward the danger to save her friend. "He's gonna eat him!"

"Save yourselves!" Sparklebutt yelled.

Hunter was about to shoo Thermia to safety when an idea struck him. "Thermia! Come here! Quickly!" He gave her the rundown, and she nodded.

Moments later, he jumped up onto the beast's tail and gripped it. As he did, he and the monster lost control of their bodies. Sparklebutt was released from the grip and fell to the ground.

Thermia pulled Sparklebutt free and then grabbed Hunter. She screamed as she the heavy man to the ground. Sparklebutt came in from behind her and helped drag Hunter away from the chimera.

"Ekio!" she screamed.

As the creature began to gain control of its body, several small trees and large branches crashed around it. They dug into the ground, forming a tight prison. As the beast struggled to move, more were added–until the prison no longer budged.

Ekio walked out from the nearby woods, smiling ear to ear. Sparklebutt rubbed at his chaffed ass. Thermia checked in on Hunter as he was regaining consciousness. He gave a thumbs up to indicate he was perfectly fine.

Cadivus strolled back through the woods, rubbing his back that broke a tree moments ago. He had a smug look on his face.

"Good job team! We did it!" Cadivus said.

Hunter tackled him to the ground and punched his chest. He grabbed his shirt and slammed him into the ground. "You maggot-brain moron! You could have got us all killed!"

Cadivus reached up to grab his fist.

"You don't want to be a leader! You want to play hero! Well, guess what? You're not!" With his fist locked in Cadivus's grip, Hunter slammed his head down on Cadivus's nose, causing him to release his fists. Hunter took his time standing, never breaking eye contact as he scowled at him.

"How was I supposed to know it was that strong?" Cadivus asked, his voice sounding muffled through the wounded nose. "Am I supposed to–"

Hunter raised his fist, but Thermia grabbed it.

"That's enough!" she said, "maybe he was reckless, but his intentions were in the right place."

Hunter grimaced. "The world is full of good-intentioned people gettin' others killed." With that, he walked away to cool off.

She knelt next to Cadivus and patted his head.

Ekio walked up, her smile fading into her signature solemn look. "Perhaps Mr. Slippery Elbows here does not realize what the outside world is like. In your small town, you might be hot shit, but out here, you are just shit!" She reached out her hand to pull him up "kusimama mbele ya mto hazuii mtiririko wa maji."

"Did she just confess her love for me?" he asked Thermia, who shook her head.

"Standing in front of lava, won't stop the flow."

He looked down. He'd never seen lava before, but he was sure he could kick its ass.

"Thank you, Ekio." He got to his feet and went to hug her, but she pointed his own dagger at his chest.

"*Please.* I know you're just trying to grab my ass." She whacked him in the nose with the pommel, to which he grimaced, and wondered how she knew.

Sparklebutt adjusted his pants once more, freeing his undergarments from their prison. Still rubbing the affected area, he walked over to the trapped beast. "What should we do with you? my sniffy wiffy friend." He looked it over for weak points, while sharpening an impromptu spear made from one of the nearby branches.

"Hold on a second." Hunter said, "when I grabbed the beast–"

"My boy got some tail!" Thermia interrupted.

"Yeah...anyways, I saw some of its past." He walked up and looked into the beast's eyes, the glowing yellow had dimmed. "This thing was not so, inappropriate, until it drank from a stream a few miles from the direction it came. I think something in that water made it go into a frenzy."

“Did someone swap out the water for ale, you think?” Cadivus asked…seriously.

“No, that’s re…That’s not what happened. But the water is infected with something. Which means two things. One, this beast is also a victim. And two–

“There are going to be more in these woods,” Ekio said.

The whole group thought about how many fanny sniffing monsters they’d have to fight off before they could make it to Pribbs.

“Well we could just leave it like this,” Sparklebutt said, “Give it a taste of its own medicine.”

The beast groaned.

Cadivus walked up to the group, readjusted his nose with a loud crack and spoke normally.

“I have another idea. It’s going to sound crazy at first, but hear me out!”

The whole group sighed except for Thermia, who was clapping excitedly.

Hours later, the group–including Cadivus–could not believe they were actually riding through the woods on the beast’s back. Except for Sparklebutt, who was tied to a stick with a rope. His pants had been pulled below his marvelous ass. He dangled just out of reach of the beast’s nose as they traversed through the woods in ease.

At this pace, they would reach Pribbs just after sundown.

Chapter 10

"Bandits!" a man shouted at the top of his lungs.

Darion awoke from his bed of sand. The sun had just barely set. The people scrambled around, as he took a long gulp of water.

"Women and children to the center!" he ordered. "Scouts, hold positions! Fighting men, assemble to the north gate!"

He also ran toward the north gate, which was just a rope wall with a small opening to pass through. The wall only partially stretched around the town, but he hoped they would funnel through the door.

"How many?" he yelled.

"At least fifteen approach!" a watcher called.

He wished he had time to build an overlook tower. In the setting sun, he could only see silhouettes approaching over the dunes.

"Hold position!"

Only nine men were grouped by the gate. No sign of Decan. That coward.

The one advantage they had was position. No sooner than the thought soothed him, did he see flaming arrows shoot toward the town. The arrows crashed around the fence, some connecting and setting the ropes ablaze. Darion watched his men grow timid. He had wasted all his efforts on the wall and now it was falling apart in a fire that lit their encampment in an orange glow.

"What do we do?" one of his men called out.

The only thing he could think to do was the unexpected. Perhaps he had read that somewhere.

"Charge!" Darion screamed, unsheathed his sword, and ran out to meet the attackers.

He wasn't sure if the men would follow him, but what other choice did he have?

As he approached the attackers, he held his father's necklace that was around his neck and whispered, "Guide me, Father."

Swords clashed with the first enemy he reached. The loud clang of swords meeting echoed by his men meeting with others around him. A smile took over his face.

He parried several blows, but his form was off from lack of recent practice. He lost his footing with every parry and found it impossible to counter-attack. One blow sent his back to the ground. As he looked up, his attacker raised his sword to pierce through his chest. Yet as the blade came down, he held up his hand, catching the blade through his palm.

Pain and fear filled him, and then he felt something else. His body warmed with ecstasy. The hairs on his arms vibrated in anticipation. The world slowed around him, and his father's words echoed in his head.

"That moment, when you decide to fight or flee, *that* is where our power comes from."

Father?

As his attacker freed his sword from his hand, he swung his sword at the attacker's legs, cutting them off below the knees. The attacker's body fell to the ground, and he pierced his heart.

The battle kept moving in slow motion, yet he found his movements were unhindered. He stood, and looked around, watching the sparks light off the steel clashing, dancing in the night. He saw the shadows the embers cast as they passed by flesh.

A pressure poked his back, and he turned to see a man attempting to push a wooden spear into him. He turned out of the way, sliced the spear in half, and delivered a strike to the spearman's neck. He could have even sliced the blood that floated from the wound.

As he ran through the attacking party, he delivered blow after blow. His sword moved through them with such ease. A thrill overcame him, and he wondered if his father had felt the same ecstasy, the same weightlessness. Although from his own lips his father would have said killing was the worst thing a man could do. He wondered if his father had lied.

Darion carried on, striking down as many as he could. After a few of the men fell, the enemies found themselves turning to watch him. His men used the distraction to create mortal wounds. He jumped toward the last group of enemies and unleashed a singular spinning blow, cutting through their vital areas. When the four men dropped to the ground, a hand grabbed his shoulder, and he turned around, prepared to strike.

"Sir!" his comrade said, his voice drawn out. "Sir, it's me!"

The passing of time made sense once more. His men just stared at him in disbelief.

"How…You fought like, Ducian."

His face covered in blood, Darion didn't have time to explain as screams and metal clashing echoed from the other side of the camp. "Defend the camp!" He raised his sword and ran toward the noise.

The men roared and charged behind him, unable to keep up, but followed all the same. Darion jumped onto a nearby roof, surprising even himself, and looked around the town for gleaming weapons in the night. Two battles taking place at the southwest and southeast sides.

He pointed at the closest man. "You, take the lead! Go southwest!" As they did, he headed in the other direction.

He punched his wound as he approached the battle. He swung through these men just as easily as the others. Pausing, he looked around to see how many allies were with him, but only found one–who was about to be cut down. He charged. When he went to pierce his enemy's chest, the enemy parried his blade.

Darion retreated and studied the enemy from several paces away.

He had a thin mustache above his smiling lips. "First time crossing blades with an anguar?" Anguars were rare, exceptional warriors who exceeded human limitations. Their speed was unmatched. The longer a battle was, the stronger they became. Ducian, his father, was the last known anguar. But he had died during the great war.

"And your last time," Darion replied.

Darion charged and traded blows with the smiling man. Three other enemies joined. In between attacks, he swung and stabbed at the others until only the two anguars remained. They held an attack pose.

"Name's Tuka," the smiling man said, bowing. His voice was scratchy. "And you're Ducian's boy I presume?"

"Well, at least you know who's about to kill you." Darion said.

Tuka laughed and held his sword arm out.

"We shall see."

Darion swung at him. He dodged and blocked the blows with grace. Darion kept the onslaught up without gaining a single blow before he was kicked in his stomach. Darion fell backwards, struggling to catch his breath.

"You're shit," Tuka said. "Not surprising really. You never had the chance for a proper tutor after all." He removed his robe. Underneath he only wore a leather thong with leather straps in a cross pattern on his torso.

Darion gagged at the sight of the old man's decrepit body and revealing outfit.

"I think you might be off your rocker, old man. You attack my camp to offer me tutelage. Is that it?"

"Mostly for supplies, but yes the thought had crossed my mind." He placed a hand on his hip and let his gut bulge out.

"Why do you think I would train with you after all this?!" Darion shouted, pointing at the chaos behind him.

"You're welcome for awakening your powers, my ungrateful apprentice. Now be a good boy and choose to come back with me to my cave and I'll show you what it really means to be one of the chosen. You'll have to take your licks as all young ones do, but in a few years time, we'll be ready to rule over this world…together." He clenched his fist.

"That sounds…awful. I'm afraid I'll have to refuse your boring offer."

Tuka rushed him and placed the tip of his steel at his neck.

"I'd like to reword my choice, please." Darion muttered.

"It's a certainty *disguised* as a choice. I didn't want to seem too forceful. Then again there is a certain thrill to holding your life in my hands."

Darion stood frozen. Any movement could be instant death.

He lowered his weapon and sheathed it. "Of course, I will give you some time to decide. An easy decision as far as I'm concerned but a big one nonetheless." He put his robe back on and kicked a pile of sand into the air, creating a smoke screen. "One week Darion," he whispered before he vanished into the night.

In the distance, his men cheered.

"Strange times." he muttered.

All the events from the evening raced through his mind. His people had thought the anguars were long dead. Tonight, there were two clashing swords. Often he dreamed of following in his father's footsteps. Now that dream has merged with reality. However, could he trust this Tuka?

As he pondered, his name echoed from the distance. He composed himself and ran toward the voices. When he found his soldiers, they cheered his name and thumped their fists on their chest. His eyes widened and his hands trembled to see how happy they were to see him. He thought of his father and his stoic stare, and tried it on for size.

"Impressive showing at the gate," one of the men said as the cheering halted. "Haven't seen any of our kind fight like that since…"

"I know. Thank you, friend." He shook hands with the men who approached him.

"What do we do now?" another man asked.

"Account for the dead and wounded, keep the guard doubled, and put out any fires still raging." He turned toward the center of town. "I'll check on the women and children."

The men nodded and turned to their duties.

As Darion walked toward the shelter, anxiety seared his chest. He hastened his pace, escalating to a full-on sprint. Once he reached the shelter, he slammed the door open and looked inside. Women and children filled the space, tears and fear upon their faces. Toonda was nowhere to be seen.

"Where is Toonda?" he asked the crowd.

No one answered.

"Where is she?!" he screamed.

"A man…took her," one of the women cried between her tears. She pointed toward a piece of paper stabbed into the wall with a dagger.

Darion walked over and read it. *One week. Tuska Point. Alone. Bring a pipe.* He ripped the paper down and removed the dagger. A familiar but forgotten feeling overtook him.

Glowing wings.

He clenched his teeth so hard he thought they might turn to dust in his mouth.

Toonda's husband ran through the door, panting heavily. He looked around the room for a moment and fell to his knees.

"No, no, no, no!" He roared his pain.

After a moment, he stood and charged Darion, grabbing him and holding him against the wall. Darion's feet hovered above the ground. "You were supposed to protect all of them!" He yelled, spit flying from his rabid mouth.

Darion stayed limp as he was repeatedly slammed into the wall. After several attacks, Doban lowered him and placed his head on his chest.

"We'll get her back, Doban," he said. "I'd die a thousand times over to get her back."

"No, Darion, you don't get to die. We'll save her, and then you'll do what she's been asking of you all these years."

Darion dressed himself in his father's stance and stare.

Chapter 11

As Cadivus's group arrived near Pribbs after nearly a full day of riding, they couldn't wait to get off the beast's back and stretch their own. Hunter used his sight on the beast once more to immobilize it, while the others hopped off, and Sparklebutt was pulled back in and released from his ropes.

"Sorry about all that, Sparkles," Cadivus said, "but it was the only way to get out of those woods, a devil's virgin."

"Actually, it wasn't that bad," Sparklebutt said, "reminded me of my good ole days." He stretched.

"I'm not sure what that means, but I am simultaneously intrigued and unwilling to ask for elaboration." He motioned for the others to get away from the beast, pulled Hunter up to his shoulder and walked him away from the beast, handing him off to Ekio. "You guys go on ahead. I'll convince the beast to leave."

The others agreed and walked through the thick trees and toward the town. Several minutes later, he walked up to meet them. In the distance, trees bent and cracked as the beast left.

"You didn't just…?" Hunter asked with a look of disgust.

"A gentleman never tells, my boy," Cadivus replied as he approached Thermia and wiped his hands on her dress.

The group pressed on. Since it was getting dark, they figured it was less suspicious to approach in the morning. To avoid detection, they also opted for no fire, which relieved Cadivus. The group all slumped against nearby trees, toward the edge of the forest, except for

Sparklebutt who curled up on the ground with his thumb in his mouth, snoring lightly.

"Ekio," Cadivus said, "lay near us please." He tapped the small spot between him and Thermia.

"In your dreams, lava boy," she said as she passed by. He grabbed her hand and whispered.

"I don't know these men well enough, and I am worried about her." He motioned his head toward Thermia.

She looked down at him, saw the sincerity on his face, and nodded. She lay up next to Thermia, who smiled from ear to ear and talked hers off. Cadivus surveyed the area one last time, observing the sleeping bait and catching eyes with Hunter. He could swear he gave him the slightest nod. He couldn't shake the feeling that there was more to this group than met the eye. Still, he had to trust their goals were aligned. It seemed fate had tied them all together.

When the group awoke the next morning, the delightful scent of distant fresh bread and butter lingered in the air. They slowly got themselves together, some more easily than others.

Thermia ran her fingers through her hair, becoming more violent with each motion. "The freaking sap got in my hair last night!" she shouted, nearly ripping her hair out in the process as she growled in her follicle frustration.

"My dear, stop this," Ekio said, grabbing her arm. "You will be bald at this rate! Let me see." She moved her fingers through her hair, noting that even though Thermia was due for a wash, Thermia's hair was still brilliantly soft and shiny. She found the spot of sap. "You'll need some strong wine to get this out. Pulling at it will only make it worse."

“I don’t mind my ass smelling like a sewer but no one told me life on the road was gonna be this hard.” Tears spilled from Thermia.

“It hasn’t even been a week…” Cadivus muttered.

Ekio quickly shifted her stance, causing him to turn his head sharply into a tree.

Stroking his head, he uttered “Yep. That one’s solid enough.” He tapped it twice before walking away, holding his forehead.

“Okay. We need to go over a few things before heading into Pribbs,” Hunter said, standing in front of the group. “First off, it would be better to cut your hair off completely, ladies, but we’ll have to settle for tying it up and hiding it under hats.” He motioned to Ekio, who slid a piece of twine off her wrist and tied up Thermia’s long red hair. He then removed his hat and placed it on top of her head. Revealing his short, blond, and balding hair underneath. After pulling some of his clothes from his bag, he gave them to Thermia, "Change into these darlin."

“Can I ask why I’m not allowed to look cute anymore?” she asked, taking the clothes from his hands.

“Well, here’s the thing…Pribbs is not like any other place in the world. I’ve only been here a few times for the odd contract but, I have learned no women are allowed here."

“Sounds like my birthday parties,” Cadivus said.

“I’d imagine so,” he said, “even more, you need to be careful how you speak. It’s dangerous to ask too many questions. And as far as I can tell this place is full of the most extreme misogynists in the realm.”

“Well that should be interesting. Up until this point I’ve only had normal massages.”

"You've gotta start asking for pleasant finishers," Sparklebutt said, "complete game changer."

"How does that work exactly?" Cadivus said, "I always chicken out at the last moment."

"Well, what I do is put the coins on the table, and then I–"

"What I mean," Hunter interrupted, "is that these men hate women more than anyone I've ever seen. As such, any woman found here will be turned away, jailed or possibly murdered on sight." He pulled a spare pair of boots and some loose pants from his bag. "Ekio, I don't have another hat for you to wear. We'll either have to make you one or cut your hair. Or you'll have to wait out here."

Ekio laughed.

"There will be no need." She grabbed her hair and gave it a strong tug, removing her wig and handing it to him to place in his bag. Her near bald head beneath glistened in the sun that passed through the trees. She also removed her earrings.

Cadivus glared at her with his mouth open. "Did that just happen?"

"What? No longer beautiful to you?" she asked.

"That might be the most perfect head I've ever seen…I don't know why you would choose to cover it up with something inferior."

She hesitated, caught off guard for a moment…

"Of course you don't understand." She then walked away putting the pants on over her tight clothes and motioning Thermia to follow her to some privacy. When she rounded some bushes, she brushed her own scalp, a sense of pride filled her. A memory of getting ready for a battle back home came. Fitting armor, sharpening weapons and applying war paint. She remembered the power it filled her with. She cringed.

“I think he likes you,” Thermia said softly as they tied their breasts down and changed into their new clothes.

Ekio rolled her eyes.

“You think?” she said sarcastically. “All men like women like us. What does it matter hmm? Not to mention, doesn’t this one lay with inanimate objects?”

They both giggled.

“I’m just shocked you don’t like him. He’s the best,” Thermia said, “he’s always in a good mood, and he always helps me out when I need him.”

“You take him then,” Ekio said, glaring at her. “You’re husband banished you, didn’t he? So, you are a free woman, right?”

“My Smokey banished us to save us from dying. He wouldn’t get rid of me unless he absolutely had to. Also, I already have the love of my life and I don’t need another, especially not my brother. That’s the dark stuff baby!” She fell over, trying to fit the oversized boot on.

Ekio pulled her up and hugged her. “I admire your devotion, Thermia. In my homeland, your love would be your spear and you would be the most formidable warrior the world had ever seen. We will stay close to each other inside this place; I won’t let any harm come to you.”

“And I make the same promise to you, Ekio.” She stared at Ekio with an uncommon sincerity, and Ekio knew she meant it. She wondered if she would feel the same if she knew the truth about her.

Cadivus’s eyes kept finding their way back toward the trees, back where the women had left.

“You need to stop doing that.” Hunter said while rearranging his pack.

"I'm sorry?" he replied.

"She's your traveling companion, not some random woman to conquer. You can't just keep throwing yourself at her like that. It's not fair to her or the group."

"I don't know man," Sparklebutt said, "I like the will-they-won't-they vibe."

"They won't," Hunter said.

"Well, let me give you some advice, Hunter." Cadivus said, "A great thinker once said, you're not the boss and mind your own fucking business." He stuck his tongue out at him.

"If you keep coming onto her like that, she's going to leave, and we need her to complete this mission. Put the group's goals ahead of your pecker."

"Oh, for the sake of fuck, my man! Oh, look at me, I'm a bounty hunter, I have a gun and I'm so fucking stoic and cool! Everyone has to listen to me! Bounty hunters don't even form groups! If there is anyone here who is the odd man out, it's you!" Cadivus walked past Hunter, slamming into his shoulder as he passed him.

When he was out of sight, Cadivus rubbed his now sore shoulder.

Not long after. The group met up one last time.

"I don't think this is gonna work with these two dames," Hunter said after staring the women down. "Maybe it's best for you two to wait here."

Sparklebutt reached into his pockets, and after a long awkward moment he pulled out some fake facial hair. A puzzled look took over Hunter's face.

"Here." He gave Thermia a red mustache and Ekio a blond beard. "Try these on. Fix em with a little sap on the back and stick em to your skin for a good minute. They won't go anywhere."

"You can't be serious…" Ekio said. She held up the blond beard to her dark skin. "He isn't serious is he?"

He grabbed it back and rubbed it into the dirt until the blond disappeared.

"There, is that more to your liking?"

She grabbed the beard and examined it once more. It *did* look more convincing now…She adorned it and looked to the crowd, standing with a perfect posture.

"It's…perfection," he said with his eyes closed.

"The beard's not a deal breaker by the way," Cadivus said.

Ekio threw dirt in his face.

"Okay, so tell us the plan now?" Hunter asked Sparklebutt.

Sparklebutt brushed the dirt with his foot and picked up a stick to draw with. He drew a square, creating a grid outline, and placed rocks at each corner.

He pointed at each position as he named it. "We're here. The vault is there. Now, to enter this vault we need three codes. Each leader has access to a unique code."

Excitement filled Cadivus's body.

"There are three leaders: Sigma, Gamma and Omega. Sigma is a brute, Gamma is a shapeshifter, and Omega is a wizard."

"Shapeshifter?" Hunter said, "those are real?"

Sparklebutt smiled and nodded.

"Very real I'm afraid, and this one is a damn sneaky one." He pointed at one of the rocks. "They all have a unique code memorized except for Sigma who will have it written down. He's a brute, but he's…how do I say this gently…retarded."

Everyone's eyes widened to comment.

"The other two…Well you'll have to force them to tell you and kill them after."

"Wait, wait," Hunter said, "we aren't killing anyone. I know we're stealing here, and I'm already uneasy about that, but we aren't going that far."

"These men are *dangerous*." Sparklebutt said. When Hunter stared at him blankly, he sighed and shook his head. "Well, fine. You'll have to incapacitate them then. If they alert the guards, they will activate a fail-safe that changes the codes to the vault, and the mission is over."

"We'll do that then."

"Wait a moment, what if they try to kill us?" Cadivus asked.

"Self-defense is a whole other thing," Hunter said, "though I'd advise not letting it get that far. If you cross that line I'm taking you in with Chronic."

"I'm feeling pretty defensive…" Cadivus said.

Sparklebutt winked at him.

"So we can steal Sigma's, send the most clever to Gamma, and I'll deal with the wizard."

"How do you plan to do this?" Ekio asked.

"Don't worry about it for now. I have my methods." He pointed at the women. "You two have enough to worry about getting Gamma's code."

The women smiled at each other.

"You two should steal Sigma's code," he told Cadivus and Hunter. "I would suggest not fighting him if at all possible. He'll have it in his chambers, and I doubt it's hidden well."

Hunter hung his head at the idea. Sparklebutt reached into his pocket and handed a key to Cadivus, who accepted it with a confused look.

"What's this for?" he asked.

"Sigma's chambers. Thought I'd make it easier for you," Sparklebutt said.

"How did you get this?"

Sparklebutt just smiled.

"You should learn to not ask so many questions, my guy." He winked. They all stood up and stared at each other. "So, that's about it," Sparklebutt said. "Everyone all set?"

They all nodded.

"Gotta say it. I'm impressed, kid," Hunter said.

Sparklebutt's smile widened.

The intrigue in Hunter's eyes glaring at the well-prepared man.

"Well, let's give those disguises a test then, shall we?" he said, "the guards at the gate will be the most suspicious. If we get past them, we should be good to go."

The group walked toward the entrance, which was surrounded by a beautifully engineered wall. It funneled everyone to a narrow archway so the guards could keep the bad eggs out. Luckily for the group, there was no one waiting to get inside. Thermia hung back and tried to mimic the walk Cadivus had taught her.

“Man, I’m so glad I divorced my bitch wife!” Cadivus said loudly as they approached. “That’ll teach her to fuck another man because I can’t satisfy her sexually!”

The three guards nodded in approval.

“What’s up *men*? It’s good to see strong *men*, guarding other *men*, instead of dumb wo*men* for a change.”

“Good day to you sirs,” one guard said, “what brings you to Pribbs? The most prosperous city in the land!” The guard waved them forward.

“We heard about this place a few towns over,” Hunter said. “Thought it was too good to be true. Decided to come take a look for ourselves. See what we may be able to offer Pribbs.”

The guard looked him up and down.

“Okay. I’ll let the lot of you in. But first, you must answer a riddle. You may take all the time you need. Some men stay out here for days, mind you…you only get one chance to get it right. Fail, and you will never be allowed entry.”

“Oh! I love riddles!” Cadivus said, clapping excitedly.

The guards unsheathed their swords and pointed them towards him.

“Watch where your pointing that thing! Your gonna poke my damn eye out." Cadivus yelled.

The guards looked at each other and nodded. They lowered their weapons.

Ekio slapped him on his back. "What are you doing?" she whispered to him angrily.

"Being aggressive and refusing accountability," he whispered back.

She shook her head.

“Yes, riddles are…good,” the guard said. “so, here it is lads: your friend just told you his father used to beat him viciously. What do you do?”

The group huddled together. Both of the ladies murmured “hug him!” and Cadivus covered their mouths.

“Sit this one out ladies,” Cadivus said, “I’ve got this.” He turned toward the guards. “I’d tell him he probably had it coming. Then we’d get drunk and fight each other.”

The brows of their group raised in unison.

“That is…” the guard's suspicious look turned to a wide smile– “Correct!”

The guards cheered and tapped a nearby keg that was somehow previously out of vision. They passed a pint around to each member of the group.

“Oh, okay,” Cadivus said, “it’s like seven in the morning, but okay!”

They drank some of their beer, except for Ekio who dumped hers out when nobody was looking.

“Damn that’s good! One for the road please!” Cadivus said.

A guard struck him in the jaw.

“No! It’s *mine*! No take!” He then sobbed uncontrollably, his comrades dropped their pints and came over to comfort him.

“She can’t hurt you anymore, Reygar!” one of the other guards said, rubbing his back gently. “You’re the prize, baby!”

Now very confused, Cadivus’s group put down their pint glasses and entered the city.

“Wait, Halt there!” One of the guards called after them.

The guards all picked up their weapons once more and walked toward them.

Reygar wiped the tears from his eyes. "As you were walking away from us, I noticed something amiss. One of you has the roundest ass that could only belong to a lady."

"Ekio…" Cadivus whispered, "it seems your most perfect posterior has alluded to the fifty."

She sighed and turned around.

"Not you sir!" the guard said, "gods! We're not racist!"

All the guards nodded in agreement.

"No, no, no. Turn around you good sir. Keep it fletched and all that!" Ekio turned back around, breathing heavily, trying to resist the urge to murder.

"Grab that one!" Thermia cursed herself out for doing all those squats recommended to her by ladies of the court. Yet when the guards approached, they grabbed Sparklebutt, and dragged him off.

"What the shit!" he screamed, "take a look at my cock and tell me I'm a woman!"

"Ew! We're not gay!" one of the guards said, "we'll take you to the dungeon until you can confess to your crimes!"

"Stop! I have a dick! I have a dick!" Sparklebutt cried out in frustration.

"Typical woman. Won't take accountability for her own actions." The guard turned to the other guards. "Lock her away and toss the key!"

The guards dragged him off through the dirt while he protested.

“Sorry you gentlemen had to see that, it’s easy to be fooled, it’s happened to all of us after all! My first wife was a chair, didn’t find out for seven years!”

The group stared at each other mouths agape.

“Guess you gotta fuck sober every now and then. I should have known no woman would be that quiet…Oh well! Enjoy your stay!”

“What is happening?” Cadivus asked Hunter.

“I don’t know,” Hunter said, “let’s just get the hell away from this entrance and figure out our next move.”

“Wait,” Ekio said, readying her hand over her dagger. “Shouldn’t we stop them? Steal our friend back and leave this place?”

“He’ll be okay for now. They’ll realize they made a mistake and release him. In the meantime we should explore the city and learn as much as we can about it.” He looked around at the impressive city. The architecture was simple, but perfect. Every building was built from the same materials, and had the same colors, tan and dark tan. “Besides, we’re here to rob their armory. If need be we can release a prisoner as well.”

Cadivus flinched.

“Wait a pigeon-fucking minute now…I just realized how insane it is that we’re planning a robbery with a lawman. I never considered it before for some reason.” He placed his hand underneath his chin and stared at Hunter’s flat face. “What happens to lawmen who break the law Hunter? Furthermore, why would you take such a gigantic risk?”

“Shut up,” Hunter said while attempting to walk away.

Ekio grabbed his shoulder and turned him around.

“I cannot believe I’m saying this, but he is right. Why do you risk your own livelihood to find this man? Or is this some clever setup for the rest of us?”

He looked each of them in the eye and sighed.

“You’re right. A lawman shouldn’t do what I am doing. It goes against everything I stand for.” He rolled up his sleeves and revealed the scars along his wrist. “What I am about to tell you cannot leave this group.”

They all nodded, Cadivus had even found some peanuts and began snacking.

“A while back I was caught in a trap by this man. Captain Chronic. Thought I had him cornered and fell right into it. He didn’t kill me though. Just captured me, blindfolded me, gagged me, brought me….somewhere. I don’t know. He told me I was to use my sight on all his men, since he could be sure which ones he could trust. When I refused, he played his little tune…"

Cadivus moaned. “Oh my god…. Get to the fucking point already! This story is boring. You’d better be fighting or fucking someone soon.”

Ekio and Thermia slapped his chest, making him cough out a mouth full of peanuts.

“One by one,” Hunter continued, “his men lined up, and I was forced to see their pasts. It was worse than that though. The music…It doesn’t just force you to use your powers, it *enhances* them. I could *feel* the visions as well. I don’t know how long it took for my mind to break, but it did. For one fella, I seen the horrible things he’d done to his own flesh and blood, and I snapped. I managed to get one hand free, gutted him with his own blade, and dug it so deep into my wrist I thought I damn near cut my hand off."

"And then out of nowhere," Cadivus interrupted, mimicking Hunter's voice, "a gang of sexy bounty hunting paramours in tight leather armor broke in, murdered the ravagers, and saved my life with their magical pussy powers."

Thermia's face lit up and nodded toward Hunter.

"I passed out from bleeding," Hunter said. "When I woke up, I was back in the Requiem. And then I got better, and was sent back out into the world."

"Wait a minute," Cadivus said, "you glossed over how you managed to end up in the capital?"

"Were you sold?" Ekio asked, "rescued? Left for dead?"

"I don't know," Hunter admitted, "my boss wouldn't tell me. She just said I was home now and that's all that mattered. That I should shut up and be grateful."

"Your boss is a woman?" Cadivus asked.

"Don't even start with–"

"She must be a badass…" Cadivus said. Wondering who she was, and what she was wearing at this very moment. "What's her name, your boss?"

"I think you would know by now. It's the Inquisitor."

Thermia and Cadivus shared a look of disbelief with each other.

Ekio looked puzzled.

"Who is this person?" she asked.

"The Inquisitor is perhaps the scariest person in the world," Thermia said.

“Not only that. After today we’ll all be on her shit list for helping her own break a law,” Cadivus said.

They all stared at each other for a moment of silence.

The Inquisitor was not to be trifled with. Chronic himself was not fit to sit in her shadow. This plan needed to work without them becoming targets of her hunters. Otherwise it would all be for naught.

Chapter 12

Cadivus's group traveled deeper into the city and found a pub to settle into while figuring out a new plan. Even in the morning the pub was quite full. The room was well lit from windows and large fireplace. The interior was wood and marble, making up the various tables, stools, and chairs. The walls held no art or fanfare. Several men sat at tables eating breakfast meats with ale.

Cadivus looked around and nodded, thinking this place wasn't so bad after all. He tapped Ekio's shoulder to get her attention.

"I think you're the only one with money on you. Buy us some food and ale, would you?" He made a sad face.

She grimaced and shook her head.

"Please…" he said. His hands clasped together as his face saddened further.

She stared at him and sighed before waving a waiter over and ordering for the table. After the food and drinks came, he took a bite and a sip and came up with an idea.

"Okay. So here's what we do," He said through a full mouth. He took another long sip. "We'll just get the other two codes while we wait for Sparks to get released. Then he can do his part." He held up his hands and gauged everyone else's reaction.

They all looked amenable to the idea.

"What happens if they don't release him?" Ekio asked. "If we take two, and they sound the alarms…" She turned toward Hunter and

Thermia, who mulled over the idea. She stared directly at Thermia. "What do you think?"

Thermia's eyes widened.

"I don't know. I don't do this stuff."

She glared at her until she found the confidence to speak.

"Well, if Sparkle doesn't get out, we're out of luck when they change the codes. So, it seems our only option is to get him back first. Then continue with the plan. I mean, we have to do all this at the same time for it to work, right?"

They all placed their hands on their chins and thought hard. Except Cadivus, who was too busy observing the waiter and the large trays of food he was carrying back and forth.

"She's right," Hunter said, which made Thermia smile. "First things first, we have to get him back."

Cadivus finished his ale, he realized everyone else had only taken a few sips. He motioned for another to the waiter.

"Okay. We'll finish breakfast first. Then I'll go and get him out." He burped into his hand and wiped it on his pants.

Hunter shook his head.

"No. Me and Thermia will go get him out," Hunter said. "You two can stay here and see if you can learn any information."

"Why am I going with you?" she asked.

"Because you put ease in a person. Could use a touch of that in this situation."

She grinned and nodded her head. She turned to Cadivus to see his reaction only to find him picking meat out of his teeth.

They finished their meals before heading out to free Sparklebutt. As the two left out the door. She shot Ekio a thumbs-up, which made Ekio smile.

“Well, well, well…It seems we find ourselves on a date,” Cadivus said.

Ekio rolled her eyes.

“How can it be a date if I am the one paying?”

He took another bite and sip, holding his finger up.

“It's a new world, Ekio. You're rich and I'm just an immensely skilled warrior." He bobbed and weaved in his seat. Shadow boxing with his empty glass. "Besides, I would have paid if you didn’t trick me the other day.”

She smiled at that.

“You're not some typical run-of-the-mill lady are you? I’d wager…” He looked at her and then leaned in as he spoke. “I’d wager, being the warrior that you are, you enjoy a certain amount of dare I say *control* over your romantic entanglements?”

She shook her head, Cadivus had come to expect it at this point.

“Let me be clear with you. I have not any time for these…entanglements.”

“What if I’m quick?”

She smiled and sighed.

“Look, I–”

“Cadivus?” a person in a dark red cloak and hood said.

“Who’s asking?” he said without looking up. When he finally did glance at their face, his eyes and smile widened. “Oh, it’s you!” He got up and hugged them.

Ekio stared at their hug, confused.

"What the heckles are you doing here?" he asked.

The cloaked person pulled up a chair and sat next to him. When they did so, Ekio got a glance at their face and realized it was a light-skinned woman. A beautiful one at that.

"Oh, I've been doing some work around here," she said, "I'm trying to keep a low profile, so don't bring too much attention to me, if you please."

Cadivus nodded. "I haven't seen you since—"

"Yeah. About that. I'm—"

"Who is this person?" Ekio asked, pointing a finger toward the intruder.

Cadivus's eyes widened, as he realized how rude he had been.

"This is…Well, her name is hard to say. Let's just call her El."

"I would know her full name." Ekio crossed her arms.

The cloaked woman shrugged.

"My full name is: Elanthoriatelleborcalliobenatar. Or Elanthoriatellebor for short. Or El for super short." She clasped her hands between her thighs and threw her cheek to her shoulder.

"See? It's El-throat-collaborator," he said.

El laughed at the jest, and touched his shoulder, causing Ekio to raise a singular eyebrow.

"Small world, it seems. Well it's good to see you anyway," Cadivus said.

"Yes, you too. The owner of this place owes me a favor. I'll tell him to comp your meal and bring more breakfast and ale for you."

"Eh, a comp is great and all, but I think I'm at my limit for drinks. I've got work to do after all."

"Oh Caddy. We haven't seen each other in *ages* and you aren't gonna have a drink with me?" She made a pouty face.

Ekio shook her head as she fell into her own seat.

Cadivus gave up a smile and playfully punched her shoulder.

"All right then! We'll do a quick catch-up but then I've gotta get to work." He laughed.

El wiggled her shoulders and along with it, her impressive cleavage, motioning for the owner to bring over more drinks.

Ekio folded her arms once more as her eyes rolled, wondering where Thermia and Hunter were.

****

As Thermia and Hunter walked through the city, she did her best to fit into the crowd and not arouse suspicion. She mimicked the patented walk, and avoided eye contact. She wasn't sure how to act around Hunter though since they hadn't spent anytime one-on-one before. A sense she could and should trust him lingered, yet the way he carried himself was so selfless and sure. Still, the long walk ravaged her feet in the oversized boots.

"I can't walk anymore!" she shouted, "I feel like my feet are gonna fall off!"

"Hey, disguise your voice," he snapped, "you saw how fast they throw people in jail here."

"My bad, bro," she said in a deep voice, which would only fool another fool. "Speaking of which bro, isn't it weird they haven't released him yet?"

"Stop saying bro so much. Have you heard any of us say *bro* this entire voyage?"

"Sorry, bro." She held out her fist for a bump, and he reluctantly obliged.

"You're not wrong. They should have figured it out by now."

They asked a nearby guard to point them in the right direction and continued their journey. Upon arriving, they noticed the jail was as clean and proper as any other building in the city. They sat in a small waiting room that had a large marble desk dividing the room in half. Yet no one came to help them. After a short while, Hunter smacked the table with his fist to bring someone out. Dead silence. Yet after a few more moments, a voice called from out back.

"One momenta!" The voice had a far north accent, farther north than Hunter's.

Soon a young man came around the corner. He had long dark hair, glasses and walked bent over with a cane. A brown shawl and cloak covered his body. "Howa might I be of assistance to ya now?" He looked at them with his head tilted sideways.

"Our traveling companion was brought here a few hours ago," Hunter said, "we were either hoping to bail him out or get some more information." He tilted his head slightly to match the man's.

"Oh, thatsa interesting. Indeed, thatsa interesting, because our cells be empty. No intake all dayo." He stared at them, then down on the floor and then back up at them once more. "Ya should get movin' on then, dontcha think?"

Thermia slammed her fist on the table and nearly lost her hat in the process. "That's not possible, bro. We saw him get arrested earlier."

Hunter gently placed a hand on her shoulder, guiding her back.

“Can we just take a peek for ourselves, one lawman to the next?” He unfolded his jacket to show his bounty hunter badge. The five point star forged in silver. Polished to a mirror like finish.

“If I doa that, I be the one in dere. So, just go on with yaselves now.”

The strange man pulled a lever that dropped a gate over the desk. Dust and dirt filled the room, and he waddled off into the back. Hunter tried to lift the gate, but found it was locked in place, which seems fitting for a jail.

“What the hell was that exactly?” Hunter asked.

“I dunno, bro.”

He glared at her.

She sarcastically mouthed, “Sorry.”

He shook his head.

“Ugh, it’s fine. Talk however you want. For now, just stand back a bit. I’m going to see what’s back there.”

“But it’s too heavy to lift,” she said, “you can’t lift it, bro!”

“You ain’t wrong about that. Lucky for me…” He grabbed a hold of the gate once more and kicked the wood out from underneath the desk. Once he made a big enough hole, he motioned for her to stay behind and crawled through.

A corpse lay on the ground behind the desk. Fresh. He couldn’t use his sight on someone dead.

Hunter ground his teeth. “I’ll be right back, if anything happens, run to the pub and find the others.”

Thermia nodded her hat toward him.

He grabbed a dagger off the corpse and carefully walked toward the cells. It was empty as promised–only six large cells and no other doors. Strangely, no sight of the strange man from before.

"Hello!" He yelled.

"Hi!" Thermia shouted from the front.

"Not you!"

"Kay!"

As he took a look around the room, something stood out in a dimly lit corner. As he walked closer the outline became more and more clear.

A pile of bodies.

He grabbed a torch from the wall and stuck his arm in the cage to see if he could make out anyone. The pile shifted, and he could see Sparklebutt's body with a metal object sticking out of his chest. He panicked. He breathed heavily as he struggled to bend the bars to get inside but found them too thick to force apart.

He bowed his head and thought carefully. He walked back to the desk and checked for keys but found none. So, he punched the wall in frustration, cracking it.

"What's the matter, bro?" Thermia asked.

"Sparklebutt…He's dead."

Tears filled her eyes.

"Something's wrong here…very wrong," he said.

"Should we get back to them?" she asked through her tears.

"As quickly as possible."

As they turned to leave, another guard walked in with a man in cuffs.

"Found this one pissing in the fountain," The guard said, assuming the two worked there.

Thermia stood in front of the hole Hunter had kicked through the counter, trying to act inconspicuous.

"Alright then," Hunter said. "Leave em here. I'll take care of it."

The guard eyed him suspiciously.

"Where's the warden?"

"You know him," he said, "ran out to fill his flask for after brunch I'd imagine."

The guard stared at him for a moment before smiling.

"Ha! Sounds like the ole coot. Anyways, here ya go!" He handed the prisoner over to Hunter, who accepted him and waved the guard goodbye.

"Can't a man mark what's his anymore!" the prisoner slurred out.

He waited for the guard to leave before chopping the man in the back of the neck, causing him to pass out. He then placed him on a nearby bench.

"Whoa!" Thermia said, "that was a close one."

"Let's just get back to the others."

He wasn't sure what was going on, but his senses were tingling. There was more to all of this than he originally thought. Sparklebutt, the city, the group…not of it made sense. He thought about cutting his losses but revenge and justice didn't always overlap. He took solace in the fact that no matter what happened, he would have a bounty to bring back with him.

Chapter 13

Thermia and Hunter walked into the pub and hesitated when they saw Cadivus chatting with a cloaked person and Ekio sitting at the table with her arms folded, glaring through them. They rejoined the group, which hushed the laughter ringing through as Cadivus explained his adventures to the woman.

"Can we be excused?" Hunter asked the cloaked woman. Cadivus threw up a hand, shrugging off his concern.

"Nonsense! This is an old friend of mine," he said in slurred speech, "she works here so we have an in to the workings of this place." He chugged the last of his ale and motioned for another to the waiter.

Thermia caught the same waiter's eyes and waved her hand, suggesting to cut him off.

The waiter shrugged with an unconcerned face.

"Who is this then?" Hunter asked Cadivus.

"This is the wondrous El," he said, "El, I'm gonna introduce you to my mate Sparklebutt. You're gonna love him." He turned toward Hunter and Thermia. "Where is the good man now?"

The two shared a look.

She hung her head low. "Sparklebutt was killed in jail, Cadivus."

Cadivus's face went blank for a moment, then he sang.

From Motob comes, a shining light, destined for a greatness
Till the dusk falls and the battles are won
We must pray for salvation
Oh Sparklebutt, he was carried off, by a beast that sought his rear

Oh Sparklebutt, he struggled through, and asked it for completion

Then, Thermia sang.

He was as cunning as a fox, he gave her golden locks

And blended them to match her grace

He was a man adorned with class

He had the most perfect ass

Any man would love to be him

Sparklebutt, the world would fear him

Then, Cadivus sang again.

Oh, how the world cries out for him today

In our hearts he will surely stay

We lost a man who was mighty with a flail

The children gather all around, just to hear his tale

Oh Sparklebutt, the world will mourn you this day

Also he was gay…

They all bowed their heads. "Well," Cadivus said, "I guess we can nix the meeting then." He made a funny face at El. She laughed and touched his arm. "Careful! I've already lost a button. I'd rather the rest remain intact if possible."

Ekio rolled her eyes.

"We need to leave," Hunter said, "the plan is done for."

"Nonsense," Cadivus said, "we have El here. We'll be fine."

El perked up. She pushed her shoulders inward and addressed the table. "What's that now? What are you up to, you little devil?" She wiggled in her chair.

Thermia blushed.

Hunter tried to hold a hand out to prevent him from talking to no avail.

"We're after the armory, legs," he said, "supposed to have some weapons we need for a quest." He poured the last suds from his pint into his mouth. "Sparks was supposed to get the code from the wizard."

Everyone but he and El sighed.

She looked at the group and smiled.

"I can do that. Easy! I've been scoping this place out for a while now. It shouldn't be too hard."

He looked toward the others for approval. They all had their reservations but nodded.

"Great! When do we get started?" El said.

"Quicker than a–" Cadivus swayed and resisted the urge to throw up, heaving in his throat.

"We need to do this quick and be on our way," Hunter said, "are you sure you can handle a wizard?"

She looked at him, smiled, and pulled her cloak back, revealing her curvy body wrapped in tight darkened red leather. She removed a dagger from her waist, held it up to her face, and licked the blade. "I think I can handle it, darling." She winked.

"I don't trust this one," Ekio said, giving her the evil eyes. She caught eyes with Thermia, and Thermia gave her a subtle shake while narrowing her eyes.

El leaned toward Ekio, placing her cleavage in Cadivus's face.

"Oh, you need not worry, my dear. A little ole thing like me. I wouldn't dare make enemies of a group as formidable as this one here." She sat back, put her arm around Cadivus and kissed his cheek. "Plus, I owe this man right here. Things didn't turn out so well the last time we met up, and it's been tearing me to pieces ever since." Her eyes teared up as she grabbed his face with her soft hands and stared into his eyes. “I’ve been longing for the chance to make it right.”

He raised his eyebrows, and looked toward the group for approval.

“Fine!” Ekio said.

“Wait a minute,” Thermia said “how are you able to exist here? I thought they hated women.” Somehow, the idea had slipped everyone’s mind.

“Well, let’s just say I have a special arrangement,” El said, “although to be honest, I’ve grown so bored of this place. This is a fine way to leave.”

The answer wasn’t satisfying. Still they knew they needed her to complete the mission.

They left the tavern, El gave them directions, and each group headed off in a different direction with uneasiness settling in them.

****

Hunter walked with Cadivus toward Sigma’s chambers. He huffed and puffed at each of Cadivus’s stumbles and distracted detours. They caught a lot of side-eyes and full-on glares in the busy streets, standing out like a sore thumb.

“Are we there yet?” Cadivus said, “my feet are all wobbly.”

“Your *brain* is wobbly,” he snapped, “why in the hell did you drink so much?”

Cadivus ignored the question, humming a song instead.

They came upon the building they were looking for. It was much larger than the surrounding homes, but made up of the same white marble design. Several guards had been posted outside. Lots of grunts and slams sounded off from inside.

"We'll need to sneak in through one of the windows," Hunter said, "I'd imagine his chambers are on the third floor." He looked back and saw Cadivus pissing on the building, waving to people passing by. He shook his head, reached into one of his pouches, and removed a black liquid vial. He handed it to Cadivus, who took it and squinted.

"Your drugs are spoiled," he said.

"Drink it. It's gonna sober you up."

Cadivus tossed the vial over his shoulder, and it smashed against the ground.

"I'm not even buzzed! Let's go already!"

Hunter slapped him and grabbed his jacket, causing him to struggle in his grip.

"I'm not fucking around anymore!" he whispered angrily. He changed his grip, grabbed another black vial, and forced him to drink it.

Cadivus choked on the liquid, falling onto his hands and knees. He coughed and gagged on all fours. Less than a minute later he stood, completely sober.

"Now stay that way!" Hunter scolded him with a finger waving in his face.

"What the shit was that stuff?" he asked.

"Old recipe. Granted, you broke the one without side effects."

"Side effects? What side effects?"

"Don't worry about it for now. We have fifteen minutes before it becomes a problem. That should be more than enough time."

He sighed.

"Now, throw me up to that window there," Hunter said, pointing to the second story window. "I'll help you up once I'm inside."

He nodded, and put his hands out for Hunter to stand on. He flung him toward the window but with too much force. Hunter crashed into the top of the windowsill, catching a blow to the back of his head. He managed to grab the bottom of the sill and pull himself in. He rubbed at the lump forming on his head and cursed the man who was now giggling. As Hunter looked around for a rope or linen to pull him up, he climbed through the window.

Hunter's mouth dropped. "How did…"

"I got good leapies," Cadivus said, "whoa! Check out this room!"

They looked around the luxurious bathroom. The bath was four times larger than normal and was already full of hot water.

"Uh oh," Cadivus said.

"Let's leave quickly." Hunter quietly opened the door and peeked out into the empty hallway.

He motioned for Cadivus to follow him, and they walked toward the stairs. As they approached, heavy footsteps could be heard on the floor above. He frantically waved his hands and pointed to a nearby room. They ran inside and found another man there wearing only a towel. The man opened his mouth to scream, but Cadivus grabbed his mouth and held onto his body. The loud footsteps passed by the door. Moments later, the sound of water splashing echoed throughout the floor.

"Make a noise, and I'll snap your neck. Got it?" Cadivus whispered to the toweled man, who nodded. "Where are Sigma's chambers?" He released his grip, but the towel man simply stood still. "Oh, you literal prick. Just talk."

"It's up the stairs and at the end of the hall," The toweled man said.

Cadivus gagged him once more, stood there for a moment, and then looked at Hunter, raising his eyebrows and motioning his head toward the man.

“What?” Hunter asked.

“Do I just kill him now?”

The toweled man squirmed and screamed through the hand covering his mouth.

“Stop it!” Cadivus hissed.

“What? No!” Hunter said, “just choke him out, and we’ll head upstairs.”

Cadivus wrapped his arm around the man’s face and squeezed. The toweled man squirmed even more fiercely, feeling his nose break under the force.

“Lower! Around the neck you moron.”

He nodded and gripped the man’s neck, who passed out after a few seconds. He gently placed him on the ground. “No wonder that’s never worked for me before.”

Hunter shook his head.

Using towels from the room, they tied the towel man up and gagged his mouth. They then left the room, sneaked upstairs, and peeked around the corner. Empty.

“There!” Cadivus whispered, pointing at the far door.

They walked over to it , and Hunter tried to open it, but found it was locked.

“Use the key Sparks gave ya,” he said.

Cadivus nodded and searched through his pockets. He then searched through them again. And again.

“Don’t tell me…”

He grimaced, pulling his pockets inside out to reveal they were empty.

"I think we've been bamboozled."

"You mean you fucked us!"

"Bah. It's fine. I'll just kick it down."

Hunter placed his hand on Cadivus's chest.

"No you won't. That there is red elm wood. It's what they make castle gates out of."

Cadivus looked at him with a blank expression.

"It's built to withstand a siege. You're not gonna break it by kicking it."

Cadivus just smiled and shook his head.

"Oh, my dear boy. Watch and learn." He took a step back and performed a sidekick. The force of the blow sent him to the ground, and the door remained perfectly intact. His body vibrating in pain as he moaned on the floor.

"Told ya. And now…you just alerted everyone to our presence here." Hunter rubbed his eyes with his palms.

"Oh, there are lots of banging noises here," Cadivus said, "I'm sure it's fine."

"There are gonna be a few more banging noises in a moment," a deep voice from behind them said.

They spun around and saw a large man in a towel. He was three times their size, and his muscles had muscles.

"Sigma?" Cadivus asked.

The bald man just smiled and laughed as he charged toward them.

Chapter 14

Thermia and Ekio approached their next location, which appeared to be a rather small building. It was barely the size of a shack.

"Who even wears dark red with leather anyway?" Thermia said, "I thought that went out like a century ago."

"Did you see her braids?" Ekio said, "Loose and haggard. Just like her pussy, I'm sure"

They both giggled. A man walking by stopped for a moment and eyed them suspiciously.

"Fuck you lookin at bro!" Thermia shouted in her tenor voice.

He shook his head and continued walking.

"Keep walking, bitch!" Ekio shouted her own tenor voice. Her beard itched, but scratching at it only loosened its hold, so she had to suffer through it.

"Something about that woman…I just don't trust her," Thermia said.

She nodded.

"Is this really it?" She pointed toward the small building. "Seems small for a leader."

Thermia shrugged, and they went inside. When they opened the door they realized it was much larger inside than it had appeared outside.

"How is this possible?" Ekio asked.

"Um…Maybe it's like wearing black?"

They looked around. The large brick room had fancy furnishings with red carpets and two spiral staircases in its center. As they approached the staircases, a fireplace lit itself.

"Who dares to disturb me?" an echoing voice called out.

Ekio and Thermia glanced at each other.

"We're reporting for duty!" Thermia yelled.

An ominous groan echoed through the large room, and the flames in the fireplace spun into a frenzy. One dizzying flame crept out and slammed into the ground. There appeared an old man in a gray cloak who held a metal staff. The staff had a pendant on it that looked like an upside-down *U*. The flame retreated into the fireplace as he stood with his arms outstretched.

"Reporting for duty?" the old man asked, the ominous groaning growing louder and louder with each passing moment. Then all the noise died, and he smiled. "Fantastic! I've been waiting all week for new help to arrive!"

He hugged the pair and walked toward a door on the side of the room. He waved for them to follow, and they did. The double doors swung open on their own. Inside the room were stacks of books, all over the place and in no apparent order. The walls were lined with red drapes and covered candles that seemed to burn despite no oxygen around them.

"As you can see, much help is needed here!" he said.

"You want us to organize these books?" Ekio asked.

"Heavens no! I have already seen to that." He walked over to the middle of the room. "What kind of wizard would I be if I couldn't organize my own books?" He laughed.

Confused, the women stared at each other, mouthing "wizard?" They were supposed to be going after the shapeshifter.

"No, no. I'm researching a new potion, a revolutionary one at that. It can keep you awake for days on end without feeling tired."

"That sounds cool," Thermia said, "wouldn't that make you super tired once it wore off though?"

"Well, so far, it's been a bit worse than that." The wizard laughed. "Getting the effect is quite simple really. Just need a little bamble root. Getting rid of the side effects however…Ah, that's the tricky part!"

"What are the side effects?" Ekio asked.

"Oh just the usual. Nausea, vomiting, hair loss, and, uh"-– his voice lowered to a mumble–"your dick falls off."

"It falls off?" Thermia asked, "like, plop?"

"Right off!" He laughed once more. "But seeing as how I'm the Omega, I'm sure it can be perfected. So, fear not my boy!" He walked over to a stack of books and placed his hand on top of it. "This here is the herbalism section. Look through these volumes here, and write down anything you can find about bamble root or dick loss." He turned to walk out of the room.

"Wait. Where are you going?" Ekio asked.

Omega turned around, looking puzzled.

"Me boy? I've many duties to attend to. Big things are happening! If you need me for anything, climb the stairs on the right side. I imagine you'll be here a few months before that however!" He left through the swinging doors, when they swung back he was gone.

"Well, let's get to work." Thermia grabbed one of the books and looked through it.

Ekio grabbed the book from her hands and threw it onto the pile. Thermia's eyes widened.

"We're not here for that. We need his code! Not to mention the fact that bitch sent us to the wrong place."

Thermia put her hand to her chin.

"She did it on purpose you think?"

"Of course she did! She kept bragging to Cadivus how she was working here and had connections. We'll show her though. We'll get the code from him, and then I'm gonna throw her in a canyon."

She nodded.

"Let's just go upstairs then. He doesn't look very strong. I'm sure you can take him!"

Ekio walked out of the room but instead of the main room, she found herself in a thick forest. She turned toward her friend.

"Thermia, I…"

Nobody was there.

The forest was familiar. The temperature was hot and the air was muggy. The sound of battle echoed in the distance. She ran toward the familiar noise, increasing her speed with each step with the wind pushing at her back. She soon came to a clearing and saw an army attacking her people. "No…"

She growled and ran to the battle. Removing her dagger, she jumped into the fray and swung at her enemies. The blade harmlessly passed through them. They didn't acknowledge her. She watched helplessly as they cut down her tribe. Again and again she tried to fight back but nothing changed.

"Aires!" her people cried out as they were cut down. Their hopeless faces stared past her.

She continued her efforts, much in vain. Panting, she remembered her family. She dashed toward her home and charged inside, passing through the front door like a spectre. Her mother and siblings were barricading the windows as the young men took up weapons. She ran towards the back and found her body in bed, unresponsive. Her heart sank. She realized this was the day…the day everyone she ever loved was taken from her. Her eyes welled with tears as her collapsing chest forced her to the ground. Only whimpers passed her lips as the doors slammed open. "I'm sorry," she moaned.

****

Thermia appeared back in her room in the capital city, Afferium. She awoke in a feather bed as the sun shone through lavish drapes. Knocking, a tall man opened her door and stepped through.

"Dad?" she said, a wave of confusion washing over her.

"Hello, my dear. Did you do what was asked of you?"

As she stared at him, her memories of this moment flooded back, memories of a long-lost love. The one she was dating before her father demanded she marry The Hybrid. The one she was planning to run away with. Her face flushed.

He sat at the edge of her bed. "Did you break it off with the boy? You'll be leaving soon. Can't have any loose ends you know."

"Marcel? I haven't seen him since—"

"Good, my dear. Now, get yourself proper. You're going to meet the man today."

A maid walked inside, carrying a beautiful red gown with such detail Thermia had never seen before. She laid it across the bed, and everyone left the room.

When Thermia picked up the dress to examine it, a note fell out of it. *My dearest Thermia* written on the outside. She opened it, and read the words she already knew. Words written on the same page, locked in a chest in Dreyhal.

Thermia, I cannot go with you as planned. My love for you runs as deep as any chasm and it would pain me to put you in danger. But I know you, I know a woman who would risk her life wouldn't be put off by such a refusal. And I know you could convince me against my better judgment. As such, drastic measures have been enacted on my part. I'll carry my love for you in the next world and present it as a gift to the gods themselves.

I'll miss our time together. Please always stay the woman you are and make your family proud. Farewell, my love. I hope you find your palace of light.

Her tears covered the letter as seeded emotions unearthed.

Outside her home, people yelled and cried out. She already knew what the noises were for. Yet she still walked toward the window to gaze out of it. But she found herself back in the bed, her father knocking as he entered the room. She thought about how she ended up here. She remembered the wizard's door, and her friend.

"Ekio!" she screamed.

****

Ekio kneeled in her home as the vision repeated over and over. Her sanity lost to the repetition. A voice called out to her, and her eyes shifted. It was distant at first, but it grew louder. Thermia's voice. She began to remember how she got there in the first place.

"Thermia!" She stood up and walked around, looking for her. "Thermia!"

"Ekio! Help!" her voice called out. The words far away and stretched out.

She followed the voice to an upstairs room with a mirror. A mirror that her family never had. When she looked into it, she saw a fancy room with Thermia inside. She pounded on the mirror. "Here!"

Thermia turned around, and seeing Ekio's image she ran to the mirror. She put her own hands against hers. Their eyes met and hope returned to them.

"Help me!" They both cried at the same time.

At that moment, their hands touched, and they grasped the other. They pulled each other close and embraced, squeezing as hard as they could. The illusion around them disappeared, shattering the dream, and they found themselves in the main room of the wizard's building once more.

"Thermia, it wasn't real…It wasn't real…" Ekio said.

Thermia made some choking noises and tapped Ekio's back. Ekio released her, and she took an exasperated breath.

"Too hard…Couldn't breathe..." She took several deep breaths and coughed.

"That bastard! He tricked us!" Ekio wiped her eyes and put her hands on Thermia's shoulders.

"Are you okay?" Thermia asked.

"I am now. Are you?" Ekio said.

"I will be. Thanks to you." She stood and brushed herself off. "I'm gonna kill that wizard!"

She caught Ekio's eyes. Witnessing the stillness of the warrior before her.

“Thermia…Leave the building.” Thermia saw that determined look in her eyes and found no reason to argue. She nodded, then walked outside.

Thermia mumbled to herself on her way out, "yeah, fuck his ass up."

As Ekio stood in the center of the room, she focused her power. Her clothes flapped as rugs were pushed to walls, and anything not bolted to the ground toppled over.

“Wizard!” she screamed, her voice carried by the torrent of wind that emanated from her.

With a bloodcurdling scream, she released her powers, pushing out through the walls and floors. Pieces of rock and wood swirled outward, as the building crumbled at her will. Even as the roof began to collapse, the debris found no purchase around her where the wind was moving at its greatest velocity. There was no need to hold anything back. She let it all go.

Chapter 15

The behemoth crashed into Cadivus and Hunter, smashing them through the door. They both kicked him off their bodies and into a wall, but he flipped and pushed off it with his feet, cracking the surface as he did. As he soared toward them he extended his arms, smashing each of his arms into their sternums. He grabbed Hunter's foot and threw him into a wall and; then picked up Cadivus by the neck with one hand and slammed him against another wall. Holding him in place while staring into his eyes with his wicked smile upon him.

"Ants? Ants in my home!" Sigma said, "I crush ants!"

Gunshots rang out as Hunter unloaded a cylinder into Sigma's back. Although the bullets barely impacted Sigma's flesh, bouncing off and embedding into nearby walls and floors. He holstered his gun and removed metal knuckles from one of his pouches. He equipped them, and charged at Sigma, and punched for his liver. The blow made the giant flinch, but Sigma caught the next swing and squeezed his fist. His knuckles cracked in the giant's grip as Hunter fell to his knees, grinding his teeth in agony.

Cadivus, still held against the wall by the neck, grabbed at the figure holding him, trying to peel his fingers off. The stubborn sausage like fingers never budged.

"Remember those side effects I talked about?" Hunter said, catching Cadivus's eyes. "Oughta be any second now…"

Cadivus's eyes squinted as his stomach growled audibly. He clenched.

Sigma tilted his head, uncertain of what was happening. The smile dropped from his face in the confusion of the moment.

"I'm going to beat the shit out of you two!"

"No need," Hunter said.

A horrible stench filled the room. Cadivus grimaced as his legs shook uncontrollably. Hunter removed nose plugs from his pouch, and clogged up his nose as the wet fecal matter dripped down Cadivus's pant legs. His trumpeting pants announcing the bile river's arrival.

Sigma's eyes rolled into the back of his head. "You nasty ants!" He released them both and covered his mouth and nose, gagging unwilled.

Cadivus took as many deep breaths as he could through his mouth. He turned and caught eyes with Hunter. Hunter nodded toward Sigma, and they both attacked. Hunter punched at the behemoth's organs and Cadivus kneed him in the nose. The combo attack caused him to flip onto his back.

"You think I've never fought with shit in my pants before!?" Cadivus kicked at his legs. Ignoring the sticky feeling on his own. "Take this!"

Hunter mounted him and rained metal punches into his face. Each blow delivering a satisfying thud as they bounced off the thickened skull.

"Get the code, I got this guy!" Cadivus said.

Hunter rolled off him, and searched around the room. Sigma tried to stand, but Cadivus punched the side of his head, which only made him slightly flinch. He grabbed Cadivus's arm, and lifted him into the air over his head.

"Bye bye stinky man!" He then threw him out a window. Cadivus's head hit the windowsill as he passed through it, and he flipped and landed on the roof next door.

Hunter looked back and saw Sigma focusing solely on him. His throat sank into his stomach as he no longer could see his partner.

"Now, you die, ant!" Sigma charged at him with his arms outstretched again, but he rolled out of the way and pulled his gun out. "You're out of bullets to bounce off me! Give up! Let me pull your limbs off!"

He smirked, flipped the barrel out and quickly swapped to another set of rounds.

Sigma laughed and flexed his chest "I'll give you one last chance!" His body widened as he spread his lats. His veins strained underneath his skin.

"Not too bright are ya?" He shot a round into his arm.

The bullet hit and stuck into Sigma's skin. He looked at the small wound and smiled.

"Pathetic ants!"

The round then exploded. Smoke and red mist filled the room as he screamed.

Hunter ran to the window to check on Cadivus, who was beginning to stand.

"Jump over! I'll catch you!" he called out.

Cadivus shook off the brain trauma and cracked his neck. "Just don't drop me! I can only land on my head so many times today."

He got some space, ran towards the edge, and leaped off of it. As he reached for Hunter's hands, Sigma hit Hunter's side, removing him from the window. Cadivus hit the side of the building, bounced off it, and fell down three stories to the alley below.

Lucky for him, a pile of trash broke his fall. He groaned after colliding with it. Feeling the diarrhea crust on his skin, he rolled out of the trash and hobbled his way to the front door.

Dazed, Hunter looked around the smoky room. A shadow ran toward him and he ducked. As the smoke left through the window he saw Sigma holding his half of an arm with his other hand, still smiling.

"For me ouchies, for you death!" Sigma said.

He raised his weapon to fire another shot, but Sigma disarmed him. Sigma grabbed him into a bear hug with one arm and slammed him into the floor, crashing through it and landing in the bath below. Hunter was held beneath Sigma, underneath the surface of the water. Sigma tried punching down, but his blows were slowed by the water still remaining. Sigma stood and raised him up. Hunter's eyes were struggling to stay open. The behemoth headbutted him, causing a rush of blood from his nose. He licked his lips at the sight of it.

He tossed Hunter outside the bath and got out himself. He stood over his body and thought as hard as his boiled brain could. "How to kill? So many ways to kill." He found Hunter's gun, at his feet, he picked it up, and examined it. Yet his finger couldn't fit in the trigger guard. He positioned one of his overgrown nails on the hairpin trigger. "This good."

Hunter looked up and sighed, taking a deep breath. Sigma's towel fell off, and Hunter saw while his upper half was gargantuan, his legs were remarkably skinny.

Sigma blushed. He refocused and took careful aim with the revolver, savoring each beat of the moment.

“Watch this dive!” Cadivus said as he fell from the floor above and landed in the bath. He had taken his pants off, which he now held in his hands and he whipped them around Sigma’s neck. He grabbed the other pant leg and pulled the behemoth down by his neck until his face was underneath the bathwater. Causing Sigma to drop the gun on the floor.

Hunter stood and held his legs so his waist teetered on the edge of the bath. The water turned brown as Cadivus’s body got washed of its excrement. Hunter, with his metal knuckles, punched Sigma’s solar plexus, causing all the air to rush out of him. Bubbles formed at the top of the water. Still holding his legs, Hunter grabbed his gun and held it to his stomach. But before Hunter needed to pull the trigger, he stopped struggling and went limp. They released their grip and pushed him out of the tub and onto the floor.

“Bout damn time,” Hunter said.

“Yeah. He was pretty tough,” Cadivus said, washing off the rest of the residue.

“I meant you. What took you so long?”

“Do you know how much brain trauma I’ve suffered today? Consider yourself lucky that I don’t think I’m a doorknob.” He got out of the bath and blinked rapidly. “Oh heavens. I think there’s shit in my eye! Not again!” He ran to a nearby clean bowl of water and washed them out.

Hunter holstered his gun and checked on Sigma. The behemoth still had a light pulse.

“Tough bastard,” Hunter whispered. “Let’s get that code and get out of here, kid.”

Cadivus didn't move, still cleaning his eyes. His bare cheeks shook back and forth as he rubbed at them.

"And let's get you some pants while we're at it…"

He turned around, placed his hand on his hips, and nodded. They went back up to the room and looked around.

"If I was a muscled psycho where would I keep my code…" Cadivus said. He rummaged through the bed.

"Even he wouldn't leave it out in the open. There's gotta be a secret safe somewhere," Hunter said, "we'll have to find it and crack it quick."

"Found it!" he said, waving Hunter over.

Under the bed's pillow was a paper with several crossed-out numbers. One set at the bottom wasn't crossed off though.

"I think this is it." He handed the paper to Hunter.

Hunter shook his head and smiled. "I wouldn't have thought to check there first."

"That's because you're not built like us," he said, mimicking flexing poses.

Though Hunter tried not to, he found himself laughing at the display. His distant stare more relaxed and near.

Soon after, they found a chest with clothing. The pants fit snugly on Cadivus, thanks to Sigma's aversion to leg training.

He admired the black pants with a white stripe going down the sides and elastic waistband. "I like it…It's freeing."

Footsteps sounded behind them.

"What have *you* done?" a man asked. Cadivus ran over and grabbed the man, but realized it was the guy they had tied up earlier. He brought him over to Hunter.

“We have business here, and we can’t have you sounding the alarm just yet,” Hunter said as he pulled a white vial from his pouch and opened it.

“Wait! Wait!” the man said. “My name is Bradley. Pleasure to greet ya. Did you really beat up Sigma?” Bradley looked at them in anticipation.

“Was that not obvious?” Cadivus said, “your captain is defeated, and your bath is defiled!”

Bradley smiled and shook his head.

Cadivus and Hunter stood there, confused.

“Oh man! What was it like? Did he cry or beg or anything?” Bradley asked his questions without waiting for an answer. “Wow, you guys must be strong! Especially this guy!” He said while pointing at Cadivus. Cadivus blushed and a smug look drew upon his face.

“Well, all in a day's work for someone like me,” Cadivus said, “my friend here nearly shit himself.”

Hunter frowned and shook his head.

“Put that vial away. This guy’s all right," Cadivus said.

“A few compliments is all it takes to gain your trust eh?” he asked.

Cadivus grabbed the man’s cheeks with one hand and displayed his face to him.

“This is the face of a good man here. I think he can keep a secret for a few more hours, can’t you?”

“Uh-huh.” Bradley said through his squeezed cheeks. He moved out of the grip. “I won’t tell a soul! I’m just gonna write about this in my journal.”

Cadivus’s eyes widened.

"Oh, a journal! I should start keeping one of those. Might come in handy when people write about my life." He rubbed his chin. "It's decided then. Retrieve me a journal, my lad."

Bradley smiled and gave him a thumbs-up.

"Hell yeah, man! We're gonna be journal-bros!"

They touched forearms, and he ran out of the room, giggling.

Cadivus smiled and sighed as he watched him leave.

"I like that man."

Hunter shook his head as the events of the past two days replayed inside it. "You're an interesting guy, Cadivus, I'll give ya that."

"And you have a lot of things, Hunter." Cadivus said with a baffling amount of sincerity.

"Uh, thanks?"

Cadivus placed a hand on his shoulder and nodded.

The two then headed off for the next part of their mission.

Chapter 16

Thermia stood outside the collapsed building, a mountain of rubble before her. Men who had heard the destruction walked around, staring.

"Planned demo! Rebuilding on a new foundation!" she yelled toward the onlookers.

The men then discussed their own demo projects as they collected together. They walked off a short while later, each waiting for their turn to discuss a time they built something. Not long after, the rubble shook.

Thermia took cover behind a large piece of debris, as smaller bits were blown away.

When the dust cleared, Ekio stood amongst the stones. She turned to Thermia and nodded. Thermia fist-pumped the air and ran toward her. Yet as she approached, the rubble shook once more, and the wizard rose, a spherical shield of translucent light around him.

"My research!" he screamed, his voice echoing off the surrounding buildings. "I am the Omega! How *dare* you!" However, his face of rage turned inquisitive. "Wait…How did you two escape the spell? No man has ever escaped it before."

Thermia pointed her finger at him while her other hand grabbed her hip. "It was simple! We just had to do the one thing men are incapable of!"

"What's that now?"

"Ask for help!"

Omega smiled, and then his angry face returned.

"That's it then? Well, trespassers…I will carry out your sentence here then." He formed a ball of water at the head of his staff.

"We'll take your code now," Ekio said, "or, you can die." She removed her dagger and held it in an attack stance.

"*Please*. You knock over a few rocks and you expect me to tremble?" he said, "I create *worlds*!" He shot the ball of water towards her, which turned into an arrow. She focused her wind on her edge of the blade and sliced upward, breaking the spell. She then threw her dagger at him, it stuck itself into his shield, the edges cracking around it. When he went to grab it, she commanded it back to her hand.

Thermia cheered from the sidelines.

"Still not trembling?" Ekio said, "I can change that." She charged and swung at him. Her blows bounced off the shield but each one left a crack where it struck.

His staff grew a blade of water that he counter-attacked with. She dodged the blows and continued her assault on the shield. Frustrated, he performed a downward strike that she dodged to the side. When she went to strike back, she found her foot was stuck. The water blade was no longer on the staff but instead wrapped around her foot.

"Shit!" she muttered.

He summoned another blade at the staff's head. "Oh, you ignorant fool. It seems you're stuck. You almost got through my shield, so I'll give you credit for that. However, it was foolish to fight the Omega alone."

She struggled to remove her foot, then looked up at him, and grinned.

"She's not alone!" Thermia yelled from behind him.

When he turned toward her, Ekio put everything she had into a final punch on his shield, shattering it to pieces. She then summoned her wind power and directed it into his chest. The force sent him flying backward. He tripped over Thermia, who was on her hands and knees behind him, and hit his head on a rock with a loud crack.

"Teamwork beats the wizdork." Thermia said as she stood and dusted herself off.

The spell around Ekio's foot broke, so she walked over to Omega to check him.

"Oh no. We need the code from him," Ekio said.

"Oh, right…Well maybe we'll find it written down here," she said as they stood in a pile of rubble. "Or maybe not."

"Wait!" Ekio said, placing a finger on his neck. "He is still alive."

Thermia grabbed the staff and tried to cast a spell, which proved fruitless. She tossed it to the side.

"Damn…so close to cool powers." She sat next to Ekio.

They both carefully watched until his head turned to them.

"I can't feel my body," Omega said, his voice weak. "Oh, my research…I'll never complete my research…"

Thermia frowned and her eyes watered, despite their previous battle. She grabbed his hand, even though he couldn't feel it.

"We need that code," Ekio said, "we'll send someone to help you when we leave."

"Code?" he asked, "who cares about a stupid vault? Power doesn't come from trinkets. It comes from within us." He turned his head to the side, looking on the verge of passing out, but Thermia gently grabbed his face, staring into his eyes so he could see her tears.

"*Please*. If we don't get that code…I can never go home," she said.

Omega closed his own wet eyes for a moment then sighed.

"6969."

She snorted.

Ekio looked puzzled.

"What is funny?" Ekio asked.

"I'll tell you later," Thermia said, winking at the wizard.

He winked at her, and they winked back and forth for an awkward amount of time before he fell unconscious.

Ekio and Thermia nodded toward each other. They left the ruined site.

They walked toward the building where Sparklebutt had said the vault was located. Yet they were both conflicted over the situation they found themselves in. When Omega was lying there on the ground, he seemed like an ordinary old man. They had almost forgotten about the torture he was happy to leave them to. They didn't talk to each other on the walk over. They were both stuck in their own heads, thinking about their ordeals. Occasionally looking over and smiling at one another.

When they saw the others in the distance, a wave of relief washed over them. Cadivus performed an exaggerated two-handed wave as they approached.

"Who's ready for a heist?" He called out.

The women noted how rough their clothes looked and how he had changed his pants.

"You guys look, and smell like shit." Thermia said, plugging her nose.

Ekio made a grossed-out face.

"We had a bit of a run in," Hunter said, "the important part is we got our code. Did you?"

Thermia giggled.

"Yeah…we got it."

"There's our fashionably late comrade!" Cadivus pointed at El, who was walking toward them. Smiling as usual.

"Okay. Everyone all set then?" El asked the group.

"Uh, no!" Ekio said, "you sent us to the wrong guy. Why did you do that?"

She and Thermia both folded their arms and stared down El.

El put a hand on her hip and smiled.

"Oh! My mistake, girls. I guess I'm just bad with directions. Hence why I'm here and not running important missions."

She and Thermia both shook their heads.

"The important thing is you did your part. So let's get inside, and I'll show you how to enter the codes."

"Hold on a second," Cadivus said, "as leader of this group, I feel like I should give a pep talk before we go inside. Listen up! I…" He trailed off as everyone walked past him and into the building. His enthusiasm waned. "Yeah, let's do it. Whoo," He mumbled.

No guards were posted at the vault. Shocked, they entered a tall stone room with a giant circular metal door at the opposite side. Large red cloths fell from the ceiling to each side of the gold carpeted walkway. Their steps echoed in the open room. The smell of sulfur becoming more apparent in the air as they continued along the path.

"I don't like this one bit," Hunter said, looking around the room.

"Oh, you worry too much," El said, "just use the dials to enter your codes. The symbols above them indicate which code goes where." She positioned each group in front of their dial.

"Wait a second…" Cadivus said, "there's a fourth dial...does anyone have a code for it?"

"1234," a voice from behind them called out.

"Thanks! Okay 1…2…"

The cloths that hung from the ceilings opened from the middle, revealing a group of guards on each side. As the group turned around to face them, they saw yet another man standing behind them. He wore fancy clothing: deep purple pants and shirt with a black jacket with white faded vertical stripes and leather shoes. He smiled and snapped his fingers.

"Cadivus burn em!" Hunter yelled. He moved to remove his gun, but a large man with one arm grabbed him from behind.

"Hello ants!" Sigma said as he laughed.

Ekio pushed Thermia toward the middle of the group and went to remove her dagger, but as she placed a hand on the pommel a strike to the back of her neck knocked her out cold. Thermia looked back. El had delivered the blow.

Thermia growled and charged at her, but El slapped her so hard that she fell to the ground.

Cadivus charged at the newcomer in the fancy suit, but guards swarmed him, each grabbing a different limb. Still, he slowly walked toward the man in the fancy suit, dragging the guards holding him. More guards ran in to tackle him, knocking him to the ground. They tied him up in chains.

Sigma picked Hunter up with his one arm and headbutted him. Blood ran down Hunter's face once more as he fell unconscious.

"Why did you do this?" Thermia asked El. "We trusted you, you leather-clad bitch!" El looked at Thermia and laughed, placing her hands on her hips and moving them side to side.

"I'm gonna let you in on a little secret." El said. Her face and body transformed into a man with pale skin and red eyes. His voice became raspy. "There is no El. Only Gamma." She laughed.

"Enough of this!" Cadivus said, "you'll release us, or you'll suffer my angry wraith!"

The guards finished wrapping several layers of chains around him and threw him to the floor, face down.

The man in the fancy suit walked over and squatted in front of him.

"Look, kid. My name's Alpha. You're Cadivus, right?"

"Oh wow! You know my name," Cadivus said sarcastically. "I feel so special."

"Yeah…Anyways, I think you've got potential, kid. This group though…" He pointed at the others. "Well, I can't say the same for them. So I'm gonna make you a one-time offer here, and realize I never do this."

"If the offer is we all get to watch you punch your own dick repeatedly, then yes, I accept."

He laughed and looked around the room until everyone else laughed with him. When he snapped his fingers, they all stopped.

"Listen, you've had a tough life buddy. Nobody respects you, least of all these people. They won't even consider the possibility you'll get them out of this. I'm guessing you have been feeling down lately, trying to figure out a direction in life. Is that true?"

Cadivus had to acknowledge there was truth to that statement.

"I know, kid. We all crave love and respect as men, hell I'll even say as people! A younger me wouldn't have. Now, what do you see when you look at me? Some guy at the head of a great city? Who has all these extraordinary henchmen? 'He must be a super villain with amazing powers!' Well, my super power is wealth…and for a small investment each month I can teach you the same strategies I've used to gain this wealth. And if—"

"Pass!" Cadivus shouted.

A shocked look came over Alpha.

"I don't fucking care about any of this dribble. Release us now, and you can larp another day."

He frowned and nodded.

"Too bad kid. Hoist 'em up!"

Guards attached Cadivus to a hook that hung from the ceiling. Hunter was tied up in ropes, and the women were strapped to odd-looking tables that were standing up with wires running through them. The guards ripped their fake facial hair off, causing their skin to turn red.

"You should have said yes, kid."

Cadivus was lifted into the air, where he could see everything. Including a large lid being removed from a hole in the ground. The smell of sulfur resurfaced. An orange glow emanated from it. Lava. It was lava, and he was heading straight toward it.

Chapter 17

Hanging above the lava pit, Cadivus thought of his next move. He saw the leaders standing around, deliberating and pointing at each other and the women. Everyone seemed to point toward Sigma and offered him high fives, which he seemed happy to receive.

"Excuse me!" Cadivus yelled.

A large booming noise echoed from outside. Everyone looked around suspiciously, until Cadivus cleared his throat to get their attention.

The guards looked up at him, confused.

"Don't you find it a little rude to exclude your captive from your plans? Honestly, I know we're planning on killing each other, but there's no need for bad manners."

The guards and leaders looked at each other and smiled.

"It's simple really," Alpha said. He pointed at the tables Ekio and Thermia were strapped into. Two empty tables were next to them. "These are transference tables. They take a woman's life energy and give it to a man."

That explained their exceptional abilities. The no-women rule also made more sense. It was merely a cover-up.

As the guards continued deliberating, Cadivus caught eyes with Bradley. Bradley held up a journal to him and mouthed, "Sorry." He pointed his head toward a dark corner of the room, where the real El was hiding behind the rolled-up curtain.

She pointed at him, struck her arm, and pointed at the guards. Like she wanted him to make a distraction.

"Gentlemen and gentlemen!" Cadivus yelled, everyone turned to face him. "Seeing as I'm about to die soon, I thought it would be proper to give my final words."

Alpha gave him a hand wave, allowing him to continue.

"When I told my brother I wanted to be a vigilante—seek out justice, protect the weak, and all that—he laughed in my face and said it wasn't meant for me."

El snuck over to the tables while he was talking and moved the wires around.

"Funny enough, he told me I'd end up getting caught and killed."

"Brothers can be jerks!" a man from the crowd yelled.

Cadivus frowned and nodded.

"Yeah, they can be jerks. As I hang here now though, I think I get what he was saying. Why, if he were here…" He laughed. "He would fill the room with a thick black smoke and force it all into your lungs. Your eyes would tear for a moment, until all the moisture was pulled from your body. You'd beg for a grasp of fresh air, but it would never come. It would be slow, painful, and, well, just *terrifying* when you think about it."

El gave him a thumbs-up as she snuck back to the side of the room.

"So, no, I might not be able to stop you. Hell, *we* might not be able to stop you. I can promise you one thing though…incurring the wrath of that particular hybrid…Well, I would advise against it."

The leaders' faces were blank, and the guards looked at each other with wide eyes.

"But hey, I'm not telling you how to be evil or anything."

"Thanks for the tip. I'll install ventilation," Alpha said as everyone laughed.

A man was carried into the room on a stretcher, looking feeble.

"Welcome back, Omega," Alpha said.

Omega looked at him and smiled.

"Thank you, my lord. I look forward to completing our research."

Alpha frowned while tilting his head.

"Yeah about that…I heard you got beat up by two chicks. Can't really have you representing us after that."

Omega's eyes widened. "No! I've been nothing but loyal to you! The dark-skinned woman is an exceptional fighter, she destroyed my entire tower!"

"Face it," Gamma said, "you no longer have what it takes."

He looked at Sigma, who just shook his head. He closed his eyes, sighed, and accepted his fate.

"I only wish I could live long enough to watch her defeat you too."

"Yeah, well I wouldn't worry too much about that." Alpha said. He motioned to Sigma, who grabbed the stretcher and held it over his head like a waiter delivering drinks.

Sigma walked over to the lava pit and slammed Omega into it head-first. A terrible smell and smoke filled the surrounding area. Cadivus gulped, realizing he was watching his own fate.

"So, we need a new Omega," Alpha said, "we already deliberated and decided it is going to be…Yorin!"

The crowd clapped as a man walked toward Alpha, smiling ear to ear. He got so many high-fives his palms turned red.

"Thank you so much for this opportunity!" Yorin said, "I won't let you down!"

"Of course you won't," Alpha said, "now, get on over there!" Yorin and Sigma were strapped into the tables. Gamma walked over and stood next to a lever between the tables. Cadivus looked at El, who met his gaze and nodded.

"Let's begin, shall we?" Alpha said, raising his arms.

The crowd erupted into applause.

"It's time for the transference! Let it be known that if you give it your all as Yorin has, you too can receive rewards far beyond your comprehension! Who else would give you the chance to better yourself for such a low monthly payment?"

"Alpha!" The crowd cheered. "Alpha! Alpha!"

Alpha smirked and nodded.

"All right! Without any further ado, let's get this party started! Drop that man! Pull that switch! Let's fucking go!"

Cadivus plunged into the lava. He couldn't form any final thoughts beyond panic.

Alpha motioned for Hunter to be strung up on the ceiling hook next. Gamma pulled the lever, and the tables glowed with light blue haze. They all watched. The men strapped in were smiling until their faces turned into horror. They screamed and shook. Their bodies trembling, and their throats expelling the contents inside. Their muscles aching beyond excruciating as their minds subsided reason.

"Cut it!" Alpha demanded with a concerned face.

"I can't!" Gamma shouted, "It could kill all of them!"

"I don't care! Shut it down!"

He cursed and pulled the lever back.

The machine stopped glowing, and the men passed out.

"What happened, Gamma?" Alpha asked.

“Someone crossed the wires…son of a…” He began changing the wires back.

“Just get it done before she—”

Ekio’s eyes opened. She took a peek around the room and at her constraints. Strength boiled inside her like never before.

“Stop her now!” Alpha ordered.

As the guards approached her, she focused her power and pushed them all back with her wind, except for Alpha who stood his ground in the heavy wind. One by one, she removed each shackle from her body and pulled each limb free from the table. Breaking free from her constraints, she fell to the ground and collected herself. When she finally stood, she spun around and punched the table towards Gamma. It collided with him and sent him and the table flying across the room.

She gazed around the room once more, her face stern. “Where is the loud one?”

Alpha laughed. “Little late for that sweetheart! Your boyfriend’s dead, and I do believe you’re next.”

She used her powers to pull Alpha toward her, but he didn’t budge. Instead he held up a glowing ring. The wind was sucked into it, and he aimed it toward her.

“Golden rule, baby. He who has the gold”—he shot her power back at her, pushing her against the wall—“makes the rules!” He laughed and turned his back on her. “Fuck it. Kill her.”

The guards took up their weapons and closed in on her. She reached for her dagger, but it wasn’t there, so she put her fists up into the air.

A thick splashing erupted from her peripheral. The lava pit erupted outwards, and Cadivus leapt from it. As he landed on the ground, bits of lava splattered around him. He sat there on one knee, his arms outstretched. His clothes had burned away, and the chains that wrapped him now only partially covered him. He held long chains in his hands. Yet his leg cramped after a moment.

He stood and rubbed at it furiously. "Ow, ow! Charley horse! Ow!" A look of relief came over his face after he rubbed it for a moment. He stood tall and took another battle stance.

"How did you survive that?" Alpha demanded.

He smiled.

"Because I *can* kick lava's ass!"

He charged the crowd and swung his chains with great force. As he swung the chains, they grew shorter with each swing. The molten metal oozed off them, flung off, and attached to the guards' armor. They had no choice but to remove their armor or else be cooked alive in it.

Ekio watched, her eyes wide.

He cleared half the room before the chains were gone. He grabbed a sword off the ground but found it difficult to hold with melted chains on his hands. He tried to scrape it off as the guards charged at him.

Ekio now charged in to join the fight. Yet Alpha caught her with a side kick at an alarming speed. The blow hit her hip and caused her to stumble onto her side.

He stared her down, putting on tinted glasses. "Wind hybrid, huh? Yeah, that seems appropriate since I just knocked the wind out of you!" He laughed.

"You're so fucking corny," Ekio said with a disgusted face.

Gamma joined his side, as his arm morphed into a veiny blade made of flesh. "Usually, I like to take my time, but let's make this quick," Gamma said.

"Agreed."

He ran towards Ekio, who took a defensive stance, but he was struck in the shoulder and reeled back. After a short delay, his shoulder exploded. She looked over her own shoulder and saw El removing the rest of the ropes from Hunter, who was aiming toward them.

"I got your nine," he said.

"Now me!" Thermia yelled, "I'm gonna trip the shit out of everyone in here!"

Gamma frowned then smiled. He stepped on his fallen arm and absorbed it back into him, forming a new arm with an even more evil-looking flesh sword. "I'll take that one!"

As he ran past Ekio, Ekio summoned her wind to push Alpha into the wall. Yet Alpha reflected the wind power to send her flying toward Cadivus, who caught her.

"Hello, lioness," Cadivus said, winking, "plenty of time for that later."

She shook her head and stood on her own.

"Use your powers on the pale one," Ekio said.

He looked at her and pursed his lips.

"Oh, don't worry. Let Hunter have some fun. He's more than capable, you know." He looked around and noted the twenty remaining fighters and their leaders. He saw El sneaking over toward Thermia, which drew Alpha's attention. "I'll take their leader. Can you take down their soldiers?"

Ekio gave him a smug look, kicked a staff off the ground into her hands, twirled it around her body, and ended in a battle stance.

"I think so," she said, "I bet I'm done before you are."

"Bet the dagger?"

She smiled. “Against your pride? Sure.”

They charged into battle.

Chapter 18

Hunter had four explosive shots left and his metal knuckles. Noting how ineffective the last round was he saved the remaining shots. He only dodged the blade arm and struck blows when he could.

The man before him wasn't nearly as strong as the behemoth he fought earlier, but he was craftier. In between Gamma's strikes his limbs would change forms, to bludgeoning weapons.

"Pathetic," Gamma said, "this is what the crown sends nowadays? You wouldn't last a day in the old times." He thrusted a mace-shaped arm toward Hunter, who caught the blow with his two hands. Yet his arm extended and collided with Hunter's chest.

Hunter was sent flying backward. He stood, watching as Gamma, who had absorbed some of his leg into his arm to allow the extended arm attack, returned his body to normal.

"Interesting body you got there," Hunter remarked.

Gamma grinned and swung at him again. He caught the blow once more and activated his sight, stunning both men. A few moments later, they regained their composure and stumbled back from one another.

"What the hell was that?" Gamma asked.

Hunter grinned.

"I just learned how to kill you, Bruce."

Gamma's eyes widened.

****

Cadivus ran toward Alpha, screaming to get his attention off Thermia, while Ekio leaped into a group of guards. She swung her air-infused staff around, knocking them about.

He swung at Alpha.

"Got you!" Cadivus cried as his blade collided with Alpha's back—before it bounced off, the vibration of the blow reverberating throughout his entire body.

Alpha blew air through his nose. "Yeah, you sure got me, bro." He continued his glare at the crowd, not paying attention to Cadivus.

Cadivus kept swinging at Alpha's body, trying to cut through it. Growing frustrated, he grabbed the sword with two hands and swung as hard as he could, screaming. Alpha slightly stumbled and turned around, angry. Alpha punched his chest, and he felt all the air rush out of his body. He was then struck in the back of the head, sending him face-first into the ground. Alpha placed his boot onto his back.

"What the actual fuck?" Cadivus groaned.

"Maybe you didn't realize it, but I'm decked out in the best enchanted items money can buy!" He showed off his outfit, several rings, a necklace, and bracelets. "I had a few things tailored to fit, which might have dampened their effectiveness a bit, but it's more than enough to get the job done."

He picked up Cadivus by the back of his shirt, lifted him into the air, and stared at him through his tinted glasses. "Oh. A siphon. Yeah, that's not gonna work on me, bud. I'm not a hybrid, you can't steal my powers."

Cadivus shook his head. "Siphon?"

His response was to throw Cadivus into Sigma's table, smashing it to pieces and freeing him from the bonds.

Sigma groaned as he regained consciousness. He looked down at his arm that wasn't repaired. His face grew angry. "Why arm not fixed?!" he growled at Cadivus. He picked Cadivus up with his good arm, struggling as he did so.

Cadivus pointed toward Alpha. "He said you can jerk him off just as good with one arm. Of course, *I* told him that's ridiculous. You can't hit the staff and satchel at the same time that—"

Sigma dropped him to the ground and bared his teeth at Alpha, who was paying attention to the other fights in the room.

"Finish him, Sigma," Alpha said without looking at him.

"I crush ants!" Sigma yelled as he ran toward Alpha. He picked Alpha up, threw him into a pillar, and rained punches onto him.

Alpha just shook his head as the blows landed. "You have two seconds to stop this."

He just kept attacking.

Once two seconds passed, Alpha caught his arm and ripped it off his body. He cried out, tears filling his eyes. Alpha smacked him with his detached arm knocking him to the ground.

"I hate to put down a good pet," Alpha said, "but you bit your master."

Sigma's roars from the ground were silenced when he stomped through his head. The explosion of blood slowly dripped off his clothing and fell to the ground around him. He looked toward the light-skinned woman and noticed she wasn't strapped to the table anymore.

****

"Thanks, traitor!" Thermia said to El as they hid behind a pillar.

"Traitor?" El said, "*hello!* I'm the one who *saved* all your asses."

Confusion filled Thermia's face as she thought about the situation. "But you sent me and Ekio to the wizard and then let Gamma pretend to be you."

El placed a hand over her mouth and giggled.

"Oh, sorry. I'm bad with directions and Gamma caught me trying to steal his code." She turned to look at him fighting Hunter. "He's tougher than he looks, and he looks pretty terrifying to begin with!"

Thermia nodded, deciding against her better judgement to trust her. "Okay then. What do we do now? It doesn't look good for us, does it?"

El pursed her lips and thought for a moment. "I think I know what has to be done, but…you might not like it." She raised her eyebrows at Thermia and then whispered into her ear.

Thermia's eyes widened, and her jaw dropped. "Are you crazy? I'm not doing that!"

She stared at her and tilted her head, letting the moment hang in the air.

"Fine! Just so you know, I haven't been able to work out in weeks." Thermia said, her arms folding.

El laughed and left, stealthily crouching around the room.

****

Ekio defeated enemy after enemy. She thought of her youth, training against multiple attackers in a courtyard. Her mind drifted back to that time. Laughing with her sparring partners. Her entire youth had been spent training for moments like these. It came as natural as braiding hair. Alpha's guards, on the other hand, lacked technique and practice.

Standing in the middle of the remaining soldiers, she glanced at her bracelet. She then narrowed at the remaining guards.

"All at once now, boys!" one of the guards shouted, "she can't stop all of us! Charge!"

As they swarmed, she thrusted her staff out, and a sternum cracked when it connected. Luckily for her, Cadivus had caused them to strip off their metal armor. She brought the staff back and swept it across the ground, tripping three guards. She performed an overhead blow to one in the middle and released the staff to shoot wind toward the other two, sending them flying over the stone floor. Her foot caught the staff, and she kicked it back into her hands.

The remaining six guards formed a circle around her, raising their weapons. Focusing, she took a deep breath. She held the staff in the middle of the shaft and parried their blows as they rained down on her. It didn't take long for their lack of training to show as their blows became slower and more forced.

She caught a glimpse of the dagger she had won from Cadivus in the hands of one of the guards. She swung up at his hand causing the dagger to shoot into the air. She thrusted the tip of the staff into his forehead, pulled on the dagger in the air, and dodged it as it came down. It stuck into the neck of a man behind her.

She tried to command it back, but it was stuck too deep. She rolled backward, removed it, and launched the staff toward the feet of the last four. They stumbled, and she moved in, dagger in hand, slicing through their vital arteries. When she was on the other side of them, she pushed them with her wind forcing them against a wall.

They grabbed at their wounds that would soon drain most of their blood.

Chapter 19

Hunter continued to dodge Gamma's blows as Gamma chased him down. Gamma changed his tactics, using quick piercing attacks instead of swings. One caught through Hunter's leg. He stumbled to the ground and caught another through his hand, preventing it from going into his head.

Gamma laughed. "You're about to die, dog!" He pulsed the bits of himself that were inside Hunter, causing Hunter to scream in agony. "I know I said I'd be quick, but I love this part." His wicked grin found ways to look even more sinister.

Hunter, once again, activated his sight powers. And again. And again. When each ended, Gamma would try to speak–only to be pulled back into it. After several visions, he withdrew his hold on Hunter. The room spun as his mind centered on reality.

Four shots rang out.

Two explosions sounded behind him and two more on his body, blowing off his leg and arm. Hunter rolled over toward him and grabbed the loose appendages before Gamma could collect them. He tossed them into the lava that he had lured him over to.

Gamma had to reform his body into a much smaller proportion. "You dog!" he said, his voice higher pitched. He stood only four feet tall with matching proportions.

"Gets a little fuzzy after visions. Lucky for me, I didn't need every shot to land," Hunter said. He drank a blue vial down. His bleeding stopped, and his wounds slowly closed.

"You think I can't kill you like this?" Gamma said, "I'll cut you to bits!" He turned all his limbs into slashing weapons and charged.

Hunter grabbed his arms and brought his foot up, slamming his heel into his chin. The leg blades cut into Hunter but not deep. The arms Hunter held onto ripped off as he was sent flying back. Hunter threw the bits into the lava, and his size shrunk once more.

"I suppose your buddy uses a serum like the one I took," Hunter said, "heals the body, including damaged muscles and makes them stronger." He put his fists up.

"I'm not gonna lose to you, dog!" Gamma said, his voice even higher pitched now. "I am eternal! I won't—"

Hunter charged and punched his head down, slamming him into the ground. Gamma's body went limp, he grabbed the limp body and threw it into the lava pit.

"Annoying bastard…" Hunter's vision became hazy. The combination of repeatedly using his sight and drinking the vial had taken a toll on his body. "Ah, dang it. I still need to—"

He fell to the ground, unconscious.

****

Cadivus approached Alpha once more. "I know this probably goes against ethics, but can you just tell me your weakness?"

Alpha pointed at him and laughed. "Redheads, kid." He got into a fighting stance, and kissed one of his rings.

"Oh, I think I like bald heads now. Well, maybe it's not the hair that matters but—"

Alpha swung at him, knocking him to the side. He carried on a combination of attacks that Cadivus tried his best to block, but the pain rang through his body. Alpha took a step back, hopping from foot to foot before stepping forward and throwing a roundhouse kick that, even though Cadivus blocked, sent him flying toward a pillar.

"You guys should just give up now," Alpha said, "there's no shame in submitting to Alpha. It's just nature." Alpha looked around the room, noting all of his subordinates were dead or defeated. He shook his head and sighed. "Why is it so hard to find good talent nowadays?"

Cadivus slowly got to his feet and grabbed a mace he found on the ground. He swayed back and forth, his body giving out on him.

"That's not going to happen. You killed Sparks. You *tried* to kill my other friends. I won't forgive your treacherous douchebaggery."

Alpha shrugged, picked up a spear from the ground, and threw it at Cadivus, who was unable to dodge the blow. Yet a rush of wind from the side pushed him out of the way and into Ekio's waiting arms.

"I guess the dagger is still mine," she said, winking.

"Yeah…I kinda stacked the deck against myself," Cadivus said, "this is a pretty good consultation prize though." He reached around to grab her hips, and she dropped him on the ground. "I'm okay."

"Let's finish this." She pulled him back up to his feet.

Alpha walked up to them, his hands in his pockets.

"Wind and siphon…interesting."

Confused, she stared at him.

"Siphon?"

"That's what I said! I think it's a clever way of saying I suck."

"That guy is a siphon," Alpha said, removing his hands from his pockets. "He could be useful to me. Well, he could have been. Now, he's about to be dead."

"Don't use your fire powers on him," she whispered to Cadivus. "He can absorb it."

Cadivus nodded, thanking the gods.

"All right. I'm bored now…time to end it." Alpha lowered his body and was about to charge when—

"Oh, hubba hubba." A voice called out from the side. There stood Thermia who had cut her pants and shirt short. With her body on display. She walked toward him.

"Sup bitch?" Alpha said, lowering his guard.

"Watching a real man in action…" Thermia said, trying her best to appear sexy. "It really gets my furnace going, if you know what I mean." She stumbled over a fallen body, nearly falling before regaining her composure. "It gets me horny for having sex." She leaned her back against a pillar and pushed her chest out, blowing her hair out of her face.

"Yeah, we all knew what you meant," Alpha said, "well, just give me a minute, babe. Work comes first."

She dropped a rock from her hands onto the ground.

"Oops!" she said playfully. "I dropped my favorite rock…guess I'll have to…pick it up."

Confused, everyone stared at her as she turned her back toward them and slowly picked up the rock. When she flipped her hair and looked back toward Alpha she fell onto her head.

"Dammit!" She cried as she fell to the ground.

Cadivus and Ekio looked toward Alpha and saw El behind him, reaching for his hand.

Yet Alpha sensed her presence and grabbed her wrist.

"El? Well, you're fired, bitch. Enjoy retirement." He punched her, sending her flying away.

She rolled across the ground before coming to a stop.

“El!” Cadivus called out to her.

In a fetal position, she held out her hand to show a bunch of jewelry, and smiled through bloody teeth. She passed out shortly after.

Alpha could sense his strength had waned and checked his body, realizing all the enchanted jewelry he was wearing was now gone. He growled and walked toward El’s body. But Cadivus and Ekio ran between them. Ekio gently pushed El with her wind, sliding her body along the floor away from them.

"Thermia, get El out of here!" Cadivus said.

Thermia shot up from the ground and ran around to El, dragging her to the entrance.

“It doesn’t fucking matter,” Alpha said as he adjusted his clothing. “You still can’t hurt me in this outfit.”

“I never thought I’d say this,” Cadivus said, “but let's strip that man down to his undies.”

Ekio snickered. “Back to your weekend festivities are we?”

They ran in, punching and slashing at Alpha. He held his arms up and blocked all the blows, a deep bass noise coming from each deflected attack.

“Retribution!” Alpha screamed.

An invisible force came from his chest and pushed Ekio and Cadivus away from him, Cadivus and Ekio groaned as they rolled across the floor.

Alpha removed a women's watch from his pocket and put it on his wrist. His body radiated a purple aura around him, and his eyes glowed the same purple color.

Ekio got to her feet and placed the dagger in front of her.

“This is it…” he said, his body hovering as the purple aura concentrated on his hands. “You lost. I won. Nothing can stop this attack, not even gods.” He placed his hands together behind him as the purple glow emanated from them, causing his body to be outlined in its hue.

Grimacing, Ekio summoned every ounce of power she had into the dagger.

“Move out of the way!” Cadivus shouted at her, pointing for her to hide behind a pillar.

Determination and anger filled her face. “I won’t! I can deflect it!” A piercing wind blade formed around her dagger.

Alpha threw his hands forward and unleashed a purple beam attack that headed straight toward her.

“Stop!” Cadivus jumped in front of her and took the blow to his own chest.

It knocked them both back, his body slamming into hers as they rolled to the other side of the room before his body landed on top of hers.

She groaned. “Get up!”

But he didn’t answer.

“Get up!” She said again, slapping his shoulder.

Still, there was no response.

Her voice trembled. “C-Cadivus…get up.” She pushed him off her, got to her knees and looked into his empty eyes. She caressed his face, where a smirk remained, and buried her forehead into his, running her fingers over his chest and feeling a warm liquid spilling from his body. “Wazimu,” she whispered to him.

“Don’t worry. You’ll join him soon.” Alpha said. His purple aura slowly disappeared. The watch he wore turned into a purple light and evaporated from his wrist.

She tried to wipe the tears from her eyes, but they kept coming. So, she sat, holding onto his body. She grabbed his hand and placed it on his chest, and placed the dagger in his palm.

Alpha continued to taunt her but his words were distant.

She stood, and looked around the room. Seeing all the bodies on the floor gave her flashbacks of the Aires trial, where she acquired her wind power. She closed her eyes and took several deep breaths before opening them again and focusing on Alpha.

“Looks like you’ve got that determined bitch face,” he said, “come here, and I’ll take care of that for ya.”

She cracked her neck and walked toward Alpha.

“What kind of victim would you be without your petty defenses?” Ekio remarked, her face blank.

“Tell ya what sweetheart, one final offer. Get on your knees and beg for my forgiveness. Then maybe I’ll let one of your friends live. You can be my special little secret guest.”

"I would sooner swim in your lava pit, vermin."

He charged. Ekio spun around him and yanked the collar of his jacket, kicking behind his knee. She pulled on the jacket while pushing his head forward. The jacket tore at the tailored seams and she threw it to the ground. He grabbed her wrist, she spun him around and ripped the dress shirt open, breaking all the monogrammed buttons free. She then grabbed each side of the shirt and slammed her knee into his chin. The shirt ripped off him as he flew backwards. He looked at her while holding the tattered remains of his shirt, and for the first time she saw fear in his eyes.

He turned to flee, but she chased him down and grabbed at his pants' waistband. She reached inside, grabbed his underwear, and pulled it up until she lifted him off the ground. The under-garment snapped, and she threw the broken pink lace onto the ground. He shrieked and tried to take off again, but Ekio tackled him from behind once more, knocking them both to the ground. She pulled his pants down and forced them off, tearing them in the process.

"Of course you would tailor objects touched by gods," Ekio said.

He sat on the ground, trying to scoot himself away as she walked slowly towards him. He held up his hands in desperate defeat.

"All right…fine! Fuck! I'll give you some money to leave." He stood and covered his private parts.

She reached out, wind-pulled a staff into her hands, and held it toward him.

"No…beg."

He laughed at the request, so she spun the staff and hit his right arm, breaking it. He cried out and fell to his knees.

"*Beg*!" she said through gritted teeth.

He looked around to make sure nobody was watching.

"Fuck…fine. Please…*please* don't kill me."

"Make me believe it." she said softly, swinging at his other arm and snapping that one as well.

"Please! *Please!* I'm sorry! I'm sorry for all the fucked up shit I've done to you just please, *please* let me live. I don't wanna die before I'm a millionaire!" He rubbed his tears off with his shoulders.

Ekio placed the staff under his chin and made him stand. “Okay…go.” She nodded toward the exit.

He looked at her, at the exit, and then back at her. As he turned around to leave, she snapped the staff in half over her knee and spun her arm around his body, stabbing his heart. She could feel the echo of his pulse fade through the broken staff.

She let the body fall to the ground and fall at her feet. She turned to see Cadivus once more, his still body resting on warm stone. She knelt beside him. "Wazimu! I told you I had it! You did not have to—" Her anger failed her as she caught a breath she almost lost. She suddenly felt so tired and sore, she laid down beside him with her head on his shoulder. She knew one day she would share the same destined fate.

Chapter 20

Darion stood in his wobbly, impractical tower. It stood in the center of the encampment, so he could keep an eye on everything. He had given orders out to everyone, and expected them to be carried out.

Decan approached his tower with his henchmen in tow. “Darion, share a moment?”

He jumped down, and his tower shook as if it was going to collapse. “I believe I can. What is your business?”

Decan shooed his men away.

“While I appreciate the progress you’ve made lately. I am here to inform you that we still plan to have an election.”

“Of course. I wouldn’t expect less from you.”

“I just didn’t want any confusion. I’m aware you're prone to it.”

“The only thing I’m confused about is why the fuck you are wasting my time telling me this. I haven’t seen you lift a finger to help anyone. What’s wrong? Lost your can-do attitude in the last battle?”

Decan smirked.

“You know, it’s going to bring me great joy when you lose. This whole pseudo-confidence persona you have now…well forgive me for saying but I don’t buy it.”

“It’s going to bring me great joy when you…” Darion mocked, “blah, blah, blah. Oh, fuck off chest-hair.” He turned to walk away, but Decan grabbed his shoulder.

“You're to save your wench tomorrow, yes?” Decan said, “do take care. It would be a shame for you to lose your head now after all the ‘work’ you’ve done recently.”

“Touch me again, and I’ll relieve you of your hand and use it to clean my backside.”

He obliged, releasing his shoulder and showing his palms.

“Forgive me.”

Darion took a step away but stopped himself. He turned around and stared at Decan with a scowl. Walking toward Decan, he forced Decan to back-pedal. He stared through his soul until Decan tripped and fell onto the ground, his men approached, but Darion drew his sword and held it out toward the goons while maintaining eye contact with Decan.

“I’m sick of all this snarky holier than thou bullshit,” he snapped, “this is the sands, Decan. People must choose their words carefully here.” He sheathed his sword and knelt. “Especially when they are on their back.” He lightly tapped his face and left.

As his henchmen tried to help him up, he threw a fit, berating them for not stepping in.

Darion walked the encampment, greeting the men, women and children who were working. Finally, he found the man he was searching for: Doban. Doban stood on top of a wall, building it up with a sand mix that was as hard as stone.

“Doban!” Darion called, “a word if you will.”

Doban motioned for another man to take his place and jumped down to greet Darion with a hearty handshake.

“You’re an impressive man, Doban,” Darion remarked.

Doban shook his head.

"Oh, cut the shit. Are you ready or not?" Doban said.

"I believe so, but we should talk away from prying ears."

They left the work site until they came upon a secluded area inside of the camp.

"So what's the plan?" Doban said.

"Doban, there's no easy way to say this…but I won't be returning with you and Toonda tomorrow."

He stared at him, confused.

"What the hell do you mean? What have we been training for?"

"A week of training isn't enough to defeat this man I'm afraid. It has been helpful, but still…I won't beat him. I'll have to do as he asks of me."

"You can't…you can't leave us now. We'll think of something. We'll—"

"We won't," Darion said, "this is the best I can offer these people."

"Oh, forget all that. If you're not here that means we won't have a camp to defend. Who's gonna…" He stared at Doban with an evil smirk on his face. "Oh, fuck that. Darion…I'm not a leader."

"You're a better man than me. I bet your cock is twice as long as mine."

"Twice as thick too, I'd imagine. That isn't gonna help us through this though."

"If I agree to be his student, he'll leave everyone alone. You'll come back and tell the people that I died in combat and you struck the final blow and saved your wife. You'll take my place as a hero. They *will* support you; They already see you as a leader on the walls. Just…spread your influence."

"It'll be a lie…You can't build a world on lies."

"Of course you can. I'm proof enough of that. You'll do it because you can."

Doban sighed and Darion put his hand out to shake. He reluctantly shook his hand, squeezing hard.

"Thank you, Darion. I always thought you were a weirdo. Now I see, we just live in weird times."

"Thanks…" Darion said, "do what you need to do. I'll meet you in the morning."

With that, Doban walked off to continue his duties. Darion looked around and realized that with his home making up most of the walls, he hadn't had the privacy to relieve himself in some time. Thinking of the possibility of dying tomorrow made him aware of his urges. He thought about buying a woman for the evening. But the thoughts of being with someone always reminded him of the one who got away. If she was still here, there wouldn't be any need to agree to a forced apprenticeship. The feeling left him, and he continued his duties for the last time.

****

The next morning, Darion waited outside the camp's north gate. The walls were beginning to look formidable from the outside.

Doban approached, dressed in leather armor, carrying several weapons. "Just in case."

They made their way to Tuska Point. The letter didn't specify a time, so they figured to show up early and wait as necessary. It took them several hours to reach their destination. The day was hot, and the sands got even hotter as the sun rose. When they arrived, they found they were the first. They sat on a rock and waited for several hours.

“Man, people should really specify a time when they kidnap a wench,” Darion said.

“Right? It is presumptuous to say a day and place.”

“If I’m ever an evil man, when I kidnap people I will state a time as well.”

“I’m sure you can offer that advice as his new apprentice.”

“I shall.”

In the distance, the silhouettes of two people approached.

“Here they come.”

As the silhouettes got closer, they could make out Tuka and Toonda. Toonda wasn’t in bonds; not that he needed her to be. Darion and Doban stood from the rocks to greet them.

“Didn’t I say alone, Darion?” Tuka said.

“Oh, you’ve got his wife. Cut me some slack, will ya?”

Toonda and Doban ran for each other and embraced in a warm hug. They then made out with each other. Tuka cleared his throat loud enough to get them to stop and walk to the side.

“Don’t leave!” he commanded the reunited couple. “We’ll settle business first.” He removed his robe once more, and Darion found himself even more repulsed in the daytime. “So, have you decided to come under my tutelage then?”

“I’ll agree to your terms, but I have some of my own,” Darion replied.

Tuka furrowed his brow and folded his arms.

“Ugh. What are your terms then?”

“We leave my encampment alone. Never return and never cause strife among my people.”

Tuka closed his eyes and slowly nodded.

"Fine! Our travels are gonna take us far from here anyway, boy."

Darion motioned for Toonda and Doban to leave.

"Wait! They weren't given permission to leave."

He stared at Tuka confused.

"I thought this was a trade. My village for me?"

Tuka laughed.

"They aren't in your village, are they? If you want to prove to me that you *are* serious, you are going to have to *get* serious."

Doban pushed his wife behind him and removed his sword.

"That wasn't the deal!" Darion screamed.

"Either you kill them now," Tuka said, "or I kill your entire village, boy!"

Darion looked back and forth between the two and clenched his fist, his teeth grinding.

"Darion…" Toonda said. "Do it, Darion. Save the village."

Doban looked at her, shocked.

"My dear, our child?"

"How many children will die if this beast attacked our camp?" She placed her hand on his cheek and mouthed, "*It's okay.*"

Doban closed his eyes tightly, shed a tear, and hugged her with all his strength. She felt it appropriate to die in her love's arms and embraced him back.

"Be done with it then!" Doban called to Darion.

Staring at the two, Darion removed his sword. He held out his blade–and pointed it towards Tuka.

Tuka laughed.

"You wanna do this again, boy? Fine! I'll kill them myself."

He charged toward the couple, preparing to plunge his sword through their bellies. But before he could attack, his sword halted. Darion had grabbed the blade and held it in place inches from Donban's back. Blood dripped from his hand and onto the sand.

"This power…it wasn't meant for this." Darion swung his sword toward Tuka's heart. Tuka evaded the blow, taking a cut to his leg instead. "Go…" he told the couple.

"We won't leave you here!" Doban said.

"You will because I order you to!"

Toonda stared at Darion and met his eyes. She couldn't recognize him anymore.

"Darion…" she said, "kick his ass." The couple turned and ran away.

"Where do you think you're going!" Tuka screamed and ran towards them again. Darion clotheslined him and swung his sword to the ground. He evaded the sword, and the blow sent a cloud of sand into the air. Darion kept his eye on the couple as they left and matched blades with him, who didn't seem like an unbeatable god anymore. They clashed blades that rang over the sands and echoed through the canyons several times.

"My, how you've grown in such a short time, young one." Tuka said.

"Witness me now. There is no tomorrow for you."

"I wouldn't be so sure of that." He pointed toward Darion's wounds. Cuts from where Tuka's sword passed his own covered his body, adding up. "Without my help, you'll never make it out of here alive, boy."

Darion laughed.

"What's so damn funny?"

"To think I value such a pitiful thing as my own life..." Darion thought about all the times he sought to throw his life away. It was easier this time, having a purpose that was much larger than him.

Tuka screamed, coming in with a thrusting blow. Darion took the sword into his stomach and grabbed Tuka's sword hand, holding him in place. He slashed his own sword upward, cutting off Tuka's other arm, twisted the blade's hilt in his hands and stabbed it through his neck. As Tuka choked on his own blood, he pressed his nose to his, staring into his eyes with trembling hate as he ground his teeth.

"Die with me, anguar!" His gaze unrelenting as he poured all his malice into Tuka's soul until the gleam in his eyes left. He removed the sword and before Tuka fell to the ground, he removed Tuka's head from his shoulders with a strong blow. He fell to his knees, a sword's hilt sticking from his stomach.

The world slowed, and the sand stopped swirling.

Darion saw his father looking at him, with pride on his face. A look he had never seen while he was alive. His eyes filled with tears, and acceptance of his fate washed over him.

Then the world darkened, and the glowing wings appeared behind his father. The archangel grabbed onto his father's neck, staring at him. He knelt there, unable to act. Simply watched his father's body turn to dust before him.

An inconsolable violent will overtook him. He screamed, louder than his voice had ever reached before. Saliva dripped over his chapped lips. The scream sapped his remaining strength, he stabbed the sword into the ground and rested his weight against its pommel. It held firm in his hands as his world faded to black.

Chapter 21

Thermia's and El's distant and distorted voices woke Ekio. She looked at Thermia's mouth and read the words *hurry* on her lips. She allowed herself to be removed off Cadivus, rolling on to her back. The other two women carried Cadivus to the table Thermia had been strapped to previously.

"Is this gonna work?" El asked.

"Yes. I don't know how, but it will work!" Thermia said, crying as she strapped Cadivus into the table. "I-It has to! Is it still intact?"

"Somehow. I just need to change a few things that they tried to fix." She swapped some wiring around and set some dials on the panel. "There!" She looked at Thermia. "I hope this works."

Thermia nodded.

El pulled the switch, and the machine went to work. Ekio looked over and realized Yorin was still strapped to the connecting table. The machine glowed as the women stepped away. Yorin's body shriveled up, and Cadivus's wounds on his chest closed. Sparks shot out of the control panel, catching flames as the power passed through. El nodded, assuring them it was fine. They all waited until the machine fully turned off. The fire sizzled the wiring before dying out in a flare. They stared at Cadivus's body and watched for signs of life.

Ekio limped over to them, observing the closed wound on his chest.

"Is he alive?" Ekio asked with hope in her voice.

"I don't know," Thermia said as she approached his body. "Cadivus…wake up…"

His body lay there motionless.

She pounded on his chest. "Wake up dammit! We need to go home!" She kept pounding on his chest until El walked up behind her and grabbed her wrist, hugging her from behind.

"I'm sorry," El said, "it was a long shot."

Tears poured from her eyes.

Ekio walked up and grabbed his hand.

"Wait." She grabbed onto his wrist. "He has a pulse…"

The women unstrapped him from the machine and laid him on the ground, surrounding his body.

Cadivus opened his eyes and gazed up at the three women.

"Am I dead? Are there foursomes in the afterlife?"

The women all sighed in unison.

"I guess he's fine…" El said as she stood to go check on Hunter.

Thermia hugged him tight, and he groaned in pain. He tapped her arm to reassure her.

"I don't know what you did, but good work, sis." As she released him, he looked toward Ekio. "I know you don't want a turn to hug me but—"

Ekio hugged him.

"Gross!" Thermia shouted. She threw a cloth over him.

Ekio stopped hugging him, confused.

"What?" Ekio asked. Thermia pointed toward the tent he was now pitching under the cloth. She turned her head back toward him in disgust.

"Well at least we know it still works," he said, raising his eyebrows.

She shook her head and stood.

Cadivus shrugged and asked for some clothing, realizing he was still naked from the lava. El walked over to them with Hunter hanging around her as she helped him walk.

"Howdy. You get all em?" he asked.

Ekio nodded, looking at Alpha's corpse. "Yeah, that's all of them."

He followed her gaze and grimaced.

"Dang miss. That from you?"

She nodded again and looked away.

"Remind me never to cross ya…"

Cadivus got some clothes from other bodies in the room, he felt it morbid but necessary. Hunter gave Ekio his last healing tonic, and she was shocked to feel its results, commenting it was a lot like her medicine from back home. After some small talk, hugs and handshakes. They soon stood in front of the vault, with one code remaining.

"Any ideas?" Hunter asked.

"He said the code was 1234," Thermia said.

"Nobody is dumb enough to have that as a code."

"Well, it's easy to remember," Cadivus said, "try it!"

Hunter looked at him and shook his head. El put the final number in and to his surprise, the door opened. They all smiled and walked inside–to a surprisingly bare room. Only a few items remained, and the reason soon became obvious. A hole had been blown out the back of it, stones in a pile around its burnt surfaces.

"Well, that explains the noise from earlier…" El said.

"Ugh," Hunter said, "this place was hit while we were fighting? What are the chances of that…"

"Better than the chances of finding clean underwear here," Cadivus said.

The few remaining items were on the stone shelves that ran along the walls. Several chests with a few coins each were here as well.

"All right, how do we divvy up the loot? I think we should go by kills, personally," Cadivus said.

"Just take what you can use effectively," Hunter said, eyeing a revolver that was like his but white and gold.

"I can help you guys decide," El said, "I know these items. I brought them here to trade."

They all looked at her in disbelief.

"Wait. *You're* the reason that guy had all those items?" Thermia asked.

El nodded and averted her gaze.

"Yeah...When you're in the guild, you do what you're told." She handed Hunter the white-and-gold revolver. "Hunter, yours is obvious. It's a revolver that doesn't need bullets. Instead, it uses your stamina to fire projectiles."

"Interesting. Bullets are hard to come by, after all." He took aim, noting it was very light. He then looked over the fine details and felt a sense of guilt for letting his service revolver look so rundown. He placed the gun in a large pouch. "Seems strange that someone would leave it behind..."

She handed Cadivus a short chain, three feet in length. She draped it over his hands.

"Cool...now I can lock up a bike..."

She frowned.

"It's a growing chain. If it heats up, it grows longer. The hotter it is, the longer it gets."

"Just like me!" Cadivus winked.

Everyone sighed.

"Well…I don't know if you saw the last fight I was in, but heated chains tend to break apart when using them as a weapon."

"Not this one," El said, "it's enchanted to be indestructible. Go ahead and try it out!"

He frowned and wrapped the chain around his arm.

"Maybe later. I'm really tired right now." He turned to Hunter. "That excuse works for men too, right?"

Confused, Hunter shrugged.

She laughed, grabbed a ring from her pocket, and handed it to Ekio.

Ekio took the ring, wondering if it was as powerful as the absorption ring Alpha had used. It fit perfectly on her finger.

"What does this one do?" Ekio asked.

"Put it on your finger and say *shield.*" she said, taking a step back and motioning for the others to do the same. All followed her lead, except Cadivus who walked over to look at the ring's design.

Ekio made a fist and examined it. "Shield…"

The ring transformed into a shield half the size of her body. The expansion hit Cadivus's forehead, causing him to stumble backward. He grimaced and rubbed his forehead as everyone else chuckled.

"Serves you right for being nosey," Ekio said.

"There's a good chance that ring is a homage to your past, Ekio," El said.

She observed its markings, and her eyes went wide as she recognized an ancient text she had read as a child. She caressed the shield, following the markings with her fingers and feeling a sense of home.

"With practice you can change the size of it. Smaller shields absorb more impact. Larger shields cover more area but offer less absorption. You can turn it back to a ring by—"

"Ring…" she said. It transformed back to its original form.

"Good…"

Thermia stood on the outside of the group, feeling left out. But she put on her best fake smile. "Cool stuff guys!"

El turned and pointed at her.

"Don't think I forgot about you, mistress." She handed her a wooden brush with red gems embedded into it. She took the brush and ran her fingers along the bristles, noting they were in perfect condition. She used it on her own hair.

"When you're brushing someone's hair with this brush, they are forced to tell the truth."

Thermia smiled. "Does the dumb slut expect me to believe that?" Thermia said out loud. She covered her mouth, dropping the brush to the ground.

El laughed, picked it up for her, and handed it back.

"Thanks…I…I like your shoes." She glanced at the brush, before going back to working on her split ends while she covered her mouth tight. Her muffled voice still tried to speak through her hand.

"Wait," Cadivus said, "what about the other cool items that guy had? Let's split those bad boys up!"

El frowned and wagged her finger.

"No can do. Those have to go back to the guild. If I go there without them, I'm a dead woman."

He sighed and put a hand on his chin.

"Are you seriously thinking about taking them from me?" El said.

He made an exaggerated shocked face and looked around the room.

"What?! I would never. I was just thinking about something else, something less punchy and kicky."

"Can we keep these at least?" Thermia said as she placed tinted glasses on her face. They were too big for her, but she held them in place with her hand as she gazed at the group. A pink hue outlined their bodies, except for El, and text appeared underneath each of them. Hunter had *sight* written below him, and Ekio had *wind*. Yet Cadivus had *two* lines of text underneath him.

"Why do these call you a siphon?" she asked.

"I don't know," he said, "the other guy said the same thing. It's unknowable to us malcontents."

"Can I see the glasses?" Hunter asked.

She handed them over.

He placed them on his face and gained a puzzled look.

"You…have two." He squinted at the fuzzy bit of text that appeared next to *siphon*. "Trigger effect: love." He turned his eyes to the corner of the room, deep in thought. "You can take the powers of people…That's quite rare…"

"What?" Cadivus said, "holy hell. That's news to me…Sounds a bit overpowering, doesn't it?" He put his hand out toward Hunter and tried to take his ability. He concentrated hard, his hand shaking. But nothing happened. "How the heck do you activate something like that? Also, is it permanent or temporary?"

"You're asking that *after* you tried to steal my powers?"

He raised his eyebrows and mouthed "Sorry."

“It’s also got a trigger condition. It can only be someone you love. So, it’s useless against an enemy.”

He swiped the air in disapproval.

“Also, I’ve read about this type of power. It’s only supposed to be temporary. Unless…”

The whole group looked at Hunter, urging him to continue, except for Ekio who looked away.

“They die…” she muttered.

They all looked at Cadivus with sympathy. He held a blank expression as he took all the information in. He tilted his head and took a deep breath.

“Well, I really lucked out on the not remembering thing! Now, let’s go team! Time to celebrate! There’s plenty of booze in this town!” He turned toward the hole in the wall and whistled a merry tune.

“Cadivus!” Thermia yelled.

He stopped and turned around, looking puzzled.

“We’re all here for you.”

He smiled.

“Thank you! I didn’t expect to see you again, you know…” He stared at the group. “I hope we can share our adventures until our dying days! Now, give me a hug!”

Cadivus placed his arms out and walked toward the group. Ekio sighed as he drew close, but he walked past her and toward El, who smirked at her. Yet he passed her as well, causing Ekio to give her a revenge smirk. Thermia closed her eyes and smiled, holding her arms out as wide as she could possibly stretch them, but he put his hand to her face pushed her out of the way.

He instead wrapped his arms around Bradley, hugging him tight. “This feels right,” he whispered.

Bradley handed him the journal he promised him.

“Journal bros always come through!” he said, “I got out of there when the fighting started. And I already told some important people in town what happened, so you’re all welcome to move freely throughout the town!”

Cadivus examined the journal, noting it was a beautiful leather-bound one. He placed a hand on Bradley’s shoulder and smiled.

“Wait. They aren’t hostile out there?” Hunter asked.

Bradley shook his head and laughed.

“Of course not! You just saved them a ton of money each month. Not to mention the fact that the whole walking-around-in-perpetual-fear-for-stepping-out-of-line thing is gone.” He laughed nervously. "Well…maybe a few guys are ticked. Don't worry about that just now though."

“See? First mission, and we’re already heroes!” Cadivus said, “at this rate, we’ll be the most famous vigilantes the world has ever seen in mere months!”

The rest of the group shook their heads.

Cadivus and Bradley walked out into the city. Loud music played, and people drank in the streets. Carts full of sausages sat at each corner.

“Is the redhead single?” Bradley whispered to him.

Cadivus smiled and grabbed Bradley's shoulder, pulling him close.

“She has a dick.” He turned around to wave at her, and she waved back, adjusting her short shorts.

“Don’t they all…” Bradley said.

He and Cadivus laughed loudly.

With the tinted glasses on top of her head, Thermia walked over to examine the blasted hole in the wall. On the outside, she found large scorch marks and some round objects with rope sticking out of them on the ground.

"What are these?" she asked as she showed them to the others.

El and Hunter held out their arms, pleading with her to be careful.

"Those are explosives…" El said as she walked up to examine them. "They tore that wall down, so please be careful. However, it seems these are well made fused bombs. I'd recommend tossing them in a bag and saving them for a rainy day."

Hunter walked over and opened a pouch for Thermia to drop them into.

"In here darlin'"

Thermia began to place it inside, but pulled her hand back.

"No. Give me the bag, and I'll carry them. You're always smoking those things. It's safer with me."

"I'll take em if you want!" Cadivus said.

"No!" everyone said at once.

Cadivus felt attacked, but then remembered his previous actions, and felt it was the right call. "You blow up one time, and they never let you forget it." He said before continuing a private conversation with Bradley.

"I got it," she said, "trust me."

Hunter nodded and handed her the bag.

Though it was a victory for certain, an immediate sense of danger and unease knowing they were on her back weighed on her. Yet she had made too much a stink about it to go back on her words now. She pushed those feelings of doubt into her dark place and joined the others as they left the vault.

Chapter 22

Cadivus's group walked down the festive streets. The breeze running past Thermia's exposed skin and their own tattered or ill-fitting clothes gave them cause to find the nearest clothing store.

"Maybe we should all wear leather so we match," Cadivus said, observing Ekio and El. He touched his womanly hips and changed his mind. "Then again, maybe we don't all need tactical chaffing." He looked at Ekio. "How do you avoid that anyway?"

"Drinking water," she said.

A half smile appeared on his face.

"Yeah. Definitely no leather then."

They entered a clothing shop, and the owner ran to meet them, going on and on about how broke he had previously been between the taxes and the monthly payment plan. He repaired Hunter's clothes to his request, while the others picked out new items.

Cadivus found a brilliant white outfit with silver trim and matching shoes. "I must have it…Oh El!" He used as much charm as he could muster. "Perhaps I could borrow some money or you can pay me back the gold I gave you a few years ago?"

She giggled.

"Oh, you're still going on about that? Let it go, man. I told you that you can go hit up the guy who owes *me* money. I think it's easier that way."

"Oh right. The ex-boyfriend. I remember you going on, and on, and on…and on about him." He was reminded of the last time they hung out, and the reason his affections for her had waned. A hand tapped his shoulder, and he turned around to see Ekio holding two pieces of gold toward him without looking at him. “Wow! Really?”

“I might be dead if not for you,” she said, “now we’re even.”

He took the coins and looked at the outfit, wondering if it was worth almost dying for.

“I hope stains come out of this thing. I’d hate to have to almost die every time I need a new outfit.”

The shopkeeper ran over to him, holding a tape measure and scissors.

“Nonsense!” he proclaimed, “everything your group gets here today is on the house!” Yet he took the coins out of Cadivus’s hands and placed them in his own apron as he said it.

Cadivus and Ekio gave him a confused look. The shopkeeper grabbed the white outfit off the rack and held it up to Cadivus. His tailor mind observed the needed alterations. “Just give me five minutes to customize this for you.”

Thermia walked out of the changing room, wearing dark purple pants with a red blouse that matched her hair. The men’s clothing wasn’t snug, so she had wrapped a white cloth around her waist to give her some figure back. She stared at herself in the mirror with a lot of uncertainty.

El stood next to her admiring her outfit and going over each detail she liked about it. She, who was used to wearing men’s clothing, also gave her all the tips she had.

Nearby, Cadivus was looking through the other clothing, admiring the tailor’s skills and thinking of his rather large closet back home.

“Why did you do that earlier?” Ekio asked from behind him.

He glanced at her solemn face but did not stop his search.

"What are you talking about?"

She folded her arms and looked away. "I could have deflected it, you know."

He turned around, his mouth open.

"Maybe you could have. The fact of the matter is…It wasn't a calculated decision. More like an instinct thing. Like flinching when someone asks what's taking you so long in the shower."

"Do you often *instinctually* try to sacrifice yourself?"

"Honestly? I didn't think a purple attack could hurt me…" he said, causing her to look at him with fake concern. "It's not a very threatening color." He pointed towards Thermia's pants to confirm his assertion.

"You didn't hear the bit about *this attack kills gods*?" Ekio said, mocking Alpha's voice at the end. She laughed loudly, drawing everyone's attention. She tried to catch her breath before falling back into a laughing fit.

"Is… she okay?" Thermia asked, frowning. "She's not laughing at my outfit is she?"

Cadivus shook his head toward her and motioned for her to turn around. He placed a hand on Ekio's shoulder as her laughing fit concluded.

"Get it all out did ya?"

Ekio wiped the tears from her eyes.

"I think your actions are withdrawn from thought," she said.

He thought over her words and smiled.

"I think your thoughts are withdrawn from empathy." He raised his eyebrows and walked away.

She thought about the response, wondering if it was the wisdom of a sage or the ramblings of an idiot.

The tailor came back out and insisted on helping Cadivus get dressed, which he obliged. Cadivus strode back out with a confident look and a wedgie. The pants were the perfect fit and stretchy for good movement, and the top was a button-up vest that left most of his skin exposed.

He stared at himself in the mirror from multiple angles.

“My gods…I’m hot!”

The tailor, wanting his garments to look their best, pulled out some scissors and approached him.

“Um, you realize I’ve killed people today, don’t you?” Cadivus said.

The tailor frowned.

“You're not gonna walk around in one of my signature pieces while looking like that. Now let me do my work. I guarantee you’ll be happy with the results.”

Cadivus sighed and agreed. The tailor went to work, cutting his long hair short while making remarks about the horrible state of his hair.

“Now, take a look, you ungrateful swine.”

He looked back into the mirror as the tailor brushed some pieces of hair off him.

“Oh wow! What a difference that makes. Who knew?”

Even Ekio raised an eyebrow at him, admiring the new look.

“Uh, literally everyone knew!” Thermia said, “I’ve been trying to get you to comb and cut your hair for years for that exact reason!”

He frowned.

“What?" Thermia asked.

"My look is gonna be ruined the second this gets dirty, isn't it?" he said, his enthusiasm fading.

"Actually," The tailor said, "Omega accidentally created a potion that we use on these clothes. Makes it so they never get dirty. Heck, even blood or sweat won't stick to it!" He reached into his apron, then held up the concoction that they used and smiled.

"Oh, fantastic!" he said, "does it work on urine too?"

"It sure does!"

He put the chain around his neck, tying the ends together with a thinner piece of metal he could bend easily.

"Can you send a barrel of that stuff to Dreyhal?"

The tailor laughed. "No. The guy who makes it died." His eyes watered, and he walked toward the back of his shop. "Time for you guys to go then! We're closed!"

They exited the shop and planned their next stop to be a tavern Bradley had told them about.

But El decided she needed to get back. After she said her farewells to the group, she pulled Hunter to the side.

"What's your deal anyway?" she said.

He looked at her with his blank expression. "Scuse me?"

She walked him farther from the group.

"A lawman robbing a vault? There's only one reason that would be permitted…without it meaning your death."

He looked at her and sighed, removing half a cigar from a pouch and lighting it.

"We need to get this Chronic guy. He's better at rounding up hybrids than the crown. I was given orders…any means necessary." He took a long drag and dropped his shoulders when he blew out the smoke. “I’d go a lot further than that to take this bastard down.” El looked past him and smiled at the group eyeing them.

“Okay. Just so you know though. If you hurt *him*, your badge won’t protect you from me.” She pointed at Cadivus who was posing for the group in his new outfit.

He considered the threat, wondering if it was worth an ounce of worry.

She held up his potion pouch and gun and handed them to him. “We have an understanding…right?”

Hunter looked at the items and smiled, gripping the cigar in his teeth.

“I’m sure we’ll have our time…but it won’t be fer that one.” He took his items back and secured them tight. “What’s your interest in him anyway? Clearly it's not a romantic one.”

“In my world…it’s mostly about one-upping and deception. Layers and layers of bullshit on a big steaming pile of evil blood clots.”

He shuddered at the description.

“It’s nice to know there are people like him…wanting to do good.”

“Didn’t you steal his money?”

El smiled and nodded.

“Yeah, and now he knows not to trust every beautiful woman who hints at sleeping with him.”

He shook his head.

“Oh, one more thing.” El held up the tinted glasses. “Tell Thermia I’m sorry, but I need to take these back with me.”

Hunter turned to look at Thermia. “Tell her yourself, why dontcha.” But when he turned back around, El was gone.

He smirked. “I’ll catch ya later.”

Walking toward the group he spotted a figure on a nearby roof, staring at them. Dusk was approaching, making it difficult to see any detail, but an ominous feeling emanated from the figure. Yet he decided to not say anything for now. They had reason to celebrate, and he didn't want to lessen it.

Chapter 23

After traveling until the lit sky went dark. Cadivus's group found a well-lit tavern near the city walls. Loud voices and laughter traveled from the inside rather than fighting. Ekio motioned for everyone to go in.

The inside was very similar to the rest of this monotonous town. The walls were stone, the wooden tables were round, and the stone bar had a wooden top with plenty of stools underneath it. As they walked around, looking for a table to sit at, a man, clearly inebriated, from another table came over.

"Hey look!" he said, "some ladies have arrived!"

The room cheered, and Ekio motioned for Thermia to stand behind her.

"Come to do some dancing lovelies?"

Hunter shook his head.

On the other hand, Cadivus grabbed the back of the inebriated man's neck, which caught the rest of the tavern's eyes.

"Good evening, gentlemen. My name is Cadivus. Indeed there are women here in your nerd world. However, while we have no immediate relations with these ladies in particular, they are of no concern to you. Why…should I even conceive of witnessing disrespect of my friends here, well, we'll do to you what we did to Alpha and the other larpers." He took the inebriated man's beer from his hands and drank the rest of it down. "But other than that, have a great time! Yay!"

He let the man go, but the commotion didn't die down. Several men came over to grab Cadivus and ask him to tell the story of killing their treacherous leaders.

Hunter and Thermia sat at the table enjoying brews on the house. Ekio, on the other hand, declined and asked for water instead.

A short while later, a group of men came over and asked the women how they ended up in Pribbs. They told the story, leaving out some of the intimate details to a growing crowd of engaged albeit respectful men. Hunter just sat back and watched from the comfort of one of the abandoned tables. He removed another broken cigar from his pouch and placed it into his mouth. Before he could light a match though, a man from beside him offered him a lit one.

"I know what you did here today, sir. I've seen a lot of broken men here in my days." The man was older, worn down. His hair was gray and white. He had a large scraggly beard, but his face seemed kind enough. "This tavern only has one room, but you're all welcome to it tonight. I've already told my previous tenant to find another pot to piss in for the evening."

Hunter lit his cigar and nodded his hat at the owner.

"Thank you...kindly." The bad feeling about the figure on the roof got to him again. As the owner turned to leave, he stopped him and handed him some gold, to which the man tried to refuse but was unable as he placed it into his apron. "Take good care of my friends here. I need to step outside for a minute. Tell them what you told me, will ya?"

The owner nodded, and Hunter watched as he walked over and explained the situation. They all looked pleasantly surprised. Seeing their smiles made his heavy heart lighten. Hunter then finished his drink and headed outside.

It was now pitch-black outside except for a few scattered torches here and there. He walked down the road, and before he even took twenty steps, he spotted the dark figure on the roof. It moved past the tavern and fixed upon him. *Good,* he thought.

He picked up his pace just slightly and moved as far away from them as he could, taking tight turns to keep the follower engaged in the chase. When he thought he had walked far enough, his cigar was almost gone. He looked for a torch and leaned against a wall near it.

"Come on out, son," he said, "ain't no sense prolonging this." Though he never stared directly at him, he knew his exact position.

The dark figure jumped from the roof and onto the ground, beyond the aura of the torch's revelation. And it laughed.

"I bet the other kids don't like playing hide-and-seek with you…" The eerie voice sounded confident, and lacking empathy. His laugh was menacing. "Of all the darkened corners in Noucant, here you finally stand at the place of your undoing." He stepped towards the torch, just enough to reveal an outline of a tall and slender man. "I guess what I'm trying to say is: have you heard the good news? Our lord and savior Tiabault, God of Lust, has returned and asked you to relieve yourself…of any confusion you might have."

"I'm a lawman, there isn't much confusion on my part at all here…Teavis." Hunter looked up, flicking his cigar onto the ground in front of the dark figure.

The dark figure walked into the light and stepped onto the cigar, twisting his foot as he did. Sparklebutt came into vision, now wearing dark and tight clothing, with a leather sash around his torso with empty dagger sheaths. He pulled his wig off, then he removed the prosthetics from his ears, nose, and chin. He removed a headband from his pocket and used it to hold back his short hair. He placed a hand behind his back.

“Shoulda figured it out sooner.” Hunter muttered.

He laughed. “Teavis? Aw, you’re a dirty cheater. Carrying around those little sheets of yours. I’ve often wondered how many people have died because an artist got a chin wrong. Imagine getting blasted in the head because you got a haircut. I mean, sure, I’ve killed people for having bad haircuts before, but not because I was told to by a piece of paper. You know, *that* would be insane…”

"Why go through all this trouble?" Hunter asked, "your whole scheme makes zero sense."

"Sense is an apparition. I took on the image of an unwanted adventurer and directed the group here so my protege could obtain the weapon he desperately needs. Then…it got boring. So when they dragged me away I improvised a little. I thought you had me pegged until that little scene in the jail. I hope you appreciate the difficulty of lying still when your nose is itching with the ferocity of thousand sores. So tell me, when did you become privy to my deceptions?"

Hunter smirked. "Something was clearly off from the get go. I figured you were dragging us up here for something nefarious. Then I thought maybe they killed ya, to keep ya silent. Once I realized everyone here was a dang wackadoo that couldn't think past their own shadow…it really narrowed it down for me. The only thing I don't understand was the explosion for the vault, why bother?"

"I didn't expect the thief to tag along. She would have taken everything in there if it were up to her. Also, explosions are so pretty don't you think? Bits and pieces tearing through the air." He bit his lip. "There is a delicate game being played here. Asking me to explain my actions is fruitless as asking a tree to bark…wait…no, that's right." His lips moved as if he was having a conversation with himself. His head nodded and shook as he carried on. "Well, I guess I could-"

"Look–"

"Wait! Give me a moment to explain myself." He cleared his throat. "You see, sometimes our paths lead us to interesting crossroads. Why, you're a lawman breaking the law, and I'm a guy who doesn't wear underwear." He slightly pulled down his pants to reveal he was indeed telling the truth.

"Can we ju–"

"The thing with intersections is that they are often violent. Shards of demons and gods brushing against each other…there's nothing more beautiful than that. I've come seeking a challenge Hunter, and I've found so much more." Teavis bowed, revealing a flail he was holding behind his back.

Hunter placed his hand on his gun.

As Teavis rose, his eyes changed from jovial to predatory.

"Can we stop all these games? If you came to kill me, let's just get this over with, son."

"Kill? *Kill*? Who…who said anything like that! Why would I ever agree to such terms? Death is so…it's so…*permanent* after all. Right, Hunter? Yes indeed it is! And I don't wish to send you to your maker, be it dirt or celestial." Teavis held out his weapon in front of him, it looked like an ordinary flail that had been painted white with red spikes…horribly. "Sorry, sir. I cannot kill you. Not on purpose, no. Now…if you did something unpredictable–like I don't know…fight back–well, then...things happen I suppose. Now, be a good little lawman and let me hit you in the face with this marvelous tool! I call it the Flail of Bloodgening." He held out the flail presenting it with his other hand. "Get it?"

Hunter looked at him, confused.

"I'd guess I'd have to write it out for you to get the joke." He rubbed his chin. "To be honest though, I don't think I could spell it properly even with a gun to my head."

Hunter removed his service revolver and aimed at his head.

"Yeah…still nothing." He shrugged.

"Understand quick. I'm not in the mood for this tonight. I've got a full revolver, and you're well within killing distance. I'll empty this whole cylinder into your head before you can take your first step. It's what we lawmen call a range advantage. So just drop the weapon, let me tie you up and take you in. Alive. Or we can do it the way it always ends: you dead and me getting another drink."

"Well, you've got me there!" Teavis put his hands on his hip.

A loud crash boomed next to Hunter's head. When the dust cleared, he quickly checked his body, which was still intact. To his right, the flail, much longer now, stuck into the wall–only a few inches from his head.

"Dammit! Who adjusted the sights on this thing anyway? I want a refund!" Teavis flicked his wrist and the flail returned to its original length. Smiling, he swung it around in a vertical circle next to his body.

Hunter, regaining his composure, raised his gun and fired four shots into Teavis's head. Teavis collapsed to the ground, dropping the flail. He looked at him from a distance and saw the stillness.

“I told you how this was gonna end, son…” He walked toward the body that was now half in the light. He thought it odd that the body didn’t twitch; they usually did from a head shot.

He walked closer with his gun still drawn, two bullets remaining. A horrible feeling came over him. As he approached the body, the chest heaved, and the body put its hand out to raise itself to a sitting position. Hunter jumped back and kept the gun trained on him.

“I tell you I don’t want to kill you and you shoot me?” Teavis said, “is this the castle’s justice? Unbelievable. And here I thought I would be getting a fair trial…Oh, how I long to hear them speak to me…” He rose to his feet, grabbing his flail. He twisted his neck, and a crack echoed through the streets. “Do you think they’ll speak to me Hunter? Do you think they ever make a mistake, and listen?” The light grew in his eyes as he asked the question.

“Why aren’t you dead? I saw the bullets go through your skull.”

“*That* is a great question…I’ve asked myself that same question oh so many times. I’ve lost count, and I can count very high I assure you. Perhaps your god has abandoned you. Perhaps I am the chosen one. No. No, that can’t be it. A whole world of order and rules, and what rules apply to me? Hmm? What good are rules if you can’t enforce them?!”

Teavis swung the flail at Hunter’s head, Hunter ducked and put his remaining bullets into his chest. As he reeled back, Hunter equipped his metal knuckles and cracked him as hard as he could in the jaw. He took a few steps back and stood as still as stone before fixing his eyes on Hunter.

“Oh, I do enjoy this part. That look on your face!” He laughed.

"Great. So you're immortal then, huh?" Hunter checked his bag for any loose bullets, even though he was certain he didn't have any left-over. He grabbed a yellow vial instead.

"So far anyways. Unfortunately I fear you are not, and you're clearly out of bullets seeing as how you've stopped shooting me." Teavis's chest wounds closed, pushing the lead out of the holes they entered. "I fear that in the end you weren't what I thought you could be. All that's left now is disappointment." Teavis swung the flail horizontally over his head, the length grew longer with each revolution.

"You're not wrong about anything Teavis."

This made Teavis gain a wicked grin.

"Except, I don't need bullets." Hunter switched guns, raised his arm once more and fired a large hole through Teavis's chest. Teavis went flying back and crashed through a wooden fence. This time, he got up in an instant and ran for his flail that was now on the ground. He shot several projectiles around the flail, the gun firing what appeared to be beams of light, thick enough to leave a fist-sized hole in anything it touched.

Teavis put up his hands and started laughing.

"I was wondering when you'd use my gift." He circled around Hunter, his hands still in the air. "Although, what can you expect from a guy wearing a fanny pack? You are looking a bit…fatigued however." He grinned. "Nothing is free, Hunter. The gun is cursed to drain your stamina." He laughed once more.

Hunter breathed heavily, feeling like he had just ran ten miles at full sprint. His forehead smooth in sweat. He tried to piece together the events of the day, but dropped it in frustration.

"Teavis, I don't think I can kill ya. So that leaves only a couple choices here."

"Let's hear them! I've been admonished for my listening skills after all."

"One, I tie you and gag you, god willing. Two, I sit here and shoot holes through you until you eventually die."

"Well, I do enjoy being of a singular piece. Then again, I do enjoy a little chitchat from time to time…Oh, this is really hard. Perhaps we'll get our friends from the tavern and get their advice on the situation?"

Hunter cocked his gun.

"No? Okay, I'll just pay them a visit after then."

His face turned to rage, and he fired shot after shot at Teavis, who's agility and speed was superhuman in nature. Teavis's movements were so sporadic that it was hard to lead a shot. Teavis went to grab the flail, and he, finally able to predict Teavis's movement, put one through his leg. Teavis did a cartwheel and threw a wooden splinter from the broken fence with his other hand. The piece of fence embedded in his left shoulder, his shooting arm. It went numb and limp.

While Hunter tried to pull the spike from his shoulder, Teavis grabbed the flail and built momentum with its swing. He flicked off the top of the vial he had pulled out and drank its contents. Teavis sent the spiked ball toward his chest, but Hunter punched it down to the dirt with his metal knuckles. With glowing pink eyes, he easily pulled the spike from his shoulder and tossed it onto the ground. He then switched his gun to his other hand.

"Now we're talking!" Teavis laughed.

He fired toward Teavis, who tried to dodge but the gun's beam was now five times as thick. It shot off a portion of his hip, and he had no time to stop and regenerate it as the shots came one after the other. Beam after beam tore through him until he fell to the ground with several holes along the sides of his body.

Hunter walked toward him.

"Want to rethink that bound and gag? Last chance."

Teavis coughed up blood onto the dirt road.

"Oh, come on!" He laughed and coughed some more. "Can't a guy in your position pull a few strings?!" He grabbed into the dirt and yanked on invisible threads.

Realizing what was happening too late, Hunter turned around, shot one of the daggers flying toward him, and blocked two more with his gun and metal knuckles. Still, another two slipped by and entered his stomach and the forearm of his good arm. As he tried to remove them, Teavis ran up behind him and placed him into a choke hold.

"Just let it happen Gunsy McGee…Oh, think of all that awaits you…"

He raised his gun and shot one of the arms holding him. As Teavis reeled back, he removed the dagger from his arm and slammed it into Teavis's eye. As Teavis pulled back once more, he removed the dagger from his stomach. Red warm fluid flowed down.

"Shit…Shouldn't of done that," he scolded himself. He looked back at Teavis who was still struggling to remove the dagger from his eye but suddenly he stopped and started laughing.

"What?" Hunter said.

"How do you spell Pribbs with one 'I'?" He pointed to his eye with the dagger sticking out of it. "P-r-i-b-b-s…" he laughed. "Get it? No, wait… that doesn't work." He yanked the dagger out, growled, and ran for Hunter.

Hunter went to take a shot, but his arms were too heavy now, and Teavis had his hands on his wrist and neck before he could react. He was lifted off the ground and carried into a nearby field. Teavis raised him higher before slamming him into the ground. His body embedded into the dirt. His vision blurry, he raised his gun to fire toward anything, but Teavis kicked it out of his hand. The glowing pink iris faded, and all the pain crept in at once.

"Fuck it." Hunter spat blood onto his own chin, his voice weak. "End it. Just leave em alone."

Teavis rummaged through Hunter's pockets. He pulled out one of his sheets, and read it before showing it to him.

Wanted: Cadivus, Dead or Alive. Murder.

"Oh mother! There's a fox in the hen house!" Teavis said, "I can't say I know for certain your plans, or your reasons. What I can tell you is this…" He grabbed his neck and squeezed. Hunter choked through the grip. "The boy is *mine!"* He released his grip and stood.

"What do you want with him?" Hunter groaned.

"Oh, you poor fragile thing. Your plans are mired in deception and trickery. While mine are far beyond your comprehension, unreliant to the whims of the aristocracy. In due time, your brethren will bear witness to my desires."

He backed up, placed his hands on his hips, and looked around. His body had already been fully restored, eye and all. He pulled his sash around his body until a skull symbol was visible. "I'd like to extend an apology of my own accord. I was really hoping to have a more gratifying conclusion to this entanglement." He grabbed a stick from under a nearby tree, carved the point into a spear, then chucked his new spear back to the ground, and readied his dagger. "Well, I'm out of cryptic things to tell you so I'm just gonna stab you in the head now." He made a stabbing motion in the air and walked toward Hunter with a blank expression.

A bolt of lightning struck the ground between them. The force pushed Teavis onto his ass.

A woman in an all-white ceremonial garb appeared. Her long white dress with full sleeves and gloves. Her hair matched the gown, and her face was fair. She looked at Hunter and slowly shook her head. She then glanced over at Teavis. "Hello, Teavis. I'll take it from here." She walked over to Hunter and gently placed her foot onto his chest.

Another flash of lightning struck, and then they were gone. Nothing but a few drops of blood remained.

Teavis rose to his feet and looked around the field for any trace of them.

"Brother!" he screamed into the night as he collapsed to his knees. He laughed. "Can you imagine it?" He laughed once more. "Oh, it would be so much more intriguing if we were of relations. I suppose settling for rivals is adequate." He stood, dusted himself off, and adjusted his wrappings. His eyes wandered around the empty field. "Gods I'm so lonely."

Chapter 24

A small boy watched a loaf of bread turn golden brown over a fireplace. The crackling of the withering flames did little to cover up the argument taking place behind him. Scarcity had been a merit of their household for well over a year now. During that time, he watched his parents' mood move through hope to despair. He had seen his dad play several card games before, but he'd never seen him leave the halls with a smile. Still, even without a cent to his name, he was kind to him. He'd joke that he had a money flu, that his mother would give him his medicine. The boy never knew what he meant by that, but he would laugh along with the joke anyways. This was a special night though. Having both flame and dough at the same time was a rare treat. The boy was dreaming about what that first bite would taste like, when their was a knock at the door.

"Just get the door would ya?" His father said. He caught eyes with the boy and gave him a half smile.

His mother closed her eyes and shook her head, wiping away the tears with her sleeve. "This isn't over. This has to be the last time."

"Yeah, yeah." He waved her off.

His mother opened the door to find two men standing outside of it. Her stiffened posture alluding to fear.

"Evening, ma'am." One of the men said, before they walked into he home together.

His father looked at the two guests and put on his best fake smile. "Larry! Yoseph! I was just looking for you guys down at the tavern. I can't believe I missed ya."

He noticed the men were wearing fancier clothes then their station would allow. Dark pants with lighter dress shirts. They wore large beige jackets that left a lot to the imagination. His head swarmed with ideas of what could be hiding inside those jackets. Their faces both had that scruffy and dirty look to them, scars over their scars.

"See. I told you he wasn't hiding from us, Larry," Yoseph said, "He was looking all over for us."

Larry's blank demeanor didn't change. He locked eyes with his old man.

"Yes, exactly right. As a matter of fact, I was just about to head out again to find ya," his father said.

"Now, Charles, I don't know how much patience I have for this game you're playing right now if I'm speaking honest. Just give me my money. No excuses, no extensions, no bullshit. Just give me my money."

His father held up a finger, then tapped his pockets. He snapped his fingers with a surprised look on his face. "Oh man. You're not gonna believe this, but—"

Larry grabbed the back of his mother's neck and pushed her to the ground. He removed a knife from under his jacket and held it toward her. She cried in a panic, placing a hand over her mouth to lessen the noise.

"I thought I said no bullshit."

The boy stood frozen. He didn't know whether to run away or charge the man. A shameful fear fell over him when he thought about attacking the intruder with the knife held to his mother.

His father fell to his knees, clasping his hands. "Please! Please, not her!" he begged, "just take me with you. I'll work it off, I promise you, I'll work it off."

Yoseph shook his head. "That's the problem with you types. You *think* you're in control." Yoseph stood silent for a moment as if he was contemplating the situation. "Take the woman. She'll work it off faster than this low life."

His mother cried out in shock, trying in vain to throw herself on the floor. Yoseph turned around to help Larry subdue her, and was struck in the back of the head by Charles's fist. Charles moved to attack Larry next but was caught by a vicious jab to his nose. The boy ran in and grabbed at the man's leg trying, ineffectively, to topple him to the ground. His efforts were interrupted by a gurgling noise from above. He looked up and saw blood coming out of his father's mouth. The blade being held in his chest pushed through deeper, squelching as the light from his father's eyes faded. They made eye contact for a brief moment before it was gone forever.

"No!" his mother cried out.

The boy ran to his mother and collapsed on top of her. Unable to think of any action that could protect her. His entire body shook as instincts took over his actions.

"Run, Hunter, run," his mother told him.

He tensed his body, refusing to give into the fear and his mother's demands.

"You're old man had a little fight in em after all, eh," Yoseph said. "How bout you kid?" He kicked at Hunter. The boy grunted with each blow but refused to move from his post. Yoseph reached his foot back and brought it into to his side with nothing held back. His ribs cracked, and he sobbed but still refused to abandon his position. "Hot damn, kid. If only we had a few more guys like you. Larry…"

Larry yanked Hunter off his mother. Her dress ripped in his grip as he pulled him off her. He threw him into the wall, then everything went black.

He awoke to the smell of burning bread. Every breath causing excruciating pain. His mother was gone, along with his father's body. He was alone. He longed to hear his parents arguing. He wondered if this was a dream he would wake up from. His thoughts had become abstract scraps of uncertainty. He shut his mind off and created a singular goal. Survive.

It would be two weeks before there was another knock at the door. His hunger pangs made the walk daunting. He made it half way before giving up and taking a seat at the table. "Come in," he said.

The door swung open, allowing the sun filled sky to fill the room. His eyes were blinded by the presence of the stranger. Her white thin robes glistening on its edges. He wondered if had died and now found himself in front of an angel.

"My dear sweet child," the woman said, "you must come with me now."

Her voice allowed his anxiety to shed. He looked at her with teared eyes and reached out. She took him in her arms, carrying him like a toddler. Her warm touch allowing him purchase to grieve his losses.

****

Hunter awoke from the memory in the castle's infirmary. The beds and linens were much softer and warmer than he was accustomed to. Groans from the unlucky few came from behind cloth screens. He was surprised to find he was capable of waking. He assumed he would have succumbed to his wounds. Then again, he's faced worse odds in the past.

It hurt to move to check his body for the damage. As he struggled to tilt his head down, his cloth screen burst open. There stood the Inquisitor herself. She gazed at him like she was waiting for him to get up and serve her lunch. He let his head fall onto the pillow and closed his eyes.

"You've been here for days now." She checked his bandages herself. "The wounds have healed nicely. You'll make a full recovery after all."

A short nurse with a face mask and a saw walked over to them.

"I think we should take his leg, ma'am. Nothing crazy, just everything below the mid-thigh."

"I really don't think that's necessary," the Inquisitor said.

"All right then. Just everything below the knee should be fine."

"No."

"An arm?"

"No…"

"A finger?"

"No! You're not cutting anything off him today."

Flustered, the nurse threw her hands into the air and dropped her saw on the floor in the process.

"I'll need a clean saw. I'll be right back." She left.

Hunter and the Inquisitor both looked at each other and shook their heads.

“Glad I could still be of service,” he said.

“Oh, you are,. For as long as I have use for you, you don’t have my permission to perish to creatures so far below you.”

“Well, got that going for me at least.” As he struggled to sit up, she just watched with her hands clasped together, remaining still. He reached for the water by his bed, but she handed him a blue vial instead.

“From your own supply, it was the last one you had left. I thought I told you to never use that battle elixir again?”

“What’s another couple years off the top?” He tried to swallow some water but the pain made him choke on it. He resisted the urge to cough, and let it slide down his throat.

“So, our reports are true then? Teavis is of immortal flesh?” She unclasped her hands and took the cup of water from him.

He downed the blue healing vial, it soothed the pain in his throat as it passed through it.

“Shoulda killed em a dozen times over. In the end, I hardly phased him.” He threw the empty vial at the wall as hard as he could, shattering the glass all over the ground.

A nearby servant quickly ran over to clean the mess.

“Why is it that all the vermin are so hard to snuff out?”

“Power will make a man pour his wicked will into the world.” She headed toward the exit.

“And what about you?”

“Me? Oh darling. I am not a man.” She smiled. “Come to my office as soon as you are able to walk. If you take too long, I’ll have your sight stripped, and you'll be demoted to jailer like the rest of the unfounded."

Hunter watched her leave before slinking back into bed. He closed his eyes and focused on the healing power of the vial he drank. In deep thought, he could speed up the process. But his mind kept finding focus on Teavis and the battle. How he had tricked him with an alter ego. His wicked face and his insane chatter. How did something like that become so powerful? Are the gods that indifferent?

"Was hoping you were dead," a familiar deep voice said from the side of his bed. "I see how it is. The scum get to become pets. The weak live to fight another day, while the real men are sent to their demise."

"Chase…"

"Nobody wants you here, Hunter, and when the day comes that she loses whatever interest she has in you…well, you know what happens then, right?" In fine satin and leather clothing, Chase folded his arms at the side of the bed. Gold and gems adorned his revolver that sat in a fancy black leather holster on a similar belt. His face was red, bearded, and worn from what looked like an eternity in the sun. His black hair was fading to gray.

"You know, Chase…" Hunter sat up and got out of the bed. In only his underwear, he stood next to the man. Horrible scars covered his entire body. He had to look up to stare him in the eye. "You can quit all this fancy talk, and we can just do this now."

"I'm sure you'd like that. What's another dead lawman to someone like you, huh? We both know what happens if I kill you now. Apparently, you're the only one who can get away with something like that." Chase bumped his chest into Hunter and left the room.

Hunter stood still for a moment before calling the nearby servant to bring him his clothing. The servant apologized and instead brought him a new outfit to wear, seeing as his old one was full of holes, tears, and blood.

"Where are you going?" The nurse walked back into the room with a new saw. "You still have all your limbs."

"It's time for me to go, darlin'," he said as he laid out his clothes.

"Why did I even take this stupid job? I've hardly cut off anything this week!"

A loud scream echoed from the hallway.

"He's got a nasty leg wound." The doctor pushed a stretcher toward the other attendees. "We're gonna have to do something soon!"

The nurse's eyes lit up, and she ran out of the room, holding up the saw.

"I've got the cure all right here guys!" She followed the doctors into the surgery room.

Hunter got dressed and left to meet with his boss. He felt at least seventy percent healed, which was about normal for him. He'd have to remember to make more vials before setting out again.

He walked through the long marble hallways of the Sinless Requiem. As he approached her doorway, he found she had doubled her guard since his previous visit. As he approached, one of the guards stopped him at spear-point.

"Sunrise over mountains," the guard said.

"Waves on shores," Hunter replied.

The guard withdrew his spear, and another opened the door. He entered her chambers.

They hadn't changed one bit since he had started there decades ago. White and black tiles cover the walls and the ceilings, swirling black-and-white patterns in the middle. Her large oak desk sat in front of shelves that contained hundreds of files she deemed important. Paintings of the history of the Speakers adorned the walls. The only new painting was high above her head, behind her. It showed the Razas' adornments in the trial of judgement, a fairly newer spectacle.

"Permission to continue duty ma'am," he said.

She didn't even look up from her scribbling. "Denied."

"Permission to continue to serve my sworn duty…ma'am."

"You are denied your personal pursuits, Hunter. Don't force my hand." She looked up from her writing, pushing the papers to the side. "Do you know what we do here, Hunter?"

"Keep the king's peace, ma'am."

"Wrong."

A look of confusion came over his face.

"If our job was to keep the peace, we'd all be long gone by now. No…We don't keep the peace. For the peace is not ours to keep."

"You point, I shoot. All the same. Not much more complicated than that." He reached for a cigar, but then remembered where he was, and thought better of it.

"Oh it matters more than you think. Without purpose…people lose sight of the important things in life. They become vagrants, sinners, and sycophants. So, no, we don't keep the peace. We pluck annoying weeds from an eternal garden. The job is never done, and the garden never sees its true beauty."

She pulled the papers back in front of her, and continued reading.

"So, I'm being reassigned, I take it."

“Yes indeed. For you have failed.”

He sighed.

“I had a chance to kill two birds with one stone, you told us if we ever get the chance that we–”

“You failed. That’s all there is to it.”

He sat forward, frustrated. “So what is my new assignment then?”

She slammed the paper she was reading down onto the table.

“Antsy are you? First I need to know something from you, and depending on your answer, you might not leave this very room.” Electricity bounced off a coil she kept on her desk for intimidation just like this.

He took a deep breath. “I’m an open book.”

“Why didn’t you do it?”

His throat fell to his stomach.

“Why did you let that boy live?”

He didn’t have an answer to satisfy her, he stared at the painting above her. A part of him wondered if he’d have to participate in the ritual and what that would mean for him.

Hunter shifted in his seat and adverted his gaze, staring into his palms. "He's not evil, ma'am."

Her eyes squinted. "Are you proclaiming yourself a judge now? Does your lowly office override the orders myself and your king?" She clenched her fist and an arc of electricity bounced to a metal coil on a stand that sat upon her desk.

"With all due respect, ma'am." His watery eyes stared into hers. "I can't do it again."

Her eyes turned away from him as she thought. When her eyes returned, she nodded and smiled. "You're reassigned as of this moment."

Hunter took a deep breath of relief. Her smile gave him pause. "Who's the con?"

Her smirk disappeared, she pulled a file from her desk and threw it to him. "A rabble rouser that calls himself Hilock. He started as an upstart, just offering a few words of rebellion here and there. Now it seems he has promoted himself to kidnapper. We're awaiting a request for ransom for the bishop but nothing has come through as of yet."

Hunter looked through the file and his eyes lit up. "A hybrid? How many are left?"

"Not many…but this one is unique." She folded her hands and turned her chair to stare at the painting above her. "I want this one alive. I have questions for him." She returned her gaze back to Hunter. "However… death is always acceptable in these matters."

"Is there time to take a few days to clear my head?" Hunter asked.

She turned her gaze solely to him. "Do you remember how we met?"

Hunters eyes shifted and he gulped a breath of air. "Yes, ma'am."

"I have a lead on those men. However, I need to know that you're still on my team before I hand over that lead…to you."

Hunter's thoughts wandered into the remnants of the memory that remained of those men. His fist clenched and his heart beat through his chest. His gritted teeth relieved themselves to his planned calm. "Consider it taken care of."

Chapter 25

"So, there I was, with absolutely no shit in my pants," Cadivus told the groups of relieved men who had surrounded him inside the tavern. "The giant Sigma was about to beat my friend to death. My friend screamed, 'Save me Cadivus! Save me!' Hearing his cries for help gave me the strength I needed to subdue the beast with a wet pair of pants. With my chimes hanging free, I wrapped the pants around his neck and relieved him of his breath."

The listening men had their mouths open, and their eyes stayed fixated on the storyteller.

"Weren't you scared of em?" one man asked as Cadivus took a long sip of his drink.

"Sometimes…there is no time for fear." he said. "Sometimes, a man just has to act."

The men had an inspiring look on their faces as if they had just heard some sage wisdom. Cadivus had actually read the phrase in a bathroom in some forgotten town a while back. "Anyways," he said, "For a good time, call me."

He caught eyes with Thermia, who he had been checking on all night. Smiling, she gave him the thumbs-up and nodded towards Ekio. He turned to see Ekio laughing at some jokes, quite comfortable in the company of men.

He approached her. The men at her table politely nodded and excused themselves as he stumbled into his chair, forgetting how many drinks he had already. Talking always made him thirsty. “How’s it going, my dear?”

Her signature half smirk adorned her face.

“It *was* going just fine.” She hid her face behind her cup.

Cadivus looked at her and then over his shoulder for an exit before turning back to her and taking a deep breath.

“What the fuck is your problem exactly?”

Her face lit up in confusion.

“I’m aware I may say some silly or suggestive things from time to time. Let me ask you this though, have my actions shown me to be anything other than a reliable ally? A friend even?”

She shook her head and stared at the wall for a moment before turning back to him.

“I know what is going on here. You found a way to be somewhat useful to me for a short period of time. Now you got a new look you feel confident in and a barrel of liquid courage in your gut, and you decided there is no better time to shoot your shot. Your shallow yearning is not something I need to consider for the sake of politeness or otherwise.”

He sat there, working through her words in his head. He opened his mouth to reply, but sighed instead.

“Ah, fuck it.” He got up.

“Aww. Hurt your feelings?” she said while making a pouty face.

He set the drink down on the table and leaned toward her.

“As a matter of fact, yes, you did. Believe it or not, I have feelings. I know…" He took a breath and lost eye contact. "I'm off. If I could fix it I would, but when I try it just comes off as fake. Then I'm just hating myself for a whole other reason so what's the point? You think everything I've done is a measure to get into your pants but the truth is we are companions on a journey and loathed though I am to admit it…you're the best hope we have to free Thermia." They both gazed over at Thermia, who was making ugly faces to a laughing crowd. "You're special to me precisely because you are special."

Ekio glared at him and her eyes narrowed. "You shallow, drunken, pampered twat. As if your feelings were worth more than my own. You are as carefree as a toddler, and as prolific as the stool you sit upon. You say one thing, but you do another. You have begun to gain trust of me, but this begging of empathy? Fuck…you." She sat back in her chair and folded her arms.

Cadivus's eyes widened, then he made a confused face. "Okay Ms. I have a tragic past so fuck everyone else. I don't know your entire story, but you haven't exactly offered that information either. You're not scared to tell me because you don't know if you can trust me, you're scared because you don't like how the story ended. Here's the cool thing about me though…you're not gonna push me away with some story of your past. Because I'm certain I've done worse. My being a piece of shit is precisely my greatest asset to you when you think about it."

He let the words sit in the air, hoping that they made sense.

He then lost his footing, causing his face to bounce off the table and for him to fall onto the floor. The rest of his drink spilled over him. "Syllables make me dizzy."

The room hollered with laughter, and someone threw a towel on his face. She sighed in relief as the tension fell away. He crawled away on all fours.

“Just…sit down already,” she said. “You’re making a scene.”

Cadivus took a seat, still woozy from the unpreventable collision. Once he collected himself, she held her cup toward him.

"To you, for" —she grinded her teeth—"for saving me today."

"No…"

An appalled look took over her face. He motioned for the barkeep to fill his cup.

"Are you sure?" the barkeep asked, coming over.

"Can't toast with an empty cup."

He poured.

"To the fallen," Cadivus said.

"To the fallen," Ekio repeated.

They clashed mugs together and drank deep.

"May we never drink to that again," Cadivus said.

A solemn look came over both of their faces.

"When did you get your powers?" Cadivus asked.

Ekio fiddled with her hands under the table.

"Ten years ago, I was seventeen."

"Wow…So young. How did…"

"Before the…We have one source of power, and it is earned through trials. Only someone who is not already fully grown can obtain this power. We train our whole lives for the trials and…and the war."

"You trained for war as a child?" he asked, "that's…heavy."

"It can't be helped. They kill children as if they were grown. You might as well learn to fight back."

"Huh?"

"What?" Ekio said, readying to berate him.

"Some of the evil out there…*We* might as well be children to them…"

She relaxed and nodded. Shaking her head to the faux deepness of the statement.

“I want to ask you something.”

Cadivus put his hand out to her, urging her to do so.

“Why don’t you use your powers? You’re not a fraud…are you?”

Cadivus took a long sip.

“Fine. You opened up to me, so I’m gonna level with you the best I can.”

He leaned over the table and spoke softly. “I have a fear of fire.”

She squinted at him in disbelief.

“I know. I survived lava—which was awesome of me by the way—I can’t be burned to death, or harmed by it even. It doesn’t make any sense. Still, when I wish to call upon it, I feel this…void inside me. And it collapses in on itself. My mind freezes, and I’m unable to act.”

"You're close to my age are you not?" Ekio asked.

"Possibly." Cadivus answered.

Ekio narrowed her eyes and frowned. "Possibly?" She laughed. "You don't know your own age?"

Cadivus stared back plainly. "Nope. I was involved in the Great War in some way but the details…I have no memory of them. Or the years before for that matter." He pointed to his head. "Must have taken a big ole smack to the brain chamber. After some of the veterans I've met, not a bad deal really."

"So…you just have nothing in your memory banks?"

"Less a void, more like a haze. Lost a lot of details, including how to use the powers."

Her eyes looked away as she considered the information. “Your brother… He never showed you? Never taught you to overcome the fear?"

“He tried. He was patient at first, but after a while he just said I was hopeless. Can’t really blame him for that one.”

Her knuckles turned white from squeezing her fist.

“That’s…not okay.” She released her fist. “It’s not so easy to control. The only way to put it in is to break you first.”

“Did they break you?” Cadivus asked without thinking.

She stared past him and into her thoughts. Her senses returned without answering the question asked of her.

“Have you ever been able to use it?” she asked.

He thought hard about it.

“A couple embers here and there with my brother. And that one…incident…that brought us here together.”

“So, it is possible then.” She held her hand to her chin, lost in thought for a moment. “I can’t guarantee anything…but I can try to teach you what I know. When you’re sober that is.”

He held his cup out for another refill.

“Wait. *Really*? You’d do that for me?”

“All that we have been through in such a short time…” She smirked. “Perhaps this is…fated destiny.”

He laughed.

“You like that one, don’t you?” he said with his eyebrows raised.

“It is hard to forget something that obnoxious…”

“Ekio.” he said, still forming the question in his head. “Are you okay? Like, really okay?”

He stared at her with his drunken eyes.

Her eyes watered before she inhaled deep.

"Some days are harder than others. This was a hard day."

"Damn right! Oh, just so you know that whole human shield trick I did…Well, I can only do that one more time, so use it wisely." He winked as he took a drink.

She tapped her ring.

"Well it's a good thing I have this then. Although I'd hate to scratch it. It's so pretty after all."

Cadivus wiped the beer that was still on his shirt, and his vest opened, revealing the scar on his chest. She reached out and ran her fingers over the scar, reliving the moment. "Don't make a joke and don't dismiss it. Just tell me why you took that hit."

He rubbed his temples and sighed.

"Ekio, I just…Look, you can say it's dumb. I'm fine with it. You are by *far* the coolest woman I've ever met. And I'm…I'm uh…" He sighed. "I'm just saying when all is said and done, and this is over, maybe we don't just go our own way. Maybe we can still, like, hang out…together. Because I think I could fall in love with you. You know…Provided the planet doesn't explode or something."

He sighed and then immediately fell into a state of cringe horror.

She still had a half smirk on her face.

"Okay then, give me your toe."

"Pardon, bitch?"

"It is a custom among my people. When a man wants to court a woman properly, he gives her one of his toes. That way, we know if a man is limping, that means he is no good. If he can balance proper, however, he is a good man." She folded her arms and stared at him, down at his toes, and back at him.

"You're fucking with me!" He laughed anxiously.

She stood, placed both of her hands on the table, and leaned over toward him.

"I am not," she said, almost like a threat. "I want that toe, Cadivus."

"What do I get for a whole foot then?"

She pulled out the dagger and stuck it into the table.

"I am waiting."

He stood and placed his hands on the table while staring directly into her eyes.

"You will die for me, but you will not give me a toe?" she questioned him.

"Well it's a bit apples and tits isn't it? I think your fucking with me. I'm not about to lose a piggy on a gag."

"That toe is already mine, Cadivus," she said with great conviction. "I *will* have it."

He took a couple steps back, glancing around the room.

"I'm just gonna—" He turned around and ran up the stairs.

Ekio chased after him but he slammed the door behind him.

"Give me my toe, Cadivus!" she screamed through the door. Banging on it.

"Thermia!" he shrieked. "Help!"

Thermia and the other men downstairs stared at the interaction, laughing their asses off. The tavern owner watched from downstairs, wondering how this group managed to take down Alpha.

Chapter 26

Hilock stared at himself in the mirror. Not to describe himself, that would be insane. Instead, he was working up the confidence to perform. He muttered to himself, adjusted his mask and clothes, and watched his chest move up and down. He glanced over his shoulder before taking his place in the middle of the room. Standing in a beam of light casting down from a small window.

The stage was set.

An illusion of himself appeared in the Afferium marketplace. Larger than life, he stood in the fountain. The women washing their clothes collectively groaned. He raised his arms as if he was embracing applause and cleared his throat once more.

"Ladies and gentlemen, I am back! I'm sorry that my last speech was tack. I've taken the moments to collect my thoughts. Now I've got even more deliberate visceral taunts."

"Oh, bugger off, you buffoon," one of the women said.

Hilock took another breath.

"Bugger off I simply cannot. Not while our lives are a frivolous thought. You see, it's not by luck that your children don't feed. We're simply stuck from carrying their greed. It's exponential in growth and seeded by crosses, while we all bemoan and remain sorry for losses."

For the first time they seemed to be listening. Some stragglers came in closer.

Hilock held out his hands. Images of crosses, gold and crowns formed in them and floated around him. The images were outlined in a white and golden haze.

"An army is forming to lead you to slaughter. They kill all your sons and fuck all your daughters. These speakers speak to those who need listen, but ask why they only speak to the rich men. There's a curse on this world and it feeds on our souls, Your autonomy was sold but a generation ago. They praise only hard work and faith. Step out of line, and they show you their wraith. Who builds walls between people they care for? Only a king with something to fear of."

The images collided into each other, and exploded in a ball of light. The familiar ritual fire, from the ritual of judgment. It pulsed with life and crackled like a wet log on a fire.

"What are we to do then?" A man asked from the crowd.

Hilock turned his face toward the man, and his mask smiled.

"Ask yourself but a simple question: who survives the ritual inspection?" The image of Hilock turned into ash as the orb of fire pulsed brighter and boomed louder. "Ask…questions…"

He released the market illusion and found himself wrapped in the beam's warmth once more. He fist-pumped the air. "Yes!" he muttered. He looked over toward the dark corner of the room. "They are beginning to listen. Not to a god, but to brethren. The facade of your power is fading, like the glimmer of coals they're straining."

He walked closer to the corner. As his eyes adjusted to the darkness, he saw the bishop strapped to the chair and gagged. But the captive was still calm. It irritated him how their ego wouldn't allow them to show proper fear.

"Would you…like a sneak peek of your empire collapsing?"

Still no response of any kind.

"Allow me…"

Hilock created an image through an oval of light in front of them. Through it they saw the citizens of Afferium gathering together with weapons. Dragons swooped on top of the walls, drawing the guard's fire. A battering ram made from tied together logs attacked the gates.

"Unfortunately for you, these gates are not rubies. I'm sure you regret ever giving up boobies."

Images of the castle set on fire appeared, walls crumbling to the ground. The throne was broken to pieces. Pikes adorned with the heads of all Afferium leaders surrounded the outside. Citizens danced, and Hilock was shown making out with a woman and grabbing her ass.

"Nice, right?" He nodded to the bishop before turning back to his image.

The woman got down on her knees and pulled his robe up. Before sensitive parts could be revealed, the door crashed in. In the midst of dust and splinters stood Hunter.

"That's enough of that, son" Hunter said, holding his gun to Hilock's head.

"Ah brave soldier, you couldn't be colder. Of idiocy and genius your former. Follow my legacy, then you'll be warmer."

Hunter shot to the side of his head.

"Not much for riddles. Just get on the ground before I have to kill you."

The bishop had a smug look on his face, even through his gag.

Hilock stuck out his tongue at the bishop and then turned to Hunter.

“Okay, lawman. I surrender. Take me in but do be tender.” He held his hands over his head.

As Hunter removed a rope from his belt and approached him, a loud bang sounded and a flash of light appeared between them. When his eyes readjusted he saw the Inquisitor standing before him.

“Leave this one to me,” she said, “it’s taken you entirely too long.”

“Sunrise over mountains,” he said.

“Don’t you dare suspect me!”

He aimed his gun at her.

“Sunrise…over…mountains.”

She smirked.

“Waves on shores…”

He fired a shot through her head, and she fell to the ground. Blood flowed out of her and ran toward Hilock.

“Are you insane? You insufferable tumor. She gave you the code, and still you shoot her? For this you’ll burn, I have no doubt. Late to learn, to take the out.”

He aimed at Hilock once more and shook his head.

“All right, I confess. The white lady was a jest. But still I ponder, how you knew? What gave away my brilliant ruse?”

“If that really were her, she wouldn’t have answered. She’d just shock me and take you in herself.”

“Pity that of my ignorance. I should have done my due diligence.”

Hunter pulled Hilock’s arm down and began tying him.

A young man appeared at the door.

“Hunter? Is that you Hunter?” the young man said. “Help me Hunter, I’m in so, so deep…I don’t…I don’t know what to do.”

He dropped the ropes and stared at the young man.

"Tavos? Tavos I…" He walked toward him.

"Why? Why did you…" Blood poured from Tavos's chest. He fell to his knees and grabbed at the wound. The blood ran over his fingers and onto the ground. "I trusted you…"

"Tavos…I'm sorry." Hunter held his body. "It was just…"

The body decayed ten years' time in his hands—into a dried-up corpse. The corpse turned to ash and blew away.

He gritted his teeth and turned around, firing shot after shot from his gun while screaming.

But the room was empty.

He screamed as the gun clicked.

****

Hilock wandered through a sewer with his captive. Dragging the chair behind him. He "accidentally" dropped him into the sewer water now and then as they traveled through.

"Forgive my loose grip. So much bread in your hips."

He made several turns before finding a round door to enter through. He dragged the bishop to the corner of the room and removed his gag. His screams couldn't reach anyone now. Inside the large chamber were stacks of books and pages on tables and chairs. All was kept above the wet ground.

He removed his mask, revealing another black cloth mask beneath it. He placed the first mask on a bust of the king that faced the bishop. The red mask had streaks of black, and the appeal of a demon. He moved toward a table and looked through some pages he had out.

"Think you're the first?" the bishop said. "You twit. Do you have any idea how many revolutions we've squashed hmm? I shit less often.” He seemed to grow angry when Hilock continued looking through his pages. “Hey! Do you hear me, peasant?”

Hilock turned around holding a page with a drawing on it. He walked towards the bishop pointing his finger at the image. The image was an orb in the center with black hands from above, and white hands from below reaching for it. Set within a mountainous backdrop.

“Do you see what I see? Do you feel what I feel? How can this be if the truth is not real? I’ve pondered and schemed and danced with delight. I’ve wondered how pristine is an obsidian night. Do you understand yet, you ripe little muppet, I’m quite aware, that the king is a puppet. Let’s grab the scissors and see what they bring. I’d like to know who’s pulling those strings.” He pulled a pair of scissors from behind him.

The bishop sweated. “You’ll burn for eternity for killing a man of the faith.”

“If what you preach is true, you’d have no fear. To your gods, I bring you near. You’ve seen my home, and lived your purpose. Now only death, can bring us closer.” He stabbed the scissors into the bishop’s stomach.

The bishop grunted and tried to remain with his pride as he stared into his killer’s mask. “As you slip away I have one gift. Listen to my final riff." He took a step back and took a theatric pose as he spoke. "Our king is not kingly, just merely a god. Our time is not simply, specifically ours. With it comes lineage, not previously heard. What of the history? Now that is absurd. Well I'm going to smash it and break it to bits, When your sore gash bleeds you'll seize all your fits. So give me the honor to lead them to light, when we're upon her we'll shut off the light."

The light faded from the bishop's eyes as his chin fell to his chest.

Hilock stared at the picture once more. "Give me your secrets, usurper."

Chapter 27

The remaining members of Cadivus's group searched and asked around for Hunter, but when he didn't turn up, they figured he must have left them for something more important. They went to the jail to ask for Sparklebutt's body, but they were met with shrugs when they couldn't procure one. A whole morning of failures was not a good way to continue a quest, but what choice did they have.

Without their guide, they traveled on the main road, heading east. Ekio and Thermia walked side by side, talking the whole time. Cadivus trailed behind them by himself, trying to come up with a scheme to fix his relationship with Ekio. Because what is love if not just really, really liking someone.

"So…heading east eh? How about that!" he said, trying to make conversation. But he was only met with a couple mean glances before they continued their own talk. "Oh, come the fuck on!"

They both finally stopped walking, turned around, and put their hands on their hips.

"I told you I'm in love with you! Now, all of a sudden, I'm the asshole here?" He put his hands up in defeat.

"If you really loved her, you would have given her your toe!" Thermia yelled, "you had your chance, big dog!"

Ekio nodded.

"Oh! Oh! Let me get this straight," he said, "I'm supposed to hinder my ability to fight, before we have the most difficult battle of our lives, while our team shrinks smaller each passing day. All on the off chance she isn't just playing some cruel joke on me to prove I'm a sycophant?"

Thermia held up a finger, and the women turned around and whispered.

He awaited their verdict.

"Okay," Thermia said, "let's say that maybe we are wrong. There is a break of trust here, and we have a quest we need to complete."

Ekio whispered something to her before she spoke again.

"For the rest of this quest, you will not pursue her romantically, and you'll keep your thoughts to yourself."

"Can I give compliments?" he asked.

"Like what?"

"Like I don't know…Nice ass-?"

They grimaced.

"Nice ass-sasination!"

The women convened once more.

"Yes," Thermia said, "complimenting achievements is fine."

"Splendid!"

They stuck out their hands to shake.

Cadivus walked up and shook both of their hands. "It's a pleasure doing business with you ladies. And might I say you look—"

Ekio shot her hand out and shoved him far off into the woods. A loud cracking sounded in the distance.

"I'm okay!"

Cadivus rejoined his place in the rear, which was much less awesome now as Thermia gave Ekio a cloth to wear around her waist, covering her perfect butt. They walked for hours, and each moment he spent trying to think of a way to prove his love. Maybe he should try the power stealing thing. What harm could come from it? Of course, if the glasses were correct that would mean that Cadivus would have to be considerate…and that wouldn't do. What good were powers if he couldn't just use them on a whim.

The women soon halted, and Ekio walked off into the woods.

"She'll be right back," Thermia said.

"Nothing like a good shit when you're on the road, eh?" he said.

"Ugh. Don't overthink it, chief. She's just gotta pee."

"Ah, also good. That was my second guess."

As they stood and waited, Thermia couldn't help but rub his elbow.

"You okay, chief?"

"Yes, I'm fine. And what's with this chief thing all of a sudden?"

"Get used to it, chief. I heard a guy using it in the tavern last night and I like it! You almost had her, chief. And then you had to muck it all up!"

"Please. You know I'm not good at these things. I just…" he grabbed Thermia's arms and started hopping up and down "I really really really really like her! I don't know what to do! I just keep trying to say anything and it all comes out wrong. Help me!"

She slapped him across the face.

"Get a hold of yourself, chief! Damn!" She adjusted her blouse and shook her head."Ugh. This sucks! I love you both, and I'm torn! Torn, I tell you!" She grabbed his shirt and shook him. She then stood still. "Okay. Here's the plan. Stop acting like a douchebag, be nice, and no more complimenting her body. We'll get this Chronic guy, drag him back to my Smokey, and declare our innocence. Then I'll suggest…" She smiled wide while raising her eyebrows. "A double date! Oh, it is perfect!"

“A double date? That’s…your plan?”

“Trust me. No woman can resist a double date, because we have to ‘win’ the double date…” Her face grew serious. “And I’ll show no mercy on that battlefield.”

“Right…Well, I have to admit my instincts are usually wrong, so maybe, trusting you is the right move here…” He put his hand on his chin for a moment, before slapping the air. “Okay, I’ll agree to your terms!”

They bumped elbows and slapped the back of their hands together.

A woman screamed from somewhere in the woods.

Cadivus ran toward the noise, collided with a body flying through the air, and hit the ground. A man with long green hair and a brown robe lay on top of him. He pushed him off and rubbed his sore nose.

Ekio stormed out of the woods, dagger in hand, with a look of murder in her eyes.

“Watch me piss, you piece of shit! I—”

Thermia ran in front of her. “Calm down! Maybe he can expla—”

“I am calm! I just…need to stab him a little…”

Thermia held out her arms to stop her, but she continued forward dragging Thermia's feet along the road. The green-haired man hid behind Cadivus as they approached.

“Oh, hell no…” Cadivus said, pushing him toward her.

She grabbed the man, her eyes wide with rage. She raised the dagger into the air and ground her teeth. The dagger came down.

“Please! Please! I didn’t mean it. I—” the man pleaded.

She halted herself at the last moment and let Thermia disarm her. Instead she kneed his balls, causing him to fall over.

“Usually, I’m the guy on the ground,” Cadivus said, “it’s way funnier from this angle.”

“Ugh!” The man cried out in pain “I’m sorry! I heard a strange noise, and I thought you were a friend of mine!”

A group of animals, including: deer, rabbits, birds and rodents, scampered out of the woods then sniffed and butted their noses against the green-haired man. They soon stood between him and Ekio in defensive stances.

“Calm down, friends. It’s okay. I made a mistake, and I paid the price for it!”

The animals retreated to him and he stood, leaning against a nearby tree and gently rubbing his affected area. “Dear gods, you’re a strong one, my boy.”

“You are still breathing, are you not?” Ekio said, “consider yourself a lucky one.”

“What are you even doing running around in the woods?” Thermia asked.

“Excuse me, madam, but I happen to live out here. You’re the ones using my home as a toilet, and you have the audacity to attack me? Unbelievable this lot.”

“Who are you exactly?” Cadivus asked.

The man held up one finger and took several deep breaths, regaining his composure. Finally, he stood straight and patted his pet deer on the head.

“My name is Bobo Daffodil. I am the vagrant who watches over these forests.” He bowed politely.

“Do these trees need babysitting?”

“Oh, you unenlightened man! Allow me to explain, through song!”

All their eyes rolled into the back of their heads.

Hey hi hoo, Hey hi hoo
What's that there? Oh, it's me
I'm watching over animals and all the trees
There's evil men, no not me!
They'll kill everything that their eyes can see
This spruce right here, it's so beautiful
I love to touch it with my genitals
What's that you ask? Yes, I can shapeshift
Into anything I can pull from my main list
If I see evil, I stomp it out
Then put my friends' privates in my mouth
Will they climax? I have no doubt
I reach around and then turn them out

"STOP! What the hell, man?!" Thermia shouted.

The man looked puzzled.

"Hold on. There's fifteen more verses. Then it starts getting *really* good!"

"I think we get the picture. You're in the woods, sucking off rabbits," Cadivus said. He looked at his comrades. "On that note, let's get the hell out here. What do you say?"

They started walked away.

"Now, just wait a berry-picking minute here!" Bobo called, "I thought I would make it up to you guys by bringing you to my home and we can have a meal together and maybe impart some obscure knowledge." He twisted his beard between his fingers.

"Well if I need any advice on how to jerk off a bear, I know where to find you," Cadivus said.

Offended, Bobo transformed himself into a large buck. His massive antlers reached towards the trees above, and he snorted and raked his hoof over the dirt.

"Allow me to accompany you then! I have skills after all. Also, I might have information that you would find useful, my boy."

The group stopped and looked back for a moment. Cadivus and Thermia glanced at Ekio.

"Oh, that's right. You're looking for the guy with the funny smelling smoke, aren't you?"

He stood tall and proud before transforming back into a human.

"How could you possibly know that?" Cadivus asked.

He shrugged and rubbed against his animals.

"Animals see everything, and they like to tell me stories. Gossip can travel fast in the animal world, can't it snookums." He rubbed a deer's cheeks with his own, kissed its lips with tenderness, and licked its forehead, causing the group to gag.

"Tell us what you know then," Ekio said.

Bobo walked around and made a motion like he was adjusting a scarf he wasn't wearing.

"I could do that, but…I want something in return." He placed a finger on his lips.

"Oh gods," Thermia said, "it's gonna be something weird."

"What do you want?" Cadivus said, sounding defeated.

Bobo traced his lips with his finger.

"All right. I want this honey pot to do something for me." He pointed at Cadivus.

Cadivus sighed and motioned him to continue.

"I want you to face that way, unbutton your top a tad, turn to me with your feet facing forward, and say: Bobo, I'm proud of you and would never try to smother you with a pillow ever again."

The groups' eyes went wide.

But Cadivus still turned around, unbuttoned his top a tad, and turned back to Bobo. "Bobo, I'm proud of you and would never try to kill you with a pillow."

"Say it right!" Bobo screamed in a growling voice, spit dripping from his mouth.

The woods seemed to grow dark with his mood before brightening once more when he smiled once again.

Cadivus sighed before continuing with his next attempt. "Bobo, I'm proud of you and would never try to smother you with a pillow ever again."

Bobo stared at him for a moment and then closed his eyes. He appeared to be breathing in the scene. His chin quivered. He then opened his eyes and cried, and ran to Cadivus.

"I'm sorry too, Dad!" Bobo said, crying and hugging him. "I love you so much, Papa! I'll be a good boy, Papa!" He sobbed deep until the tears and snot ran out of him. When he finished and let go, another deer came over and licked the snot off his face while he wiped his tears.

The group grimaced, Ekio gagged.

"All right." She gagged once more. "Out with it then," Ekio said.

Bobo gathered himself.

"Yes, I did see the man you're after. Heading east. He had some rather exceptional talent with him. If you walk into his camp in this state, well, you'll all die, my boy."

The group looked at each other with uncertainty.

"And I have a vested interest in a positive outcome for your lot."

"And why is that?" Cadivus asked.

"This farm grows larger every month, and it's pushing into my territory that I protect," he said, "If they are left alone, there is no telling how much carnage they'll cause for my friends and lovers here."

"So, how are you gonna help us then?"

As Cadivus asked the question, the whole world appeared to halt. The wind stopped, and the trees stopped moving. An ominous voice groaned from the heavens.

"What the—" As he turned around in place both Ekio and Thermia came into view, standing next to him.

"I don't like these wizards," Ekio said.

Thermia nodded.

"Any idea what's happening here?" he asked, "my ass is starting to get itchy."

The wizard appeared behind them with the rest of his animals. The look on his face had grown serious.

"I will be accompanying you whether you will it or not. The matters at stake don't only concern you."

Cadivus looked at his group, and they sighed. "All right, Bobo. But…we need some ground rules here."

The forest changed back to its original state.

"Anything!" Bobo said, "you name it, and Bobo will make it reality."

"No weird animal sex stuff while we're traveling," he said as he and the women folded their arms and stared the wizard down.

Bobo closed his eyes and took several deep breaths, moving his head back and forth. His face switched between grimacing and smiling as he muttered under his breath. Finally, he opened his eyes wide with a smile.

"Okay! I can see how my enlightenment with nature could make lesser souls uncomfortable, and it is unfair for me to show off the love I garner in this world. So with that said, I will alleviate your jealousy. Provided you'll allow me a few moments to get ready behind those bushes over there where my travel gear is stored."

Cadivus said nothing, only motioning with his hand for him to hurry.

"This one is doing something gross in the bushes. I know it…" Ekio said.

"I think I'm gonna throw up," Thermia said.

"As much as I would like us all to high-tail it out of here right now, we might actually need him for the showdown," Cadivus said, rubbing his chin. "Seeing as how we're down two traveling companions now."

They waited for an uncomfortable amount of time before Bobo popped back out of the bushes without his entourage of animal friends and a backpack strapped to him.

"All right. Let's go stop some evil then, shall we?" Bobo said as he walked down the path, whistling his merry introduction tune.

The group sighed, and followed along.

Chapter 28

In his chambers, Hilock sat with his thoughts. The old adage of leaving them wanting more was a powerful one. He hoped he had garnered some intrigue at his last showing. Once the wheel was in motion, it couldn't be stopped, he thought.

He stared at his plans, going over every detail. The guards were already checking the sewers and houses. When they came through his area, he had just cast an illusion of a room filled with shit. They dispersed and never returned since then. His thoughts roamed from his past to present. Would Marcus be proud of what he has done? Did the Hybrid ever hide in a sewer while formulating his own plan?

He carefully walked through the bowels of the city. He took long routes in case some unseen force was following him. It also gave him a chance to collect his thoughts.

He walked for hours through the sewers. Finally, he approached a ladder that led to the market's outskirts, and left his robe and mask behind. Underneath them was a poor set of clothes. He'd have to cast a face on since he'd be too recognizable if he walked around. He rubbed his fingers on his bumpy and ridged flesh, and it echoed pain even after all these years.

He cast another image above him so nobody would see him entering from below. Yet no one was around to see him enter. He found it odd he couldn't hear or see anyone. In the distance, children ran towards the…*Oh no*. Following them, he approached the ritual grounds, where they carried out the ritual of judgement. A sand filled arena, surrounded by stone fences and seating for thousands to spectate upon. The outer walls adorned with images of gods and demons battling over our souls. They asked for our aid and we fought alongside them, in return they granted us something more. Without ever telling us the cost. All divinity betrays us. Hope is a lie to keep us docile while they latch onto our souls.

He followed them, walking as fast as he could. A crowd gathered in the distance. At the ritual grounds. Both cheering and booing echoed down the street. He joined them, listening in on their conversations.

"Another one for the gods to sort!" one woman said.

"This is an abomination!" a man said.

"I pray they get all the bastards!"

"Why don't the people trial him, eh?"

"This is a disgrace to divinity!"

"Praise the listeners! Praise the speaker!"

"Now they speak..."

They were divided. He had to make them see. To know that this was wrong. But what could he do? He wasn't blessed with strength or fighting ability like the others. He had to think quickly as the guards walked the accused man to the slab. They approached from the road that led directly to the dungeon. Entering through a large metal gate.

The guards walked the man out onto the ritual grounds, his face cast defeat. He was washed up, but one could see how emancipated his body was. They had to drag him the final few yards to the slab. They tied him to it with chains and shackles, tightening and securing them from behind. The man slouched in the bindings, refusing to to stare at anything but the grains of sand that surrounded his feet. A sand mixed with shards of glass made by intense heat. Hilock had a jar full of the glass back in his sewer home.

Horns echoed through the grounds as the king approached. He wore ceremonial white metal armor with a purple cloak. The metal for the armor was rare; there were only two sets of it in the whole world. Nobody knew where the other one resided, lost in some battle in some distant time. The king stood on a platform high above the crowd with a wave and a smile. The horns blared a final note as he held his hands out to the crowd.

"Greetings!" the king said into a device that amplified his voice, "hope you're all enjoying that bread we gave out!"

"What bread?" the crowd shouted back.

"Oh, right…This bread!"

He threw his arms up in a *Y* shape and wagons of bread were pulled into the arena. Guards tossed armfuls of bread to the crowds.

"Savor it, my friends!"

Many attendees found themselves with a loaf in each hand. The crowd erupted in cheers and shouting as they scavenged every bit they could get a hold of.

"Now let us begin, shall we?" He motioned for the ritual priests, called the Razas, to come out and take their positions.

While softly chanting, the priests—wearing orange and yellow hooded robes—moved forward, standing across from the slab. Their eyes were not visible, hidden in the darkness of their hoods. The three Razas formed a triangle and held their arms out to each other without touching hands. A shadow formed between them.

"We once again humble ourselves in the embrace of a sliver of divinity. Boratir stands accused of treason, of planning to commit violence against the city. We have heard both sides of the story and deemed it so that this ritual take place. The gods are just and true, and their judgment is the only one we need seek. If he is innocent, he shall walk away from here a free man. Save innocence, his soul will be given to the gods, and his body will perish. Now, they speak!"

More of the crowd cheered than booed. Repeating the prayer. They chanted "Now they speak."

The Razas chants grew louder, inhuman in tone. A small ball of orange and red light appeared between them and grew bigger with each passing second. The larger it grew, the louder the voices became. Those in the front row covered their ears, less they bleed from the noise.

When the orb had grown to the size of a large boulder, the Razas moved themselves behind it and seized their chanting. Their tone became melodic, almost comforting. Many in the crowd formed tears in their eyes to the beauty of the sound. A final hum came from them and it crept toward the slab and flashed a bright light onto the onlookers. They shielded their eyes but found themselves momentarily blinded by the flash. When they regained their vision, they saw the king himself was strapped to the slab.

"Stop this!" he screamed, "stop this now!"

The guards scrambled to get into the arena to free their king. All while the light crawled forward, pulsing as if it were yearning to embrace the accused. The king continued his screams as they loosened the chains.

"My king!" one of the decorated guards cried as he charged the orb. He threw his shield up to halt it.

The orb pressed him back, and his feet dug through the sand. His shield melted, and his armor heated.

He took a step back, threw what was left of his shield down, released several straps of armor, and tossed his sword aside. He charged the orb with hands outstretched. “Judge me instead! Judge me!” He dug his arms into it and screamed as the orb accepted him, consuming his body. The Raza’s continued their chants, altered in a dramatic flair.

It pulsed. Slowly—and then with speed—-a throbbing boom increased until it was a single note. The light burst once more.

Hilock used the distraction of the illusion to free the man on trial. He had his hand over the mouth of the man that was set to be a part of the ritual. “It’s simple to fool the devoted, one need only give them motive.” He took his hand off his mouth and pointed for him to run.

The man did not speak. He simply got up and stared at him. He then ran towards the arena.

“What are you doing?” Hilock screamed. He tried to run the man down, but the man somehow found an ungodly strength in him to move his scrawny body towards his death. “Shit, shit, shit.”

When the dust in the arena cleared, the soldier who sacrificed himself to save his king was still kneeling in the middle of it. Smoke rose from his hands, and his wounds were healed. No sign of burning on his skin. The king was no longer strapped to the slab. Instead, only empty chains remained. The crowd erupted into thunderous applause mixed with cries of sorrow. The noise soared to a crescendo as they spotted a man in victory's pose.

The king who was up on his platform, jumped down gracefully to the arena. Farther than a man should. He walked toward the soldier who sacrificed himself and held out his hand. The soldier took his hand and was raised to his feet. The king smiled at him and bowed his head before kneeling. The attendees followed suit, each kneeling before the brave soldier.

The king rose once more, grabbing the soldier's hand and raising it high in the air. "Survivor!" he shouted.

The crowd roared as tears of joy streamed down the survivor's face. He hugged his king, and the king hugged him back.

Hilock lost track of the man he was chasing around a turn. Yet when he turned around a corner he saw him talking to guards and pointing in his direction. He gasped and turned heel. After obscuring his body to be invisible to prying eyes, he ran on harder dirt so as to not leave footprints. He kept running till he was out of breath. When he saw an entrance to the sewers he took a breather against a nearby home. Catching his breath and calming himself. As he made the final steps toward home, a loud bang echoed.

His leg felt hot and collapsed. He looked around to see his attacker but instead he found a metal barrel pressed against his head.

"Cute show back there. Try anything, and I'll plug you again," a red-faced man said.

Hilock thought as hard as he could and cast an angry mob coming toward them. Yet another bullet entered his left shoulder.

"I wasn't bluffing. If you wanna keep trying, I'm more than happy to keep this up."

"Seems I've been bested by a red-faced warrior," Hilock said, "tell me, how did you manage to reveal my invisible aura?"

"Well, to tell it plain. I was told you cast visual and auditory illusions, but they aren't perfect." The red-faced man began tying his body with ropes, starting with his hands and feet. He held a purple vial to his mouth and plugged his nose, forcing him to drink the liquid.

A moment later, his face illusion disappeared revealing his grotesque features.

"Ugh. Remind me not to do that again. You're one ugly son of a bitch."

"My illusions are an art mastered in secret lairs. Tell me, how did you see past your human stares?"

"You live in a sewer…I can smell the stink five hundred yards away."

Hilock froze and then let his head fall to the ground. Wondering how could he be so careless?

"So where do we go now? Let me be privy to how…To the king's blade or a hangman's rope, tell me how they execute a dope."

"Oh no. This here is what we call a special circumstance. You'll go to the big boss."

He smiled at that. Perhaps there was a chance to continue his work after all. Yet his heart skipped a beat when he realized that meant the Inquisitor. His days were numbered, and they would be filled with agonizing pain once more. Unless, he planned for just such a thing to happen.

"Tell me your name, my brilliant foe. Who you are? I'd like to know."

"Chase." The red-faced man slapped his face, picked him up like a duffel bag, and walked toward the outskirts of the castle. He hummed as he walked. "S'pose I should thank ya for making Hunter look bad. That man is on the death spiral." He laughed to himself. "I'm sure you'll have fun with her though. Wouldn't try those illusions anymore. She's…well…she's a bit unstable."

"So I'll remain in a prisoner's den. I think it'd be nice, to see her again." He smiled.

Chapter 29

Cadivus and Thermia were enjoying an afternoon respite by the side of a pond. They laid back in the soft grass with their hands behind their heads and observed the clouds from the shade of the large trees that surrounded the forest oasis. The aches in their feet melted away while they listened to the birds and frogs serenade them.

"Just like Dreyhal, eh?" Cadivus said.

"If you think a pond is the same thing as a river that flows over a massive waterfall into the ocean…then yeah, same thing." Thermia replied.

"I am starting to miss the food. I can tell you that much."

"Shut up! It's literally all I have been thinking about." She grabbed at her stomach. "If I don't get my hands on a flavored cake soon, my ass is gonna fall off completely. I can feel the damn bone rubbing into the ground." She wiggled her hips to confirm the claim.

Cadivus laughed. "Yeah, my gut is starting to go down too. I almost have those stomach bumps my brother has." He slapped his stomach, it jostled slightly.

"I think Hybie just exercises a lot, like everyday a lot. I peeked in on it a few times. It was pretty hot." She giggled.

"Ew." He threw some loose grass at her to which she panicked and rubbed it off quickly.

"Hey!" She protested.

"Keep your smut inside your diary."

"Pfft, you're just jealous that you don't have any *smut* to call back on." She stuck her tongue out at him.

"Oh, you'd be surprised." He grinned.

"I would?" Thermia said with great excitement and intrigue. The possible bit of gossip gave her a rush like no other. The hairs on her arms rose, her mouth salivated and her fingers shook.

"No, not really. Just wanted to sound cool." He shook his head.

Thermia groaned. "I'm being serious, don't ever tease gossip if you don't have any. I *will* destroy you."

"Oh yeah? You and what army?"

"Ekio."

Cadivus laughed. "Yeah, that might be enough to do it. Unless…I did this…" He shot up and ran to the water, jumping into pond. He stood thigh high in the water and moved his hands around in circular patterns. "Super water attack, activate!" He splashed the water at her. She screamed and shot up from the ground.

"You…dare!" She put her hands together and closed her eyes. "Secret technique—hey what's that over there?" She pointed to the other side of the pond.

Cadivus turned his head to see, but could find nothing. "I don't see—"

"Surprise attack!" Thermia leapt from the side of the pond and landed on Cadivus's chest in her cannonball form. They crashed under the water and Thermia got to her feet first and started splashing it in his direction. Cadivus rose from beneath the pond's surface and found himself unable to open his eyes in the onslaught. He held his arms out to shield himself but could find no reprieve.

"No! It's my one weakness! Light splashing!" Cadivus said with dramatic flair. "How did you know?" He grabbed at his chest.

"I read it in your diary, next to the part where it says: Cadivus loves Ek—i—o, Cadivus loves Ek—i—o." She teased him in song, the ultimate insult.

"No!" Cadivus cried out. "The embarrassment, the ridicule, the debauchery…I'm…I'm." His body went stiff and he fell back into the water, falling beneath the surface.

Thermia threw her hands in the air and screamed in her best manly voice. "Victory!" She pumped her fist, before taking on a more stoic demeanor and bowing her head. When suddenly she felt something grab her leg. She shrieked. Cadivus lifted her into the air and tossed her slightly so his hands were under her feet. She stood uneasy in his palms high above the water, wildly throwing her arms to maintain balance. "Wait, wait. Draw!"

"Hey Thermia, would you like to play flying fish?" Cadivus said as he smirked.

"You better not! You better not!"

"Sounds like a yes to me! Here we go!" He pushed her into the air and she sailed through to the middle of the pond. Her limbs flailed and she screamed the entire journey, before crashing through its surface. A splash of water shot up high and the noise scared the birds from the surrounding trees. Cadivus cackled so hard his stomach hurt. Thermia swam back up and groaned.

"I hate you!" She shouted.

"Sure thing. By the way, you might want to hurry back. There are probably alligators in this pond." He waved his hand, calling her over.

Thermia's eyes went wide. She swam back as hard and fast as she could. The still pond proving to be no match for someone who had practiced her technique in a river. She made it near the ponds edge and stared at him blankly. "Truce?"

Cadivus eyed her carefully. He rubbed his chin and tried to see beneath the murky water. "What are you holding?"

Thermia's blank stare melted into narrowed brows and a wicked smirk. She held up her hands that were now full of mud. "A peace agreement."

Cadivus held up his hands. "Fine, you win this time. Thanks for taking it easy on me. I hope to avoid such escalation in our countries' future."

"Oh yeah? Avoid this!" She brought her arm back to throw the mud into his face, but a loud splash behind her caused her to pause.

A large reptilian beast rose from the pond. It's long jaw filled with sharp teeth, short arms to each side, the entire body wrapped in scales worn from years of battle. "Get out of my pond!" The beast screamed. Thermia shrieked and ran towards the pond's edge, her heart beating so hard it felt like it might break skin.

"Cadivus, help me!" she cried out. Only to look up at him and see him shaking his head. He pointed behind her to reptilian beast. Who was now performing dance moves and repeating "Get out of my pond" in musical tone. "Bobo! You rotten..." She splashed water at him and trudged the short distance to the shore.

Bobo stopped dancing and moved up the shore as well, he switched back into his human form and laughed. "You townsfolk make it too hard to resist. Oh, the look on your face...marvelous!" He spun around in circles in his merriment.

"So much for a relaxing afternoon," Cadivus said, "I'm sure Ekio is almost back from her hunt by now, why don't you wash that mud off your pants and *I* will make a fire." He put his hand on his hips and posed.

"Two things, chief. One, I'm proud of you for learning to control your powers. Two, that isn't mud," Thermia said. She raised her arms and observed her outfit in disgust.

"Ah, I see." Cadivus made a pained face. "We'll just go this way and uh, let you clean this whole thing up." He grabbed Bobo's arm and pulled him away as he waved good bye to Thermia. Who was throwing a mild tantrum as she removed her cloth belt.

The two men walked through the shaded woods, blocking out the sun that broke through in fragments. Cadivus found the sight calming and familiar. "Where are we going?" Bobo asked.

"Back to camp, getting things ready for dinner," Cadivus said. He took a deep and calming breath. "These forests are amazing aren't they?" He looked around and smiled. He thought of a simpler time that seemed so long ago now.

"Yes. Yes. Yes! I have taken great care to keep them that way," Bobo said, "the history, the smell, the thousands upon thousands of lives…it must be protected at all costs."

"I can see why, Bobo. I sure would like to retire in a place like this."

Bobo stopped and laughed. "I'm afraid not, my boy."

"What I'm not allowed? You wouldn't let me have a place out here?" Cadivus asked.

"It's not that, my boy," Bobo said, "I read your diary and—"

"Has *everyone* read my damn journal?"

"In your *diary* it said that you wanted to be some…famous vigilante." Bobo held his arms up in dramatic flair. "I'm sorry, my boy. Most of those kind tend to die at the end of swords and spears, they don't retire."

The fragments of sun disappeared into solid shade as they continued toward the camp.

"I don't plan on dying anytime soon, Bobo."

Bobo scratched his beard then held up a finger. "Are you sure? Because in your diary it said that you basically did already…"

Cadivus groaned. "Yes, true. But Ekio killed that guy, and the item he used to do it is gone."

"Will she always be around to protect you, my boy?"

Cadivus stopped and found a tree to lean against. Bobo joined him, leaning on another tree across from him. He pulled out a pipe to smoke and waited for the mood to settle. "Do you want that, Cadivus?"

Cadivus sighed. "Yes, more than anything else. I want that." He forced a smile as he thought about how far from that goal he actually was.

"Forgive me, my boy. I don't see the attraction," Bobo said before taking another long puff from his pipe.

"What?" Cadivus said in bewilderment, "are you insane, old man? She's a hybrid like me, a particularly badass one might I add. She's got this ferocity about her. A great sense of humor. And that's all before mentioning the fact that she's probably the prettiest woman I've ever laid eyes on." Cadivus grimaced as he gestured to Bobo.

"Meh," Bobo said.

Cadivus shook his head. "Meh? That's your rebuttal, meh?" He folded his arms. "I suppose she'd have to have feathers or scales to attract someone like you."

"Or a soft tail."

"It's pretty soft alright." Cadivus said while grinning. "How in the hell is it so soft?" His mind wandered as he thought about her…*tail.*

"To each their own, my boy," Bobo said, "does she have these same feelings for you?"

Cadivus pursed his lips in thought. "Maybe? She's a little hot and cold with me. I think I get under her skin a bit."

Bobo laughed. "Oh, I see now." He laughed again.

"What? What do you see?"

"She likes you, but she doesn't *want* to like you. Basically…you're beneath her."

Cadivus grimaced. "You know, I stand to inherit a large town with a castle and everything."

Bobo scoffed. "And she lead a country…" He raised his brow and pursed his lips.

Cadivus put his hand to his chin. "Kinda true…" Cadivus sighed and lowered his head.

"Look, my boy. Males need to attract their mates in ways that seem quite silly from the outside. I've seen dances, colors, scents, brawls to the death! One grand gesture, and you're in. Then you just have to not muck it up."

"What kind of gesture could I make?"

"Something you can do for her that no one else can. Otherwise, leave her be to find a more suited mate."

"Well…shit. I might as well give up now and let my brother wed me off for land."

Bobo laughed. "No, no, no. Love is a precious and sacred thing, my boy. Always remember to love. Without it, well…I can't imagine what kind of apocalyptic wasteland we'd be living in." He took one last puff of his pipe before snuffing it out and putting it away. "You still have time to figure something out. According to your diary the journey back should take several weeks."

Cadivus raised a fist. "It's not a—" He put his hands up and stopped himself. He held up a finger. "You're right, Bobo. Plenty of time."

They talked for so long that Thermia rejoined them. They made the short trip to the camp to find Ekio placing cut up meat flanks near a roaring fire. She did not meet there eyes as they approached.

"So let me get this straight," Ekio said, "I have to hunt the food, prepare the food, make the fire, clear the camp, cook the food and serve it to your lazy asses? I guess I am a servant which is weird because I do not have the salary of one, and another thing…" Ekio continued on, berating the late arrivals as Thermia ran over to help.

Bobo leaned in towards Cadivus and whispered into his ear. "The rest of your life with that noise?"

Cadivus looked at her and smiled. "Absolutely."

Chapter 30

Ekio and Cadivus sat across from one another. Their eyes closed in the seclusion of the forest. They had spent several hours a day trying to help Cadivus use his power.

"It is important to remember, the intruder on your soul is also yourself," Ekio said, "feel the power surging inside and grasp it in your mind." When Cadivus didn't answer back, she opened an eye to peek at him. She saw his face covered in sweat that was unexpected of a cold morning. "Cadivus?"

He broke his concentration with hard breathing, catching eyes with her and sighing. "My brother wasn't far off after all I guess." He shook his head as he clenched his fists. "This shit is stupid anyway, let's just do some sparring and get back to the group." He unclenched his fist and stared into his palms.

"When I was seventeen, I won a competition. Me and two of my closest friends actually. Zalika and Toma. It was a team event of sorts," Ekio said.

Cadivus looked up to her, but her eyes stared off into a distance beyond him.

"Njia ya Moja. That was what they called the place where we were to receive our prize." She looked to him and her eyes teared up. "We were so happy, so proud. We were to meet with the Aires of our tribe. The man who held the power that I now possess. He-" She stopped herself, Cadivus placed a hand on her foot.

"Continue. Please."

"He told us…only one person could return to the village. That person would be the new Aires. 'This is the way it has to be' he said. Of course we refused at first. Then my friend, Toma, slit his own throat. We knew then, there was no turning back." Her chest heaved several times before she regained her practiced composure. She stared into Cadivus's eyes, noting the pink of his iris. "You run from the darkness, but it is that darkness you must embrace. You cannot fight it, it is you now."

Cadivus felt like a cold hand wrapped around his heart. He looked to Ekio. His voice quivering. "I'm…"

Ekio nodded and leaned in toward him. "You can allow it to consume you, or you can consume it instead. The choice is yours alone to make."

Cadivus closed his eyes, the shadows of his past cast over his thoughts. He allowed those shadows to surround him. He pushed past every instinct that told him to run, to close his eyes, to escape this place. The shadows took on an image he could inspect. Images of himself, in various forms, surrounded him. With calming breath he allowed them to approach and merge with his subconscious self. A warmth filled him and he allowed it to flow toward his shaking hands.

"Now make your will known," Ekio said.

Cadivus pushed with everything he had. Every fiber of his being wrapped around itself, his fingers tingled, his stomach turned and finally…he gave up.

Ekio sighed. "Performance issues?"

Cadivus shook his hands. "I haven't been sleeping that good, work's rough lately, not enough water." He smiled. "I'm closer than ever, just you wait."

"We need to go back to the group. Practice while we walk, just remember…embrace it. Stop being a pussy about it." She winked at him.

He laughed. They sat their for a moment in what felt like a weightless world. A calm that could only exist after intense trauma.

"What was your friend, Toma, like?" Cadivus asked, "and who was the other person there?"

"Toma and Zalika." She smiled. "They were…complete fucking assholes." They both laughed. "At first. I was barely able to run before we began training together. They were a year and two older than me. They beat me senseless for months. Everyday I would go home crying to my mother 'they hate me mother' I would say, 'they hit me as hard they can, they bully me'." She adjusted her bracelet, running her fingers along the beads. "My mother said to me 'Ekio, do you not hit these kids as well?' I would answer, yes of course. 'And do you hate these kids?' No, mother, no. 'What do you think that means?'"

Cadivus smiled and listened. He had never heard Ekio talk about her past in this much detail previously. He realized also, that he had never asked. The thought saddened him.

"Of course, I did not understand what she meant. Everyday I would say the same thing to her, and she would repeat those same words back to me. It took over a year before I was able to beat Toma in sparring. I thought he would be upset with me, I prepared to have his anger unleashed upon me. Instead, he smiled and congratulated me. He told the whole class I beat him, and they all congratulated me. He had no hate for me, he just wanted me to be better, he had to hurt me to do that."

"What about Zalika, did you ever beat her in a duel?"

Ekio laughed. "Not once. She played with me like a cat plays with a lizard."

"But the cave—"

Ekio held up a hand. She stared into his eyes with her piercing intensity. "Not once."

"Your friends sound cool. I often wonder if I had friends as a lad, maybe I'll run into one someday."

"You are still claiming memory loss? You seem pretty unbothered by it. It is strange of you."

Cadivus shrugged. "It's probably for the best. Everyone seems to have fucked up childhoods anyways. I think I should consider myself lucky."

"Lucky? You are a mess!" She laughed.

Cadivus grimaced with exaggeration. "You can fuck all the way off, back on, and then back off again. I've seen you fight. You've got some unresolved 'anger issues' as well."

"Oh yeah? I have seen you fight and you have some unresolved 'skill issues' as well."

Cadivus stood up and took a fighting stance. "You sure about that?" He waved her over.

Ekio stood, and put a hand behind her back, standing tall. "As sure as—"

Cadivus tackled her mid section and they fell to the ground. They rolled down a nearby hill toppling over one another.

"Wazimu!" Ekio shouted as she elbowed his sides and shoulders.

Cadivus grabbed onto the arm striking him and held it firmly between his body, he delivered a fist to her rib cage that made her shoot a breath out. He looked to her reaction and found a smile. She twisted her body causing them their roll to take them airborne then she twisted once more, while holding onto his neck, continuing to smile. His back crashed against large tree and horrid gasp escaped his lips. They slid down to tree to its roots, with Ekio still grasping his throat.

Ekio spoke, "Nice cheap sho—"

Cadivus kneed her in the stomach, causing her to lose her breath and collapse on top of him. With his neck free of her grasp, he was able to find air once more. They each lay their wheezing through collapsed lungs. Cadivus pulled her close to him and rubbed her back while gently seizing her waist. She buried her head into his shoulder and listened to the quickened pace of his heart, which became more frequent with every breath he took.

"If I could forget everything except for this moment. That would be okay." He said. He could feel her lashes rub against his chest as she blinked. If only the world could melt away and leave them there for what remained. Why couldn't this be what life was? Or was the moment granted sweeter by the prospect of danger that loomed over them. He pushed the thought aside and let his mind go blank. He wouldn't be the first to pull away, he knew that much to be true. Perhaps that was enough.

Several hours later, after they rejoined the group, a spark of hope ignited.

“Look, look, look!” Cadivus yelled as they walked through the last light of the day. In his hand was the smallest flame. Sweat covered his face, and his eyes were closed as he held his arm out away from him.

Everyone stopped and gasped. The training and patience was taking hold, to the surprise of all the companions. He shook the flame from his hand and collapsed onto the ground, breathing heavy.

Thermia ran to hug him.

"Way to go, bro!"

"I see my teachings are paying off," Ekio said.

He held back to the urge to scream and instead tried to feel their comfort. Although, in his mind, it felt as if he had done something very wrong. Guilt washed over him, and visions of smeared shadows entered his brain.

"Those leafers won't stand a chance," he finally managed to say through baited breaths.

"Yeah," Bobo said, "we'll just have you light their funny smokes and smack em on the head when they're lost in the great void." He ran his fingers through his beard.

Bobo had, surprisingly, been rather delightful when he wasn't talking about placing animal genitals in his body orifices. Yet he had no delight today.

"You know, you've been awfully testy today," Cadivus remarked, "is this what happens when you don't get a gopher to sit on your face for a few days?"

He shot air through his nose.

"You think it's easy having this much love to give? It's a curse more than anything! What I would give to be living in a tiny wall in which no emotion could leave or enter—like yourself. I guess I'll just have to live the rest of my life happy instead. Oh well." He looked off the beaten path for a place to camp for the evening.

"I don't think we'll be able to count on your powers for this fight," Ekio said, pulling Cadivus to his feet. "It's good you're making some progress, but it is not enough."

"Well, I've made it this far without using them," Cadivus said.

“Didn’t you die not too long ago?” Thermia said.

He shrugged.

“Only for a few minutes…Considering how long I’ve been alive for, the odds are really in my favor for continuing to do so.”

“Well, we did not come all this way to quit,” Ekio said, “we will find a way to get our vengeance.”

“Justice, you mean,” he said, eyeing her.

“Same thing, lighter boy.” She clenched her fist and turned away from him.

Bobo called out from the woods, and the trio walked toward him to make camp. Which consisted of brushing some debris to the side and finding trees to lean against. Thermia, having learned her lesson, wrapped her hair in the cloth Ekio had given her to prevent the sap from getting on it. Bobo turned himself into a bat-like creature and hung upside down from a tree. He vigorously cleaned his private area before tucking himself in. Cadivus waited for everyone to fall asleep before walking into the woods.

Several hours later, in the pitch of night. Ekio felt a hand on her shoulder, shaking her. She removed her dagger and held it out toward the intruder.

“Whoa! Easy!” Thermia whispered. Ekio put the dagger away and Thermia took a few calming breaths.

“What is the matter?” Ekio asked.

“It’s Cadivus, he’s missing. Look.” They searched the area, including the tree he was sleeping against, and found no sight of him.

“They might have kidnapped him. Quiet now, and follow me.” Ekio stood and looked for signs of footsteps. She found some stepped-on plants, and motioned for Thermia to follow. They only traveled for a few minutes before they could hear a voice in the distance. She put a finger to her lips to signal silence. They drew in closer until they could hear what the voice was saying.

"We retrieved all these codes, and then we naturally went to the vault for our reward. Only to find that the whole thing was a setup. We were caught with our pants down, metaphorically, then a little later on, literally."

Cadivus sat on a ledge over-seeing the forest with a view of the stars. He scribbled into his journal while narrating his writing.

"Everyone with me performed spectacularly. Except for Hunter, he just did okay. We almost had them all. Just the leader, Alpha, remained standing. We quickly found out our attacks had no effect on him. He had all this cool enchanted gear that gave him protection and strength."

"He's using the journal. Maybe it's a good thing?" Thermia whispered.

Ekio hushed her, wanting to eavesdrop on the entry.

"You guys would have been proud of me, I think. Alpha had a trump card. A powerful attack that couldn't be intercepted or dodged. He shot it at Ekio, and just like in the stories, I took the blow for her. I died in the process, but these things happen from time to time I suppose. Honestly, it might be the only thing I've ever done right in my whole life. In a way, it made me feel close to you."

Thermia pouted, as Ekio looked on.

"In a matter of days, this journey will be over. I will get the justice you guys deserve. Hedal, Toasty, Lumpy. I wish you could know me now, and in the future. I wasted so much time doing nothing. But I still have the rest of my life to live stories worth telling. I'll get you the justice you deserve, no matter what it takes." He folded the book closed, and stared at the sky.

"I told you he's awesome," Thermia said.

"Always the wing woman, you are," Ekio said.

Thermia and Ekio traveled back to the camp, pretending to sleep. Cadivus returned shortly after and laid against a tree. The women looked at him through half closed eyes.

"Oh, go to bed you nosey shits." Cadivus said as he curled up into a ball and fell to sleep. The women rolled their eyes and followed suit, stifling their laughter as they did so.

****

A couple days later, Cadivus's group arrived at the outskirts of the farm. Bobo turned into a bird and scouted the area. He soon returned. "Nearly fifty people working the fields. And there's a home with several guards carrying various weapons around it. Their goats are hideous by the way." He turned his nose. "I saw our guy though. He is here. It's…not going to be easy to win this thing."

"How hard can it be?" Cadivus said, "we just charge the outside guards, beat them up, and when the guys inside come out, we beat them up too!"

"Or perhaps we can use our brains this time," Ekio said, "if that's okay with you, fearless leader."

"I suppose it couldn't hurt. If the thinking thing doesn't work out, we always have my plan to fall back on."

"What's the biggest animal you can turn into?" she asked Bobo.

He stood still, thinking for a moment.

"I can turn into a giant jellyfish!" he said excitedly.

The group stared at him, lacking amusement.

“How the heck do you plan on moving around on land as a jellyfish?” Thermia asked.

“Well, you didn’t say anything about that…All right, let me think about it for a minute.” He sat on stump, pulled out a pipe, and puffed away.

Ekio walked over to him and slapped it out of his hand.

“Are you crazy? Do you know what we’re trying to do here?”

“What? I agree he’s a dick about how he does business, but this shit *is* prime.”

She stomped his pipe and the dried leaves inside until it was all just powder. The scowl upon her face softened into a smile as she finished her work. Only to look up and see him smoking another pipe. “You know I still owe you a knife in your heart right?” She placed her hand to her waist, where her dagger was sheathed.

He raised his eyebrows and shrugged.

“I think you’ve probably tried to kill just about everyone you’ve ever met.”

Thermia and Cadivus both nodded behind her. She turned around and stared daggers, and they abruptly stopped. She turned back to Bobo and went to pull out her dagger, but Cadivus grabbed her arm before she could unsheathe it.

“I get what you’re going for,” Cadivus said, “I do. You’ll have plenty of stabbing to do soon enough. Ideally you wouldn’t waste it on one of our few allies on this earth.”

She shrugged his arm off and moved her hand away from her dagger. She held her arms up in the air.

“Bout' time,” Bobo said.

He moved her out of the way and punched Bobo’s ear.

Bobo dropped his pipe, grabbed at his ear, and shrieked.

"What gives, my boy?" he said as he rubbed at it.

"Stop antagonizing. That's my job. Just tell us how you can be useful today."

He stopped rubbing his ear, and his eyes darted upward. Finally, a smile came over his face.

"I have a few ideas…but you're not gonna like it…" His smile widened.

"It's gonna be some gross sexual thing isn't it…" Thermia said, defeated.

He laughed as he stood and danced.

"Oh…it…will…be…glorious!" He slid across his knees, throwing his arms up in triumph.

Ekio dry heaved in her throat, trying her best to keep her mouth closed.

Cadivus covered his face with his hand, leaving an opening for his mouth.

"Okay. Let's just hear what you've got and work off that," he said, wishing he had just run in guns blazing. Or better yet, run in with him blazing.

Bobo explained his plan. After their stomachs settled, they were ready to end this, once and for all.

Chapter 31

Hilock remained suspended in the air. His body hogtied. He was left staring at the floor. It was almost too dark to make out the stone tiles beneath him.

He had no idea how long it had been. Days? Weeks? He couldn't say. They force-fed him. Well, he had them believe he was being force-fed. He wanted them to *believe* he had given up. In reality, he was starving and desperately wanted each scrap they gave. He still had the pleasure of being suspended in ropes, which reminded him of a life long ago.

A light crept into the room, blinding him.

"Ready to talk?" a woman's voice said.

"She asks me if I'm ready to speak. I'd much more enjoy a peek. Lift that dress and show some leg. Don't make me float and beg."

She walked over to him and rubbed the back of his head, running her fingers over his coarse skin.

"Disgusting. The only thing I'd have you beg for is your life." She slapped him. "You'll talk, or the pain starts. Of course, I'm going to recommend the latter."

"Very well. You have me in a corner, I'll tell, and spare you from being a mourner."

She turned around to leave the room. "You'll be seeing her shortly. Make your peace with the gods."

"It's the gods who should ask for peace from me." Hilock spat toward the ground.

The door closed and he was left with his anger.

A group of men soon entered and covered his head in a loose sack. They removed him from the hook suspending him and carried him through the halls. He could vaguely make out the tiles through the mask, and he knew exactly where he was.

“Eww. I think his pecker’s attending,” someone said.

The guards laughed.

“Fucking little weirdo, ain’t ya?” another man said.

“Excuse me, men,” he said, “I just wanted to be ready. If she wants answers, she’ll have to give some head to me.”

A punch slammed in the back of his head, making him dizzy.

The guards opened the double doors and threw him onto the floor.

“Ow!” He rolled to his side. “Landed on my shaft…”

“Leave us,” the Inquisitor said plainly, “I want you all fifty paces from the door.”

The doors closed behind him.

Heels clattered as she walked toward him. She removed a knife, cut off his bindings, and removed the sack covering his head. She didn’t even flinch at the sight of him; she had seen far worse in her days. With a wave of her hand, she motioned for him to have a seat in one of the leather chairs in front her desk, which he obliged.

“Beautiful office you have here,” he said, “tell me what you want, dear.”

“I’m going to ask you this once. Do you want to die today?” she asked as if she was offering a side of butter.

“Whether I want death to conclude me, depends on the life that presumes me. Though I’d prefer to walk and yearn, I’d rather see this whole castle burn.”

She stared at him and showed him a piece of paper with the image he had shown the bishop: a circle wrapped in thorns and resting on a pedestal. A hand from the heavens reached down to touch it as a hand reached up from the fires below.

"Do you know what this is?"

Hilock stared in disbelief, how could she know about that?

"I find it intriguing," she said.

She removed a tray with a cover from behind her desk, brought it over to him, and removed the top. On it lay several meats, cheeses, fruits, and a cup of wine. He didn't care if it was poisoned; he ate as much as he could and slurped down the wine, enjoying the lightheaded rush. Yet he left the cheeses on the platter.

"A wonderful meal," he said, "sorry to not finish, my stomach is small, my hunger has diminished, due to equal stalls."

"Now, we have found your little hideout," she said, "I want to know where you found all the documents."

"I'm sure you have guessed, it isn't just coincidence. To find me with these papers, you surely already know my labors."

"I don't waste my own time. It's the most valuable thing in this whole damn city. Don't bother trying to use your little spells either. You've just ingested enough soul tonic to prevent it for days." She had hoped using the last supply they had of it would prove fruitful. She'd have to convince Hunter to make more.

"Might I stand? It's easier for me to command…my thoughts." Perhaps a little too much wine, he thought.

She nodded.

He stood and walked around the room. "My captor has asked of me compliance, even though my soul screams defiance. However, she treats me like an honored guest, so only gods could predict what comes next. I'll give you my secrets, and all that I ask—is that you leave the other citizens to task." He stood on her desk. "There once was a world, where demons were harnessed. Or angels instead, whatever we were promised. In an underground lair, not unlike a mausoleum. We cast out the fair, and the dead were ideal. They cast despair and ambition, the smoke was allotted with a now lost system. They put halos on beasts, and blended their souls. They couldn't know then, what their futures would hold. Of my own scars that adorn me, inflicted by the woman before me. Pain was all that could precede it, to mix, they must be defeated. But above all of this rhetoric and feeling so tender, it is you my dear that I never fail to remember. You fucking bitch!"

He jumped on her, wrapping his hands around her neck and knocking her chair onto its back. She grabbed his wrists and sent pulses of electricity through him, kicking up and sending him crashing through the table that held the platter. She teleported to him, grabbed his leg and threw him toward the window. He crashed straight through it. The stinging pain of each shard embraced his skin with bitter despair.

She teleported above him and grabbed his neck as he fell. Gravity betrayed his ambition as the fear took over his fibers. Nearly inches from the rocky path below, they reappeared in the office once more, and he fell onto his face.

His body was alive with a pain he had forgotten about. He rubbed his fingers together, feeling the slippery blood.

"Still pathetic, I see," she said.

The guards ran inside to find her standing over his battered body. Blood stained her outfit, standing out against the vibrant white.

"Take him back to his chambers. I'll file an execution order and alert the king that I've found the culprit."

"Yes, ma'am!"

The guards grabbed his body and dragged him out, and a thinning trail of blood followed. They picked him up and threw him inside his cell. His head bounced off the ground. A large latch crashed down securing the door as the darkness enveloped him once more.

He reached into his pocket and felt around.

"It seems she's bold and maybe forgotten, that I am after all, lactose intolerant…" He removed the cheese and devoured it.

Chapter 32

Chronic stood on his porch and looked out onto his ranch, admiring everything he had built. When he decided he was going to settle in this area, he bribed the right people and sent out the bat signal for the rest of his friends to join. Now, he had more resources than he'd ever need and could profit off the farm itself in a year or two.

Everything was going perfect, but the mundanity of it all still bothered him. He had made enemies—powerful ones at that. Killing them might be the last thrill he'd ever have. Then what purpose would life hold?

"Gimme one of those," he said as he reached toward his butler, who removed a golden lid from a golden platter to reveal a large stack of rolled sticky leaf. He put it in his mouth and another man lit it for him. He puffed it to life. The troubles and anxiety rolled away as he exhaled. "If you see a three-legged ape, come get me immediately!"

The servants bowed their heads.

Inside the home, his friends were discussing plans.

"Where is that skinny bastard you were hanging out with a few years ago?" Silverhand asked. He fidgeted with the pommel of his sword as he awaited an answer. He stood with perfect posture. His long silver hair fell onto his shoulders. Regardless of how casual an encounter was, he always wore his chainmail chestpiece and thick leather pants.

"Travis? I don't know man," Chronic said, "I had a few letters sent to Esteval so we'll see."

"Esteval eh? Now that was a fun week..." Gorstin said, puffing his cigar. Gorstin was a short and stout man. He wore a less formal tuxedo with white gloves. He took particularly good care of his mustache that flowed past his jaw. "Remember that stabby dame they had running around there?"

"*Had* being the key word there," Tristan said. Tristan was by all accounts average. He wore colorful designs to stand out. His pants and shirt were made of patches of various colors. "Bitch was like a frightened wolf baring its teeth. Bound to happen sooner or later." He raised a glass, took a long sip, and grimaced at the drink's burn before adding a few ice cubes.

"All those Esteval bitches were wild!" Chronic said, "freedom's what it's all about." He took another long drag before putting the joint out in a drink of a man walking by.

The man gave him a crooked eye.

"Do something!" he said, puffing out his chest.

The man sighed and walked off.

"Is anyone else seeing this?" Silverhand asked as he stared out the window.

They all joined him to see guards and workers running to what appeared to be a gathering of elk with large antlers. They made loud noises that Chronic was able to imitate back to them.

"What the hell are they doing there?" Tristan asked, taking another small sip and grimacing.

"Oh shit!" Chronic yelled, "those elk are sucking and fucking each other! I'm going in!" He ran out the door. As he ran across the field, he stopped, jumped, and pumped his fist before turning back to the house. “Gay elk orgy!” He continued screaming as he ran toward the elk, his voice fading in the distance.

“Never seen anyone that excited for anything in all my life…” Gorstin said, shaking his head. “And I’ve sold a stable of whores to virgins.”

“To be fair, how often do you see a giant gay elk orgy on your own property?” Tristan said while handing his drink to one of the servants.

Silverhand drew his sword and looked around the room carefully.

“Oh gods. You're like a dog before a storm. Calm down.”

“This isn’t something that would happen…ever,” he said, “it’s a trap. I’m sure of it.”

The room laughed.

“How many times have I heard ole Silver say that, *it’s a trap!*” Gorstin said.

Everyone had a few more laughs, but Silverhand walked around the room searching all the doors and corners. After he checked them all, he sheathed his sword once more.

“Better safe than sorry,” he said.

“You are such a f–”

The back door smashed in as two figures charged into the room. Gorstin quickly drew a wand and fired mud balls that shot from behind them. One of the figures summoned a shield that blocked the attacks.

“We’ll give you one chance to run away and never return,” Cadivus said as Ekio withdrew her shield.

“Are you dense?” Tristan asked.

Cadivus looked down at his pants.

“Not at the moment…”

“I’m guessing you're here for Chronic, right? Well, if that is the case that means you caused that interesting distraction somehow and lured him outside alone, near only a few farmers and hired guards.”

“Yes. It was a genius strategy. What of it?”

“If you had him alone…outside, why would you come in here?”

Cadivus and Ekio both looked at eachother.

“I told you,” she mumbled.

“Be more assertive next time then,” he muttered.

“It doesn’t matter your plan.” Silverhand said as he held his sword out. “Your lives will be extinguished in mere moments. Meet thy maker.”

“Well at least we get to beat up an emo kid,” Cadivus said.

“I’m not emo!”

“Sounds like something an emo guy would say,” she said, “I think if we wait a few more moments, he might use the blade on himself.”

Silverhand shrieked and charged, Cadivus deflected an overhand slice attack with the chain on his arm, kneed him in the stomach, and slid underneath him while kicking him towards Ekio. She bashed the tumbling man in the face with her shield, knocking him to the ground. She removed her dagger. As she swung down the man exploded off the ground and found footing on the ledge that ran near the ceiling. His long blade now reached between the ground and his new location.

“I suppose I’ll take a do-over,” Silverhand said, grinning.

****

“Holy shit! Look at the dong on that one!” Chronic shouted as he grabbed a farmer and pointed toward a well-endowed elk being fellatiated by a green elk. “Nature is crazy!”

“Yes, boss,” the farmer said, “very crazy.”

"It's not crazy to show your love!" the green elk shouted back.

"These fuckers can talk?" Chronic yelled, "I have the best planta—farm ever!"

The green elk spit onto the ground and stood tall. He turned his nose up toward the sky, closed his eyes, and then let out an unusual call for an elk. When the call ended, the other male elk stopped throwing it back and looked toward Chronic. They snorted air through their noses and took off at full sprint, making calls of their own.

Chronic screamed as the elk darted toward him.

****

Cadivus swung his fist at Tristan, aiming for his head. Tristan blocked the blow with his arm and grabbed his hand.

"Take," Tristan said.

Cadivus's vision became very blurry. He backed away and rubbed at his eyes.

"What did you do to me?" He checked his blurry vision and rubbed them again.

"I can steal people's senses or give them my own. Chicks like the latter."

He stopped rubbing his eyes and took a fighting stance once more.

"It's basically already over. Nobody can fight without vi—"

He kicked Tristan in the dick.

Tristan grabbed at his balls and turned to Gorstin. "Avenge me, G."

Cadivus swung the small length of chain around Tristan's neck and threw him to the ground, his head bouncing off the floor.

"How the hell did you pull that off?" Gorstin asked.

"Think I've never fought drunk before?" Cadivus replied as he charged Gorstin.

Gorstin pointed to his left. When Cadivus turned to look, several mudballs struck him, pushed him against a wall, and stuck to him. He struggled to break free.

“I think I’ll just wait for one of these guys to gut you,” Gorstin said, “I hate getting my hands dirty, ironically enough.”

“Well, in that case, you’ve forced me to use my secret weapon.” Cadivus said as he stared down the mudslinger.

Gorstin’s eyes lit up. “Oh? And what’s that?”

“Ekio! Help!” he screamed.

****

Silverhand made piercing attacks with his enlarged sword that Ekio either dodged or blocked with her shield. She threw her dagger at him in between the blows but he shrank his own sword and knocked it away before continuing his attacks.

She jumped backward and prepared for the next flurry of attacks, but they stopped.

“Get closer, loser,” he said, waving her over with his hand.

She looked at him and the distance between them.

“Ah, I see. Don’t worry. I bet it happens to lots of emo swordsmen.”

“Ha, ha, ha,” he mocked. “You think you're a better warrior than me?”

He jumped down from his position, she charged at him, increasing her speed with a push of wind. She held out her shield to smack the side of his head once more, but he placed the tip of his blade in the middle of it and extended the sword, sending her flying across the room. She crashed through a hanging wall.

She punched the ground and stood up just in time to block another attack. He had a smug look on his face as she tried to close the distance once again.

Yet his smug look disappeared as the wind lifted him off the ground. He struggled to stay upright and control his blade. She charged in and threw a spinning elbow directly into his liver, causing his body to shut down. His blade fell to the floor. She then kicked his chest, sending him into a wall on the other side of the room.

"Ekio! Help!" Cadivus yelled out.

She looked to see him stuck to a wall. She grabbed the sword off the ground and threw it toward him. It collided with the mud, freeing one of his hands. He grabbed the sword and cleaved off the rest.

"This is pointless for you two," Gorstin said as he summoned a giant wall of mud in front of him.

Cadivus and Ekio both charged toward the mud wall as the ground rumbled. The mud wall fell and showed the two other henchmen grouped beside Gorstin now, all staring out a window.

"Oh…fuck!" Tristan shouted.

The elks charged through the doors, windows, and walls. The surprisingly thin walls crumbled beneath the elks' massive weight and power. Silverhand was trampled. Two separate sets of antlers struck Tristan through his chest, and his body hit a pillar as each elk ran to a different side, tearing him in half as he screamed.

Cadivus's vision returned, just in time to grab Ekio before she was trampled. He leaped to the far side of the room, and they pushed themselves up against the wall. As they watched the chaos, they spotted Chronic riding one of the elk through his own home.

"This is my shit!" he shouted, "Whoo! Let's trample some mother fuckers!" He exited out through the other side.

As the raid died down, a green elk approached them.

"Aren't ya glad I came now?" Bobo said.

"Isn't that kind of your thing?" Cadivus asked.

Bobo laughed and turned back into the green-haired wizard.

"What did you do anyway?" Ekio asked.

"Psh. Easy. I just made a call for the girls over in Tobias Woods to come out into the fields to come get some." He brushed off his sleeves. "With all those male hormones in the air, they couldn't resist. The boys like to get riled up, but when females are around, they just see red."

"It's gross and clever, I'll admit," Ekio said.

Bobo nodded and transformed back into an elk.

"Wait. Where are you going now?"

"Honey, you gotta get it while the gettin's good. I'm sure you two can clean the rest of this up." He sauntered off, shaking his tail in the air and making more odd calls.

Ekio and Cadivus stared at each other, looking into each other's eyes. Cadivus leaned in to kiss her but was met with a hand on his mouth.

"Yeah. Not exactly good timing," she said.

He mumbled something into her hand.

She removed it. "What?"

"That's between me and the hand."

She rolled her eyes.

He regripped his new sword and ran toward the two downed men. As Silverhand moved to get up, he swung the sword down at his neck.

Silverhand dodged the blade and grabbed the back of it, preventing him from moving it.

"It'll be a cold day in hell before I die to my own blade," Silverhand said.

He grunted as he struggled to move the blade, pulling and pushing in every way he could think of. He then gave it a mighty push downward. Silverhand released the blade, and the cold steel sunk into Cadivus's own flesh.

Chapter 33

Cadivus grunted, the blade stuck in his own foot. Silverhand got to his feet and grabbed at the sword's hilt. The blade moved back and forth in the wound, and Cadivus cried out. He got his foot free and headbutted Silverhand as hard as he could throw his head. Silverhand's head went dizzy, and his vision blurred. Cadivus released the blade from the floorboards and—in a fluid motion—sliced upward, cutting open Silverhand's chest and splitting his chin in half. A few choking noises later, Silverhand collapsed onto the ground, bleeding out.

Cadivus reached down toward his left foot and removed his boot. A piece of his foot had been cut off. He held it up in disgust, slightly nauseous.

"Well, well, look at that," Ekio said, "looks like you've decided to give me your toe after all."

"Relax, psycho. I'm not giving you this toe…maybe I can sew it back on or something."

"Be a man and fulfill your promise. You owe me that much, mzungu." She held out her hand.

"I'm not giving it to you."

"Give…it!"

"No…thanks!"

Ekio reached out to grab it, but he closed his fist around it and placed his arm back and over his head.

She grabbed at his face and reached for it.

"Give me my token!"

He lost his footing and fell backward over some rubble. She stood over him, toe still in his hand. He looked up at her, back at the toe, and then back up at her again.

"Don't you dare!" she threatened.

Cadivus shoved the toe in his mouth and swallowed it, a look of victory intertwined with disgust on his face. Her jaw dropped, and her scowl transformed into a…wide smile. She laughed, doubling over. Her eyes filled with tears.

"Have you completely snapped?" he asked.

She tried to talk through her laughter, but it was unintelligible. She finally caught her breath and was able to get out a few words.

"I…was…was just…" She laughed some more, holding up a finger. "Messing with you…And…and you ate it! Idiot!" She fell to her knees, laughing.

He sat there, dumbfounded.

"You know what the worst part is?"

In her laughing fit, she shook her head and mouthed, "No."

"It was kinda tasty, and now I'm worried."

She laughed even harder.

He laughed with her. "Please make sure that's the last time I do that. I'd hate for it to be my thing."

"I will try my best." She rubbed the tears out of her eyes.

He closed his eyes and sighed deeply when her lips pressed against his. He wanted to grab her and pull her into him. Instead, he just softly kissed her back and let the moment pass.

"Gods your nasty," he said.

"You have no idea," she replied.

"Well I'll say this—"

The floor beneath them turned to mud with different consistencies. Cadivus was stuck, but the floor beneath her was slippery. She struggled to stand and hold her footing as Gorstin barreled toward her, threw her to the ground, and tried to choke her out.

"Killed my brothers, you bastards!" Gorstin screamed, "I'll end your miserable lives with my bare hands!"

Ekio, feeling the grip growing stronger, turned her body around so her face was buried in his chest. She placed her knee up against his body and used the leverage to drive her fist into his stomach. She kept punching until a crack sounded, and his grip loosened on her. Now free, she mounted his pained body and rained down punch after punch.

Cadivus looked on to see his mud-covered woman straddling a mud-covered man.

"Is this really appropriate?"

"Shut up!" she shouted between her punches. She kept up the relentless pace until she spotted her dagger in the upper corner of the room. She reacheddown with her left hand, choked Gorstin, and summoned the wind behind the dagger to draw it toward her free hand. It didn't move much. With a loud grunt, she forced it into her hand. She slid the dagger into his neck and continued choking him as she twisted the blade.

First, his grip on her arm faded. Then the struggling chokes subsided.

The mud around them retreated slightly, and Cadivus found that it no longer had its sticky nature. He crawled over to her, who was breathing heavily with a thousand-yard stare. She rubbed at her neck.

He gently grabbed her face.

“He’s gone. It’s over,” he repeated until her eyes met his.

She nodded and slowly stood, still taking deep breaths.

He hugged her muddy body. “Good work, bucko,” he said.

“Eh, it was okay. Not really a fan of getting my hands that dirty though!” a voice called out from behind them.

Chronic stood in one of the new openings made by the stampeding elk. On his finger, he spun a golden harmonica.

“Seems you're having a rough go at it. Having to be in front of me twice.” He stopped spinning the harmonica and grabbed it in his hand. “Won’t be a conspiracy this time at least. I’ll make sure to finish you off after.”

Ekio tapped Cadivus shoulder three times.

“Run!” he shouted as she tried to drag him outside. “No! Not me! Let go! Just run!”

“I’m not leaving you!” she shouted back as the tune played.

He struggled, but she dragged him out of the home.

Chronic finished his tune as the two left and turned the corner. He closed his eyes, flared his nostrils, and raised both of his fists in the air, setting off an explosion of fire on the other side.

Chapter 34

Thermia stood among a group of guards and workers that were watching the elk orgy. After they stampeded across the field, they all turned to go back to work.

"Wait a second, guys!" she called out, "what are you going back to, exactly?"

The workers looked at her, confused.

"We need money for our families, miss," one of the men said, "I thought that was obvious."

"There will be hell to pay if we don't get back to work," a woman said.

"Well, I guess you guys didn't hear the bad news…" Thermia said, and the crowd drew in closer. "This place is closing today. There is no more work here."

Everyone threw their tools to the ground, talking among themselves.

"Oh man, what a bummer! I have the worst luck!" a man said.

Thermia looked toward the man with a familiar voice. "Bradley?" Thermia asked, seeing the man she recognized from Pribbs.

He smiled.

"Oh snap! What up dick-girl?" He shook her hand. "The new outfit is tight as hell, dude."

"Uh, thanks. What are you doing here? And how did you get here before us?" she asked.

He laughed.

"Well, I had some gambling debts I couldn't pay back, so I just hitched a ride with some people here and...got to work." He waved at one of the farmers. "It's not as fancy as my last job, but I enjoy it. What brings you here?"

Thermia grimaced.

"Um...We have business with your boss, again."

"I see. Say, are you guys gonna kill my boss every time I get a new job?" He stared at her, then laughed. "I'm just yanking your stick, don't worry, I always land on my feet."

"Well, speaking of jobs. I actually have an idea for everyone here," she said.

****

Chronic bobbed his head to imaginary music as he walked toward the explosion. His shoulder, arm and hips joined the dance as he drew closer. He found some rolled-up sticky leaf on the ground but discarded it because it was covered in mud. He walked outside, looked to his left, and saw burn marks from the blast and a few small fires—but no bodies.

As he stepped closer, faint footsteps sounded behind him. He tried to bring his harmonica to his mouth, but a punch to his jaw spun his body around. A kick to his stomach knocked the wind out of him. Followed by an arm wrapped around his neck.

Ekio stood before him. She snatched the harmonica from his hand and threw it toward the farm's tree line.

He was forced to his knees, and the grip on his neck loosened. "Who else are you here with?"

She looked at Cadivus and raised her eyebrows.

“She’s still with me, fuck face,” Cadivus said as he slapped his head.

Chronic grinned.

“Let me guess…you found a way to block your ears…”

“Lucky for me, one of the gentlemen in there left plenty of thick mud to use. Frankly, I’m not sure if it was worth it. I’m still waiting for them to pop. Have you any idea how annoying this feels right now?”

“So you must have had an explosive device as well, I take it?”

“Well, I guess this guy really is a genius. Good ole lighter boy at your service.”

“We can thank Thermia for finding unexploded bombs back at the vault,” Ekio said.

Chronic smiled as he understood how he was tricked.

“Where are the rest of my guards and workers?”

“They’re with our friend, she convinced them not to work for you anymore. I doubt it was too hard considering the working conditions you likely kept them under.”

“Please, bitch. What are they gonna do without me to feed them?” he said, annoyed.

“Oh you know that place you tried to take down? Dreyhal?” Cadivus said, “well they got a whole thing for taking in migrants. So we’re sending them that way with some of your food stores.”

Chronic smiled and laughed to himself. Ekio punched his face, causing his lip to bleed.

He licked the blood on his lip and spat it onto her boot.

“So what’s the plan here, guys?”

“We’re taking you to trial in Dreyhal,” Cadivus said, “you’ll tell them what you’ve done, and free me and Thermia from our exile.”

“And why the hell would I agree to that?”

“Because if you don’t, the other plan is to let her smash you into a million pieces.”

Ekio lightly slapped his cheek with a smug look.

“Wait a second…Don’t I know you?” Chronic asked her.

Growing angry, she raised her hand to strike him again.

“Hold on a tick, love. Don’t knock his block off just yet,” Cadivus said.

She reached down and grabbed Chronic’s cheeks with one hand and squished them together.

“Just pay attention, and only answer the questions we are asking,” she said.

“Give me a moment to think about this,” he said. He looked at their faces and found no wiggle room, no empathy. He glanced at his empty fields and food stores. His dead friends in his damaged home. He grew angry inside, but kept cool on the outside.

“It’s not that we don’t have time for this,” Cadivus said, “it’s more that it’s boring to watch you think. Hurry up.”

“All right. I’ll go with you guys. Just don’t do that lame thing where you tie me up with rope and then tie yourselves to me. That’s so played out, dude.”

On queue, Cadivus began tying his hands together and wrapping his arms to his torso while Ekio held the dagger to his neck, ready to strike.

Chronic stood still and stared into her eyes, trying to remember where he knew her from. He finally remembered, and accidentally moved his eyebrows. Ekio noticed the movement, and a look of worry came over her face. He turned back to look at Cadivus and then back at her once more. It wasn't worry. It was…fear.

"Upsy-daisy, Mr. Hazy," Cadivus said as he lifted Chronic to his feet. He tied two ropes around Chronic and the end of those ropes to his and Ekio's wrist. "You do know you always smell like rotten ass, don't you?"

"I got some nasty good shit, son!" Chronic said, "it is what it is."

They walked toward the tree line where they could see Thermia waving from the shade of the trees.

"You know what's nice about owning property?" Chronic asked while they walked toward her.

"It would be my pleasure to gag you," Ekio said.

"When you own your own property, you learn where all the ditches are!"

With that, he threw his body into a deep ditch, and the binding ropes on their wrist dragged them with him. After landing, he whistled a tune. Thermia ran toward them.

Ekio realized what was happening.

"Cadivus! Cover your ears!" She looked around the mangled mess of bodies to meet his eyes. He was on the ground in the fetal position, clenching every muscle in his body, his eyes closed. He was already under the spell, struggling to fight it off.

Chronic had cradled his face in between his legs. A few hard kicks from her did not stop the whistling. Her mind raced. She directed wind towards Cadivus, and his body was swept up in it, rising into the air above them, tethered to theirs. Concentrating, she pushed until his ears bled. The pain in his ear drums seemed to overtake the pain of his powers releasing. Still, his body released flames, and he shrieked, trying to rub the flames away. The chain on his arm rapidly expanded and coiled onto the ground beneath him.

The rope around his wrist caught flame and snapped, sending him flying out of the ditch. His soaring, inflamed body collided with Thermia, knocking her out cold.

Ekio, now enraged, grabbed Chronic's body and threw him into the side of the ditch, knocking all the wind out of him. He raised his head from in between his legs, but she held his forehead down and stuck her hand inside his mouth. She grabbed his lower jaw and pulled down, breaking it.

His suffering filled her with a rush of adrenaline, and she smiled.

She grabbed his body again and threw him out of the ditch, toward Cadivus. She tried to jump out herself, but a sharp pain sparked from her thigh. A dagger stuck into it. She hadn't even noticed.

She yanked the dagger out, sheathing it back. She then used his body as an anchor as she climbed up the rope, and pulled herself over the ledge. Beyond him, Cadivus sat in the dirt with a thousand-yard stare on his face. She walked over to him, dragging Chronic along with her. He groaned with every stick and rock his body slid over.

In front of Cadivus, she sat and put her hands on his face. He still didn't seem to notice her. His eyes were dry, he looked as if he would start sobbing any second. She wished he would.

"Hey, hey, hey," she spoke softly, "everything's fine. Everyone's fine."

His eyes stopped fixating on the distance and looked directly into hers.

"What!" he screamed in her face. "I can't hear you! You need to speak louder!"

Her face scrunched together.

"Everything's fine!" she yelled. "Nobody was hurt bad!"

"Okay! Good!" He gave a thumbs up. "My ears are ringing!"

"I know!"

"I said my ears are ringing!" he yelled even louder.

She placed a finger over his mouth and nodded. She then hugged him. "I'm glad your okay," she whispered.

"Your leg!" he screamed into her ear, pointing at the blood.

She jumped.

"You okay?"

"I'm fine!" she yelled back.

"Ah! Not so loud." he said. "I think the ringing stopped…well, most of it anyway." He looked past her and saw Chronic lying on his side, the lower half of his face covered in blood. "Interesting solution. I'm impressed. Is he?"

She glanced over her shoulder.

"He'll live. He won't be able to whistle, but he'll live."

He held her hand and hung his head.

A rope wrapped around her neck, she couldn't breathe. Cadivus jumped up to help, but Chronic pulled her down on top of him and held the rope tight. Cadivus couldn't get his fingers under the rope to break it, nor could he loosen the grip of the hands holding it. Chronic's gargled laughter echoed. As her face turned purple, he placed his fingers on the rope and summoned what little piece of flame he could.

"Come on! Come on!" he screamed as it nipped at the bindings.

Her eyes drifted away.

"Burn!"

Light flashed, and the rope snapped.

He grabbed her and dragged her away, thankful to hear her gasping for breaths. "I'll take care of this. Just give me a minute."

He then faced Chronic, who now stood in front of him. Chronic pulled his hands apart, breaking his bonds. Cadivus did not hesitate and charged toward him. He went to tackle him to the ground but was met with an elbow to the back of his head. He was sent to the ground, tasting the grass. Chronic grabbed onto his back, and lifted him up, and threw him into a bale of hay.

"Don't think I've forgotten what you did, fucker." Chronic said, his voice sounding odd without his lower lip.

Cadivus got up, cracked his neck, and stretched out his back.

"You don't get it. You weren't ever supposed to forget it. If you did, there wouldn't be any need to drag you back to Dreyhal. So, I'm going to hit you just hard enough, so you don't lose that precious memory I need."

Cadivus charged back in and was met with a sidekick that cracked two of his ribs. Hid body lifted into the air and was met with a roundhouse to his head before his feet touched the ground. His world went blurry as the taste of blood filled his mouth. A tug on the back of head pulled it up from the ground. He looked into the bloodied face of Chronic unable to discern any emotion on the demonic face.

"Pathetic," Chronic said. He coughed out blood and spit it into Cadivus's face, covering it. He picked him up over his head, preparing to bring his back down onto his knee. Cadivus glanced over to see Ekio still on the ground, her chest rapidly rising and lowering with her head tilted to the side.

"I fucked up." He thought to himself. "I'm sorry, brother. I really fucked up."

As Chronic let out a wet scream, Cadivus found himself falling to the ground at an awkward angle. He was released from Chronic's grip, laying on the ground. He looked up to see green antlers aimed toward Chronic.

"That's enough!" Bobo said, "this is still my domain after all. You'll turn yourself in to my friends here, or I'll smash your bones into dust." Bobo doubled in size before Chronic, his muscles growing ever more taught.

Chronic stared at the giant elk, unmoving. Suddenly, he laughed and held his arms to his sides while bending his knees. He charged toward Bobo, who swiped down with his antlers. Chronic, leaped and grabbed onto one with a grunt of pain. He stomped his foot down several times before running along the spine as Bobo spun in circles. Chronic brought his foot straight up into the air ready to deliver a large blow to the elk's back. Bobo quickly shifted into a large green bear, causing Chronic to fall to the ground. Bobo swiped at him and caught his left shoulder with three claws, scratching only thinly beneath the surface.

Cadivus got to his feet and readied himself for another attack. As he charged in, Bobo stepped in front of him.

"He's beyond your abilities, young man. Just wait here," Bobo said.

"I won't stand by and do nothing! This is my fight!" Cadivus cried out.

Bobo let out a deep sigh. "Fine. Just try and stay out of my way, it's hard to see my surroundings with such large bod—" A kick to Bobo's rear leg interrupted them. The loud snap echoed throughout the field. Bobo fell to the ground, as Cadivus charged in once more. This time he watched for the sidekick which came as expected, he dodged to the left and balled his left fist, sending it straight into the ribs of Chronic. Chronic fell to the ground for a moment then rolled into a backwards somersault to get back to his feet. He brought an upper lip smile up to Cadivus.

"Interesting," Chronic said, "that's what I call a good warm up."

"For the love of all that is sober and true, I cannot understand a word you're saying right now," Cadivus said, "stop trying it's grossing me out."

Chronic leapt into the air as a large green cat soared underneath him. The cat dug into the ground and leapt backwards, transforming into a large eagle. It flew towards Chronic talons first and grabbed onto his leg. The eagle swung around in the sky and released his talons. Causing the body to sail towards the ground at incredible speed. A cloud of dust rose out of the impact, obscuring their view. Bobo flew to the ground and transformed into a large and leathery horned beast. He charged into the dust, lowering his horn as he did. From outside Cadivus could hear the impact which caused the dust to clear. It revealed Chronic holding the beast by the horn as they each struggled for ground.

Cadivus found himself awed by the display of strength from both of the fighters. A feeling of impotence fell over him, an uneasy despair soon followed. These fighters were on another level, and he had never even heard of them before. His previous world felt so small, as if seen from far away.

Unable to gain any ground, Bobo transformed into a giant ape causing Chronic to stumble. Bobo brought both of his large arms over his head and down in a smashing motion. Chronic dodged backwards, barely avoiding the attack. He dug into the ground and sprung forward, bring his knee into the nose of the giant ape. Bobo, roared and grabbed the jaw-less man from the air and threw him to the ground, he he brought hammer fist down onto his body in rapid motion.

"Oh, no. He'll kill him," Cadivus said to himself, "Wait! Don't do it. I need him!" Cadivus shouted and ran towards Bobo while waving his arms.

Bobo looked towards Cadivus with his fangs bared. He hid the fangs behind his lips and his eyes seemed to calm from their rage. He nodded.

Cadivus sighed a breath of relief. Short lived as a fist came up from the ground and struck Bobo in his lower jaw, shattering the teeth in his mouth and sending the ape falling to the ground. Chronic stood up and dusted himself off. He pointed at Cadivus, and then at his own eyes before looking back at the green ape. He then took several steps backwards before holding his hands out as if he was ready to be bound once again.

"He's giving up?" Cadivus said, "Perhaps that beating before was too much." A wave of relief washed over him. He began to walk towards Chronic, ready for anything other than what would happen next.

Chronic clapped.

Cadivus's eyes shot open and he ran at full pace. The clap was followed by another, and another. Three claps. Cadivus halted himself when he heard the screams of agony from Bobo. His body rolled around on the ground switching from form to form. Instead of perfect transformations, these were damaged and rotten versions. Organs and blood flew about the field. The screams changing in pitch and level as his body did. Cadivus watched with baited breath, unable to do anything. Bobo changed into his human form, sitting on his hands and knees as his cries continued. The skin from his body fell away starting from the appendages and working their way in. He caught Cadivus's eyes.

"Remember to love, my boy," Bobo's final words were soft, yet they reached Cadivus all the same. As the last of his skin melted off of him, his body turned inside out and it fell to the ground. An uneasy amount of red cascaded across the field for the green wizard.

Cadivus fell to his knees. The world slowed until it seemed no moment would pass ever again. He thought of all the deaths he had seen so far. All the people he had hurt and even killed. A terrible fear wrapped around him and pushed down on his shoulders, holding his knees into the dirt. He wanted the world to melt away from him so that he might find peace in solitude. A horrible clicking laughter interrupted his grief. He caught eyes with Chronic who tilted his head in faux sympathy.

"Wazimu!" Ekio shouted from behind Cadivus. Several things happened at once. Chronic performed an encore, clapping his hands together once intending for three. Cadivus turned his head to see Ekio throwing the dagger she had won from him at the tavern they once met at. Cadivus caught the dagger by the pommel and a light toss placed the blade in his hand, then he threw it towards Chronic with all of his might. The feat reminding him of a wet basement from what felt like years ago. The dagger sailed through the air, two claps, he stood and ran toward Chronic as the third clap was interrupted by the dagger.

It caught Chronic in his right hand, pinning it deep inside his rib cage. He grunted in pain, his confident eyes turning angry. He charged toward Cadivus, catching him off guard. He threw his good shoulder into his chest at center mass. Cadivus was sent flying backwards, rolling in a reverse somersault before landing on his stomach. His shrill gasps reached for breath he couldn't find. A yank on the back of his shirt pulled him to his feet, arms wrapped around his waist and held him up right.

"He is the same as us. You need to understand that," Ekio said into his ear, "that strength is not his." She pushed air gently into his lungs and he gasped.

"He's strong like my brother." Cadvius said while coughing and searching for more breath. "I never beat him either. I never—"

"I am here now," Ekio said, "I need you for this, Cadivus. No dying this time." Her arms squeezed his waist.

All of his anxiety dripped away from his body. Falling to some abyss so deep he couldn't be sure it ever existed. The chain on his arm extended and he wrapped it around his knuckles. "Paper airplane me."

Ekio smiled. She put her hands on his back and buttocks and pushed him into the air towards Chronic, who moments before was struggling to free his arm. They caught eyes as his body hurled towards him. Cadivus brought his wrapped hand back preparing for a strike. Chronic met the fist with this own, causing his momentum to halt before Ekio slid in from behind Cadivus, catching Chronic in the shin, causing him to fall to the ground. Cadivus landed on his feet and prepared another strike on the fallen foe, while Ekio flipped her body over and prepared for the same. As they closed in on Chronic, he snapped his fingers and a powerful burst of wind from Ekio sent both her and Cadivus sliding backwards away from on another.

"Don't let up!" Ekio yelled. They got their footing as Chronic rose back to his feet. Cadivus released the chain from his knuckles and let it hang, as Ekio pushed a cloud of dirt ahead of her. She ran back in, rolling to the ground when she heard another snap from the cloud, she felt a beam of fire pass over her. Cadivus grunted and swung his chain forward and overhead. Chronic raised his arm and caught the chain as it wrapped around his own arm. Chronic yanked on the chain, causing Cadivus to fly toward him, he was preparing a powerful kick when he heard Ekio behind him. Instead, he stepped out of the way of Cadivus's body allowing him to travel towards her. As Cadivus soared by, Chronic saw Ekio palms facing his chest. Her teeth clenched, as the dust around them swirled. The chain rang out as it grew taught and Ekio roared as she pushed air into his chest. On the other side of the chain, Cadivus had landed and pulled with all of his might. A short moment of tension, before the chain whipped towards Cadivus, carrying the freight of Chronic's arm.

Chronic screamed in pain. He roared and brought his head down into the forehead of Ekio, who fell dizzy to it. He threw another powerful sidekick, that Ekio managed to roll sightly, allowing it to glance off her.

"Down!" Cadivus called from behind her.

Ekio dropped to the ground as the chain came whipping in from the side and wrapped around Chronic's neck. She turned her ring to a small shield and struck upwards at his chin with all her strength, knocking him in the air as Cadivus pulled and swung Chronic toward the ground at incredible speed. His body collided with the hard dirt beneath the topsoil. Barely conscious, Chronic felt a few more pains before he passed out. A boot on his chest, the dagger pulled from his ribs, his thumb removed from his remaining hand, and the heat on the amputation's wound.

Chapter 35

Cadivus used his remaining rope to bound Chronic tightly within it's grasp. He placed a tourniquet on his stump of an arm. He stared at the man wondering if he could find any sympathy for his current condition. None came to the front of his mind, neither did any joy or relief. The long journey home would be perilous as it was, the burden of having to keep a careful eye on the criminal would weigh them down greatly. He turned to see Ekio sitting down and cleaning the dagger's blade. There was no smile on her face either, in fact she seemed scared. He knelt down in front of her and waited for her to look up at him. She gave him a forced smile as he lost himself inside her eyes, observing the lines of pink that stood out of the brown like veins of power.

"We should have just beat him bloody when we caught him. That tricky little bastard," Ekio said. She looked past Cadivus to the man tied on the ground, she spat what blood remained in her mouth.

"Well, when my brother has him executed, I'll put a good word in for you to be the executioner," he said, causing her to smirk and nod. He stood up and dusted off his clothes while noting the battle had not left a single stain upon them. As was promised by the tailor in Pribbs.

"Great." Ekio said while reaching for Cadivus to pull her up to him. "Go and grab Thermia. Let us go have a rest in the shade. We could all use a minute."

Cadivus nodded, and Ekio pulled Chronic's unconscious body across the field. She smirked to each groan he made over the bumpy terrain.

Cadivus walked over to Thermia and shook her. She groaned and took light breaths. A bruise had already started to form on the side of her head. Her eyes opened with a squint in the bright light of day. He picked her up and walked toward their meet-up spot. Making sure she couldn't see the remains of Bobo on the battlefield. There hadn't been enough left of him to bury. He thought of words to say over a fire to honor the man who had saved his life. A man who he bore the responsibility for getting killed.

"We need to get you a helmet, sis." Thermia smiled at the words then drifted back to sleep. He could of sworn he had seen her eyes turn black before they closed, but tossed it up to his head trauma. The bruise turning into an egg on the side of her head as if a horn would spout out at any moment.

Ekio placed Chronic against a tree, undid her wrist strap and secured him to its trunk. Cadivus laid Thermia down and poured some water on her face. He wasn't sure why but thought it might help. It accomplished nothing. He fanned her off with similar results.

Ekio sat next to him and bandaged her leg.

"That sonofabitch said, 'I hope you don't tie me up and then tie me to you two,'" Cadivus muttered, "so, of course, I was thinking that was exactly what I was gonna do because he didn't want that. Who would've thought that it was a dastardly trick the whole time? Some kinda backward talkology. I guess Hunter was right about that whole genius thing after all."

“He is not a genius,” Ekio said, “He is just a lucky thug.” As she pulled the bandage tight, her face lightened. "I'm sorry about, Bobo. I know you two were getting close."

Cadivus took a deep breath. "He wasn't so bad you know? Very weird…but I don't think the world is better off without him."

A groan sounded behind him.

“I do know you…” Chronic’s strained voice said, “I…know you. Ekio. Aries Ekio.” His upper lip curled as if he was trying to smile. The gesture made him cough weakly.

“Shut it!” she snapped and threw a handful of dirt at him.

He laughed.

“Aires Ekio…The survivor. Why did you come all this way, Ekio?” He tilted his head and glared at her as if memories were being poured into his head.

“You know why I am here, scum.” She pulled the bandage tight and stood, her fist clenched at her side.

“Next time you’ll think twice before you get a whole village addicted to your sticky leaf and ruin them,” Cadivus said, “or more preferably, never get the opportunity to do it all. Yes! Never at all.”

“Whole village?” He laughed and coughed. “No, no. For some reason, your people didn’t like my plants, did they? Interfered with the training…”

“I said shut it!” she pointed at him with her shaking hand.

“What is the pissant going on about now?” Cadivus asked. He looked at her eyes that seemed to promise retribution for any more words uttered by the villain tied to the tree. The distant stares of the day replaced by focused strain.

“Nothing. He’s just trying to get under my skin.”

“What did you tell this man?” Chronic laughed again, swallowing blood. He coughed even harder. “Oh, Ekio…Did you lie to this man you so dearly love?”

She pulled out her dagger and walked toward him. Her whole body shaking with a rage on the needle's edge of boiling over and smothering the world around her. “I will take your tongue next if you don’t stop.” She said the words through clenched teeth.

Cadivus looked on, trying to understand what was happening. Of course this could be another trick from Chronic, but her anger towards him gave tremendous weight to each word that was uttered by the man with a broken jaw. His heart started to sink into his stomach. “What does he mean by you lying to me?”

She refused to meet his eyes, keeping her focus on Chronic. Her chest heaved as a gasp escaped her clenched teeth.

“You said he’s responsible for the death of your entire village.”

“He is!” she screamed, turning towards him. Tears formed in her eyes as the declaration fought for truth within her. Her saddened lips tried to retreat to an angry scowl.

Cadivus looked down to see the dagger pointed at him now.

“You can trust me,” he said softly, “we all have pasts we aren't proud of. I understand what you're going through right now.”

She scoffed. "You? Your memory is short. Five years?" She turned the blade to point her finger at him. "You have no idea what it's like." She started to yell. "What's happened to me! Wounds from my enemies! Pain from my tribe! Losing everything! You do not fucking understand!"

She turned away from him, placing a hand on her hip and another on her mouth. Cadivus stood still as stone as the words washed over him. He wasn't sure what to say or what to do next.

"I could tell him for you…" Chronic said.

"I am not gonna say it again jus—"

"Let him talk," Cadivus interrupted her. "I need to hear this. If he lies, just tell me he's lying, and I *will* believe you."

She turned away from both of them.

He motioned with his hand for Chronic to continue.

"Where she comes from, there is always war. Aires is necessary to keep the balance." He coughed, his voice growing raspier. "There's stress in being a leader, *the* leader. She asked me for help, so I helped her. Gave her some of my product, and something a little *stronger* if things got tough." He spit more blood onto the ground.

"So she took the edge off? So what?" Cadivus said.

Chronic shook his head.

"Biggest battle yet. Scouted days in advance. A tribe killer. When the fighting started, Aires was in her bed, unconscious from taking too much."

Cadivus looked at Ekio, her arms wrapped around her still body.

"They hid her. But the battle…They killed everyone. She wasn't there to lead…to fight. They all died, or were taken prisoner. I guess she blames me for that."

"Because it is your fault!" Ekio turned toward him. "If you never came, that would never have happened!" She yelled words in her own language, her voice a mix of devastation and anger. "You never told me." She fell to her knees. "What would happen, what it does to you."

Her breath caught in cry. "You are a liar!" She fell to her hands and her tears fell into the dirt below.

Chronic rolled his eyes.

Cadivus walked over to her and lifted her up to him. She refused to look at his face, so he cupped her cheek and gently lifted until their eyes met.

"This doesn't change how i feel about you," he said, "if this is the worst of it then you have not lost my love, Ekio."

She pushed him away, her crying ceased. She looked directly into his eyes and he watched the sorrow melt into an emptiness that pained his heart.

"Your words are weightless." She held her hand toward Chronic. Her bracelet jostled on her still wrist. "You love me?" she asked with a tone of challenge.

The wind began to stir around her. The noise of the bracelet intertwined with the crusted leaves on the ground as they fled the eye of the forming storm.

"Yes…" he whispered.

The wind around her picked up speed, gathering bits of dust and dirt that circled around her. The debris formed a dome around her body as rocks joined gale shield. She reached out her other hand and placed it onto her colorful bracelet.

"A bead for every life lost that day…" She ripped the bracelet apart and the beads flew in the dome around her. They created a blur of colorful stirring beauty. They danced around her and serenaded her power. "Every life that *you* stole that day."

Chronic eyes flashed fear as he stared at the tempest. He struggled to free himself but could find no means. He closed his eyes and laid his head back against the tree he was bound to.

"You don't have to do this!" Cadivus said, "please! You don't have to do this!"

Still the wind's intensity increased with her standing tall within it. The trees that surrounded them swayed with a violent energy. Their leaves and branches either consumed or blown away.

Cadivus tried to push through the storm but pulled back after receiving several deep cuts on his hand and arm. Her power offered him no sympathy. He knew if he entered the sphere he would be torn to tiny shreds. He got on his knees and held his hands together.

"Please. We *need* him!" He yelled over the sound that was ever increasing. Wondering if even his words could penetrate it.

She turned to him, and met his eyes.

"You love me?" She asked once again, her voice now quivering.

"Yes!" he answered as he stared into her eyes.

"Then take my power."

Cadivus was caught off guard. But still he closed his eyes, trying to remember the feeling of Chronic releasing his fire powers, and focused it on his siphoning abilities. In his mind's depth he saw a string to pull on, but when he reached for it, he couldn't grasp it. No matter how hard he reached it would move further away. His entire body tensed and flames lit on the tips of his fingers. He opened his eyes to find her staring at him. He closed them once more and kept focusing as hard as he could, grimacing and grinding his teeth. He grunted and screamed.

“Come on!” he screamed. His face was drenched in sweat. The veins in his neck tightened and he turned red. “Fuck! Come on!” He touched the edge of the string and felt it press back against him. He reached out one more time to grasp it and his hands and arms went up in flames. He pulled them back to his body and the string disappeared completely. He opened his eyes to find his arms were not engulfed. He looked back at her with a face full of despair and regret.

She gave him a small nod as her lips formed into a frown. She turned her head back toward Chronic. She felt a heavy weight on her heart as her eyes heated and watered once more. She pushed the weight into her soul and strengthened her wind one last time. She aimed her palm toward Chronic and sent the beads hurling toward him at sound-breaking speeds.

Chronic shut his eyes tight and screamed as tiny bits of shrapnel tore through him. She screamed with rage as the color that danced around her found its way through him. They erased his body as if it was turning to dust. All that remained of him was the liquid inside of him that had clung to the now porous tree.

The wind around her disappeared. She looked down at Cadivus, her face solemn and her eyes now dry.

“Why would you…” he said.

She leaped into the air, summoned a large shield, and pushed the wind beneath it to propel her high and away.

He watched as she disappeared from his sight. An unrelenting emptiness returning to his world as his heart screamed into his nerves, doubling him over. He cried. For the first time he could remember, he cried.

Chapter 36

The Inquisitor and Yuda sat in her office, discussing what to do with Hilock.

"Ma'am, you should just kill him now and be done with it," Yuda said.

The Inquisitor stared at her, considering the proposition. Hilock didn't seem very cooperative, and they already had all his belongings. She searched for a reason to let him live and could not find one.

"I agree, Yuda. Let's get this over with."

They left the office and headed toward his chambers. The guards outside it stepped aside to let them through. When they opened the door, they found Hilock curled into a fetal position in the corner of the room.

"Tie him to the hook." Yuda grabbed him off the ground and wrapped his hands with rope. She then placed the rope onto a hook before pulling him to his toes with the pulley mechanism.

"He stinks like shit, ma'am. Don't get too close." The Inquisitor approached him, looking sorry for the wretch.

"Last words, Hilock…"

He slowly looked up into her face, days without food or water had drained him.

"Just be done with it. I've had enough breaths."

"You are sentenced to death, to be carried out immediately. May the gods judge you justly. Now they speak."

The Inquisitor raised her hand and sent a surge of electricity from her fingertips and through Hilock. After only a few seconds, the pain and the screams stopped. His body slumped over.

"Take his body to research and, for gods' sake, wash him."

As the words left her lips, the image of Hilock on the hook distorted. His body changed to Yuda's, and behind Yuda stood Hilock, having removed Yuda's dagger and holding it to her stomach.

"She's not yet dead but close. Use your head and don't act verbose." With his other hand, he pulled a piece of cheese from his pockets and showed it to the Inquisitor. "You'll swallow this down, and step aside. Else I'll show you what her insides look like." He tossed it over to her, and she caught it.

"*Please*," the Inquisitor said, "I could replace her as easily as ordering lunch. You should have picked a better hostage."

He pushed the blade into her stomach—just enough to draw some blood.

The Inquisitor grimaced and her eyes narrowed. "Fine! Just so you know though, I'm going to make it slow next time." She chewed the piece of cheese, and with a nod from Hilock, she proved she swallowed it.

"My dear lady, it's not death I fear. You already killed me. I'd need not shed a tear. What's left is a shell that has but a single purpose, to remove all your masks and bring a usurper."

He cut Yuda free from her bindings and let her fall to the floor. Even without the Inquisitor's powers, he knew he couldn't take her in a close-range fight. He wouldn't make the same mistake again.

"I'll alert the guards if you don't kill me," she said, smirking.

“Yes they’ll come, and try to kill me, but who will they actually be stabbing? While changing the past is your ambition, the present is mine, and your place is this prison.” He changed Yuda back to him and himself into the Inquisitor. “I’ll take my leave, and you’ll take your stay. Show your mouth reprieve, and she’ll live another day.”

Hilock left the room and motioned for the guards outside of it to follow him down the hall. It was a long walk out of the Requiem. He tried to wear her scowl as best as he could, so nobody would interrupt him.

As he journeyed down the hallway, Chase walked toward him in the distance.

He panicked. “Stop that man!”

The guards, although confused, complied. Chase’s eyes widened at the detainment.

“You! Wait in my office until I return”

Chase shrugged and made a hand sign, extending his index and pinky finger out. Hilock responded by putting out his middle and ring finger. He nodded and proceeded with the guards. But as they walked past Hilock, He punched Hilock’s face. The guards, unsure of what was happening, jumped on Chase and took control of him, while Hilock, after a moment of being dazed, ran past them all.

“That was him!” Chase screamed from the ground. “He didn’t know the call sign! Get off me!”

The guards hesitated.

Fed up, Chase kicked one guard off him and put the other in a choke hold. The guard passed out in seconds. He then rolled over and elbowed another guard’s nose, knocking him unconscious. He chased after Hilock, who was still running down the hallway.

Hilock took a right down another hallway. Chase approached the corner cautiously and peeked. The white garment was talking with another guard. He pulled out his gun and shot out Hilock's knee. Hilock fell to the ground.

Chase ran up to capture him, but when he got there, he realized it wasn't him. It was another guard crying in pain.

"My fucking knee!" the guard screamed. "Why did you do that?! Argh!"

Chase pulled out a bandage and handed it to the other guard there.

"Here! Tie him off! I have to move!"

The guard took the bandage and worked on the injured man. "Asshole," he said.

Chase took a second to breathe. He knew Hilock was trying to leave, and there was only one path to do so. As fast as his legs could carry him, he ran down that path.

Hiding in another room, Hilock watched as Chase ran past him. While common sense would say to leave out the only exit, he knew he would never make it out alive that way. Plus, there were far too many guards to trick between here and freedom. His last trick would make Chase more cautious, which he counted on to backtrack.

Still disguised as the Inquisitor, Hilock ran back toward her office. He passed over the guards on the ground, entered the office, and ransacked her papers. Several folders were thrown around. He had to find the file he allowed himself to be captured for.

The office doors burst open, and Hunter entered in. "Jig's up, Hilock."

Without another word, Hunter fired into his left shoulder. He fell to the ground and grabbed at his wound. There—underneath the desk—

he saw the folder he was looking for. He grabbed it and stuffed it into his shirt.

More bullets flew over the desk.

"I'm getting impatient," Hunter said, "and when I get impatient, I tend to miss and hit vital organs…"

Hilock stood, Hunter fired through his head. The image disappeared.

"The real one now."

Hilock stood for real this time.

"Good to see you again, brave one. Glad to see you found closure and then some."

"What are you doing, Hilock? What's your goal here?"

He held up the folder he had been seeking for ages. He smiled with his ragged face. "What a delight to become entangled, in the embrace of an archangel." He turned the folder around to reveal the name Cadivus aka "Archangel" written upon it. "Of course she sent you to smite him, but your labors are uncertain. Instead as friends you invite him, without pulling upon the curtain."

Hunter bared his teeth. "The kid's popular alright. What's your play in all of this?"

"This veil won't prevail when the chips are fully down, guidance for the finest specimen of the crown. My duty is to aim the battlements of the wicked, back at its creators that created their self destruction."

"Speak…plainly."

Hilock sighed. "The fate of us all depends on this ritual stopping. I don't mean our lives, I mean our very existence!" He threw the folder at the wall. "This Cadivus is connected I know it, I feel it! MY bones are vibrating I'm so close to the truth. I have to know, Hunter. I have to know why they did this to me!" He revealed his disfigured face, the skin red and green looking as mixed color candle had melted. "We have to stop it. There can be no other goal while this one persist!" His chest heaved as he stood.

"Okay." Hunter lowered his weapon. "I'll help you."

Hilock wiped the water from his eyes as Hunter extended his hand toward him to shake. Hilock walked toward him and shook his hand. Hunter leaned in and breathed deeply through his nose, as his grip tightened. Hilocks's breath fell out of him.

"What are you…" Hilock muttered.

Hunter grabbed his neck with his other hand, and squeezed. "The smell, you can't change the smell," he said softly.

Hilock grabbed at the hand and altered reality around them. Visions of demons, ghosts and even his late parents. Yet Hunter never faltered.

"The man you showed me before. He was my partner, a youngin' I was meant to train. He fell into the wrong in the worse kind of ways. I killed him. He came to me for help and I killed him." Hunter's eyes watered, offering a reflection for Hilock to examine his now purple face. "Following orders. That's what I repeated to myself at the bottom of every glass of liquor I could get my hands on. That girl loved him and I killed him." Tears fell down his face. "I won't do it again. You may not deserve this now, but I reckon it's the only way for me to do what I need to do."

Hilock stared into Hunter's eyes. On the verge of death his mind sparked to life as it never had before. He could see it, see all the threads and how they were pulled. He smiled as he realized his own fate. He was never a knight, never a hero, not even a soldier in this fight. He was merely a pawn. A pawn that lived exactly as it was meant to. A pawn meant to die here in this exact moment. His final thought was a farewell to his own hero. *Goodbye, Marcus.*

Chapter 37

Darion awoke in a bed, an unfamiliar softness. Unknowingly to him, residing in Toonda's home. He tried to call out but his mouth was too dry. Instead, he just made an awkward moaning noise.

Toonda entered the room and gasped.

"Donban!" She called out as she ran to Darion's side.

He pointed at his mouth, and she grabbed a pitcher of water and splashed it onto his face in her excitement. He caught some of the splash in his mouth, and moistened his tongue and throat.

"Ah," He moaned, "that's never tasted sweeter…"

She stood there motionless as he reached for the pitcher. She put it in his hands, and he drank the last drops from it. When he finished, she hugged him. Strong. He could feel her tears on his cheek.

"Too…tight," he croaked out.

She hugged him even tighter.

Doban entered the room and separated them.

"Don't kill him now," he said, embracing her. He smiled at Darion, who was still piecing everything together.

"How?" Darion said. "I…I…died. The…sands."

"We heard a scream," she said, "and well…we came back to help and found you on the ground with a faint pulse. I can't believe you recovered after that…It's beyond reason."

"One tough bastard," Doban remarked with a smile and nod.

Darion tried to sit up, but pain shot through his body. He relented and laid down instead.

“Not tough enough to sit even…” Darion said, “how long…has it been?”

Toonda and her husband looked at each other.

“It’s been two weeks,” she said, bowing her head. “You…missed the election.”

“Fuck…Doban, you didn’t…get voted leader?”

“Afraid not. Decan is…very persuasive after all,” Doban said.

Darion rubbed his eyes and tried to focus on anything but found it impossible.

“Don’t worry about that. Just rest for now,” Toonda said, placing a wet cloth on his head.

He grabbed her hand and looked into her eyes.

“I never say this, but thank you. Thank you for taking care of me all these years. If I were you, I would have quit on me a long time ago.”

“That’s because you're used to being a quitter. But…my father left me with a purpose before he died.”

“What purpose?”

“To watch over you. He told me you’re gonna do big things one day.” She wiped the sweat from his forehead. “I just didn’t know how needy you were gonna be, or I would have told him to stuff it!”

They laughed at that.

“I think it was five years ago that I cut that noose from your neck, and brought you back to life.” Tears slipped down her face. “That’s all over now, right?”

Darion nodded. Then he coughed and buried his head into his pillow.

“Rest now. You still have a purpose here, Darion.”

With those words, he fell back to sleep.

Several days later, when Toonda came by to feed Darion, she found him dressed and standing at the bedside, folding the sheets she had given him.

"What the hell do you think you're doing?" she asked.

"I've gotta do something," he said, "I can't hide here."

"You can't…"

He walked over to her to show his progress.

"As spry as ever!" he said. His face fell solemn. "I've got to get out there. Let them see me."

Toonda hesitated, but helped him walk toward the door. Before they opened it, she stopped him.

"Make them see the real you, Darion."

He nodded and left. The glare of an unfamiliar sun blinded him. He let the heat kiss his skin as he closed his eyes and embraced it. Invigorated once more, he could still feel the pain in his body, but he walked with his chin high as if he felt nothing. The sand running over his toes made him smile.

It didn't take long to find a crowd gathered around Decan. It seemed to have grown in Darion's absence. The crowd's voices quieted down as Darion approached him.

"Welcome back to the living, Darion" Decan said, extending his hand to shake.

"Good morning to you, Nomad."

The crowd refused to meet his eyes. He took this as a good sign.

"Have you come to congratulate me?" Decan said, "it is quite an honor for your first voyage out of that shack to be to me."

"Yes, the honor is all mine. In fact, I feel honor is indeed the word of the day. So now I ask. Will you honor all the old ways?"

"Of course! That is why I ran for election in the first place."

"Good. Then you'll have no problem honoring a proposition of mine."

"Anything you need Darion, consider it done."

"I'd like to challenge your leadership by means of combat."

The crowd whispered among themselves.

Decan closed his eyes for a moment before eyeing Darion's injured body.

"Surely you jest, cripple? Say it true, and I'll spare you the embarrassment."

Darion revealed his sword by his side.

"I'll take my chances."

He looked around the crowd, and then smiled wide.

"Let the gods decide then!"

As the two men shook hands, trumpets and drums sounded out in the valley. They stared each other down as the crowd became frantic. They could hear someone screaming from far away.

"The king's banners!" One of the guards shouted from far away.

Panic grew among the crowd. Their smiles dropped as the two men headed toward the town's entrance to greet the uninvited. Fancy caravans with royal guards protecting them stood there instead of an army. The horns and drums performed a spectacle of a finale as the caravans halted. One of the doors opened, and a plump man jumped out of it and waddled toward the entrance, which had now been fashioned with a simple gate and a tower.

"What's your business?" a guard called out to the plump man.

"King's orders." The man reached behind him, and another man ran up and placed a scroll into his hand. He unrolled it. "It has come to the lord's attention that robbery and murder are commonplace in these lands. By order of the king, peace is to be brought to the sands. Meet with an anointed leader and establish the king's justice in the sands by any means necessary—with great efforts to be focused on civility and diplomacy. So says the king. Now they speak."

Darion and Decan stared at each other, confused. "What?" They both said.

"*Ugh.* Invite me in, and we'll have words. As a peace offering, we've brought some supplies for your people." He snapped his fingers, and several barrels were unloaded off the caravans and carried toward the town. "We brought water, pickled fish, smoked meats and a smattering of wine."

One of the guards handed the plump man a small cask. With it in hand, the plump man motioned for his request to be granted. The camp's guard looked toward Decan for orders.

"Open the gates!" Decan shouted.

The guards went into action and stepped aside. Barrel after barrel was stacked inside the town. Everyone in town came to see the spectacle, and cried tears of relief and joy as they were handed cups of water and food.

The plump man approached Decan and bowed.

"Greetings. My name is Astarian. Whom do I have the pleasure of speaking with?"

"Decan." He reached out to shake his hand.

Astarian eyed his dirty hands before shaking it.

"What's all this about now?" Decan asked.

"I thought the decree was clear enough…Well, the king has taken an interest in your barbaric ways of life. He finds it unpleasant. And of course, he is a great man and has devised a strategy that doesn't involve bloodshed."

"What strategy is that?"

Astarian looked around at the onlookers and leaned toward Decan.

"Perhaps, we should discuss business alone and in the shade? If you find it wise."

As the two men retreated toward Decan's new home, he waved Darion off before Darion could join.

Inside his home, Astarian wiped the sweat off his face, took off his jacket, undid some of his shirt buttons, and downed a glass of wine. "It's a little warm here." He poured himself another cup.

"I'm going to need details, Astarian." Decan said.

He smacked his lips as he held up a finger, taking another long sip.

"Of course, it is only prudent to require such a thing. Basically, peace needs to be made out here. Now we understand the nomadic nature of your kind, very interesting indeed. However, when we were informed one of your kind was building a town well, it deserved a closer look. While your efforts are endearing they are..." He put his hands up and looked around the poorly built home. "I'll just say it...It's pathetic. You clearly lack knowledge or taste to build such things. It is forgivable."

Decan laughed.

"Aye, I'd agree to that. Hence why we are preparing to continue our nomadic ways and leave this place once and for all."

"Decan, Decan, Decan...While returning to the old ways is a commendable thing, I'm afraid you lack knowledge of your surroundings. Even now, several groups are poised to strike you down, and while you were in need of the supplies we brought, they do make you a rather large target. Also, might I say, good luck convincing a parent not to feed their children with it."

"You're a colorful snake, Astarian..."

Astarian smiled and shrugged, sipping more wine.

"It's what I do best, sir." He raised his cup to Decan and they finished their drinks. He poured another. "I know you think it in bad taste, and of course it is. It's also the best chance you'll have at cementing your legacy as the greatest leader of the sands in all of history."

Decan's eyebrows shot up.

He continued, "after the first election to ever take place, the newly appointed leader, Decan, established a treaty with the king himself and led his people to prosperity beyond what they ever deemed possible."

They took a sip.

"Why, mothers will name their sons after you, fathers will tell the tale over dinner across the world. I'd say. I'm rather jealous of your position. What luck."

"Go on, good sir." Deacon smiled.

****

Darion stood outside at the gates, and watched as the last of the barrels were brought in.

"Two weeks too late..." Toonda said, coming up behind him.

"Yes..." he said, "it's interesting how that worked out."

"What do you think Decan will do?"

"He might be stubborn, but he's also a pompous fool. They'll tease his ego, and he'll agree to their terms."

"So...we won anyway? That's a good thing right?"

"I hope so, but something doesn't feel right about all this." As he said the words a royal guard approached him.

"Darion?" the guard said.

He nodded.

"We'll have words with you." He stood to the side, pointed his spear out of the town and raised his chin. "This way if you please."

Darion tapped her shoulder, and walked toward the caravans. A door opened to one of them and a man waved at him, beckoning him.

As he drew closer, the man hopped out and bowed.

"In here, sir."

Darion couldn't see inside the dark caravan but thought it safe since they didn't seem interested in disarming him. As he entered, the door slammed shut behind him.

Darkness surrounded him, too dark to make anything out. Then a match lit, revealing a man's face as he lit a pipe. He used the remnants of the match to light several candles.

"Greetings, friend," the man said, smiling in the dim light. "A little over dramatic maybe?" He opened a window, letting plenty of light inside. "That's better, I think."

"Who are you?" Darion asked, confused. "What do you want with me?"

"Oh, we'll get there. You're looking strong and confident, Darion!" He slammed his fist onto his chest. "I'd say you are indeed ready."

"Ready for what, exactly?"

The man smirked and took a long puff of his pipe.

"Tell it again, Darion. Tell me the story they don't believe."

"Look…I don't know what this is, but I think I'm just going to leave, if it suits you."

“Your king orders to stay.” He puffed his pipe once more, raising his eyebrows. “Decan is signing the treaty now, and I am your king as of…four seconds ago I'd wager.”

Darion closed his eyes and sighed.

“I know, right? What was he thinking? You would have never agreed to that.”

“Well, you’re not stupid at least.”

He laughed at that, then he motioned to some proper steaks next to him, but Darion shook his head. “Smart lad. Now, tell me that story if you please. The one about your father…”

Darion gritted his teeth, but felt compelled to answer.

“If it pleases. My father was killed by a hybrid, one with glowing wings. It latched onto him and turned his body to ash. The others, they don’t remember what I do. They think he died in his sleep. It’s driven me near madness.” Darion snarled, then collected himself. “If you brought me here to mock me, I can assure you my skin is thick from previous taunts.” He grabbed a glass off the table and poured the fanciest bottle into it. It burned down his throat.

“Marvelous. Indeed quite a marvelous story.”

“It’s not—”

“It’s not the creativity of a child, I can tell you that. It’s a matter of fact and truth. Not many are aware, but that is indeed the truth of things, Darion.”

“Surely you aim to humiliate me.”

“Any other man…but not me. No, my aim is not my own, Darion. What I aim is you, and what I aim you at is what you desire most.”

“I’d request you to speak plainly, sir.”

The king took another long puff from his pipe, closing his eyes and savoring the tobacco flavor.

"The man who killed your father still walks these lands. I can give you a name, descriptions, and a location…All I ask is that you bring me the woman who is with him."

Darion trembled as he stared through the king. All this time his father's killer was out there. He figured he had died in the war, having not heard of a hybrid with glowing wings since. Finally, he could put an end to his nightmares.

"I can feel your rage washing over me. Quite impressive." He poured himself a drink and raised his glass toward Darion. "Is that something you desire?"

Darion commanded his body still and tapped glasses with the king.

"Consider it done."

They drank together.

"I'll have that information," Darion said.

"Certainly. The man's name you seek is Cadivus."

"Cadivus…" The word oozed past Darion's lips. He finished his drink and threw the glass at the wall. "I'll learn everything you know about this man."

The King told him everything about Cadivus and his last remaining traveling companion, Thermia. He gave him descriptions and told his location.

"You wouldn't lie to me would you?" The thought had crept into his mind as he handed him everything he wanted a silver platter.

"It's beneath a king to lie, Darion. I assume we have an agreement then?" He held out his hand to shake.

Darion grabbed his hand, and held his head down during the shake. When he looked up, tears were in his eyes. He tried to turn his head away, but the king reached out and pulled his chin toward him, staring into his wet eyes.

"Never turn from passion, Darion," the king said, "it gives you strength."

Darion nodded and wiped tears from his eyes before exiting the caravan. Before he closed the door, he turned to face the king.

"Thank you, my king." He bowed before turning around to head toward his camp.

The king smiled as he watched him walk away.

"Oh, I always loved this part…"

Chapter 38

Cadivus walked in a forest with Thermia in his arms. Where, how far, or which direction? He couldn't say. He just knew they had to leave. He couldn't see the path before him, only the vision of Chronic—and any chance they had of restoring their old life—being torn to shreds.

"You fucking dumb bitch!" He fell to his knees and yelled as loudly as he could until his throat hurt. "Why?! Why?! Why?!" he coughed, the screams having torn his throat into pulled meat.

Thermia stirred in his arms. He laid her down on the ground and rubbed his neck.

"What the frick…" she muttered, "what's going on? What happened?"

He didn't know how to answer.

She threw her head to the ground and collected her thoughts, groaning through her headache. "Cadivus, talk to me…Say something. Tell me—"

"We can't go back to Dreyhal," he said without looking at her in the eyes.

"What? No…The plan… It was working. What happened? I remember he dove into a ditch and…Where's Ekio? Where's Ekio?! Is she…No, don't tell me." Tears formed in her eyes.

"She's alive and well," Cadivus said. Thoughts raced through his head of what to tell her next. He didn't want to hurt her image of Ekio. "We had Chronic caught, and…things got out of hand."

"Oh, Cadivus…don't tell me you lost control of your powers again."

His eyes darted up.

"Yes, he tricked me again. Only this time, he was a victim of his own wickedness."

Saving Ekio from indignation, and thinking Thermia would forgive him…It was the perfect plan.

"What is *wrong* with you, Cadivus?" She held her hands over her eyes to cover her tears. "You killed Chronic and scared away one of my best friends!" Still on the ground, she kicked and screamed, flopping from side to side. "Dammit!" Her anger seemed to leave her for a moment. She just covered her eyes and softly cried into her hands.

Cadivus sat next to her, debating on whether or not to offer his hand.

"How am I gonna convince Smokey I'm innocent?" she finally said.

"I'm sure you'll be fine. It's me they blame after all, isn't it?"

"Don't even!" She turned to face him. "You're not leaving me there by myself! I'll never be allowed to leave the castle again!"

"This isn't a debate. I don't know what else to do here. I don't even know where I am."

She stared at him with all the intensity she could muster.

"What do you want me to do?!" he yelled.

She kept staring.

"I…can't….fix….this!"

"You can try, can't you?" she said.

He wanted to turn the dirt around him into quicksand and suck them both deep into the earth. Instead, he kept yelling, loudly.

"Fine! I'll go back to Dreyhal, escort you through the gates, bend my neck on a stump, and wait to be beheaded!"

"Was that so hard?" She got up, and stumbled for a moment, underestimating her head wound. She caught herself on a tree. "Why are bodies always flying all over the place?! I'm sick of being unconscious all the time!"

Cadivus stood, took her arm, and placed it over his shoulder.

"Which way is home?"

She stared at the stars in the night sky.

"Oh, fuck me. I really should have paid attention when they taught me this shit…" she walked toward a constellation she recognized, but after a few steps, she vomited on the ground. "Okay…Maybe a small rest would be okay."

He laid her down against a tree and sat beside her.

"Are we okay?" he asked.

"I don't know *what* we are. I just know we need to get back home. He needs us there. Chronic or not, we need to be home."

She stared at the sky, remembering her first few nights in Dreyhal. How her Smokey would take her to the roof and point out the brightest stars in the sky, even offering stories about them.

She remembered the story about the dimmest of the major stars, Titeenius.

A mother had three sons, their father had died in a war over some land. She focused all her attention on the two older boys, letting the youngest fall behind on his training and studies. One of the older brothers went off to become a respected general, and the other became a revered scholar at a most prestigious school. The younger brother stayed behind, tending the gardens, and trapping small wildlife.

When the mother got sick on her deathbed, she asked the youngest child if he hated her for what she had done. He smiled and said no, for he had the privilege of caring for the mother of two of the greatest men in all the land. He served her food and cupped her hands. She grasped him tight, and tears fell down her cheeks. My sweet son, she said, it is not the blade or the book that nurtures the soul. As I drift into the afterlife, my greatest pride I take with me is you.

He went on to care for others who found themselves alone at the end of their lives. On his own deathbed, nobody was there to hold his hand. The Goddess of Light took pity upon him. She reached out and pulled him toward her, promising him a place in the night sky forever. All he asked was that he not be too bright as he didn't want to distract travelers.

Thermia teared up, thinking about the story. Other people seemed to know who they were meant to be, but she had no idea. She would have been married to a lord in the royal city if yelen's disease hadn't destroyed her womb. She would have married her childhood sweetheart if his breath still lingered in his lungs. It was only by chance that another lord who had no care for having children existed. She longed to be with the man who allowed her freedom to blossom. "I miss him so much, Cadivus…" She cried, and he hugged her as long as she needed.

"Why are we so obsessed with being near this dick weasel…"

They both laughed.

"When my family gave me away to him, he was kind," she said, "he told me he would take care of me forever, whether I chose to be with him or not. We talked a lot on that first trip, we told each other everything. In fact I think we talked for at least twenty hours straight before falling asleep the first time. He was just…a real person."

"I don't think I've ever talked to him for more than a few minutes…"

"He is stern and cold at times, but…you feel safe when he's around, don't you?"

"Yes. Maybe that's it."

She took a deep breath. "Cadivus?"

"Yeah?"

"I should tell you, in case something goes wrong." His ears perked up. "Me and Smokey well…We love each other as best friends. Not as a husband and wife does."

"What? I don't understand what you're saying."

"I'm saying…We don't perform our marital duties…"

"Yeah, I've never seen you cook or clean anything. So what?" She slapped his shoulder, and he flinched.

"We don't fuck each other! You numbskull!" She folded her arms.

Cadivus sat back, grimacing. "Does his dick not work? Does he even *have* a dick?"

"Of course he has a dick!"

"How would you know!?"

They both became flustered, and turned away from one another. Cadivus turned to look at her and sighed.

"Why keep this a secret?" Cadivus asked, "why be so…performative about your *entanglements*."

She brushed her hair back. "We couldn't have people thinking otherwise. He was scared to tell you because, you know, you're a drunken loudmouth."

He nodded. "Well, fuck me that's weird. So, you have a connection beyond your loins. What is it that binds you?"

She looked him in the eyes. The playfulness in her eyes faded into an emptiness that was unbefitting to her.

"We both lost someone."

His smile fell. "Oh…I see." His heart ached knowing he never bothered to ask either of them the question. He wanted to ask for more details but, his eyes felt so heavy.

They laid down to sleep. He looked to his side, hoping to see Ekio. But she was still gone. His heart felt empty. He wondered if he missed her like Thermia missed his brother. Could he ever love someone so relentlessly as she did? He grabbed onto a nearby root and pretended it was Ekio's calloused hand. He closed his eyes and fell to slumber.

When Thermia awoke in the morning, the world was still there.

Her head still aching, she moaned for water, and kicked Cadivus until he woke up to fetch it from a nearby stream. His hand was cramped from gripping the root all evening. He watched her gulp down the water he retrieved, only pausing for heavy breaths.

"Home?" she held out her hand, and he lifted her up.

"Home," he agreed.

They set off on their voyage—through an unfamiliar but seemingly peaceful space in the country. The forest was calm, the sun peeked through the needles and leaves. Distant calls from the wildlife serenaded them as they walked. Chronic had picked a great place to retire it seemed.

Cadivus kept picturing the vision of Chronic being torn to shreds by Ekio, like watching sand blowing into the wind.

"Hey," Thermia said, "distract me while I walk."

"All right. I've always been a good distraction. Let's see…what if I didn't stay with you in Dreyhal?"

Her mouth dropped.

"What? What else would you do? Are you going after Ekio? Are you going to make things right with her?"

"I…I don't know. I think…there are things that have been hidden from me. Somewhere out there, the answer lie in wait."

"Hey. I can't say I won't miss you. But, if this is something you have to do. I will support you fully. You have so much potential, you could do anything you set your mind to. I'm sure of it."

"All right. So, whether my dream is to be the best prostitute in the capitol or the most revered poet, you'd support it all the same?"

She giggled a little.

"Yeah…I mean I would have questions, but you know, it's your life."

"Let me ask you this then, what will you do if you're not allowed back into Dreyhal?"

"Well I would—"

His ears picked up the noise of footsteps. He put his fingers to her lips and whispered.

"Be quiet. Someone else is here."

Frightened, they glanced around. Leaves rumbled all around them.

"Run!" he shouted.

Thermia took off, and the men left the shadows and pursued her. Cadivus went to give chase, but a hand caught his shoulder. He turned around and punched the person in the face, feeling the skull crack upon his fist and sending them flying into a bush.

He counted the men chasing her. Four. He quickly caught up to one, slammed him into a tree from behind. Cadivus removed the man's sword and stuck it through his back. He then grabbed the man's face and whispered in his ear. "How many men are there?"

"Fuck you!"

He twisted the blade and pulled it through his body "Five!" he grunted. He ran the blade over the man's neck and left. Three left.

Thermia ran without remembering the pain in her body. Loud footsteps thundered behind her, so she gave it everything she had.

Her and Cadivus had come so far. Only to fail over and over again.

Someone jerked her hand and pulled her to the ground with such force. All the wind left her.

Nearby, Cadivus closed in on the next chaser. "Wait up!" he yelled.

The man turned around, and made a surprised face at him. Cadivus threw his sword and caught the man through the leg. The man tumbled onto the ground and landed on his back, screaming. Cadivus unwrapped his chain and wound up a heavy swing onto his chest. He grabbed at his ribs, taking short breaths.

"I actually still need this. Hold on." Cadivus grabbed the sword's hilt and pulled it out. As he did, blood gushed out of the wound, mudding up the dirt around him. The man tried to use his hands to stop the bleeding, but he slammed the hilt into his nose, knocking him out cold.

"Two?"

Thermia tried to catch her breath as someone dragged her foot through the woods. Rocks and roots dug into her as she passed over them. "Stop! If you're gonna kidnap me, at least pick me up!"

“Eh,” the man said, “you look heavy.” He laughed and continued dragging her.

She reached out, trying to grab anything from the ground, and found a fist-sized rock in her hand. She contorted her body and slammed the rock into the hand holding onto her, making him release her and cry out in pain. She threw the rock at his head but missed, so she opted to run in the opposite direction instead. Yet she found herself standing in front of a hundred-foot drop.

Her kidnapper held up his good hand in a fist, clenching his teeth. “I’m gonna bash that pretty little face of yours in!”

“I think you're forgetting about something,” she said.

“And what’s that?”

She pointed behind him.

Cadivus ran in and kicked him in the balls.

The kick sent him airborne over the edge. The man reached out and grabbed a root on his way down, but the root gave way and he continued to plummet to his death. With the root pulled out, the dirt crumbled away.

The ground under Thermia moved.

“Cadivus?” she said.

The cliffside gave out, and she fell. He jumped toward her and caught her hand. His chest lay on the edge of the fallen earth. They both screamed for a moment before realizing he had made the catch.

“That’s my boy! Pull me up, please!” she said.

“Working on it! Weird angle!” He started to lift her, but pain stabbed through his back. Air fell out of him, and what remained of his strength left him.

“It’s your lung…” a voice whispered behind him. “It’s been pierced. You’re not gonna be able to talk. You’re not gonna get the chance to say goodbye. Same as I.”

Hanging off the edge, she only saw part of Cadivus’s torso hung over it.

“Cadivus? Pull me up.” She stared into his empty eyes. “Cad…What…what are you doing? Pull me up! Please!”

His grip lessened.

“Another innocent dies in your hands…Archangel,” the voice in his ear spat.

Cadivus tried to breathe in short breaths. His face turned purple. The strength in his hands fell into the abyss of the pain in his chest.

“Cadivus… I didn’t mean anything I said! I’m sorry! Please don’t let me fall! Please!” Her pleading turned into angry tears. “Cadivus! Why are you doing this? Don’t!”

He slowly shook his head, and tried to mouth the words “I’m sorry.”

“Farewell…” The voice whispered.

He lost his grip, and she fell.

Her eyes were wide, and her face full of despair. She never looked down. That despair radiated into his mind through her gaze. Although his senses were blurry, he knew the moment her screaming stopped. When her movement stopped. Her stillness haunting him as her body lay upon the ground below.

“Oh, this wasn’t part of the plan by the way,” The voice said, “just an improvisation. I have nothing against the woman.” The man removed his sword from Cadivus’s lung, grabbed his leg and flipped him through the air.

Cadivus's back slammed into the ground. He knew someone strong was manipulating his body. He could only watch and listen as his body failed him.

"You know, I'm pretty disappointed. I was hoping to have a duel of the ages. I thought we would battle in the morning sun until the greater man overcame the other. I thought you were someone worth fighting. Now, you just look like any other *nobody*." The man stabbed his sword into the ground, and punched Cadivus's battered body.

Pain. He could still feel the pain.

"This…this is how you ended it." The man grabbed his throat, lifted him into the air, and walked him toward the edge of the cliff.

"You seem to be confused. A lot of people are but not me. My name is Darion. You see, seven years ago, you killed my father. For years, I've held a hatred in my heart that I couldn't begin to understand. A killer instinct I couldn't quench. A sadness I couldn't mend. But now…" He punched his chest until his fist was slippery with blood. The open skin leaked out blood and tubes held beneath it. "Our past—our misdeeds—will always come back to haunt us! My blade is the will of justice! My actions are benevolent prose! My pain dies with you, fallen angel. You won't—"

Cadivus placed a finger to his lips, and slowly shook his head. A weak smirk upon his face. The world around slowly fading to an eternal blackness.

Darion knocked his hand away, growled, and threw him over the cliff. His eyes watched until his body hit the ground. Near the girl he laid, bleeding in to water that flowed near them. Trembling, he stared at him until he felt satisfied—He breathed heavily trying to savor his revenge and felt a hole he couldn't fill. He stared at his sword and forced a smile. Sheathing it before turning around and walking away from the edge of the cliff.

Chapter 39

The woman's sweet voice sent warmth into Cadivus's heart. A warmth that trickled throughout his body. He reached out and pulled the distant voice close.

The sun, must rest, so it can shine
The moon, must succeed, the one true light
Today's troubles, are fading away
Without words, I hear you say
Goodnight, and know
For you, my soul
The son, must grow, so it can find
The truth, within his waking mind
Yesterday's troubles, are present now
His actions, to whom he bows
Goodnight, and know
For you, my soul

Cadivus awakened in a dark tent. Naked. He couldn't move, tied to a log that supported the structure. Several men huddled around a brazier that dimly lit the dark and small space. They looked like soldiers with wornout uniforms, weapons, and their tattered insignia. Some chewed on what looked like rotten meat.

A greasy, large man walked toward him. His eyes menacing and uncaring. The mail armor on his chest was starting to rust. Cadivus recognized them as a militia once hired by the crown. He remembered seeing their insignias in Afferium years ago.

"Ey, boys. I think he's awake…" the greasy man said.

The crowd gathered around him, the men smiling and laughing.

"I think I might know the answer, but tell us your name, boy."

Cadivus looked around the room, at all their dirty and pathetic faces.

"Me? Don't remember your own father? Pity. What a disgraceful and small peckered son I have."

Nobody laughed. They just raised their brows and hands as they backed away.

The greasy man got closer. His face was weathered, and one of his nostrils had been cut off and scarred over.

"Funny boy, ain't ya? Well, I've got jokes too. Except me jokes…involve taking me small pecker an' shoving it deep in your asshole, boy." He walked behind him and sniffed his neck. "Luckily for me, they washed you up some. Hate to get the stench of death on me wee pecker."

Everyone laughed.

"Well, I thank you for the wash," Cadivus said, "I'm sure your two inches of uncircumcised fury is going to tear me a new one. While that's happening, perhaps one of your fluffers here can tell me what's happening, where's the woman?"

The greasy man squeezed his butt cheek and circled back to the front of him.

"Woman? Do you think I'd need to fuck you if we had a lass here?"

They laughed again. "Gods, we still be running train on er' if we had a woman." He licked his lips and continued. "Ya Cadivus, ain't ya?"

"Why would I tell you shit badgers anything?" Cadivus said.

“We prefer ya didn’t, if honest; Gives us a chance to ask a little harder.” He pointed to one of the men in the middle of the crowd. “You! Get me knives…”

“Get em yourself,” the man said, “what do I look like?” He gestured to the man standing next to him while shaking his head.

The room went quiet. Other men stepped away from the one refusing.

“What ya just say, cadet?” The greasy man walked over to the smaller man and got in his face. “I think you’ll suck me till I’m hard, so I can have fun with our friend here.”

“Eh, I’m good. Haven’t had the taste of shit in my mouth for weeks. Don’t plan on breaking my streak anytime soon. Unless…no, no it's preposterous.

The greasy man faked a laugh and went to strike a blow to his head, but the traitor caught his hand.

“Oh, I guess this is mine now.” With nothing but boredom in his eyes, he pulled on the arm until it separated from his shoulder.

The greasy man stared at his wound and cried out. He attempted to strike the traitor with his other arm, but the traitor drew his sword and cut the arm off at the elbow. He then clubbed the greasy man’s head with his own arm, knocking him to the ground.

He continued the attack after he fell. “Quit hitting yourself! Quit hitting yourself!” He laughed as the greasy man bled out on the floor.

The other four men in the room removed their swords and axes and took a battle stance.

“Seriously?” He cracked his neck and turned to face them.

His voice changed to a deeper, more lively tone.

“My, my. While I have an admiration for your bravery, I cannot help but feel deflated. For I’ve shown you my inclination for violence, and yet, you still believe you could best me. While a time existed where you could leave, and live out your short and ill-tempered lives. Now, you’ve forfeited the possibility of uniting your piss shooters to your palms ever again.”

“Put your hands up!” One of the men said, his voice shaking. “Y-You’re under arrest!”

“Yes, sir!” As he saluted, he swung the arm at the men, letting the blood fly off and land on their faces. He then charged and clothes-lined two of the men. Pulling two daggers from his waist, he spun around and stabbed one into a man’s chest. He threw the remaining dagger into the last man’s eye.

As they groaned in pain, he grabbed one man’s axe and swung it through all the men, separating their heads from their bodies with every swipe. He then looked at Cadivus and raised the axe in his hands.

Cadivus watched the man restrain himself from swinging the axe down on him.

“Well, I guess we’ll just go our separate ways now…” Cadivus said, half admiring and half fearing the man.

“I know it’s you, Cadivus. You’ve nothing to fear from me…Not yet anyway.” He slowly lowered the axe to his side. “My apologies. Reigning it in can be…difficult at times, as you know.”

“Who are you?”

“Me? Well who I am is not who I’ve been. Who I’ll be is not who I am currently. Furthermore, well suffice to say, a longer explanation would only confuse us both. And then I get stabby.”

“Makes perfect sense. Can we discuss this when I’m not tied up?” Cadivus wiggled in his ropes.

“Perhaps.”

An awkwardly long silence took place.

“Tell me more…” Cadivus finally said.

“Forgive me…I am a…fan. Of course, I have arrived with a purpose, and that purpose is to meet you.”

“Well, here we are.”

“Indeed. Now, I’m afraid I must ask some hard questions, not dick hard or torture hard like our armless friend here proposed, no. These are more…philosophicalological in nature.”

“Well, that’s a real word, and I have nowhere to be. Proceed”

“You’re weak. Why are you so weak?”

“Bad diet?”

He collected his knives as he continued talking.

“I would take a great interest in having a protege such as yourself…”

Cadivus thought he would agree to just about anything the crazy bastard said and then run when he had the chance.

“I accept.”

“Denied.”

“But you *just* said—”

“I know you’ll run if I free you, a few more moments are needed to garner your loyalty, I’d imagine. And I think I know what you want most in this world. Care to wager?”

“The terms?”

"If I guess correctly, you become my loyal protege. If I'm wrong however, I'll cut you loose, and you can leave. I'll never bother you once more."

Cadivus wondered if he knew about his plan to find out what happened to Thermia or about his other plan to kill that Darion guy. He still hadn't decided which he would pursue first. Or how to go about it.

"All right. Tell me then. What is it I desire most?"

"What you want…" He stared into his eyes like he was reading his soul. "You want to know who your parents are. More specifically, you want to know what happened to your mother."

Cadivus's heart sank deep into his chest. He began to ponder the question. The question he forgot to ask for so long now. His face was warm. "My mother? You…knew her?"

"There is much to be learned in this big world of ours. Come with me, and I'll help you find the truth they don't want you to see. Yes, you'll have the power to decide your fate, young one. A story of your own."

The sounds of soldiers walking and shouting orders came from outside the tent.

"I'll give you a moment to consider. However, If you want to come with me, you need to perform one simple task."

"What task?"

"Simple. Break free your constraints…usurper of fire." The man walked backward toward the door as his smiling face fell into darkness.

Like any other time he tried to use his powers. Cadivus felt an attack coming on. However, the pain felt duller. The wall…thinner.

The traitor left the tent, closing the door flap behind him.

"What's going on in there, soldier?" An officer from the crowd outside asked. His shoulders were adorned with golden epaulets to signify his high rank.

"Oh, you know the boys like to get frisky…Bunch of horned up fanny chasers this lot," the traitor said.

The crowd made a disgusted face, save for a few men who tried to peek into the tent.

"Step aside, cadet. I'll see for myself." The officer stepped toward the tent, but the traitor didn't move. "Step aside!" he repeated with authority.

The traitor folded his arms and stood tall. "The thing about that is…no."

"Kill this unloyal swine!" The officer shouted.

The group charged in, swinging their weapons. The traitor laughed louder and louder as they stabbed and bludgeoned him. He fell to his knees, taking all the blows with a smile.

"Cadivus! What is your answer?!" he screamed the words, his voice echoing through the valley they found themselves in.

A loud crackling noise came from inside the tent.

Yet the soldiers still pulled the beaten traitor to the side and continued to swing at him. The officer went to open the tent, but as he pulled the cloth door aside, a giant flame arose and engulfed the large tent in fire. It glowed as a sun had risen over the dark valley. Between the inferno's flames a roar echoed. A pained voice cried out to them.

The soldiers backed away until the heat became manageable. Within the flames, a silhouette of a man walked toward them. In his right hand, he dragged a long chain.

"Take him!" the officer shouted. He poured water over his singed face, and steam rose off his skin and armor.

The soldiers charged with their weapons drawn. Cadivus raised his arm holding the chain and cracked it forward, caving the officer's face in. He pulled the chain back and swung it from his side, sweeping it through the crowd. Soldiers either flipped over it or were knocked down by it. Some of their bones cracked, and many lay on the ground, screaming in agony. Soldiers outside of the attack ran away.

Cadivus walked into the middle of the fallen soldiers and stood. The ground around him became a circle of flame that reached out to the edges of the remaining soldiers. Fire rose within the circle, licking at every bit of flesh inside it. A circle of infernal rage enticed their screams for a few mere moments before their lives were forfeited to the intense heat.

Screams echoed in the distance. "Hybrid! Retreat!" A horn sounded.

He stood letting the blurry images of his past fill his mind. The flames…they stoked an understanding that his memories were missing…taken. He grit his teeth and tried to take them back but, they remained hidden away.

From the ground, the traitor smiled wide, watching Cadivus fall to his knees and stare at the carnage around him. The inferno consumed the trees, the tent, and the bodies. His heart lightened as he watched him amidst the flames lashing out to consume all before them.

Cadivus's face changed from blind rage into terror. "Ah! Fuck! Get me out of here!" The fire drew around him. He shrieked and huddled into himself, rocking back and forth.

"What the fuck?" The traitor muttered. He walked over to Cadivus, picked him up, placed him over his shoulder, and walked out of the fiery carnage. He walked until he couldn't feel the heat on his back and then dropped Cadivus onto the ground. He stared at him for a moment. "Aren't you fireproof?"

Cadivus opened his eyes and looked around to make sure it was safe. Then he sat up.

The traitor laughed. "Afraid of a few dead bodies, are ya?"

Hyperventilating, Cadivus sat there for several moments before speaking. "No…I just needed to leave is all."

"Speak truth to me. I am your master now, after all."

Cadivus bit his lip, debating what to say. He decided to just come clean. "I have a fear of the fire, is all. So what?" He folded his arms and looked away.

A second later, the traitor laughed so hard he rolled along the ground, grabbing at his sides.

"Go ahead. Have a laugh," Cadivus said without looking at the man.

He continued to do so, much louder this round.

Irritated, Cadivus stared at the man and then tilted his head. "Where are your wounds? I'm pretty sure I heard the sounds of them…killing you…"

The traitor stopped rolling around and stood.

"I'm getting *real* tired of being asked that all the time."

"You're a hybrid then?"

"Yes. A much stronger one than yourself, mind you. Consider that if you think about welching on our deal." He put his hand out and pulled Cadivus up to him. Then he shook his hand and smiled.

"You never answered me. Who are you?"

“My name is Teavis. And I don’t want you to only think of me as your master. Just think of me like a friend. Except if you don’t do what I tell you to, I’ll kill you.”

He raised his eyebrows and smiled the biggest fake smile he could manage. Remembering him from the sheets Hunter had shown him. As he looked toward the bodies smoking on the ground, he wondered if he would come for him now.

“Okay…” Cadivus said.

“I’ll promise you this however.” He got close to Cadivus's face and stared into his eyes. Nearly pressing his lips to his own. “If you stick with me, I’ll help you grow stronger than some other notable members of your family.”

Cadivus thought it was a jest at first, but his eyes spoke the truth. His mind raced with his failures. He was alone now, truly alone. All because he wasn't strong enough. “Okay. I’ll work with you.”

“And *boy*…go get your fucking clothes, your hairy cock is distracting.”

Cadivus looked past him and at the blazing fire. He figured the outfit he had gotten from Pribbs was locked away in a tent somewhere.

“Let’s just catch our breath for a moment. Let the fire die down. It’ll be easier to find.”

He spotted the chain laid out toward the wreckage. It shrank in size, losing links one at a time as the heat left it. The metal disappeared like a lit fuse.

****

Thermia opened her eyes in a dark room, her body heavy and weak. She looked around but could find no shapes in the darkness. She recognized the void, a place she entered when her consciousness failed her. A place that felt…safe. The emptiness hugged her tight and she felt comfort in its grasp. Her mind was empty of all that preceded this moment.

"Where am I?" she called out to the nether. Her voice echoed over and over.

"You know where you are…" a voice answered back.

She looked around at the emptiness as a familiar feeling fell over her.

"My dark place."

Chapter 40

The Hybrid stood at his round table in his Dreyhal castle, discussing strategies with his most loyal advisors. The city had fallen to terrorism and rebellious attacks since he exiled Cadivus and Thermia over a month ago. They were *still* trying to figure out how to handle the situation.

"Why don't we just call them back and execute them?" One advisor asked.

"Let me be clear: their death is off the friggin' table," The Hybrid said.

The advisors all spoke among themselves.

"I got an idea," one said, "why don't we just have a bake sale but give a twenty-five percent discount to the rebels? Then when they get the discount, we gut em like fish."

"Shut up! Duncan!" everyone shouted at once.

"Forgive me for thinking out the box…"

"I thought Cadivus and Thermia would have returned with the leader of that dang leafer village by now," The Hybrid said, "the fact that they aren't back yet…Well, gods only know what happened to those numbskulls. Any reports from scouts or spies?"

He turned to another advisor, who sighed before reading a report.

"Cadivus and Thermia have not been spotted since Pribbs, and we only know that much because we found the journal of one of our spies on his body outside of the town. Something is not right about any of this, my lord."

He stared off into the distance, thinking the report over.

One man ran into the meeting room, screaming as loud as he could. "Fire! There's a fire, sirs!" He doubled over and breathed heavily.

Everyone inside walked toward the small castle's entrance and observed the news. Several large fires were lit all over the town. Panicked screaming and crying came from all directions.

"All members of the guard, douse those fires now!" The Hybrid ordered as he summoned the smoke toward him. His teeth clenched as he summoned his soul into action.

As the guards prepared to leave, a large crowd gathered outside the gate, chanting.

"Down with hybrids! Down with hybrids!" They banged on the gate with a battering ram until it broke open. When the doors blew open, over two hundred people walked into the courtyard, continuing their chant.

The guards drew their bows and held position. There weren't enough arrows to stop them.

"Calm," The Hybrid said, and they stood down. He approached the crowd on his own. "Who's you're leader?"

A brown-haired middle-aged man stepped out from the crowd with a sword in his hand. He pointed it toward The Hybrid. His shaking hands betrayed his angry scowl.

"We've had enough of the tyrannical lord! Over a hundred dead, and the killer roams free…We won't stand for it." The middle-aged man turned back toward the crowd for approval.

The Hybrid stepped forward, staring into the man's eyes. Allowing time for the middle-aged man to look away. "So, you've decided to burn down the homes of the innocent to teach me a lesson? Is that the idea?”

“Well, yes, that was the idea. We had to show you how serious we were.”

“Let me get this straight. You depose me and then install yourself, I’m guessing. Do you arrest the people who set the fires once you’re the leader?” He turned his gaze to the crowd as their brows unfurrowed.

The middle-aged man looked back towards the crowd and rocked his head side to side before nodding. “I would imagine some amnesty is in order, yes. Why do you ask?”

“No reason. Just wanted to be sure the people I’m about to kill are damned fools! If there’s one thing I can’t stand, it’s hypocrites!”

The brown-haired man laughed, turning to the crowd urging them to laugh with him, which they did. He then aimed his sword at The Hybrid once more.

“I’ve heard the stories, sure, but I’ve heard stories of unicorns saving kids from wells too. I don’t believe a word of your bullshit legend.”

“Stories,” The Hybrid closed his eyes and shook his head, "I wish they were mere stories. Stories have endings. This..." his eyes watered.

The brown-haired man, thinking he had an upper hand, charged in and swung his sword down. The blade passed through The Hybrid’s body. Once it was through, The Hybrid swung his own sword once, slicing the brown-haired man’s neck. He fell to the ground and bled out at The Hybrid’s feet.

The Hybrid looked toward the crowd, hoping the display would make them retreat. However, they screamed and slammed their weapons to their shields repeatedly. He looked past them, at the many homes engulfed in flames. The image reminded him of Cadivus, and of her.

“Your discount militia has made a serious error on this day. Revenge was never yours—" he looked down as the crowd charged toward him, “it was his.” He held a finger up to the crowd.

As the crowd charged, he crashed the gathered smoke down before him. They paused in the dense cloud—unable to see their enemy and unable to find their breathe. He lowered the cloud to the ground, giving them a few gasps of air, before wrapping his tendrils around their necks and entering their mouths to fill their lungs. The coughs transformed to gasps and wheezing. The sound of weapons and shields falling to the stone ground emanated form the cloud. It wasn’t long before they succumbed to his smoke's vial grasp. When the last body went limp, he released them and sent the smoke back to the skies with a mere thought. He wanted to feel sadness for the act found nothing of the sort inside himself.

“Now, douse the flames,” he told his guard.

The guards stared at the bodies on the ground for a moment. A loud thump from Gerald's spear hitting the ground startled them to their duties. They ran past their lord and carried out their orders.

He continued to stare at the corpses. Worse stories crept into his mind. The small glimpses of events long passed were in tandem with slivers of the emotions present at the time. “Have I been idle for too long? How long have I sat behind these gates?” He clenched his fist and gazed far into the woods beyond. Where everything more important to him than Dreyhal held an unknowable fate. "I need to tell him…" The sliver transformed formed into a terrible ache in his heart and a terrible pain assaulted his side.

“I’m sorry, my lord,” Gerald said, his spear piercing The Hybrid. “I can’t continue to witness your kind’s wrath against us. You let him leave. Then you kill twice as many," he choked up for a moment, "It ends now.”

The Hybrid looked down at the blood on the spear's tip, he held lightly onto the shaft. “Gerald. It's a kindness you have granted me." The spear was twisted and pulled back through him. His body fell forward before he caught himself on the short wall of the moat. The blood pooled at his feet. He turned to face his attacker.

Gerald shook his head as he readied another strike. "You know this has to stop, don't you?" He said.

The Hybrid looked to him and smiled. Then he frowned. "I fucked up, Gerald." His eyes growing more distant, "My son is as lost as your own." His eyes watered. Smoke rose from his body, as if abandoning him at his time of need.

Gerald's eyebrows raised. He watched the smoke hover above them. He wondered if his fate was to be the same as the crowd.

The Hybrid continued.

"That poor girl. What is in store for that poor girl?" the Hybrid said, his voice turning to a whisper. He found Gerald's eyes as they watered. "What kind of deal have I made?" He turned to the water running below him and reach out toward it.

"You've taken many lives," Gerald said, "and you'll keep taking them without any thought of people like me and these folks here. People who have friends and family that they'll never see again, never hug again." Gerald screamed. "Don't act all sad about it now! You're a devil spawn!"

"You don't understand." The Hybrid turned and stared into his eyes, his own wet and slippery. "I'm know what I am. I doomed us all. I made a deal to protect him from his past, from what I did to him. If he ever learns the truth, the world will be become ash and dust."

"All the more reason to stop you now." Gerald readied his spear for another thrust.

"Ash or oblivion…those are your options now…" He coughed and blood dripped onto his chin. "You can only hope to serve one final purpose to me."

Gerald clenched his teeth. "I don't serve you anymore." The words pulsated with his vitriol.

The Hybrid smirked. His brows furrowed as he stared the man down. "Do what needs to be done."

Gerald screamed as he charged in slamming his shield into his face with every fiber of his rage. His body went limp as it fell back over the railing into the rapid waters below. His eyes scanned the river as he watched the remains flow to a waterfall, where it would fall hundreds of feet the rocky ocean floor below. His body stiffened. He turned to see the smoke behind him formed into a semblance of a man. The figure pointed toward him and spoke in his mind with an inhuman tone.

"Vessel…" The voice deep and echoing in his mind. It's utterance delivering a sense of euphoria to the hairs of his ears. In that moment his body felt empty, a void that yearned to be satiated.

The words ached as they echoed throughout his skull. A calm came over him as he felt the creatures intent. His eyes widened and he smiled. He dropped his spear and shield to the ground and held out his arms. "Yes!" The creature wrapped around him and poked into his body without creating wounds. His ecstasy was replaced by pain and horror as the creature bonded with him. Visions of events no one had ever seen permeated his mind. He felt the pain of people he had never met. He wanted to go numb and weak but his adrenaline spiked as his teeth ground together. He squeezed his fist so tight he thought they might explode. He tried to scream but no noise would leave his body, disallowing even that small relief. After what felt like days of excruciating pain, it finally stopped as he fell to his hands and knees. He panted on the ground and found it easy to catch his breath. He stood and stared into his hands as a dark smoke radiated from his skin. He clenched his fist once more and felt their power. The void in his eyes stared into eternities. "Cadivus."

****

Darion rode home by his lonesome. Even though he lost his men, a great sense of happiness carried him.

He never thought of his village until he was a few hours away. The whole ordeal then spun over and over in his head. He wondered if he had nailed the monologue.

He breached a dune and for the first time in weeks he saw his home. The walls were strong, and plumes of smoke filled the air. The deal with the crown proved to be fruitful after all.

As he approached the gate, the guards above halted him.

“Halt! What business have you?” one guard called down.

Darion lowered the cloth wrapped around his face. When the guard saw it, he screamed for the gate to be opened. The gate soon opened, and there stood Toonda with her husband. She held a baby in her arms.

He jumped off his horse and greeted them, shaking hands with Doban and hugging her. She handed him the baby and he held the child and smiled.

"Is it over Darion?" Toonda asked.

He handed the baby to Doban.

"Yes…it's…it's finally over." A small glimmer of emptiness betrayed him, yet she smiled all the same.

Behind them, the guards shouted orders, and bows were drawn.

"Halt! What business have you?" the guards shouted.

"Excuse me. Duty calls." Darion told the couple before he ran toward the gates. When he approached them, he saw a dark-skinned woman standing in the sands before them, her skin covered in sweat and her breathing heavy. "Ekio?"

Epilogue

Adverity awoke to a crippling pain in the middle of her back, as well as the front of her head. Her aches berated her for the night spent drowning in paperwork and wine. She slipped onto the hard stone floor, landing on her cushioned bottom. The dim light permeating through the hung sheets taunted her existence. She squeezed her eyes tight while her hands fumbled around for a bottle that still had a swig of relief. Her lips quivered when she found a half full bottle and she drank it down before curling up underneath the desk. She embraced the cold stone against her skin while feeling the goosebumps rise. A semblance of serenity washed over her.

The door slammed open. The light from outside bid her eyes closed.

"Good morning, Mistress!" the darkened silhouette shouted, "Oh, what a lovely day it is!"

The plopping of papers on the desk echoed inside Adverity's head. She groaned.

The silhouette bent over at the waist and peeked under the desk with a big smile. "Have you eaten? It sure looks comfortable under there. Did you know today is a special day? Do you know what day what it is? I'll give you a hint. No, wait, I can't hold it in. It's your leadership anniversary!" A swift movement saved her head from a flying bottle. It smashed against he opposite wall. "You dropped something!" She laughed.

"Lydia. Get…the frick…out!"

"I'm gonna get you the fudge *out* from under there." She walked around the desk and grabbed a foot. She dragged her along the floor. The sound of rolling bottles filled the room.

Adverity kicked up at her in vain. She relented and opened her eyes fully for the first time. Dark green eyes and sunken cheeks below dirty blonde hair stared back at her. Her perfect smile incited rage inside Adverity.

"Like the new robe?" Lydia said. She curtsied and twirled to show off the royal blue garment.

"It looks the same as always." Adverity said as she reached out to be pulled up. Noticing her own white robe with silver trim was stained with dirt, ink and wine drops.

"Wrong," Lydia said with a ringing tone, "I cut an inch off the sleeves so I could show off a bracelet," she smiled suggestively, "if I had one." She raised her eyebrows as she grabbed the hand with both of her own and pulled with all of her might.

Adverity assisted her effort and made it back into the chair at the desk. While Lydia collected the trash from around the room, Adverity thumbed through the new papers. She rolled her eyes and grimaced at each request. Her jaw dropped. "What the frick!" She punched the table.

"Let me guess…you found the Gossipari request?" Lydia said as she carefully placed the empty bottles into crates for refilling.

"Twenty more members? There's only 500 of us here! Why the frick would we need 30 Gossipari?" She bit her hand as the pain in her head returned.

"Actually there's 508 of us but, who's counting?" Lydia paused. "Oh right, me!" She laughed. She returned to the front of the desk and stood with her arms folded. The stance pulled the loose robe to a form fitting reveal.

Adverity glanced at her wide hips sitting below her thin waist and clenched her teeth. She slammed the paper down. "Obviously, the answer is no." She stamped the bottom of the page several times. She looked up to see Lydia grimacing.

"Don't you fricking…dare."

Lydia pulled out another page from the bottom of the pile. She covered her eyes with one hand as she handed it to her. Then she quickly covered her ears.

Some say Adverity's cries of anguish could be heard from thousands of feet away. Of course, this was a rumor. The furthest recorded distance was only 508 feet. The women found it very poetic.

Adverity clenched her teeth and hyperventilated. Her battle cry brought no relief to her psyche. She slammed her head into the desk and immediately regretted the hasty decision to do so.

Lydia ran up besides her and massaged the back of her head. "There, there, Mistress. It's not the first time the Matriarchal Order has preemptively vetoed your veto." She moved her massage to her back and Adverity flinched, causing Lydia to pull her hands away. "I'm sorry, Mistress. I forgot." She bowed her head.

Adverity could feel the heat in her eyes. She took in a deep and shrill breath to push it away. "They want a fight? I'll give them a damn fight." She flipped the veto for wrote down all of her reasons for disagreeing with the proposal. She muttered to herself with every whip of the quill. She furiously dabbed it in ink as her tongue hung outside her mouth.

Lydia smiled as she watched her work. She looked to the sheets covering the large round window and squinted. "Mistress. Perhaps you should allow the Goddess of Light to assist you in your efforts?"

Adverity snorted. "A lot of help she would be, eh? Maybe instead of watching me do *actual* work, she can help the order find reason instead of their blasted ignorance." She continued her efforts while mumbling ever more so, and crossing out several lines.

"Mistress. To blaspheme is to not dream. Without dreams, we have no goals. And without goals, we have no—"

"Purpose…Yeah, I got it," she said in a hushed tone.

"Oh, I have an idea! You should join my prayer circle," Lydia said, "You'll love the girls and the cats. We pray, sing songs, eat snacks, gossip, sew, arm wrestle—"

Adverity slammed the table. "Stop!" She bared her teeth to Lydia. She looked down to see ink spilling onto her desk. She gasped. She took some of the other papers and tried to soak up the ink. It bled through the thin pages and onto her hand. She balled up the pages in her grasp and screamed. "Frick you! Frick this! Frick your fricking poop! And frick the Goddess of the Light!" She flipped the solid wood desk over. When it crashed against the ground, the sheets fell from the window. The sun filtered in through the circular frame and her eyes surrendered to its light.

Lydia's eyes went wide. "I think she heard you," she said with a ringing tone.

Adverity looked away from Lydia and into the light. "Lydia," she said in a rasped voice tortured from her previous wail. "I can't shout anymore but, I'm still angry. My only remaining recourse is…" She turned to face Lydia, her eyes darkened with an empty look upon her face. "Is violence."

Lydia turned away at once. A quickened pace with arms to her side. She closed the door behind her and left Adverity to her lonesome once more. "I love you," she shouted from down the road.

Adverity reached for her throat and rubbed at it with care. Where the desk once stood she found an unopened bottle of wine. She drank half of it down and let out a sigh of relief as she caught her breath.

A knock at the door interrupted her respite.

"Lydia, if you don't—"

"Mistress?" a new voice called through the door. One that was older and more stern. Saria.

Adverity recognized it immediately. Her eyes went wide as she looked around the room at the mess she had created. She tried to lift the desk but it sat flush against the stone floor. Trying to push it from the top only made it screech across the floor.

"Are you okay?" Saria said through the door.

"One second!" Adverity stood and spun circles in a panic. She walked to the door, tied up her brown hair and dusted her robe off. She opened the door just enough to jump inside and slam it closed behind her. She nearly ran into Saria who stood on her small porch.

The woman's eyes went wide as a toothy smiled Adverity greeted her with a hug. Of course, Adverity never noticed the eyes or any other features of her face. Saria was the leader of the Gossipari, women who were in charge of keeping tabs on the small town, who wore masks. The masks offered utility in adjustable zoom lenses and hearing amplification which could be directed by a device that attached to the underside of their wrist. All concealed by a purple gown with swirling blue patterns throughout. Saria wore a silver sash to display her rank to onlookers.

"Greetings, Saria," Adverity said with a soft feminine tone, "it's such a pleasure to make your acquaintance on this fine morning." She smiled with big eyes.

"Oh child. How sweet of you to indulge me so. Spare me the false manners of the trained mare," Saria said.

Adverity's brow furrowed. "Just making sure you still got it, Saria."

"My knees ache from a long walk, let me in to sit would you?" She reached for her back as she leaned back.

Adverity motioned to a green field. "There's a bench not far from here. Lydia farted in there before she left and the odor lingers with great pungency."

Saria's head shot back. "Oh that's what that noise was? I thought somebody got some bad news they didn't want and decided to flip over a solid wood desk. I guess I am getting old after all. Shall we then?" Saria walked towards the field as Adverity stared daggers at her from behind. "I see that."

Adverity's eyes widened and a smile returned to her face. She caught up to Saria and took her arm. As they walked, Adverity looked out over the town that was spread out across a large grassy plain. Stone and wooden homes lined dirt streets. Their roofs already falling to disrepair. The roads required less maintenance since they no longer had cattle or horses. Which made the crops difficult to harvest. Still, a guild of fisher-women had made great strides in their tactics and hauled in loads of fresh protein to suffice for weekly rich meals. A large crowd of woman gathered in the town square, where duties would be handed out for the days work. They reached a bench that sat over looking that town square.

"We need more eyes and ears, Mistress," Saria said plainly.

Adverity sighed. "Do you see what I see, Saria? We are already falling so far behind. We can't triple the size of a group that's mainly for, let me blunt, distractions at best."

Saria laughed. "It was good while it lasted, Mistress. However, these recent days bring tides of peril."

Adverity placed her hands on the bench and stretched her neck behind her. "What kind of peril?" she asked while yawning.

"The men, Mistress. Of course I mean the men." She held out her wrist to the homes below.

"What do I care if they get laid now and then? We could use the child labor at this point." Adverity leaned forward to rest her chin on top of her fists. "Tell them not pull out."

"They are staying longer…and they are soldiers."

Adverity sat up straight. "Soldiers. How long, Saria?"

"Some have been here the entire week. Hiding in the homes. The women either go without food, or steal more to feed them. And…of course there is the matter of…"

"I know. I remember their ways." Adverity clenched her fist. "What the hell is happening to us?"

"Time heals the wounds. Time calms the anger. Time comes for our apathy and turns it against us." Saria placed her hands on her knees.

"I'll drag them out of here myself. See if they can still get a boner after being humiliated by me dragging their naked ass down the dirt road to the bridges." Adverity smiled.

Saria laughed. "If only it were that easy, Mistress."

Adverity fell to tears. She reached her hand up to wipe them away and Saria grabbed a hold of her wrist. The mask stared into her. The lenses retreated and revealed the green eyes hiding inside. Matching all the other women in the small town.

"These eyes witnessed a great horror on your behalf," Saria said, "To place a bench here in this spot…you must relive it everyday…Adverity, why?"

"The square? The one where my former husband disrobed me, humiliated me, beat me bloody and left me for dead?" Her tears steamed away amidst the rage upon her face. "'You need me.' He always used to tell me. 'Without me, you'd be dead.'" Adverity clenched her fist. "What a fate that awaited them. Lying dead on some unknown battlefield, fighting over dirt." She paused. "Of course, we all have similar stories, often behind closed doors. I grew to hate the sound of that door closing as I'm sure other sisters have as well."

"The exile that you gave the few remaining men was an act of mercy most wouldn't," Saria said, "it might not be enough in the near future."

"We will do what is necessary to protect our own," Adverity said, "That has always been the most our important task. How are our food stores going to bear this burden?"

"We have enough stores of food to get by for months," Saria said, "focus on farming technology, build more boats for fishing and let me have the women I need to quell this."

"It is difficult to deny you, Saria. I will make it work somehow. Just…don't say anything yet. I have a bone to pick with the matriarchal order. I believe they owe me some concessions for agreeing with their law to add more gossipari to our ranks. Perhaps they can convince me?" Adverity smirked.

Saria's mask covered the eyes with lenses once more. She shook her head and moaned. "Playing your own mother." She sighed. "You're a bitch. You know that right?"

Adverity put her head back and allowed the sun to caress it. "Fuck yes, I am."

Adverity bid Saria farewell as the gossipari went back into town. She closed her eyes as the events of the day washed over her. She focused on the nearby river while listening to the sounds of the water breaking over the rocks and past the trees roots. A splashing noise caught her attention and she jerked her head to see a leg sticking out from behind a tree. As she walked closer, groans of pain grew louder until she could hear the fettered breaths. As she walked around the trunk, she found a pale skinned man wrapped in a dark cloak. His bare feet dug into the soft earth, as he turned to meet her eyes. He held a wound near his stomach where his cloak was stained red with blood. She clenched her teeth. "What are you doing here?" She asked the wounded man.

The wounded man sighed. "Please. I need you," the words came out slowly, "I'll die without your help." He coughed, which made him grab at his wound once more and shut his eyes tight.

"You need me," her former husband's echoed in her head. Adverity knelt down and studied the man. His eyes as brown as the tree he lay against. She looked for weapons and found none. She snapped her fingers as his consciousness started to drift. "Who are you? What happened to you?"

"Marcus," he said, "I…I…" His head fell to his chest as his consciousness left him. She started to walk away but stopped remembering his words. "He needs me?" She looked at the all but lifeless man slumped against the trunk. "Goddess, save me…and I will save *him*."

www.ingramcontent.com/pod-product-compliance
Lightning Source LLC
LaVergne TN
LVHW010558100826
845148LV00014B/2756

9798218469122